'Women's fiction doesn't get any better than this . . . Sharp, funny and touching' *OK!*

'Acutely funny and wonderfully observed, Annabel Giles' debut is a cracker . . . *Birthday Girls* takes in fame, infidelity, alcoholism and childbirth through a cast of brilliantly drawn characters. Sharp, endlessly entertaining and slyly smart . . . Very big, very clever' *Hello!*

'The stories are cleverly woven together and there's a great twist at the end' *New Woman*

'This cleverly plotted novel strings together six loosely interconnected lives . . . also perceptive, funny and has some outrageously entertaining plot twists which shackle disparate characters ever more bizarrely together' *Daily Mail*

'*Birthday Girls*, a funny, intriguing and sometimes touching story of six women as they each celebrate landmark birthdays' *You*

'Six women, six birthdays and six chapters . . . [*Birthday Girls*] shows off Giles' ear for repartee and empathy for all matters hormonal . . . The literary equivalent of a goodie bag' *Independent*

'A black comedy that's both touching and frequently funny, *Birthday Girls* is a refreshing look at whatever happens to us all as we get older – whatever age we are' *Heat*

'This zippy, sparky novel from Annabel Giles about the lives, loves and dramas of six related women . . . is funny and unexpectedly moving' *Sunday Independent*, Dublin

So far, Annabel Giles has been a model, TV and radio personality, actress and comedienne. She is now an author – her first novel, *Birthday Girls*, was published by Penguin in 2000. She has two children and lives in London.

Crossing the Paradise Line

ANNABEL GILES

PENGUIN BOOKS

PENGUIN BOOKS

Published by the Penguin Group
Penguin Books Ltd, 80 Strand, London WC2R ORL, England
Penguin Putnam Inc., 375 Hudson Street, New York, New York 10014, USA
Penguin Books Australia Ltd, 250 Camberwell Road, Camberwell, Victoria 3124, Australia
Penguin Books Canada Ltd, 10 Alcorn Avenue, Toronto, Ontario, Canada M4V 3B2
Penguin Books India (P) Ltd, 11 Community Centre,
Panchsheel Park, New Delhi – 110 017, India
Penguin Books (NZ) Ltd, Cnr Rosedale and Airborne Roads,
Albany, Auckland, New Zealand
Penguin Books (South Africa) (Pty) Ltd, 24 Sturdee Avenue,
Rosebank 2196, South Africa

Penguin Books Ltd, Registered Offices: 80 Strand, London WC2R ORL, England

www.penguin.com

First published by Penguin 2003
3

Typeset in 12.5/14.75 Monotype Garamond
by Palimpsest Book Production Limited,
Polmont, Stirlingshire

Printed in Great Britain by Clays Ltd, St Ives plc

For Naomi,
with thanks

1. Departures

The TV is on. Looks like yet another documentary. Some people quickly reach for the remote, see what else is on.

*

'I wouldn't mind, but I didn't even want to go on holiday in the first place.' She smiles. 'I wasn't very adventurous in those days, you see. It was my ex-husband's idea. Our daughter had just finished her GCSEs, and he thought she deserved a treat. And as Jeremy's an airline pilot, he can get cheap flights. I was still a bit reluctant to go, but then he offered to pay for the whole thing, and so I thought – well, it'd be silly to turn down a free holiday, wouldn't it?'

A young-ish woman, thirtysomething, is talking to an invisible someone, who is sitting just to the right of camera. Her hair is bleached stripy blonde, and she has pale, watery blue eyes. She is neither beautiful nor pretty, but attractive.

'Tessa Holroyd', it reads along the bottom of the screen, 'Musician'.

'But I only agreed to go for Sammy's sake,' she appeals.

I

'Sammy?' asks the off-screen voice.

Tessa's face floods warm. 'Samantha. My daughter.' Pause. She realizes she is supposed to say more. 'We hadn't been getting on that well, you see – I thought a holiday might help.'

'Mum was, like, really getting on my tits.' Oh.

A young woman: 'Samantha Holroyd' apparently. 'Teenager'. Like it's her full-time job.

'She just couldn't accept that I wasn't a little girl any more.' Mum must be blind – girl on the screen with full set of bosoms, panda kohled eyes and bumpy skin on nightclub pallor. She sighs, shakes her head. 'Didn't want me to grow up. Just, like, trying to arrest my development, in order to satisfy her own childhood limitations.' She shoots a look skywards. 'Mad.'

Blimey.

*

Jeremy was looking as handsome as ever. How annoying of him, thought Tessa as she watched him carefully but masterfully loading their luggage into the back of his new sleek BMW. He was wearing his pilot's uniform, which had always been a bit of a turn-on for Tessa, and he was looking even more like the illegitimate son of James Bond than usual. He was nearly forty now, and still looking good. Even the grey hairs glinted a more glamorous silver, as they streaked through his dark thicket hair; and where other men his age were beginning to spread their bellies out like barrels of beer, Jeremy had made sure his still came in a six-pack. This was a man who was born with a natural tan – in fact, his mother had always said that he'd been born with such a lovely golden glow, they'd had to keep checking he hadn't got jaundice – there were no unsightly pink or purple blotches on his smooth skin. Yes, still a delicious man. Unfortunately.

As he drove his 'chicks' (as he used to call them) towards Edinburgh airport, gloating at the lines of festival traffic coming the other way, they all slipped effortlessly into their old family movie, the 'just-we-three' screenplay they'd always been in; Jeremy took the part of 'The Big Man', Tessa played 'The Little Woman' and Sammy, of course, 'The Baby Who Must Be Obeyed'. It was good, it felt right. For a few stolen miles, Tessa allowed herself to believe that they were still the happy smiley people they used to be.

Only, of course, Sammy had to go and spoil it. 'Da-ad,' she cooed, like the sweet little girl her parents still wanted her to be, 'I wish you were coming with us . . .' Pop! The bubble burst.

Tessa sighed and looked out of the window.

Jeremy kept his eyes on the road and said nothing.

Tessa knew he was clenching his teeth, making his temples flicker, even though she wasn't looking. Warning. Take heed, Sammy.

But no. 'I mean it would just be so cool, wouldn't it?'

Tessa said nothing. Let him deal with it this time, she

had to fend off this kind of onslaught every bloody day. Sammy had perfected the art of saying the wrong thing at the right time.

'Dad?' Sammy leaned forward, and pushing her head between their two leather seats, dropped the little girl voice now. 'No seriously, why not? You could, like, help me celebrate my GCSE results when they come through, we could get really wankered together –'

'Sammy!' roared her father, as they all knew he would. (Leo.)

But she kept going, as they all knew she would. (His roar was worse than his bite.) 'But it would be fun; all of you could come out, sounds like Mona and the twins would love it there! Mum wouldn't mind, would you, Mum? Oh, come on, Dad, it'll be a laugh! We'd be one big happy family . . .'

'Oh, Sammy, just leave it will you?' Tessa was cross and excited all at once, she secretly enjoyed watching Jeremy squirm on Sammy's hook.

'No, I won't leave it, actually,' she continued. 'Have you, guys, like, any idea how boring this is for me? I've got to go on two separate holidays, which means I'm away for most of the summer, so I can't see my friends hardly at all. It's just so selfish of you, I can't even believe you're doing this to me . . .'

Nor can I, thought Tessa. I never wanted this for you either. One family, one holiday. Just us.

'Oh don't be so bloody spoilt, Sammy!' Jeremy snatched the chance to change the subject. 'You're lucky to be going anywhere; when I was your age, I'd have given my right arm to be going on two summer holidays.'

'Ah yes, you say that, but would you?' She sat back in her seat. 'I mean, what kind of holiday would it be, with only one arm? How would you swim? And what if your bloodied stump didn't heal properly in time, you'd attract sharks ... waterskiing would be a big problem, how would you –'

'Oh Sammy,' said both her parents at once, 'Shut up!' And they looked across at each other, and smiled, and one of them wished more than anything that this was for real, while the other went back to staring at the road ahead.

God, what a mess.

*

Gina hadn't wanted to go on holiday either. The boys had made her. Do her good, they'd said. Get her out of herself. Or was it take it out of herself? There were some parts of the English language she had never mastered. It was a *lingua stupida* sometimes, it made no sense. Italian was so much easier, so much more simple. Or was it simpler? Simplier?

Doesno matter now. He's not around to correct her, not any more. But she still heard his voice in her head, of course. Sometimes she got angry with him. Told him to go away. But then she'd be sad when he did, because she'd want him back. She'd give anything to have him back. She was in charge of him now, you see, and she didn't like it. Didn't suit either of them. All wrong. He was the big boss, and she was the little boss, and that was the way it had always been.

As she washed her hands, Gina did her best not to look in the (dusty) mirror above the little guest basin. She'd been trying to keep out of her own way, hadn't looked at herself properly recently, hadn't wanted to. Or needed to, what was the point? There was no one to look nice for any more.

But she was going to be spending the next couple of weeks with other people, most of them strangers, so she had to keep up the appearances, Alfie would expect that. He'd be upset if she let the family down. Look at your flection, *Mamma*, keep looking.

She was surprised by the woman staring back at her, she thought she'd have started to look her real age now. She felt so old nowadays, you see. And tired, all the time, so tired. Tired all day, awake all night. All wrong. But no, she could still pass for the late sixties. On the outside, anyway.

Papà's customers used to tell her that she looked just like Sophia Loren, but Gina always suspected that was the only Italian woman they knew. Or they thought she'd been named after *La Lollo*, who was only a couple of years older than Gina, but she never corrected them, of course not. She was still a good-looking woman, she knew that. She kept her hair brown because it made her feel younger, but it needed tinting again now; Fabio said there was a hair salon where they were staying, she'd get it done there.

And she'd kept her figure; since having her babies, she'd put on a bit of weight of course, everyone did in those days, but she hadn't let herself get fat. No, he wouldn't have liked that. Her strong bone structure and a *tipicamente* Roman nose had helped keep her foreign-looking, as Alfie says. Used to say. But he'd loved her eyes most of all, they were like she was on fire, made him passionate, he loved that. So had she, she'd enjoyed their love-making – sex, they call it now, a horrible word – it was a way of making even more love between them, you see, that's how she saw it. And they'd made their love right up until he couldn't any more ...

But these weren't her eyes staring back at her from the mirror – the fire had gone, the spark had died with him, she'd fizzled out. Nothing in there now. This was the face of an empty woman whose heart had been stolen, taken away from her soul. A woman without love.

Gina folded her wet flannel into the handy Safeways polythene bag she'd saved for just this job, rustled it up, tucked it into a little space down the side of the suitcase, closed it up to shut. There. All done.

Now what?

She sat down on the edge of the bed, beside her suitcase. Save her legs. Long day ahead. She hadn't slept that well. Not used to sleeping in a single bed, you see. Wasn't going to get used to it, either. She'd keep that bed, their bed, no matter what. They won't take that away, I won't let them. That bed had been the centre of their world. They'd laughed, loved and cried together in there. She'd given birth in that bed. He'd died in it.

Anyway.

So much time now.

Too much time.

All quiet outside. Well, it was only half past six in the morning, too early for London to wake up, probably. London was more of a late night place. She looked around the bedroom. The nanny's room, normally. Nice room. Small. Should be easier to keep clean. She'd been

7

hurt to see that nice china figurine of a shepherdess she'd given Felicity for Christmas a few years ago gathering dust on the little shelf above the fireplace, but the cheerful primrose of her porcelain skirts did brighten this basement room up a bit. And she must tell her daughter-in-law that those spittoon curtains didn't go up and down properly, the cord was broken, that would be helpful.

But at least this room was still quite comfortable. Not like the rest of the house, which was almost completely bare now. Gina had been shocked when she'd arrived last night. The last time she'd visited it had been a normal cosy home with nice fitted carpets and squashy sofas and all the usual family clutter. But it looked like the place had been gutted, everything had been stripped away; they hadn't even got a new carpet yet, they were still walking on bare floorboards (which as any proper housewife knows are impossible to keep clean, the dust keeps coming up through the cracks, you see); and the soft furnishings were now hard ones, in bright primary school colours, with not so much as a nice pattern or even a flower in sight. (And she'd thought she was saying the right thing, complimenting Spike on his painting over the fireplace; how was she to know it hadn't been done by her little grandson, but by one of these modern art people, she'd felt so foolish.)

This 'new look' Felicity had gone for was so unwelcoming, so unfriendly. And she'd felt like she was just cluttering the place up when she'd arrived late last night, standing there in the hallway with her coat on for a full ten minutes before Cliff had finally offered to take it for her.

Though maybe she'd felt awkward because she always felt a bit – well, you know, 'in the road' when Felicity was around. Gina had really, really tried with this daughter-in-law, honestly she had. Alfie had liked her, always said his son's wives got better each time. But she just couldn't make herself.

It wasn't that Felicity was a wicked woman, not at all; it was just that Gina wanted more for 'Cliff', as he liked to be called now. A man like this needed a nice woman, one who was happy and willing to look after him herself, not a woman who paid other people to do it for her. He even did the cooking most nights, can you imagine?! Or she telephoned for a takeitaway, like last night. That wasn't *pizza*, that was cotton wool on a cardboard circle. It wasn't right. These want-it-all women were just plain selfish, you see. And lazy. Though, of course, Gina would never say as much –

'Where's Rebecca?' demanded a small boy in Bob the Builder pyjamas and no slippers, *poverino*, who was standing in the open doorway, hanging on the handle, about to pull the door off its hinges. 'Who are you?'

Gina smiled at his stick-'em-up hair, as her boys used to call it. 'You remember me, don't you?' She held out her arms, for a hug. Please.

'No,' said the boy, scowling. Just like his dad used to. 'Where's Rebecca?'

'Who's Rebecca?'

'My nanny.' And he wasn't budging till he found out. 'You're not her.'

'No, I'm your *nonna*.'

'What's a *nonna*?'

9

'A funny name for a granny, that's what.' Felicity appeared in the doorway behind her son looking like an old man in big, baggy, crumpled, tartan pyjamas. Poor Cliff. Gina wanted to get the iron out. And the hairbrush. And the eye make-up remover. 'She's gone back to Australia, you know that.' She yawned, not even bothering to put her hand up in front of her mouth.

'No, I didn't know that! Why didn't you say? Why didn't she say bye bye to me?' He started to cry. 'I want Rebecca, I want my Becca!'

And that was how their holiday started. Spike was feeling distraught, Felicity was feeling exhausted, and Gina was doing her best to feel nothing at all.

*

Feeling a little shaky, Cliff knocked on the green door and braced himself.

Penny was looking as pinched as ever. She took up her customary stance, leaning against the doorway with her arms folded. She was taller than him, all his birds were, but today she seemed to be taller than ever. How had he ever got off on those mean little tits, Cliff wondered. 'You're late!' she announced, triumphantly.

'Yes, I know. It was me who phoned you ten minutes ago, to tell you that I would be,' he said, trying to keep calm. 'She ready?'

'Christabelle!' she called, without looking behind her. 'Your father's here, At Last.' She glared at Cliff. 'Expensive, is it?' she disdained.

'Is what?'

'Your holiday.'

'Well – um . . .' This caught him by surprise, he hadn't been expecting a financial inquisition. 'Er, you know, it's er –'

'Yes Cliff, I do know. It's bloody expensive. I looked it up in the brochure. I know exactly how much it's costing you, and I think it's a bloody disgrace.' Her nostrils were flaring. 'How dare you!'

'What?' Where the fuck was Christabelle . . .

'Spend all that money on a holiday!'

'But –'

She had gone to second position now, filling the door frame, arms outstretched to either side, like Samson holding up the walls of the temple, bearing down on him, preparing to work herself up from ice-white anger to red hot fury. Here we go.

'*If* you have that kind of money floating about, Cliff, don't you think it would have been nice to have asked me if Christabelle needed anything? *Perhaps* you could have offered to pay for the guitar lessons she really wants, or get her room decorated any colour other than black, contributed to her very expensive freshly squeezed orange juice habit, maybe? And I'm sure you know perfectly well, Cliff, that the *pittance*' (she was spitting all over his new Joseph shirt now) 'the *pittance* you give me to support your daughter is just not enough! Teenagers Cost Money, you know!' Her eyes had narrowed into slits, her face was bulging with rage. She looked well rough, what had he been thinking back then? 'But of course you need all your spare cash, don't you, to support *her* guacamole lifestyle. *We're* supposed to somehow eke out a living from that *pathetic* amount you so-called "*support*" us with' – and she did the fingers to go with that, of course – 'while you go swanning off round the bloody world topping up your tans, is that it?' She nearly had his eye out with her jabby finger. 'Well, I've got news for you, Cliff Clifton; when you get back from your *un*-earned break with your silly little *millionaire* friends, there's going to be a solicitor's letter for you waiting on the *bloody* door-mat of your *bloody* enormous Kensington *bloody* mansion, which will be asking – no, excuse me, *demanding*, that you take full financial responsibility for your daughter, once and for all, do – you – *under* – S T A N D?!'

Fuck me, thought Cliff, it's only seven o'clock in the morning.

'C'mon Dad!' Christabelle had somehow slipped out of the house under her mother's raging armpit, and was standing by his dear old Jag (a bank robber's car, Felicity called it) with her tatty old rucksack, shivering.

Without looking at Penny's face again (well, he didn't want to spoil his breakfast, did he), Cliff turned on his Gucci loafer, and quickly walked back down the path, being extra careful to shut the gate the right way. The sooner he removed himself from the path of this particular speeding train, as Felicity would say, the better. And besides, he was buggered if he was going to admit to his second wife that the holiday was being entirely paid for by his third.

*

Fabio came inside Michelle, and immediately climbed off her. He had to get this over and done with, he'd been putting it off for far too long.

Propping himself up on one elbow, he idly tweaked her nipple, as you would a knob on a radio set, only he knew exactly how to find the right station. She started to moan again. He stopped. 'Listen, babe, I'm going to have to cool it for a bit.'

Michelle opened her eyes. 'What d'you mean, cool it?' She giggled. 'You sound like something out of the seventies!'

This was the trouble with the young ones, they didn't always get the message straight away. 'I think I'm going to have to back off for a while.'

'What d'you mean, back off? Back off of what?'

'You.'

Michelle frowned as she sat up in the nest of sheets, and turned to face him. She folded her arms, in that way slim women do to give themselves a bit of cleavage. Her pert little pinkie breasts poked out from underneath, as she swished her long unnaturally red hair over her shoulder. 'I'm sorry, but I still don't get it,' she said, looking down at him blankly.

Fabio would have sat up with her, but he was getting that post-orgasmic rush of having to be horizontal, no matter what. 'It's over.'

'I know, I'd better get a bloody move on, I've got to sterilize my instruments, and top up the creams, and sort out —'

'Michelle.' Jesus H Christ, do these girls understand nothing? He was going to have to sit up after all, to hammer it home. (But hadn't he just done that?! Now that's funny, he'd have to tell Bruno that one.) Fabio placed a manly hand on Michelle's mini shoulder, and cleverly avoided her gaze by staring into the sheet covering his limpening dick. 'I'm talking about us. It's finished, Michelle.' He tried to sound sad. 'I'm sorry.'

'Oh don't be silly, Fabio,' she chirruped, 'it's only just started. We're only at the beginning of the season, and we've got the whole summer stretching ahead of us, I'm not stopping this now! I only like powerful men, and you're the boss, there is no one higher than you out here. And anyway, I don't fancy anyone else.' She laughed at him. 'You'd be stupid to dump me. I mean, let's face it, I *am* the most attractive member of staff. What's the matter with you?'

This caught him by surprise, he hadn't been expecting her to argue back. 'But I want to split up.' He frowned.

'Yes,' said Michelle as she eased her tiny firm twenty-something fuckybuttocks out of bed, 'I'm sure you do. Whatever. But,' she pulled on the tiniest piece of g-string Fabio had ever seen (and he'd seen a few) which just about covered her perfectly groomed pussy, 'I don't.' She smiled at him. 'I'm sorry Fabio, but I'm just not having it. Now you'd better hurry up and get dressed, you've got a holiday camp to run. We won't mention this again. Ooh, dear me, what's that on the floor?' And turning her back to him she bent right over, to pick something up.

Oh I'll have a word with her later, he thought to himself as he approached her behind from behind. Try again. Somehow, I've got to get her out of the picture, before Mamma turns up this evening.

But in the meantime – well, if in doubt, fuck it.

*

'Bastard!' Bonnie had known this was going to happen. 'That's so unexpected, I'm so shocked!'

'So'm I, Bee.' Michelle wept daintily into her tissue, dabbing at the corner of each eye gently so as not to smudge her make-up, because that would be unprofessional.

'Well I think you did the right thing, Michelle,' said Bonnie as she forked the coffee gateau that nobody else liked into her soap-scrubbed face – for her to wear any make-up at all would be unprofessional.

'Do you?' Those pretty little hazel eyes looked up at her friend. Both of them wondered what their mums would say to do in this situation.

'Yeah, course. Don't let 'em get away with anything, that's what I always say.' Bonnie was an expert on sexual relationships – god knows, she'd seen enough marriages close up to know that all husbands were crap and all wives were shit. Especially on holiday – this was her fourth season, and she'd seen it all.

'Thanks, Bee, you're such a good friend to me. I still can't quite believe it, you know. No man has ever spoken to me like that, it was such a shock. I don't know how he had the nerve.' Michelle had finished crying now. 'Right. I'd better get on, iron my towels and that.'

'Yeah,' said Bonnie, easing her big frame up from the table, 'I've got to brief those lazy bastard nannies again. Should be a busy week – we've got two Camillas, three Justins and one poor little bugger's been called Spike, can you believe it? And there's one family whose names have got to be a misprint – I mean who in their right mind would call their little boy Feather?'

Both girls parted company, sighing and tutting as they did so – another week of hell in heaven coming up. So boring.

2. Arrivals

A lively-looking woman, FELICITY CLIFTON, with big bushy orange-yellow and white streaky, curly hair, which she has somehow contained within a smart business suit look, is talking very quickly at us.

> FELICITY
> When we were on the plane, I remember saying to Cliff that I really hoped the other passengers weren't going to the same place as us.

The caption reads 'PR Guru'. She's late thirties, early forties. Busy.

> FELICITY
> I was appalled when it became apparent that they all were. [She smiles.] I thought some of them were just dreadful.

*

'MAL-COLM!' yelled a lumpy woman with a bubble perm, in the direction of a child who was twirling himself round and round and round the pillars in the Arrivals lounge.

'COME 'ERE! NOW!' The boy ignored her. The woman said to what must have been her husband, standing there in a green Heineken T-shirt with a shaved head looking gormless, 'Go and get 'im will ya, Stew? I've got to take 'er to the toilet.' And she set off, dragging a red-faced little girl wearing too many clothes behind her.

'Right then, is that everyone safely through customs?' An extremely handsome young man with a Seaside Villages clipboard looked up and flashed a perfect smile. A big bell rang in Sammy's head. 'Mmm, he's fit,' she said out loud, by mistake. To her *mother*.

'Yes, well, I should think he gets a lot of exercise out here,' Tessa replied.

Random, thought Sammy, who was keen to employ the teenage vocabulary at any opportunity.

'Um, excuse me, we haven't got our luggage, it doesn't seem to have come off the plane yet,' ventured a normal-looking couple. A boring-looking couple, thought Felicity.

'Oh, OK, you'd better come with me to the Enquiries desk,' said the one-man boyband, flashing another Top Ten smile. 'Would the rest of you like to start getting on the coach, please?'

Felicity hadn't been on a coach for years, thank god, but Spike thought it was very, very exciting, and announced in a loud voice that he'd not been on a bus before, ever. He wanted to sit with his nannygranny Gina, which was fine by everyone except Felicity, who thought that surely a little boy who didn't get to spend much time with his mother should want to sit on *her* knee. But Cliff performed his usual peace-keeping smooth; and rather than make a fuss, Felicity stared out of the window at the scorched scenery, trying to cover up her hurt by applying goal-setting business strategies to her relationship with her son, so that he would damn well *want* to be on her lap for the return journey. Christabelle sat on her own, towards the back, away from her step-family. She preferred being on her own.

'Good afternoon to you, ladies and gentlemen, my name's Bonnie and I'd like to welcome you on behalf of Seaside Villages!' A big fat she-devil of a woman, with thin shoulder-length mousy hair and a large nondescript swollen face, was towering over them. Felicity could tell Bonnie thought she was giving them her warmest smile, but it came across as more of a menacing grimace. A small child began to cry.

Bonnie was wearing the Seaside Village uniform of bright blue shirt and red shorts, both necessarily huge (prompting Cliff to recall an old Billy Smart's joke, which Felicity informed him still wasn't funny), and she was lurching about at the front of the coach, using a microphone as her weapon of choice. She nodded at the driver, who pressed a button on his radio, and a wobbly jingle wibbled its way over the distorted speaker system. They all knew it off by heart, it had been haunting their television screens during the adbreaks since five minutes after Christmas. 'Hooray!' shouted Bonnie. And again. 'Hooray!'

Good god, thought Felicity, what the hell am I doing here?

'Now as I said, I'm Bonnie,' said Bonnie, 'and I'd

like to say a big welcome to all of you! So – welcome! We do hope you're going to enjoy your stay here with us.'

'Enjoy' is not the word I'm thinking of, thought Felicity.

'And so on behalf of Fabio and the team –'

In the seat behind, Gina said into Spike's little ear, 'That's your uncle! He's the big boss!'

Cliff snorted to himself with disdain, Felicity stifled a smile.

'– I'd like to say a big welcome from Seaside Villages – the village beside the seaside, beside the ...!' Bonnie beamed at her captive audience, and cupped a hand around the back of her ear. Silence. The small child started to cry again.

'Now that's not very good, is it?' scolded the big girl.

'No,' said a little boy.

'Come on, let's try that again, shall we?'

'No,' said the same little boy. People laughed.

'That's better!' Bonnie smiled with relief. 'You see, you'll have a much nicer time if you join in. Now I'd just like to say, that we're nearly there now –'

'Hooray!' shouted an audacious dad.

Bonnie ignored him. 'And I just want to say, that once you've been shown to your rooms and settled yourselves in and everything, there's a meet-and-greet cocktail party at five o'clock in the Bucket and Spade, which will be incorporating a short briefing session about the Kids Klubs and the Waterfront and stuff like that, OK?'

Nobody bothered to ask what the Bucket and Spade was because at that particular moment nobody wanted to know. The atmosphere on the bus had dropped from eager anticipation of nearlytherenow, to dread and fear of what was lying in wait for them. They hadn't thought it was going to be like this.

*

Gina liked the way they greeted you at the Village, it was very friendly. It wasn't every day that she got off the bus to be serenaded by lots of smiley young people clapping and banging tambourines, shouting 'WELCOME!' at her. (Maybe she should mention it to whoever's in charge of Southend public transport.) Reminded her of those Harry Cushion bald orange people with those tiny bells who they used to see every year Up West, when Alfie'd drive her up to see the Christmas lights along Oxford Street. She'd always worried they'd catch their death, poor things, with no hats on and no sign of a thermal. But he'd always laughed at her, said their god kept them warm. She could hear him laughing now in fact; that cheered her up a bit. Oh love, wish you were here.

'I am not going to let you do this,' Cliff said to Felicity, as he followed her up the stairs that led into the hotel foyer.

'Do what, exactly?' Felicity turned near the top of the steps to challenge him.

'Cancel. Go home. Get the first flight out of here, etcetera etcetera.' He sighed. 'Your usual trick.'

'But this is going to be awful!' she despaired.

'How the hell do you know?' Cliff passed her, to stand on the top step, so that they were eyeball to eyeball. 'You haven't even gone inside yet.'

'I don't need to,' sniffed Felicity. 'I'm sorry Cliff, but I only allow myself a limited amount of time off a year, and I don't intend to spend two precious weeks of it at a middle-class Butlins! You've got to admit, it's not like it looked in the photographs . . .' Blimey, it must be bad, she looked like she was going to cry. 'Honestly, Fabio could have said something.'

'Look, come on, darlin' –' He went to stroke the side of her face which had always been a winner, but she moved out of the way. 'Please? Won't you just stay for little Spike? He's really been looking forward to this, all three of us together, in the same place at the same time . . .' She was softening. 'At least let's see what the food's like – it is free, after all. And so's the wine, and the beer, and the childcare, and the evening entertainment, and the watersports, and the sun and the sea and the sand – oh come on, Fliss, we can have a laugh, all inclusive!' Nothing. He lowered his voice. 'And anyway I thought you wanted to steal the Seaside Villages PR account? I thought you were here to spy, spot the loopholes, so you could pitch for the business when you got home?' She was melting now, he knew he'd get through to her, he always did in the end; but she'd been a tougher nut to crack of late. 'Tell you what – when we go back, I'll book a weekend at the Manoir for just us two. Have a little grown-up break, eh? No kids, no mother-in-laws, just us. Come on doll, just give it a go, eh?'

Felicity thought about it. 'Oh all right then, I'll try. But that's all I can promise. I'll give this place forty-eight hours. But business or no business, if I still don't like it after that, I'm out of here, OK?' And she huffed off inside, to kick some ass in Reception.

Women!

*

'I can't believe I've got to share a room with you,' complained Sammy as Tessa inserted the key into the lock of Room 211. 'Dad promised me I'd get a room to myself, it's like, so unfair.'

'Why is it, Sammy, that all your sentences go up at the end? You sound Australian, you've been watching too much *Neighbours*.'

'What?' Sammy pushed past her mother as she opened the door, and strode into the room. 'What d'you mean? Everyone talks like this, we're teenagers, it's, like, our job, we – oh wow!'

They were both knocked out by it. This was one of the best views either of them had ever seen; it certainly beat the Edinburgh grey they looked out on every day from their little flat – this was in colour. Directly beneath them the red-and-white striped awning over the sun terrace gave way to the turquoise-blue swimming pool, which had just the right number of people around it (not too many, and not too few) with the obligatory couple of squealing little girls wrestling with an inflatable dolphin.

Beyond the pool were a few waving palm trees, giving some welcome shade to the fresh green lawn, complete with children's playground and cricket stumps, and there were a few buildings disguised as straw huts which dotted the way down to the beach.

It was yellow sand, no, gold, a golden and sparkly

beach with big straw parasols and rows of glistening white sunloungers, just waiting for you and your book; and by the shore, pointy kayaks and little boats with big sails were lined up all ready to whisk out to the sea, which was cleanly glittering and shimmering, winking up at the sun who was happy to smile back.

Some distant figures in yellow life jackets were chatting way out there on the bobbing pontoon, waiting for the waterskiing boat to come back and give them a turn. Amateur windsurfers dotted the near horizon. The sky was brochure blue, clear blue, dreamy blue.

'Ooh, fancy a swim?' Tessa kicked off her shoes – the cool, tiled floor sent a chilly thrill up her spine. It was quite a sparse room; two single darkwood beds with a little cupboard in between, and over on the opposite wall hung an oval mirror with a wooden frame, probably carved by a local artisan. Underneath it sat a built-in darkwood dressing table. Its chair had an incongruously plush red velvet seat. There was a huge built-in wardrobe as well, with enough space to hang every item of clothing that Tessa owned. Which was just as well, because that was exactly what she'd brought; Jeremy was always complaining that she didn't know the meaning of travelling light.

'A swim? Yeah right, I don't think so,' said her daughter. 'You know I'm nil by water.'

'Yes but that's at school,' said Tessa, who was amazed that the P.E. teacher still hadn't worked out that Sammy's periods seemed to last for a whole term. She laid claim to what was going to be her bed by lying down on it, and allowed the unwinding process to begin, wriggling her toes free of their sockery. 'Oh come on Sammy, the whole point of coming here is that there's loads of watersports and sailing and tennis and stuff like that to do, and they're all built into the price of the holiday, so you might as well give everything a go, Dad's already paid for it. We thought you'd love it, there's no chance of getting bored here.'

'Oh don't be ridiculous Mum, I'm just not going in the water ever, OK? Besides' – she went to open the door as someone had knocked on it – 'I haven't even brought my swimming costume. Oh –' she said, the cute guy from the airport was standing there, holding their bulging baggage up with virtually just his little fingers. 'Hi.' Overcome with unaccustomed shyness, Sammy looked down. At his feet. He was wearing those really gross sporty-type sandally things. And they were orange.

'Hi, I'm Jamie, here's your luggage!' and he beamed at her, like the jolly member of the Seaside Village community he was trying so hard to be.

'Thanks, that's so great!' sarcasted Sammy as she lugged the suitcases in. 'Bye now!' she grinned, just like an American teenager in a sitcom, and with a little wave she slammed the door in his face. Ohmigod, he was gorgeous!

*

The Bucket and Spade turned out to be the beach bar, with a couple of horse brasses nailed up here and there to give it a village-pub effect. As the new arrivals gathered for the welcome cocktail with complimentary briefing, they eyed each other up with suspicion. Those who'd already been here one week had really gone native; they were scantily dressed and shamelessly relaxed.

'So strange to see white people again,' said a man sitting at the next table to Felicity's, sporting a pair of brown bosoms almost the same size as hers.

'Is it,' she said, but with no question mark at the end of her tone.

'Yes,' he laughed, and so did his man-tits, 'you people look a bit grey to me. All stressed out, and running about like headless chickens, complaining about everything before you know how it works. Very funny.' He shook his head and knocked back his weak Tequila Sunrise.

'Hey, Marcus, d'you want my cherry?!' A red-faced woman clutching a tumbler of pina colada lurched towards their general direction. 'Ha-ha-ha-ha-ha, oh dear, what are we like,' they both laughed at each other. This is quite unbearable, decided Felicity. I am surrounded by Friends of Kathy.

Saved by her husband. 'Why didn't you wait for me?' Cliff plonked himself down beside her, kitted out in clean black T-shirt with khaki shorts and his old favourite brown leather moccasins that she'd thrown away twice, and he'd pulled back out of the bin twice.

'I didn't know how long you were going to be,' grumped Felicity.

'But I was only having a shower – give me a break, it's not as if I was going to be ages doing my hair, is it?' He took a plastic cup of cocktail from the gurning tray bearer, Felicity declined. Cliff sighed. 'That was supposed to be funny.' He put his hand on her knee and rubbed it. 'Come on, babe, what's the matter?'

'I'm sorry, I'm trying to be open-minded, I really am, but I just think this is going to be awful.' Her face was stricken, she was looking around like someone who'd got out of the lift at the wrong floor. 'I think we've made a terrible mistake.'

'It's too loud, isn't it?' Gina shouted at Cliff, as Spike dragged her over to his parents' table.

She sat down, just as the music ended abruptly, and on came that Seaside Village theme again, not wobbly this time, just annoying. Ah – Gina spotted Fabio at last, arriving late, ducking down behind the bar.

. . . *beside the seaside, beside the sea!* sang out the wretched jingle.

'Ladies and gentlemen, boys and girls, please welcome your host during your stay' – Gina would know her own son's voice anywhere, he was announcing himself in an American accent for some reason – 'Fabio Clifton!'

Fabio appeared from behind the bar and leapt up on top of it in one smooth movement. He smiled his most winning smile, and as they looked up at him standing there above them, most of the women instantly loved him unconditionally, while most of the men instantly loathed him, also unconditionally.

Fabio was classically tall, dark and handsome. And what with his long, dark, shiny hair billowing back off his handsome tanned face in slow, rippling motion, and his magnificent tanned torso, teasingly visible through his open white linen shirt, and his long legs encased in flowing sandy linen trousers, he looked like a modern-day god standing up there, beaming down at the assembled throng beneath him.

Gina waved up at her son excitedly – she hadn't seen him for ages. He didn't seem to notice her, so she called out 'coo-eee!' and she waved again.

He flicked her a wink and carried on with his welcoming speech. '... So it gives me great pleasure to welcome Bruno, who's our resident Tennis Coach!'

As blond, moustachioed, once-attractive Bruno waffled on in a thick German accent about tournaments and dress codes and returning balls to the clubhouse, Felicity whispered to Cliff, 'Good grief, what's happened to Fabio? He's changed a bit, hasn't he?!'

'Looks like a fucking poof,' muttered Cliff, who had not been physically blessed with any of his Italian mother's genes except tannable skin; in all other aspects, he was an exact copy of Alfie's British bulldog.

'He's so ten years ago!' declared Felicity with delight. 'Designer stubble, the lot – hilarious!' Things were looking up. 'It's like being in a time warp, he looks like David Ginola in the hair sponsorship days!'

The Watersports department were a joy to behold as well – Sammy noticed that the fit guy from the airport who'd delivered their luggage was something to do with waterskiing. Oh no, their paths might never cross again. She might have to get wet after all. Shit.

Everyone sat up to listen to Bonnie's speech about the Kids Klubs, paying good attention, as for most of them that was the whole point of this holiday – round-the-clock childcare while the grown-ups got to play too. The children's groups were named after English country garden flowers, starting with the babies in Daisies, and working up to the teenagers, the Sunflowers. All the dads perked up when the nannies were lined up and introduced, like shy beauty contestants; several men secretly allotted themselves someone to think about later.

Then it was Michelle's turn. Fabio hadn't managed to find her all day, but he had to admit, as she came up to take her turn with the microphone, she was looking extra fuckable tonight. She virtually snatched it from him, scratching his hand with one of those sharp nails that he'd asked her to make blunt, many times, but she'd refused.

'Hello, everybody,' she smiled, hibiscus blossom perched prettily behind her ear, shiny maroon hair scraped back into a perfect bun with just the right amount of little bits sticking out to make it modern, stylish and fashionable. 'I'm Michelle, and as Fabio said, I run the Beauty and Hairdressing Salon here. But even though it's called the Village Gossip, I can assure you, your secrets are safe with me!' She giggled at her own little joke. 'Ladies, do please come and see me to make an appointment for all your usual services; and, gentlemen, we can get rid of all your executive stresses – I am also a fully trained masseuse . . .'

I bet you bloody are, darlin', thought Cliff. Even though he hadn't said it out loud, Felicity still knew to whack him on the arm.

'. . . all treatments, depilations and hairdressing requirements catered for.' Big smile. 'Now before I go, I'd just like to say that is there a Mrs Clifton here?'

Felicity reluctantly identified herself. God, Cliff must have arranged a little surprise for her, how embarrassing.

'Well, I'd just like to extend to you an especially warm welcome. I have here a gift voucher, for your own personal use, at a time of your choosing, in the Village Gossip, during your two-week stay with us. Ladies and gentlemen, please welcome our boss Fabio's mother!'

The boss did his best to quell the hearty applause, and explained that Felicity was in fact his sister-in-law, and that actually Gina was his mother, but it was too late. The damage had been done.

*

'How many are you?' asked the girl at the restaurant door.

'Um, one,' said a confused Tessa, who was standing on her own. She'd wanted to eat with her daughter, at least on the first night, but Sammy had insisted on 'chilling' with the other teenagers, who had all gathered on the beach. However, there was a certain amount of negotiating yet to be done between mother and daughter, about what was an acceptable level of alcohol for a sixteen year old, and what was unreasonable controlling behaviour from a parent. And Sammy had taken advantage of her mother being too tired to start bargaining tonight; she'd left the room before Tessa had had the chance to say, 'Please come and eat with me, I don't want to be on my own.' Well, fair enough, Tessa reasoned, it was Sammy's holiday too. And it was probably just as well, Jeremy was always saying Tessa should be a bit more independent – and she didn't want to lean on Sammy too heavily either. She was still very young, and Tessa could well remember the pressure her own parents had put on her, being an only child herself –

'*How* many?' asked the girl again, incredulous.

'Just me,' answered Tessa, feeling more solo by the second.

'What, just one of you?' asked the girl in disbelief.

'Yes,' said Tessa, confused as well now, perhaps the girl was deaf and wearing one of those invisible hearing aids. 'Just the one,' she said a little louder, holding up a finger to demonstrate exactly how many that was.

'Are you waiting for someone then?' said the girl.

'No,' said Tessa, reddening and praying that her chin wasn't going to start wobbling, 'I'm here on my own.' And actually, anything the matter with that? If only she was brave enough to say it out loud.

'Really?' The girl stared at Tessa, as if she was a freak. 'Wow!' And then she looked at the now quivering wreck in front of her, all sympathetically and patronizingly, and said 'ah'. She put her head on one side and tutted. 'Ah, shame . . .' and she wrinkled her nose. Picking up just one roll of blue napkin with knife and fork from the basket, she said, 'You'd better follow me then,' and strode off into the seating area.

I won't have a starter or a pudding, thought Tessa, as they weaved through the busy outside terrace of the restaurant, full of people clearly having a great time, drinking and laughing with their partners and families and friends. Then it'll be over quickly. I can run up to my room, and read my book until I fall asleep.

'Here you go!' said the girl, 'you can sit with them!' A bemused couple with food in their mouths and drink to their lips looked up at Tessa, who thought she was going to be sick with embarrassment on to their table, right there and then.

'This lady's here on her own,' announced the girl to anyone within earshot and some without. 'I think she'd like to sit with you.' And she busied off, to find a chair for the gooseberry.

'Sorry,' said Tessa, still standing there like a lemon.

'Don't worry about it,' said the man, who had a very sunburnt nose, which looked like a purple parsnip.

'I'll find somewhere else,' said Tessa, who seemed to be rooted to the spot. And, of course, she felt duty-bound to use the chair that had been fetched for her.

'No, don't!' said the wife, who had a little red radish for a nose. 'Sit with us. We don't mind, really.' She looked as if she was telling the truth. 'Please.'

Hoping she'd be able to hold it together in the face of such kindness, Tessa sat down. 'How long have you been here?' she asked.

'This is our second week,' said the Radish, 'we're really enjoying it, aren't we?' she asked her husband, who nodded as he ate. 'We came here last year, just for a week, but the children loved it so much we've booked for three weeks this time.'

'Is there a menu?' Tessa asked.

'It's a buffet tonight,' he said, 'in there.' The Parsnip somehow managed to point indoors with his head. 'It alternates you see,' Radish explained, 'tomorrow's waitress service.' It soon became obvious that they were the kind of couple that explained everything together, did everything together, were quite literally each other's other half.

It wasn't bad food, but it wasn't good. Everything was served in big stainless-steel catering-sized trays, with underheaters on white tablecloths. The lids didn't sit properly on top of the tureens because the big serving ladles got in the way, and so the food was sticky warm rather than piping hot. (Tessa made a mental note to come down for dinner a bit earlier tomorrow night. It was only the bright-white new arrivals who were helping themselves to what was left, the nutty brown people had nearly finished already.)

Just inside the restaurant doorway was a trestle table groaning under the weight of about fifty opened wine bottles and a big steel keg of lager. People were helping themselves to two, three bottles at a time. Tessa thought she'd just take the one – a crisp local white, should go well with the chicken breast in a yellow-ish looking sauce that she'd gone for, even though the little notice underneath the tray called it *poulet sportif*, and she didn't know what that was.

'Oh no, you don't want to drink that, it's like paint stripper!' Radish said, when Tessa brought it back to the table.

'We like the rosé,' Parsnip explained.

Tessa would have preferred white spirit at this stage, and so she gulped it down anyway. She was feeling very new girl, and a bit shaky-tearful with it.

'So brave, to be eating all on your own,' said the Radish, in awe. 'I don't think I could do that, I'd be too scared,' she giggled across at him.

'Well,' said the Parsnip, as he put down his knife and fork, 'hopefully you'll never have to, my darling.' And he put his hand out to touch hers, as they exchanged an intimate secret smile. Tessa began to feel nauseous.

'He's such an old romantic,' the Radish confided, 'honestly, he's hopeless! Look what he bought me for our last anniversary.' She proudly showed Tessa a pretty diamond bracelet. 'Isn't it lovely?'

'How many children have you got?' Tessa asked, trying to change the subject.

'Just the two,' answered the Radish.

No need to ask their names and ages, thought Tessa as she threw more turps down her throat –

'Daniel's three, and Sarah's seventeen months.'

– because she's going to tell me anyway.

'You?' asked the Parsnip.

'Just the one, Sammy, she's sixteen.'

'Gosh!' exclaimed the Radish, 'you don't look old enough!'

'No, well, I had her when I was very young.'

'And what about her father, is he here?' asked the Parsnip.

'Oh, er, no.'

'Is he coming out later then, to join you?' Her turn.

'No.'

His. 'Oh, why not?'

'We're separated.'

'Oh dear, how awful.' Both of them together. 'You poor thing,' added the Radish, with true feeling.

'It's not that bad,' said Tessa, who had begun to eat as fast as she could. 'There are some good points to being a single parent.'

'Like what?' They really wanted to know.

Put on the spot like this, Tessa couldn't think of one. Well, nothing sensible. 'You get to choose what you watch on TV!' she finally announced, triumphantly. And stupidly.

They exchanged a Look between themselves, and Tessa realized that their togetherness wasn't only making her feel sick, but a tiny bit jealous too. And OK, lonely. She wished Jeremy was here, so that she could exchange those looks with him. Even after five years, she really missed being part of a couple; for all her brave talk, she still hated being on her own.

'Great,' they said. 'Thing is,' they said, 'we both like the same programmes, don't we, so that's not much of a problem for us, is it?'

The rest of the meal was taken up by them recounting how they met, how long ago that was, where they'd lived, how happy they were to become parents, and how they still loved each other just as much today as when they'd first met. More, in fact. Just as Tessa was contemplating pretending to have a fishbone stuck in her throat (which, she realized later, would never have worked as she was eating chicken), she was rescued by the startling sight of one of the nannies holding aloft a small blackboard, which said, 'Baby needs a hug in Room 146'.

'Uh-oh, that's us,' said the Radish to the Parsnip. (Was it the boy Turnip or the baby Swede? thought Tessa – who'd already christened this lot the Root family.)

'It's a brilliant system – the nannies take it in turns to sit on each floor of the hotel, and every fifteen minutes they go round listening at the door of every room to see if any of the children are crying. And if they are, they come and get you!' they explained, together.

'Look, I'll go and see to them, and then I think I'll probably go to bed; you two stay here and chat – don't worry, I trust you with him!' Radish said to Tessa, who trusted herself too – for god's sake, look at him. 'Don't be too late, will you, honey – remember it's your turn to take them to Kids Klub in the morning! And try not to wake me up when you come in – unless you make it worth my while!' And she actually winked at him.

'God, I love that woman so much,' sighed the Parsnip, as he watched his wife weave her way out of the restaurant, waving to some of their new-found friends as she went.

Tessa left it, ooh, about thirty seconds after the Radish had gone to make her own excuses and leave, trying her hardest not to break into a run.

3. The First Day

'CLIFF CLIFTON' says the caption. 'Photographer'. A stocky-looking man, in his mid-
fifties, with very short, cropped white hair
and jiggly brown eyes. He is not as handsome
as his brother, but certainly has something
for the ladies. A faded blue tattoo is just
visible on one arm, poking out from his black
Ralph Lauren polo shirt.

                    CLIFF
    To tell the truth, I didn't think she'd
    last another day. It just wasn't her
    sort of thing. See, I could tell this
    was going to be a bloody nightmare,
    even then.

                      *

It had been a while since Felicity had been woken up by
the sun squinting through shutters. Normally her sleep
was shattered by her screaming alarm clock, and then
the back-up one over in the far corner of their bedroom
on top of the tallboy, plus her mobile on ring and vibrate
rattling in the metal wastepaper bin, if she was really tired.
And if she still wasn't up, Spike was allowed to come into
their bedroom after he'd had his breakfast, before being

taken to school – though Cliff didn't really like that, as he didn't want his son 'seeing something he shouldn't'. Fat chance of that, thought Felicity, those days were long gone. Although they had had a very drunken quickie a few weeks ago, but that didn't count as she'd been thinking of John Cusack at the time.

She opened one eye, and looked across the pillow at her sleeping husband. A wave of sadness swept over her – he was still a decent-looking man, a bit crumpled around the edges perhaps, but he was getting on a bit now. Fifty-five next birthday. He looked pretty healthy too, even though Felicity knew it to be just a T-shirt tan. Once he could have claimed it was from shooting in exotic locations all year round. Now she knew it was from walking the dog in Kensington Gardens every day. Still, he looked fine, all things considered. But it was the 'all things' that had begun to bother her. In fact, they were making her mad as well as sad. But why?

The facts: Cliff was a good dad, but a bad husband. He'd been great until Spike came along, they'd had a lot of fun together, but then he'd switched all his attention to the baby. Which meant that he'd lost interest in his career, so she'd had to work even harder. And the balance of power had shifted. Which meant that she'd lost respect for him. Which meant, in a nutshell, that she didn't fancy him any more.

She knew she should, he looked the same as usual, but she just couldn't. He'd tried it on last night, but she'd feigned tiredness and god love him, he'd stroked her hair until he thought she'd fallen asleep – which had just irritated her further, she didn't like him touching her any more, and that made her feel even worse.

'Mummy!' Spike jumped on the bed and the door flew open, all at once. 'We're on holiday! Where's the beach? Where's my bucket? Can I have chocolate, pleeeeeease? Wake up! Mum! I want an ice cream!'

Cliff was awake in a trice. 'Hello mate!' He sat up in bed. 'Exciting, isn't it?' He nudged Felicity, she grunted, pretended to be sleepy. She couldn't face Spike's high-octane energy quite yet. 'What're we going to do today then?'

'He's supposed to be at the Kids Klub by nine o'clock,' Felicity told her pillow. 'What's the time?'

'Seven thirty,' yawned Cliff. 'He must have jet lag.'

'Oh don't be ridiculous Cliff, it's only an hour's difference.'

'It was a joke.'

'Well not a very funny one. Where's Christabelle, anyway?'

'Here,' said a quiet voice lurking in the corridor, neither in nor out of the room.

'You can come in, you know,' called Felicity, trying to be Welcoming. Her stepdaughter shuffled into their bedroom, dressed more like a black rapper from Harlem than a young woman from Twickenham.

'Could you be an angel and take him down to breakfast for us?' asked Felicity, trying to be Nice, although they all knew she'd only agreed to Christabelle coming if (a) she shared a room with Spike, and (b) was Helpful.

'OK.' Did this girl ever smile?

'Gawdon Bennett, I've got a cracking hangover – that local wine's bloody filthy, I'm sticking to beer tonight. Tell you what, I'll come with you, I fancy a fry-up,' said Cliff.

'OK.'

Nobody moved.

'You go now, I'll see you down there.' Pause. Cliff indicated his nether regions to his daughter. 'I haven't got anything on under here.'

'Oh. Right.' She took hold of Spike's hand and led him out of the room.

'You've gone bright red,' the little boy said. As they walked into the hotel corridor, he began to cry.

'What's the matter?' Christabelle asked, as she shut the door behind them.

'It's not fair,' his parents heard him wailing loudly down the corridor, 'I wanted to see my daddy's willy! I hate you! Where's my nannygranny?'

*

In her room next door, Gina had been up for hours. She had woken to the usual split second of feeling all right, and then the grief had punched her in the heart, and the stomach, and had kept on punching her, until she remembered and felt all the pain, enough for it to invade her whole body for yet another long, long day.

But this morning was going to be a little different, she was going to have a ray of sunshine in her life, just for a short while; she'd arranged to meet Fabio for an early breakfast, they would get some time alone together at last. It would be the first time they'd been alone since the night before Alfie's funeral. She'd spoken to him since then of course on the telephone, but it wasn't the same as being with him. Poor Cliff had tried to help her through this, but he just made her feel worse. Holiday indeed. For all his big gestures, he was like a little dog wanting a pat on the back all the time, and she had nothing to give right now. Besides, he wasn't able to make her feel better, not like Fabio could. She'd only agreed to come here to see Fabio. Fabio knew her so well, you see. He understood.

You shouldn't have a favourite, Alfie said in her head, *you should love them both the same.* 'So should you,' she said out loud. 'But we both know that we have one each, don't we?' No reply.

It wasn't that she didn't love Cliff – of course she did, everyone did. He was just like his father, a good man, the do-anything-for-anybody type. They were like that dog in the Tom and Jerry cartoons, you know, the one that keeps rescuing his puppy son and says, 'Dat's my boy!' with such pride. They were a team those two, Alfie and Cliff, right from the word go. Two peas in the shell. Which was right, father and son should be together. And anyway, she'd been busy, she'd had to look after Papà, once Mamma had passed away. She'd been lonely, though. Until, after ten long years of disappointment, Fabio came along.

Ah, he was a *bello bambino, bellissimo.* They soon became a team as well; he looked more like her son than Cliff ever did. Big brown eyes gazing up at her lovingly from his pram, he smiled at everybody. She could see him now as if it was yesterday. She used to walk the streets of

Leigh-on-Sea so proudly, stopping to let everyone have a good look at him. 'Blimey, Mrs Clifton,' they'd say, 'you've got a right bonny bouncer there!'

Gina smiled as she tidied up before going down to breakfast. Who'd have thought, her baby boy, in charge of all these people – the boss! She was as proud of him now as she had been when she was pushing his pram all those years ago. As she opened her door, to step out into the rest of the world, she took a deep breath and held her head high. She must be brave for Fabio, she mustn't upset him when he's so busy. She must do her best to hold her breaking heart together, even if it did feel ready to crack wide open with the pain of it all.

*

'But maybe she'd like to meet me properly, as your girlfriend,' protested Michelle, dabbing the sides of her little pouty mouth with a corner of her serviette. 'I think we'd really get on, you know.'

'No.' Fabio was determined to keep these two apart over the next fortnight. Mothers mustn't meet girls like this. 'Look, Michelle, I would appreciate a bit of privacy, please, babe? Mamma is coming down here any minute now, and I'd like to spend some time with her alone, if you don't mind.' Michelle opened her mouth to protest, but he said, 'Look, she's upset, she's grieving. Give the woman a break.' But she was still looking unconvinced, so he said as firmly as he could, 'Go. Now.'

'Ooh, masterful,' she smooched, as she slipped off her breakfast bar stool and slotted herself in between his legs, with one hand on his knee and the other on his bedenim'd crotch. She kissèd him, on the lips, in full view of all nearby villagers and more importantly, the restaurant staff. She tried to shove her tongue down his throat as well, and he automatically began to go for it, but suddenly came to his senses and stopped. He let her hand stay clamped on to his cock though – until he spotted his mother over her shoulder. Pushing Michelle off to one side, he sprang up and walked towards her, arms outstretched. 'Mamma!'

'Hmm, she's pretty,' commented Gina as they dis-embraced and her son led her towards an empty table. 'Too thin for childbirth though. She'd have problems.'

'Coffee?' he asked as he pulled out a chair for her.

'I've brought my own.' Gina produced a packet of *Lavazza*. Smiling, Fabio handed it to a passing member of the catering team. 'Big pot, please, Mandy, cheers.' Mandy smiled, keen for the excuse to get into the kitchen and pass on the Michelle-Fabio-In-Almost-Snog-Shock-Horror gossip.

(Affairs between staff and villagers were a sackable offence; affairs between staff and staff usually ended up being a regrettable offence. Mandy and Howell the chef knew this only too well, having had a bit of a secret fling that had ended nastily last season. Both had been horrified to find themselves posted to the same resort this year.)

'How are you, Mamma?' Fabio reached out for her hand and held it tight as he sat down.

'I'm fine, just fine, *mio piccino*,' Gina replied as breezily as she could.

His beautiful brown eyes searched into hers, right

down to the deep of her soul. She tried to fend him off with a smile.

'Hey, Mamma,' he spoke softly, 'it's me.'

'Yes, Fabio, I know it's you.' She tried to laugh, no sound came out. 'I'm fine, really, I am, I am ...' her voice trailed away, let her down. She wished he'd stop looking at her like that.

'You don't fool me, you know,' he said, softly, 'I can see how sad you are.'

'Fabio, please,' she begged, 'don't be nice to me. Let's talk about something else —'

'No, Mamma, no. It'll do you good to get it out.' He squeezed her hand. 'Would you like to go for a walk with me, along the beach?'

The intimacy in his voice began to fill her eyes with those round fat tears once more, they were brimming —

'Fabio!' It was that big girl from the coach, trying to weave through the tables and chairs without bumping into anybody, and not succeeding.

Fabio apologized to his mother with those irresistible eyes, and said, 'What, Bonnie?'

'I can't find the key to the Kids Kottage anywhere,' she puffed. 'D'you know where it is?'

'No, I don't. Who last had it?'

She sighed. 'If we knew that, I wouldn't be asking you, would I?'

'Well, who last locked up?'

'Tania.'

'Tania?! Tania the Village Idiot? You gave her that kind of responsibility?' Fabio sighed. 'Have you asked her what she's done with it?'

'Of course I've asked her!' She was quite cheeky, this nanny girl. Gina didn't like her tone.

'And she doesn't know where it is?'

'No!' Bonnie glanced at Fabio's mother, who could tell that she wanted to swear but didn't dare. 'It's lost.'

'Right.' He shrugged his shoulders.

The big girl took a big breath. 'So can I have the spare key?' She tried to smile. 'Please?'

'Oh, yes, right. Is there one?'

'Yes. Nikki, your secretary, keeps a copy of every key in the safe in your office.'

'Right, yes, well, go and ask her for it.' He turned back to his mother. 'Sorry about this.'

Gina didn't mind, she was grateful for the diversion. The flood was subsiding.

'And then shall I bring it back to you straight away?' Bonnie volunteered.

'Yes!' He patted her on the arm. 'Good! Go and ask Nikki for it, and then you bring it back to me immediately, OK?'

'Or I could give it back to Nikki, who could put it back in the safe, where it belongs.'

'Yes, whatever. Just go and do it, OK?'

'OK.' Bonnie half-smiled at Gina as she turned round, and lumbered her way out of the restaurant, tutting, and taking a couple of empty chairs and a tablecloth with her as she went.

'Sorry about that.' Fabio found his mother's hand again. 'Now where were we? Oh yes.' His face changed, he was serious now. 'So how've you been managing?'

'On the outside, quite well,' Gina replied. 'But I can't

lie to you, Fabio – I'm just pretending. Other people want you to be over it quickly, because they can't bear to see you in such pain for too long. And so for their sake, you try to look like you're feeling better. Only it's so strange, you see, inside it gets more difficult as time goes on, and not more easy. It hurts more every day, and so every day you have to pretend a little more.' She managed a weak smile.

'Oh Mamma, you don't have to do that with me,' Fabio said, with such kindness. 'You can tell me the truth, you know.'

'I know, I know.' She squeezed his hand, and felt a surge of love wrap round her, like a blanket. She knew he'd know what to say, she felt safe with him.

Mandy arrived with the coffee. 'Thanks babe.' As Gina poured some into Fabio's cup, he said to his mother, 'I'm sure being out here will help you; you'll get over this, quicker than you think.'

'No, I won't,' replied Gina, but Fabio didn't hear.

'Aha, here you are!' It was one of the sports men from last night, carrying lots of tennis rackets under his arm, looking just like Stan Smith used to on Wimbledon.

'Bruno!' Fabio leapt to his feet and smacked the palm of his hand against Bruno's. 'All set?'

'Game, set und metch!' Bruno winked, man-to-man. He was beaming, really grinning in fact. Gina was surprised, she didn't think the Germans were a happy people.

'No! You sly devil!' The tennis coach must have won a very difficult match.

'Oh yes. Und it didn't take as long as you thought that

it vould, in fect she gave in qvick, and what a goer, I can tell you –'

'Have you met my mother?' Fabio interrupted him, he obviously didn't like this boasting either, very unsportsmanlike.

'Oh, hello dear lady, ver charmed to meet viz you,' said Bruno as he took her tiny hand in his big paw and shook it hard. He looked like he'd once been what Alfie calls – called – a 'playboy'. Very brown, very smooth. 'I em epologizing, I can not stop to chat and take tea viz you, because today is the first day of tennis school for der new people, and I hev to be up at the courts just now.' He turned to Fabio. 'See you later, yah? Tell you all about it!' Another wink and he was gone.

Fabio shook his head, and smiled at his mum. To his dismay, he could see that she was about to cry, right here in the dining room. 'Mamma, hey, no, come on . . .' He moved his chair, trying to shield her from general view with his body.

'I'm sorry.' She looked down, tears splashing into her lap as she fumbled inside her dress for her handkerchief. 'It was just such a shock, Fabio.'

'But, Mamma,' his tone was soft, gentle, 'we knew he was ill, you knew you were going to lose him.'

'But I still feel so bad that I wasn't with him, at the end, he was alone, all on his own . . . I'm sorry, I'm sorry.' She looked up at him, her olived face shiny with watery grief. 'I didn't mean to do this, I'm sorry, I want to be strong for you . . .'

'It's all right,' he reassured her. 'Look, let me get you a tissue or something . . .' She tried to tell him she'd got

47

her handkerchief, somewhere, but he'd already left the table to look for the pile of spare paper serviettes that Mandy always left lying about.

'Oy! Boss man!' shouted a man sitting a couple of tables away. He was a DV (Difficult Villager) of the highest order, Fabio had spent most of the previous week avoiding him. 'I didn't come all this way to have marmalade that's been manufactured in France, mate!' He was wielding a foil-topped portion for one on the end of his knife. 'Whatever next? Coals from Aix-en-Provence?' The other couple sitting with them snickered, he was quite the wag.

'I'm very sorry, Mr Oakeshott,' said Fabio in his coolest tone, 'I'd have a word with Catering right now, only I think they're still busy trying to track down the Marmite you requested. And the baked beans. And the chicken tikka massala with pilau rice.' Of course, Catering were doing no such thing, instead they'd threatened instead to wooden spoon the fucker, but Mr Oakeshott needn't know that right now. 'We're still working on it,' assured Fabio, as he spotted a catering-sized kitchen roll sitting exactly where it shouldn't be, on the breakfast bar.

But by the time he'd made his way back to the table, Gina had gone.

*

Having skipped breakfast completely, Tessa selected herself a likely-looking sunlounger by the pool, and prepared for a full morning of sun, without sea and sand.

She'd forgotten how stressful all this being on holiday

business was. First there was the de-hairing thing. She'd had her legs waxed, as per normal, but this time she'd been brave enough to have her bikini line done as well. But unfortunately her hair follicles had gone into shock or something, because she'd come out in a bumpy bright-red rash where that woman had brutally wrenched it all away; and now, two days later, it was showing no sign of abating, but was still looking all spotty and sore and not just angry, but downright furious. She'd tried to cover it up with concealer just now, but it was the wrong colour, and it looked like she had a pigment problem in that area. So she'd walked down to the pool this morning with not only her diaphanous sarong wrapped around her seductively, but also a bloody great towel casually draped over her arm in front of the offending area, in case the sarong slipped off.

And then there was the business of suntan lotions. Having not been on a proper holiday for a number of years, Tessa was an alluring shade of blue-white, the same colour you'd paint a dingy cellar to brighten it up. She'd probably shine in the dark, she was luminous white. She'd brought several bottles of lotion with her of course, all part of the new M&S range; a factor 15 for the first few days, then once she'd established a basic tan, her plan was to go down to the 10, then the 8 and then the 6, and she'd bought a small bottle of Ambre Solaire 4 for the last couple of days, in case she felt daring and wanted to go for the burn. Plus a total block for the nose and lips and tops of ears and, if necessary, nipples.

Which was another worry. Was this a topless desti-nation, or not? She looked around the pool for clues.

Would you believe it, not one other woman there yet. They were probably busy checking their children into the clubs. There were a couple of dads, white skinny office-bound ones clutching broadsheet newspapers like security blankets, both looking up from their loungers at an overbearingly posh nutty brown man, who seemed to be scaring them to death, as he touted for volleyball volunteers.

So, should she get her tits out or not? Tessa didn't know what to do – she hated having those awful white marks, but neither did she want to be considered a tart. She looked over the swimming-pool fence, down the lawn, to see if she could see what the women on the beach were doing – no, too far away, no way of telling.

Being a sensible person, she came up with a sensible solution. Lie on her tummy, of course! That way, she'd avoid the bikini line and the bosoms being unnecessarily exposed, until she knew what the other women were doing. Phew.

So. She tied her hair back with one of Sammy's old scrunchies, and put her new Accessorize flip-flops with the big flowers back on (she'd read a terrible article in a magazine on the plane, about a woman who'd burned the soles of her feet and spent the rest of her holiday in a wheelchair), and arranged the back of the sunbed so that she wasn't at too uncomfortable an angle; then she put her beach bag underneath the sunlounger, in the shade, in case the suntan lotion melted; took out the book that she'd started last night, which had started off nicely enough but had now become a bit rude, in fact this sentence was obscene; perched her new rather flashy sunglasses on to the end of her nose and now, well now Tessa felt she really deserved a holiday, she was exhausted.

'Honestly Spike, I don't believe you sometimes!' An angry woman with a shock of orange hair bundled a little boy in through the swimming-pool gate. 'The whole point of us coming here was so that you would be looked after by those nice nannies, so that Mummy and Daddy could have a holiday too!'

The little boy was crying. 'I don't want to go in there, I don't like it!' he wailed. 'That big lady's really scary, I don't like her!'

'Oh don't be so ridiculous,' his mother snapped, 'you don't even know her!' She flumped down on to a sunlounger two along from Tessa, and appealed to the small boy. 'Look, all the other little boys and girls have gone in there without a fuss, why can't you?'

The little boy mumbled something Tessa couldn't hear.

'What?!' His mother hadn't understood it either.

'*I said,*' said Spike slowly, and loudly, with more patience than the grown-up had managed to display, '*I want to be with you.*'

'Oh.' This seemed to discombobulate the mother completely. 'Right.' She smiled, uneasily. 'Well, fine then, yes, OK. Um – let's stay here shall we, until lunchtime anyway, and then see how you feel after that.'

'Yesss!' The little boy jumped up and punched the air as if he'd just won the world cup. 'Come on, Mummy, let's go for a swim!'

'Oh no, Spike, not quite yet – it's a bit early for me. I've got your armbands though; you go in for a bit by yourself, and maybe I'll come in later.' If he was disappointed, he didn't bother to show it.

Tessa pretended to be reading more of her book, as the Blowing Up Of The Armbands Ceremony got underway. Fortunately the dad arrived just as the mother was about to lose it. He seemed like a nice man, quite a bit older than his wife, and quite a lot shorter, and he and Spike were soon splashing about ducking each other underwater, and doing that spitting thing with a big loop of water that only boys can do. Meanwhile, the mother got on with her own stuff; applying Clarins sunspritz, painting her toenails whilst reading what looked like a London property magazine, occasionally responding to a 'Look, Mum!' by pretending to be interested with a half-hearted, 'Oh yes, darling, well done.'

Tessa was reminded of family holidays they'd had. Only she'd been the one in the pool with Sammy, and Jeremy had been the distant figure on the edge of things, wanting to join in, but not quite able to let himself go.

'Coo-ee, Spike!' An older woman was standing on the other side of the fence, waving to the little boy.

'Hi, Mum!' shouted the dad, as he honeypotted into the deep end, splashing the bright-white office men and their important newspapers. They were too polite to complain, but his wife wasn't: 'Cliff! What the hell do you think you are doing?!' He ignored her; his son was doggy paddling his way over to his father, giggling so much he was close to drowning.

'Do that again, Dad, do it again!'

But the father got out of the pool, and went over to talk

to the older woman, his mother. Tessa noticed that even though it was a boiling hot day, the lady had a cardigan over her shoulders and was holding it close to her. She must be unhappy, thought Tessa, who'd recently seen a Discovery Channel documentary on body language.

After a little chat, the grandmother was persuaded to come and join the rest of the family. She looked nice, thought Tessa, she had a kind face and the little boy was clearly very fond of her.

She went back to her book and read that same disgusting sentence again. She'd just managed to get past it at last, when she heard a loud and familiar, 'Hey, Mum!'

Sammy was leaning lasciviously over the swimming-pool fence, surrounded by a group of lurking teenagers. 'Wotcha doing?'

Tessa ignored that deliberately stupid question, and beckoned Sammy to actually come into the pool enclosure, if she wanted to talk. To her great surprise, she did, followed by another rather sulky-looking bigger girl, dressed head-to-toe in baggy black long sleeves and trousers. She even had boots on, in this weather.

'Hi,' said Sammy, looming over the end of her mother's sunlounger. Tessa turned over to look up at her daughter, shielding her eyes from the sun with her hand. The other girl just sort of hung round, behind her.

'Have you had breakfast, Sammy?'

'Nah, too late.'

Tessa tutted and sighed and gave up, the way parents of teenagers do. 'So what are you doing now?'

'Well, according to the Sunflowers *timetable*,' she

slopped the word out, 'I'm supposed to be sitting in a damp kayak, developing a nasty case of thrush. But we're not going to do that, are we, Chris?'

'No,' said her shadow.

'What are you going to do instead, then?' asked Tessa.

'Dunno. Drink and smoke heavily, probably.' Tessa opened her mouth. 'Just kidding.'

'You could always come and sit beside me, do a bit of sunbathing perhaps?' suggested her mother. 'At least you might give the impression of being healthy with a bit of a tan, even if you do live on a diet of Wagon Wheels and Coke.'

'Tempting though that is Mum,' said Sammy, 'the alternative is hanging out all day with people of my own age who know that it's Limp Bizkit and not Limp Wristed, and who are as good at doing nothing constructive with their time as I am. Hmm, let me see' – she weighed up the possibilities with each hand – 'Mum, other teenagers; other teenagers, Mum – hmm, tricky . . .'

Tessa couldn't help but laugh. 'Oh go on then, go away, you wretch!' She gently pushed her daughter off the lounger with her foot, and watched her and the shadow walk back towards the pool gate. The overly tall spotty youths, who had been gangling in wait for Sammy, laughed as she did her admittedly brilliant fake limp.

'Oi, Christabelle!' The father from the family next door called out. To Tessa's surprise, Sammy's dull friend turned round and said, 'What?'

'You all right?' asked the man, quite kindly.

Tessa expected a Kevin-ish response, and so was surprised when the girl replied in a perfectly decent manner, 'Yes, thanks. See you later, Dad.' No smile, of course, that would be too much to expect.

'Hey, Mum!' shouted Sammy, just as the herd of teenagers was beginning to move off, 'that rash is looking a lot better now!' And giggling, she led them all away towards the beach.

Positively glowing with a mixture of embarrassment and fury, Tessa flipped back on to her stomach as quickly as she could, and found herself back at that same sentence, yet again.

*

It was just like any other day in paradise for employees of Seaside Villages.

Fabio spent far too much of the morning on the phone chasing up two hundred and forty croissants which hadn't arrived yet. He secretly enjoyed shouting at the local gardener he'd found chatting up that very pretty new chambermaid, instead of dead-heading the geraniums, but secretly loathed having to listen to his secretary, Nikki, drone on about her lovely boyfriend Sean at home, who was going to be faithful the whole time she was here, because he'd promised.

The internet connection was a bit dodgy, as usual, so it took Nikki a while to retrieve his emails. There was one from Head Office, which turned out to be one of those silly Forwards called 'Chinese Love Puzzle'; it was from that Martine, who'd got a bit of a thing for him; they'd had a fling when he was last in London, for that management training course. He'd thought she'd understood that he didn't want to take it any further;

and anyway, what sort of woman falls for a man who's just about to spend the next six months out of the country? She'd be better off getting engaged to one of those American prisoners in the orange boiler suits on Death Row. He deleted it, just like he'd deleted all her others, without bothering to read it. Silly girl.

Head Waitress Mandy came in to his office next, to complain that the chef had called her a cunt – Fabio told her to just ignore him, she burst into tears, and shouted something about not needing this, before slamming the door so hard that Rob from Maintenance had to come in and stick the doorframe back together again.

One family's luggage still hadn't arrived, so most of the afternoon was spent on the phone to the airport, trying to track it down. First, they'd said it had gone to Boston, then Bucharest. The wife of the family was getting quite upset, they'd had to wear the same clothes for a second day now, and had spent a small fortune on new swimwear from the Village Shop.

One of Bruno's girls, in a short white tennis skirt and baseball cap (just like the Athena poster girl in fact), popped by to say that they were still losing their balls; Fabio cracked what he considered to be a hilarious joke about that; she just shook her head quietly and left.

Howell the chef (a big broad man from North Wales) stormed in to say that he didn't need all this shit from a fucking dollybird; as he was talking, Fabio suddenly realized there were fresh bloodstains all down his white overalls, and a meat cleaver in his hand.

Turned out he was chopping up spare ribs, thankfully not Mandy's.

*

Meanwhile, in the calm and soothing aromatherapeutical atmosphere of the Village Gossip, Michelle was preparing to give a facial to a lady who'd just arrived yesterday. She was still suffering from the side effects of a busy, stressful, chaotic city life. They'd already established that her name was Olivia, she was thirty-five, and she had three children to look after. Her husband had come for the sporting facilities, the children would enjoy the Kids Klubs, and she'd come for a rest. An absolutely typical Seaside Village client, really.

Michelle had done her best of course to put this lady at ease. She'd dimmed the lights, lit the incense burner, started up the miniature Japanese water feature and even put on the Pan Pipes tape, which she personally hated, but not even that was working – this poor lady was still very tense. Her eyes were so wide open, she looked like she'd got riggermurtis, even though she wasn't actually dead.

'Ooh, you're stiff as a board,' said Michelle, as she rubbed some warm oil on to her hands in preparation. 'Now just lie down and relax,' she smiled, making the most of her sibilant 's' that Fabio found so cute and 's'exy. 'I'm not going to hurt you, you're supposed to enjoy this!' She sat herself down at the head end of the bed, and studied Olivia's skin closely with her professionally-trained beautician's eye. 'Now, you've either just had your period, or you're just about to have it, am I right?'

'Um, yes,' said the woman. 'I think so.'

'I thought so,' said Michelle, scratching, with her French manicured fingernail, at some of the flaky skin littering the upside-down forehead in front of her. 'And I think you like a bit of a tipple as well, don't you?'

'Well, not really. I'm not a big drinker.' Michelle didn't say anything, just waited. 'Well, you know, just the odd glass of wine here and there.'

'Yes, I thought so. Do you drink enough water?'

'Um, probably not, actually.'

'Definitely not, I'd say. Your skin is really bad.' Michelle plopped some dollops of runny cream on to the neglected face in front of her. 'And who's been plucking your eyebrows for you?'

'Um, well, me. I do them myself.'

'Yes, I thought so.'

Silence. The pan pipes carried on, trying to soothe the unsoothable. The woman was still rigid. She was going to need more help.

'So how's your relationship with your husband?' asked Michelle, massaging the ear lobes, leaving the woman's mouth free to reply.

'I'm sorry?' She sounded quite shocked – they usually were, Michelle was quite psychic in many ways. Very quick at getting straight to the truth.

'D'you still talk to each other?'

'Yes, thank you.'

'Still having sex?'

'What?'

'You getting enough orgasms? They're very good for the inner well-being, you know.'

'Um well, you know, no more or less than anyone else, I suppose.' The woman closed her eyes, and began to frown. Complete giveaway. Closing off, she was. Not an open person.

'Yes, sex is very good for the skin as well, you know. Gives you a nice rosy glow. And there's lots of protein and nutrients in the bit you can digest, if you know what I mean!' Michelle giggled. 'I make sure I have full sex at least twice a day, and you'd be well-advised to do the same, Olivia. Just see it as a beauty treatment if you like – the more you do it, the better you'll look and feel! And now that you're on holiday, well, you should be doing it all the time, shouldn't you? I would be, if I were you.'

'Really.' She didn't sound very grateful for this advice. 'Do you have any children, may I ask?'

Michelle laughed loudly. 'No, of course not! Do I look that stupid?!' She laughed some more. 'Ooh no, you wouldn't catch me running round after that lot. My friend's the Head Nanny here, I've seen all I need to, thank you very much, dear me no.' She laughed a bit more. 'I mean, think about it, I could end up as clapped out as my clients!'

And over in the Kids Kottage, Bonnie was in the kitchen, having a bit of trouble with Tania, the stupidest of all this season's nannies, the one who'd lost the key. She even knew she was called the Village Idiot, but it didn't seem to bother her. She was a very pretty girl, and Bonnie suspected she'd got away with not having to use her brain for far too long.

'So, let's retrace your steps, Tania. You locked up when the afternoon session was over, and then what happened?'

'Um, well I went over to the circus tent, to meet Otto.'

'Why?'

'Because it was five o'clock, and that was the time I was supposed to meet him there.'

'OK, then what?'

'He wasn't there.'

'So what did you do?'

Tania looked at Bonnie as if she was the stupid one. 'I waited for him, of course!'

This was worse than asking a three year old what he'd done with a missing felt-tip lid. No wonder the kids loved her, they were all on the same planet. Taking a deep breath, Bonnie asked slowly, 'And did he turn up?'

'Yes!' Tania smiled. And said no more.

Not for the first time, Bonnie understood baby batterers. 'And then what happened?'

'He taught me some circus skills!'

I'll bet he did, thought Bonnie, who knew Otto to be unfaithful at any opportunity to his stringy wife Helga, who wore herself out running the circus school for him.

'He said I was really good at the trampoline.'

'That's marvellous, Tania, I'm ever so pleased for you,' said Bonnie, flatly. 'And then what did you do?'

'Um, went back to my room, had my shower, went to the welcome drink, had my dinner, went to the Trivial

Pursuit evening in the Village Hall, won first prize and went straight to bed.'

'Now, Tania, one thing you just said isn't true, is it?'

Tania would have looked disconcerted, if she'd known what it meant. 'What thing's that?'

'The bit about winning Trivial Pursuit.' Bonnie adopted her you've-just-told-a-fib-and-we-don't-do-that-now-do-we look, very effective with bears of little brain.

Tania looked relieved. 'Oh no, we did, there was a guest on our team who's done a lot of travelling, and he knew everything about Geography, so we won! Yay!' What she didn't add was that she quite fancied him, and even though it was against the rules, she'd been flirting outrageously with him during the competition. She had a thing for older men, especially ones who knew more than her, which she had been delighted to discover was most men out here.

'Tania!' A pony-tailed Otto and his glinting gold tooth appeared at the Kids Kottage Kitchen doorway, which was split into two, like a barn door, in order to keep the little buggers from helping themselves to sharp and dangerous objects. He was dangling a bunch of keys, on a Power Puff Girls keyring. 'I found zese on ze vloor!' he said in his East European accent. 'Zey must have tropped oud of your pockette, ven you were hanging upzides down on trepeze.'

Nowhere else in the world would you hear a statement like that, thought Bonnie, despairingly. She was stuck out here with a load of freaks.

'Ah, there you are Bonnie!' a junior nanny, Angela, appeared behind the gurning Otto in the doorway, she looked desperate. 'One of the new little girls has just done a poo in the sandpit, because she was pretending to be their cat ...'

Ah yes, it was just another day in paradise.

4. Making Friends

FABIO is talking to the camera. It is hard to
concentrate on his actual words, as his beauty
is so distracting. He is saying something
about not having worked as a resort manager
before, but he thought he'd give it a go, being
the type of guy who was up for anything . . .

*

It was early evening. As she watched herself smooth
milky aftersun into her poor burnt shoulders in the
bedroom mirror, Tessa realized that she was starving.
Not only had she skipped breakfast, but she'd hardly
eaten anything at lunchtime either. Once again, she'd
been made to sit with a couple. But this had been even
worse than last night's experience, as their badly-behaved
four year old had tipped her plastic beaker on to Tessa's
plate, thereby drowning her quiche and salad in a pool of
weak orange squash. The child's parents had apologized,
of course, but Tessa could tell they thought it was naughty
but cute, rather than bad and on purpose. Surprised at
the ferocity with which she was able to hate a little girl
with curly blonde hair and big blue eyes, Tessa had taken
herself off at that point, and left the restaurant, grimly
clutching a banana and a bruised orange.

Having sussed out the pool in the morning, she'd

decided to spend the rest of the day on the beach. (It turned out that only the older women with big saggy African tribeswomen breasts took their tops off; the younger ones kept their undoubtedly more aesthetically pleasing chests to themselves. Not knowing which particular camp she belonged to, Tessa compromised by undoing the straps when she was toasting her back, and keeping those little triangles in place as best she could when grilling her front.) She'd got a bit further on with the book, which was turning out to be much better than she'd thought, having been written by some D-list celebrity, probably trying to revive her flagging career. But she'd spent most of her time staring out to sea, Thinking. Well, OK, Worrying. And Feeling Sad. All the usual stuff. It was so hard being her at the moment; she got depressed when she thought about the past, and anxious when she thought about the future.

And today she was tired. God only knows what time Sammy had got in, but it must have been late, as Tessa had been awake for most of the night thinking about Things. Stupidly, she'd forgotten to pack her herbal sleeping pills, and so she'd thrashed about with the sheet for hours – the last time she'd turned on the light to look at her travelling alarm clock it was 2.47, and Sammy still wasn't back. She'd thought about getting dressed again, to go out looking for her, but the great thing about being here was that they were all fenced in with a security guard at the entrance – it was a holiday camp or a prison camp, depending on how you looked at it – so she couldn't have gone very far, and anyway Tessa wasn't sure she wanted to see Sammy doing whatever it was she was doing at that time of night. Jeremy would be horrified if he knew, but he wouldn't ever know, and so he could just keep his horror to himself on this occasion, couldn't he, it was nothing to do with him now anyw—

Stop right there. Tessa could feel herself lurching down the I-hate-him-but-I-love-him path again, and she'd done quite enough of that last night. He was still taking up so much of her space. If she was a computer, he was taking up too many megabytes, too much of her memory. She tried to think about something else as she watched people fall off windsurfers, struggle to get back up, only to fall off again a few seconds later. (That car sticker was wrong; windsurfers couldn't stand up long enough to do anything.)

Yes, she must stop obsessing about her husband (not ex-husband, they weren't there yet, thank God) and concentrate her mind on something more useful, perhaps. Like what she was going to do with the rest of her life. But she didn't want to think about that now, this was a holiday, she should be relaxing.

If only she could. Tessa knew that she should be using this time usefully. She should be creating a new, better, more fulfilling life for herself now and so on, but unfortunately she also knew that she just didn't want to. She wanted her old life back, please. Or at least the same circumstances again; she'd do things so differently, if only she could be given another chance.

Dressed now, in a strappy frock she had thought far too young for her, but Sammy had made her buy it anyway, Tessa lay down on her bed for a few minutes, before facing the dinner debacle that was surely waiting for her downstairs.

Shutting her eyes, Tessa found herself mentally switching on the computer at home, in the little study alcove. It was Jeremy's old laptop, he'd given it to Sammy for her exam revision. OK. Create a new folder, call it 'Now What', start a new document. Type in 'Options', block it, bold and underline. Lovely. No, change that heading to 'Choices', sounds more positive.

Hmm.

Um . . .

Nothing came to mind. She couldn't think of anything to type in. She'd even remembered to take the bold and underline off as well, in preparation. It was no use, all she could see was a blank screen with an impatient cursor, flashing on and off at her. *You're-crap-you're-crap*, it was saying.

Trouble was, Tessa was afraid of making the wrong decision. She did occasionally come up with a plan, but somehow she managed to talk herself out of it again. Like that time when she thought (well, actually it had been Jeremy's idea) it might be good for her to work alongside more people, and she actually went along to that interview – but she'd felt so intimidated by the swish offices made of glass and chrome, not to mention the level of general hubbub, that she'd come across like a gibbering wreck. Even if they'd given her the job, she wouldn't have taken it, it would have been too much. She wasn't used to that level of activity, the hustle-bustle; she much preferred the peace of the ticking-clock, antique partner's desk and beautiful oils at Sir Andrew's apartment, the muffle of the tranquil cream carpet. And anyway, that big company would never have let her sneak off early, if it wasn't busy, to meet Sammy from school. Or pop home at lunchtime, bunk off early if it wasn't busy. Not like Sir Andrew, who wasn't there most of the time, so he didn't even know. No, her little job was just fine for her right now. Nice and manageable.

So Work didn't need to change, then. Home was OK too, she couldn't imagine living anywhere else. Their cosy attic flat with the slopy ceilings was tiny, and hopelessly cluttered with all their family memorabilia, and she still hated going up and down that bloody stairwell; but it was those same steps that had taught Sammy to count, they were the path up to safety and sanctuary at the end of a bad day, this was her stairway to heaven. 'Stairway to haven', as Jeremy would say – he loved a pun. And besides, living up in the rooftops of Edinburgh meant that her parents couldn't come and stay for too long, because of Mum's legs, so that was a bonus.

And the neighbours were fine. The young couple on the first floor were nice and quiet, and she'd got used to those students from the university now, a different lot every year, with their Friday night parties on the floor below. Sounded like they were having a whale of a time, and so they should at their age. Tessa wished she'd let her hair down a bit more, before settling down to marriage and motherhood. She'd actually been quite jealous of their fun at first, but now she'd got used to stepping over the splats of sick on the stairwell every Saturday morning, with all the smugness of the hangover-free.

And of course the flat was within walking distance from Princes Street, and Jenners, and Waverley station (not that she ever went anywhere), and it was comfy and cosy and the thought of moving house filled Tessa with panic. She couldn't possibly pack up their life into boxes, not yet. And she could tell that Jeremy still felt comfortable there, even though it wasn't officially his home any more. But they both knew it was really, he didn't belong in that big house with her, she'd conned him, it was called entrapment in fact; and anyway he obviously wasn't happy with Mona, otherwise he wouldn't be –

No! Stop it. Don't go there.

Oh, this is no use! Tessa snapped the mental laptop shut and sat up. She'd better just go down to dinner, get it over and done with, and then she could get an early night. Think about all this tomorrow, after a good long sleep.

She knew she was going to get a Thing about the restaurant if she wasn't careful, but a girl needs to eat, and so Tessa had decided to take her book down with her; that way she could just read, instead of having to answer endless questions, as to why she was here on her own. Too bad if everyone thought she was rude – she wasn't here to make friends. Sod 'em. Ooh, brave! Yes, well, she was here to spend some quality time with her daughter.

Which she would be doing, if she knew where Sammy was. They'd managed a quick five-minute chat this afternoon, when Tessa had gone to buy a bottle of water from the Bucket and Spade – Sammy was there holding court at a table, surrounded by lots of other teens, but she'd had to be nice to her mother, in order to get an ice cream. Tessa had asked various questions, but had found out enough sketchy details of what she'd been doing last night to make her never want to ask again. Hmm. She had a nasty suspicion that they were going to see even less of each other here than they did at home.

Thank god this is only for two weeks, Tessa thought to herself, as she smiled politely at yet another happy bloody family waiting to take the lift down to the restaurant. A wave of homesickness hit her as the doors opened, and she found to her alarm that she wanted to cry.

Gritting her teeth to stop the vulnerability from getting out, she steeled herself for the dinner queue. Turning the corner, she saw there wasn't one. Phew. But that po-faced, patronizing, punchable girl was there again.

'Just the one?' she smirked, picking up just the one rolled-up knife and fork.

'No, two. Me and my book.' And she held it up in front of her like a shield, to prove it. 'We'll have a table to ourselves tonight, please.'

Tutting, the girl turned tail as she muttered something about Tessa suiting herself, and led the way to an isolated table inside the restaurant, just beside the mens' washroom.

Flushed with the success of her aggressive campaign, Tessa waited until the girl was out of sight, and bravely stood up again, to find a better table. There was one outside, on the vine-covered terrace where everyone else was sitting, tucked away in the corner, covered with a red-and-white checked tablecloth. It even had a twinkly candle, which was winking at her invitingly. Ignoring the stares of her fellow diners (had they never seen a woman on her own before?) Tessa sat herself down.

There was a menu lying on the table, and now that she was in a decisive mood, Tessa quickly made up her mind. She was going to have melon to start, followed by *Pollo alla Lido Villaggio*; and as it was only the second night, which gave her about twelve days to get rid of the consequences before she went home, chocolate mousse. Feeling really quite empowered, she began to read her book, as she waited for someone to come and take her order. Bliss. Peace at last.

'D'you mind if I join you?' asked a man's voice.

Oh for god's sake! Tessa sighed, put her finger on her place in the book, and looked up. There, standing in front of her, was the most good-looking man she'd seen since – well, yesterday, waving her off at Edinburgh airport. She didn't quite know what to say, nothing sensible came to mind, and so she said 'sorry?' instead.

He laughed. 'I asked if I could join you.'

Tessa didn't seem able to say yes either, and so she indicated the place setting opposite with her hand, and nodded instead. 'Be my guest,' she said. Which sounded ridiculous, like that Disney song Sammy used to love. Only he was the Beauty and she the Beast.

'Don't let me disturb you,' he said as he sat down, 'it must be a good book.'

'Oh no, not at all, it's rubbish,' said Tessa, shutting it up and putting it under her chair. 'It'll be nice to have some company for a change.' She couldn't quite believe this was happening. He was just beautiful, incredibly good-looking. Old-fashioned handsome with a modern twist.

Long, dark brown hair, dark brown skin, dark brown eyes. Square-jawed. Sort of Jesus meets Action Man.

'Are you here on your own, then?' He didn't look at her, just studied the menu, scrutinizing it in fact. Obviously loves his food.

'Yes!' answered Tessa, suddenly thinking that perhaps it wasn't such a bad thing after all.

He looked up at her. 'We haven't met before, have we?'

'Er, no, I don't think so.' I'd have remembered.

'No, I didn't think so. I'd have remembered.'

Smooth. Blushworthy as well.

He smiled. He really was impossibly gorgeous. 'You weren't at the welcome drink last night then?'

'Oh god no, I hate things like that. Can't stand drinks parties, everyone standing around talking about nothing, holding some horrible sickly sweet warm drink.' Quite a speech, she congratulated herself. Marbles returning.

'Yes, they can be like that.' He was smiling at her again, she wanted him to stop and not stop, all at the same time.

'I used to have to go to lots of them with my husb— well, you know, in the past, ages ago, especially at Christmas, corporate stuff, you know . . .' She smiled. She was so crap.

'D'you know what you want yet?' It was the bossy seating woman, with a pad and a pen, glaring.

'Yes, please, Mandy,' he smiled up at her. Obviously on a first-name basis with the staff already, Tessa noted. Womanizer? 'But perhaps you could try that again, with a little more charm?' Good grief, the man was fearless.

Mandy sighed, shifted her weight on to the other foot, and took a deep breath. 'Sorry.' She smiled through gritted teeth. 'Excuse me, are you ready to order?'

Once she'd headed off towards the kitchen, Tessa leaned across the table and said in a hushed voice, 'I've been having trouble with her ever since I got here.'

'Really,' he plunged his fingers into a soft bread roll, 'why?'

Tessa explained. He was obviously a very protective man, he was really quite cross about her treatment from this Mandy woman. 'But everyone else has been nice to you, have they?'

'Well, actually, I've not had much to do with the rest of the staff yet – I was going to do Aquarobics in the pool this afternoon, but I fell asleep on the beach and missed it. But my daughter seems to know all their names already.'

'Yes, the little ones seem to love all the nannies.'

'Oh no, she's not little – she's sixteen! And she's got a huge crush on someone already, a lad who works here – he's called Jamie, I think . . .'

'Sixteen!' He was genuinely staggered. 'You don't look old enough. No, really, you don't.'

Tessa was going to pretend Sammy was adopted, but thought better of it. 'Well I certainly feel old enough. I had her very young,' she smiled, by way of explanation. She didn't want to say that she was thirty-five, as he was one of those people of indeterminable age. 'Honestly, they grow up so quickly these days! They want the lifestyle of grown-ups; you know, mobile phones, designer clothes, full set of highlights, cinema and pizzas, travelling round on public transport in the dark, etcetera, and yet they still want to be waited on hand and foot, like eight year olds. They want the freedom of an adult, but without the responsibility.'

'Ah, now that would be nice, wouldn't it?' He looked like he wanted to pontificate on that, but Tessa was on a roll.

'And of course the worst thing about it, is that they *look* like grown-ups. Did you see that article in the paper the other day, about a man who picked up a girl in a nightclub, took her back to his place, offered her a lift in the morning, she said yes, he said "where to", she said "school"! I mean you can't blame the men – at Sammy's school parents evenings, it's impossible to tell the girls apart from the teachers sometimes, some of these girls look about twenty-five!'

'Yes,' he said, sincerely, 'I know.'

'Are you a parent yourself?' Tessa asked.

'Er no, not yet.' He caught the attention of a waitress over on the other side of the restaurant with a flashing smile. 'Not that I know of, anyway!'

'Well, you've got all that to look forward to. Fortunately, we're quite close, in that she tells me what's going on, but I suspect that's only because she enjoys shocking me. The trick is to keep quiet, even if mentally your hair is standing on end. D'you know, last night, they all sat talking on the beach until 4.30 in the morning, with their parents all thinking they were safely tucked up in bed? Honestly, you'd think the staff would put a stop to that, wouldn't you? They seem to have a very laid-back attitude here as regards

73

that age group, I think it's quite badly run in that respect.'

He ordered the wine, and did that thing that men do when they're being masterful – ordered her food as well. She told him, and he told the waitress. It was as if the waitress was deaf to other women's voices, and needed a man to translate for her. Tessa knew she was supposed to feel robbed of her womanhood or something feministy like that, but actually she quite liked it. It was nice to have a man in charge again.

*

Felicity shut Spike's door very quietly. She wanted to run up and down the hotel corridor, shouting and cheering, but knew this to be inelegant behaviour for a mother who'd merely got her son off to sleep. Millions of women did this every night, she knew that. But she hardly ever had to put Spike to bed, she was always at work. And tonight he'd been particularly difficult, he'd wanted his nannygranny to do it, and Felicity had forgotten to pack any storybooks, and she'd not done very well with making one up. Spike had said it was stupid, and quite frankly, he was right. She had no idea what little boys liked, and why would she? Cliff had offered to help, as he usually did the whole bedtime thing – Felicity was either too tired or on the phones – but she'd insisted on doing it herself this evening. Just to prove that she could, even though she wasn't sure who exactly she was proving this to.

She knocked on the door of their room, and waited for Cliff to come and open it. Further down the corridor, she saw that humungous head nanny put a chair on the landing, with what looked like a puzzle book tucked under her arm, obviously preparing for an evening's babysitting. What a waste of human life, thought Felicity, who despised all nannies. What kind of mindless moron would do that for a job?

Cliff opened the door with a bath towel wrapped around his waist. ''Allo darlin', you come to service the room or just me?' (He was incapable of just doing something normally, he always had to make a so-called joke of even the most mundane operation, such as opening a door. Felicity used to love this about him, but now it got on her nerves.)

She marched past him into the room, and said, 'You're going to have to have a word with Christabelle.'

'Why?' He closed the door behind her.

'That room is a disgrace. Her suitcase looks like it's blown itself up all over the room; there's anonymous items of unwashed black clothing all over the floor, CDs out of their cases everywhere and batteries that Spike could put in his mouth within easy reach; the loo looks like it hasn't been flushed since we got here and the bin is overflowing with dirty tissues, some of them with blood on them, from her spot-picking I would imagine; yech, it's disgusting!'

'Oh dear,' said Cliff.

'And by the time I'd cleaned the bath in order to run it for Spike, he'd unwrapped all her tampons, and was wearing them as earrings.'

Cliff knew not to laugh when Felicity was 'on one', as he called it.

'Honestly, Cliff, I only said she could come if she was

helpful with Spike. I wouldn't mind, but I haven't seen her since this morning at the pool, have you?'

'Well, no, love, but he has been in the Kids Klub all day, so she hasn't really been needed, has she?' He took the towel off and rubbed his head with it.

Felicity sighed. 'No, Cliff, you're wrong. He wasn't in there all day at all, as you well know, we had to have him for the morning, which was hardly relaxing for me. And, anyway, that's not the point!' Felicity turned away and started to take off her day clothes, ready to shower. 'Christabelle should ask if we need her first, before going off and having a nice time at my expense.'

'Is that what this is about?' asked Cliff, peeking out from under his towel. 'Money?'

And so they launched into one of their old favourites, the financial fight. Same words, different order. Tried and tested examples of when you were bad and I was good, from both sides. Stuff she'd stored up from years ago, stuff he'd not even noticed at the time. Stuff that was incredible to both of them, but for different reasons.

Normally their rows ended with one or other of them storming out: Cliff to walk the dog, or Felicity to walk to work. Unfortunately, they were in a hotel room now, and so there was nowhere to go. There was quite a lot of to-ing and fro-ing in and out of the bathroom instead, but rather too much 'and-another-thing' for that to be really effective.

Eventually, they ran out of old material to draw on, and a thickly cloying silence sat still in the room, like cigar smoke in a cupboard. As she sobered up from the adrenalin fix of a good fight, Felicity realized she'd skipped the shower, and was completely dressed, ready to go downstairs for dinner; whereas Cliff was still naked, apart from the bath towel, which had been travelling around his body throughout the argument.

'Hurry up, Cliff, your mother will be waiting.'

'Look, Fliss, I don't want to fight with you.' He looked really sad. Hangdog. Pathetic.

'Well then, don't. I'll see you down there.'

And she left him to get ready, wondering, as she walked down the corridor, why everything she held of value was sifting like sand through her fingers. Her marriage, her relationship with her son, her hard-earned cash – the lot. All slipping away. Felicity was not the sort of person who dealt with insecurity well. She determined to do everything within her sizeable power to regain control of her life, oh yes, she'd do it, whatever it took. She just needed to make a few minor adjustments, probably. By the time this holiday was over, everything would be back on track again. She'd make sure of that.

*

Tessa hadn't had so much attention in years. She'd assumed when she'd first seen him that as this man was so beautiful, he was bound to be a bit thick – he wasn't, but neither was he what her mother would call 'educated'. Like I care, thought Tessa, who was really enjoying herself for the first time since she'd arrived.

'And do you work?' he asked.

'Well, yes, sort of.'

'What d'you mean, sort of?'

77

'Well, it's not an important career or anything –'

'So?' He shrugged his square shoulders. 'Do you enjoy it?'

'Yes, I suppose so.' Tessa hadn't really thought about that. 'In a way. It's not what I thought I'd end up doing, but it suits me fine.' He was smiling at her, her insides were positively melting.

'So?'

Mmm.

'What is it that you do?'

'Oh, sorry, yes – I'm a PA.'

'Sounds like very important work. What d'you have to do?'

Tessa wasn't sure if he really didn't know, or was just being kind, giving her the opportunity to talk. She decided to be kind back.

'Well, I'm a Personal Assistant. To Sir Andrew Wilson.'

He looked blank.

'The composer.'

He looked blanker.

'Oh yes, you know – he wrote the Safari Symphony, which is often on BBC2, and he does lots for the Scottish National Opera, and he writes special pieces for royal occasions, that sort of thing . . .'

He looked the blankest yet. 'No, sorry, I don't really know much about classical music and that sort of thing. I'm not very good on the arty stuff, I'm afraid. Just don't get the time.' She knew there'd be a catch. Nothing in common. But when he's that beautiful, who cares?

'Anyway, it doesn't matter. He's a hugely successful man, and I run his life for him, basically. I'm a sort of office manager, cum secretary, cum florist, cum house-keeper, stroke substitute wife, really.' She'd had to change the last 'cum' to 'stroke', because every time she'd said that word, his smile had got a bit bigger, and alarmingly, so had hers. So embarrassing. She felt so silly. She gulped down some more rosé, in an attempt to hide her blush. 'I'd only heard of him because I used to play in an orchestra, years ago.'

'Really?' He looked suitably impressed. 'What instrument?'

'Clarinet.' Encouraged by his enthusiasm, Tessa decided to tell him. 'And I play the piano too. Haven't done for ages, though.'

'Oh, why not?'

'Lots of reasons – we haven't got a piano at home, for a start.'

'Well, we've got one here, in the Village Hall. You must play for us.'

'Oh no, I couldn't.'

'Why not?'

'Oh, it's a long story. God, let's stop talking about me. What about you? What d'you do?'

'Oh, I've done lots of things in my time. Let me see, I've been a ski instructor, a nightclub bouncer, a deep sea diver, I ran a go-karting track once – I was a stunt man for a bit . . .'

'Wow,' said Tessa, who forgave his lack of cultural references immediately – clearly the man was never in – 'really?'

'Yes,' he laughed, 'mad, isn't it? When I was a little boy,' he topped up her wine glass, 'I wanted to be one

79

of those men who worked for the fairgrounds, y'know, the guys that spin the Waltzers, and make all the girls scream?'

Tessa did know, and she already had a suspicion that he would be very good at that. She could see him now, in a dirty cap-sleeved T-shirt, big muscly arms . . .

'But in the end I decided not to do that, d'you know why?'

'No, why?'

'I didn't want to leave my mum!' He grinned. He knew how cute this was.

'Ah, bless you,' said Tessa. Inside her a little voice was screaming NO, STOP IT, DON'T; she decided to drown it out with more wine.

*

Upstairs, Bonnie was having trouble with two sets of twins. They were little buggers, multiple births; you'd get one off and the other would wake up, and vice versa. Or they spent all night waking each other up. Fortunately, she was used to twins; IVF was very popular with Seaside Villagers, and there had been loads of them in South London when she'd worked there. All to do with old men marrying younger second wives, and career women leaving it too late. She shouted the relevant room numbers down the stairwell to the ground floor, to the nanny on blackboard duty, and settled back in the spindly chair, to get on with her Wordsearch.

'Bee!' A flustered Michelle leapt out of the lift in front of her. 'Thank God! What're you doing here? I thought you didn't have to do this bit, being the boss and all.'

'Tell me about it,' said a fed-up Bonnie. 'Alison reckons she's got flu, so I've had to step in at the last minute.'

'Flu? In this heat?'

'Exactly what I said, Michelle, who's she kidding? And it's not like I haven't got anything better to do, neither,' said Bonnie, who couldn't think of any examples right now, but never mind. 'She better be really ill with this, or else,' she added.

'Or else what?' asked Michelle.

'Or else, or else, there'll be trouble.' Bonnie couldn't think of anything better than that right now either. 'Anyway, what's the matter? You look like you've seen a murder or something.'

'There'll be a bloody murder soon if I get my way,' threatened Michelle.

'Sssh!' hissed Bonnie, 'you know I can't swear when I'm on duty. What's happened?'

'Well, he's only chatting up some bloody punter, isn't he?'

'Michelle!' scolded Bonnie, 'I am going to have to ask you to stop swearing' – she lowered her voice to a hiss – 'because not all the buggers have gone down to dinner yet. Shut the fuck up.'

'Sorry, Bee.'

'And anyway, you know perfectly well we're supposed to refer to them as Villagers . . .' she teased.

'Yeah right, well whatever, he's in the restaurant right now, chatting up some blonde bird, bold as you like, for all the world to see. Mandy's just crowing about it, Bonnie, crowing – he's making a mockery of me!

Honestly, what are people going to think? That I can't keep a man?'

'Right.' Bonnie closed her puzzle book, there was no way she was going to complete this Wordsearch tonight, she could see that. 'First of all, Michelle, calm down. This is not the end of the world.'

'Maybe not to you it's not, but I feel a right fool —'

'Michelle!' Bonnie's tone was unusually sharp. She smiled at a very tanned mother as she came out of the lift, they exchanged a heavenwards look and the woman walked slowly up the corridor, reluctant to be interrupting her evening to sort the kids out. 'And second of all, it is part of his job to talk to the punters, you know that.'

'Villagers,' said Michelle, who couldn't resist it.

'Whatever.' She let it go this time. 'And the third thing, is that nobody even knows for certain that you're going out with him, so who are you making a bit of a fool of yourself in front of, exactly?'

''Course they know,' said Michelle. 'And anyway, I decided to give them a hint. Mandy saw me snogging him at breakfast this morning.'

'But I thought we decided that I would let people know, when we thought the time was right?' Bonnie shook her head, she knew it would go wrong if Michelle took matters into her own hands. 'What does she look like, anyway, this woman?'

'Well, that's just it,' Michelle started to pace up and down the landing, 'she's not a patch on me. Quite mousey really, just, y'know, normal looking. Not too thin, not too fat, wearing a frilly dress that's far too young for her — I just don't understand it, Bee, what's he playing at? I mean he was looking all lovey-dovey at her, even using his special smile and everything.' She was near to tears with indignation. 'I mean, I do make sure I look good all the time, y'know, it's not like I'm a dog or anything . . .'

'He's obviously gone barking mad,' said Bonnie, in her best comforting voice. 'We're going to have to come up with something, Michelle. I'm off at midnight, give me till then and I'll have a plan.'

'Cheers, Bee, I knew you'd help me out. You're such a good friend. Listen, I know you're not supposed to drink on duty, but I could sneak you up a glass of wine, if you like . . .' She was so pretty when she smiled, her little elfin face just lit up.

'Oh go on then, why not?' The lift doors opened and a pair of newly arrived white parents burst out of it, all concerned. 'Oh, hello there,' said Bonnie, 'it's all right, I think I've got the situation under control. I'm not sure one of them hasn't got a temperature, actually, you'd better go and see.' The parents ran off up the corridor, and Bonnie winked at Michelle as the lift doors closed on her. She went back to her Wordsearch. Now, where the hell was 'obstreperous', and what did it mean?

*

'. . . and then he eventually admitted it, well he had to once her twins were on the way, and so we had no choice but to split up.' Tessa was surprised at how matter-of-fact she was being about the whole Jeremy Thing. It almost sounded like someone else's story, something you'd read in a magazine. Quite a normal one, too. Unimpressive, no twist at the end. Unremarkable.

Her whole life, in a few sentences. It's easy, if you don't include the pain.

'That must have hurt.' He'd listened to her story, hadn't interrupted, just let her talk. THIS IS TOO GOOD TO BE TRUE! shouted the little voice.

'Oh, well, you know,' Tessa lied as she swigged, 'you get over these things.' She hoped she sounded as carefree as she wanted to. 'What about you, what's your situation?'

Everything Tessa had was crossed except, she hoped, her eyes. She'd already noticed there was no wedding ring. But it was ridiculous to even imagine that he was single. And you couldn't have a relationship with someone who'd never read a book. But you could have a bloody good time with them for a couple of weeks ...

'Well,' he ran his fingers through his long, thick hair, 'I've never been married.' He smiled at her. 'Never met the right woman, I suppose. I don't know why not —'

'I just came to say goodnight, Fabio.' An older lady was standing by their table. Tessa instantly recognized her as the unhappy woman from the swimming pool that morning.

'Mamma!' He stood up and hugged her. 'Why are you going to bed so early? You must stay, have a coffee with us.'

'No, no,' replied the mother, 'I don't want to interrupt.' She smiled at Tessa, but not for very long.

Eventually, Fabio (what a terrible name, thought Tessa, so cheesy) (ARE YOU SURPRISED? retorted the inner voice) insisted that they all three go and sit with the mum and dad from the swimming-pool family. And so, after much fetching of chairs and budging up, Tessa was transported from what had been a rather intimate candlelit dinner for two, to sitting bang-smack in the middle of a full-on dysfunctional family.

The woman with the big orange and yellow hair, Felicity, explained who was related to who and how. Tessa realized she was a bit pissed by now, and couldn't quite follow. Not only was this woman a bit scary, but she also spoke really quickly, and had a peculiar knack of firing off endless questions at the same time as Tessa gave the answers.

'So, where are you from? Which part? Hmm, early August, must be filling up with festival people now, good time to get away. D'you work? What as? Really? Of course I've heard of him. Children? No, you must have had her when you were about nine! Actually Cliff, how old's Christabelle? Cliff!'

Fabio caught Tessa's eye as she was being cross-examined. He smiled. Felicity saw that too. 'So, where's your husband?'

'Um,' spluttered Tessa, thrown by this line of direct questioning into answering truthfully, 'back in Edinburgh with his bitch girlfriend.' Oh God, that wasn't what she meant to say at all.

'Bastard!' shouted Felicity, causing a few people to turn. Her husband, who was talking to Fabio and their mother, nudged his wife in the ribs. She ignored him, and really focused in on Tessa now. 'So you're a single parent, are you?'

'Yes.'

Changing tone completely Felicity asked in a hushed

voice, 'What's it like? Is it hell? Are you very poor?' But as if she really did want to know.

'Well –'

'Mum!' Sammy was weaving her way through the dining tables towards them, followed by her unisex friend. 'Whassup?'

'This is my daughter, Sammy,' explained Tessa to the rest of the table.

'And that's my stepdaughter, Christabelle,' sighed Felicity.

'Have you got any money?' demanded Sammy, self-consciously, aware that all eyes were on her.

'What for?' Tessa tried to regain some control of the unravelling muddle she felt she was in.

'They won't take proper money at the bar, it has to be turned into shillings or something.'

'Oh yes,' said Felicity, turning to Fabio, 'what's all that about? Don't you think that's taking the olde worlde village theme just a little too far?'

Fabio shrugged. 'Don't ask me, I don't make up the rules.'

'Yes, but you are the boss here, you could change it.'

'No, I can't; Squires aren't allowed to change anything in the village without full written approval from Head Office.'

'Squires?!' Felicity squealed with vicious delight. 'We're supposed to call you Squire! No, you're joking – that's ridiculous, that is just too much – were you aware, Tessa, that you were dining with the village Squire?!'

Yes, she certainly was now. But Tessa didn't answer Felicity, she was too busy retracing her words, and phrases like 'badly run' were popping up. No wonder that cosy corner position had been free, it was probably reserved for him. Which was why everyone had stared. Oh my god. She'd helped herself to the captain's table. If only it had been on the *Titanic*.

Fabio ignored Felicity's taunts, and carried on talking to Sammy. 'If you take some "real" money to Reception, they'll change it into shillings for you. And, hey, Christabelle, ask them to give you a fiver's worth, and stick it on my tab.'

'No need for that, mate,' said Cliff, digging in his pockets, 'I think I've got it covered – here you go, doll, a tenner.'

'Thanks, Dad. Thanks, Uncle Fabio.' Even though she was pissed, Tessa detected some tension between the two brothers. How predictable.

'Mum?'

'You can have twenty pounds,' said Tessa, hopefully with largesse. 'Get it put on the room.'

'Are you pissed?' Not needing a reply, Sammy was making boggle eyes at Fabio, big boggle eyes, so that everybody could see. 'Well? Aren't you going to introduce us?'

'Yeehah!' A shout rang out.

'Yeehah, yeehah, yeehah!' Big Bonnie was crashing her way through the tables, dressed up as Woody from *Toy Story* in full cowboy gear and galloping on an imaginary horse. Behind her was Michelle, in tight white jeans and pink gingham shirt, neat little cleavage and a big white Stetson with rhinestone trim, the porn star kind. Michelle did Dallas very well indeed.

'Line dancing in the Village Hall right now, people!' announced Bonnie, in a strange accent, more Birmingham twang than Southern drawl. 'Grab your pardners by the hand, and git on down with Craig and the rest of the Seaside Village Entertainments team. C'mon now, ladies and gents, it'll be big fun! Yeehah!'

Nobody moved.

'Hello there, Mrs Clifton,' beamed shiny little Michelle, 'Mrs Cliftons. Can we interest you in a little dancing? It's really easy to learn, I promise. You'll love it, my gran does.'

'Well, I don't really think –'

'Oh come on, Mum, you'll enjoy it,' assured Cliff. 'You and Dad used to love dancing.' And he stood up. 'Come on you lot, don't be so bloody boring! We're here to enjoy ourselves, stop being so bloody British!'

'It is a great laugh,' agreed Fabio. 'I admit, I have to go because it's my job – but most of the staff attend the evening entertainments just because they want to, even the Waterfront team . . .' He winked at Sammy, who turned to her mother, open-mouthed in horror.

'I'm game,' said Tessa, also standing up. 'Well, you know, for dancing.' Shit.

'Oh what the hell,' agreed Felicity, whose lips looked like she'd been drinking ink, 'they've got red wine over there, have they?' And as they left the restaurant she linked arms with Tessa, muttering under her breath, 'This should be hysterical.'

*

Even Gina had to admit, as she chatted to Alfie before

going to sleep (at ten past one in the morning, if you please), that she'd enjoyed herself. And so would he, if he'd been here. It had quite tired her out, too. So she kissed him goodnight, as she always did, every night, and hoped to dream with him as she slept.

Felicity spent the night throwing up, probably the result of too much strong sun and cheap wine. But before that, she and Cliff had got closer to having sex than they had for a long time; she'd tried to think of Paul Newman this time, then she'd thought of Cool Hand Luke, then she'd thought of all those hard boiled eggs, and then she'd been sick.

Michelle and Fabio, on the other hand, only got three hours' sleep that night. As did Bonnie, whose room was next door to theirs.

Tessa hardly slept a wink, as she had even more to thrash about than usual; Sammy fell asleep at daybreak, lusting after Jamie, even though he was a really crap dancer.

Christabelle was having those strange thoughts again.

In fact, the only person who slept like a baby that night was Spike.

5. Snapshots

TESSA is talking to the invisible INTERVIEWER
again.

> TESSA
> I really wasn't sure about Felicity
> at first, I thought she was too loud,
> too aggressive – not my type of person
> at all. In fact [she smiles at the
> thought] I was a wee bit scared of
> her.

Cut to FELICITY.

> FELICITY
> I thought Tessa was a bit of a dullard,
> actually. She was so quiet, timid. And
> she laughed at all my jokes. I decided
> she'd make the perfect holiday com-
> panion for me.

She throws back her mane of manic hair, and
laughs heartily.

*

'Now there's a woman with a hangover, if ever I saw one!' shouted out Felicity, as she walked through the white picket gate into the pool enclosure the next morning.

Tessa was sitting very upright on a lounger in the shade, with a big donkey straw hat and sunglasses covering her throbbing head, clutching her beachbag to her tummy, as if it was a cushion from the sofa.

'Phew, what a scorcher!' Felicity said, as she plonked herself down on the end of the nextdoor sunbed. Which caused it to shoot upwards, depositing her rump-first on to the harshly tiled ground. 'Ow!'

If last night hadn't been an icebreaker, then this was. And if Tessa was being honest, she wanted to get in with this woman, as she had a direct line to the gorgeous Fabio. So she waited for Felicity to laugh until she did. 'That's God getting you back for speaking so loudly to a woman with a sore head!' she giggled.

As Felicity picked herself up, and began to retrieve the contents of her Joseph raffia bag – lots of gold-topped cosmetics, not one but two tiny mobile phones, an Afro comb, a huge jar of horsepill vitamins, a very serious-looking hardback book and hundreds of loose shillings, which had scattered everywhere – the nutty brown man Tessa had already seen terrorizing the bright white men around the pool, pounced.

'Good morning, ladies! And how are we, this fine morning?'

Neither of them replied, but he didn't seem to notice.

'Now then, can I interest you in a game of volleyball?'

'No,' said Felicity firmly, as she surfaced from retrieving a pack of Marlboro Lights from under Tessa's lounger. 'Definitely not.'

'Now, now, ladies, there's no need to be like that – volleyball is a marvellous game, very energetic and jolly good fun, y'know!'

'Who for?' asked Felicity as she squinted up at him, sweeping her busy hair away from her face.

He looked a little confused. 'Well, you, of course.'

'I don't think so,' she said as she flumped on to her sunlounger at last. 'I would rather stick pins in my eyes, than break a nail trying to flip a heavy ball over a tiny net. Far easier to walk round and give it to the other person, if they want it that badly.'

Tessa thought that if he hadn't been so tanned, he would have paled at this suggestion. 'Is this a women's lib thing?'

'No, it's a free country thing.'

'So I take it you're not a sportswoman?'

'That's right.' Felicity opened her big grown-up book.

'And you don't like volleyball either?' He was looking at Tessa, who managed to shake her head, thickly.

'So you're not ball players,' he was smiling now, 'in fact, you're ball breakers! Hahahahahha,' and he actually snorted, 'hahahhahhahahahha!' And he left, repeating the line over and over again, telling himself it was really very good as he went.

'Bloody Friend of Kathy,' declared Felicity, once he was nearly out of earshot.

'I'm sorry?' Tessa didn't understand.

'Oh, it's a thing Cliff and I used to say. You know gay men are referred to as Friends of Dorothy's?'

Tessa nodded, even though she didn't actually know that, but she didn't want to look unsophisticated.

'And recovering alcoholics in AA ask each other if they're Friends of Bill's, right?'

Tessa hadn't known that either – why would she – but anyway.

'Well, we used to know a remarkably unfunny woman called Kathy, who was the only person who laughed at her jokes. But they weren't even jokes, they were just very bad puns. Real groaners. So anyone who thinks they're hilarious, but isn't, is always known as a Friend of Kathy. It's code for Just Not Funny.'

Tessa laughed. 'The sort of person who'd make jokes about Germans and deckchairs, that kind of thing?'

'Exactly!' squealed Felicity with delight. 'Only she'd say it was really hunny, instead of funny.'

'Oh god!' groaned Tessa. 'Where are they, by the way?'

'Who?'

'The Germans. And the French, and the Italians.'

'Company policy,' said Felicity as she dabbed a bit of thick white sunblock on her nose, 'it's only us Brits here. Supposed to be a corner of home abroad, or something. Stinks, doesn't it? So xenophobic.'

'Yeah,' agreed Tessa, even though to be perfectly honest she didn't really know what that meant.

'Hmm,' said Felicity, looking round, 'there's quite a lot needs changing round here. They think they're so up-market, but in reality it's a bit naff, isn't it?'

'Oh yes,' replied Tessa, who thought it was OK actually, and had already mentally composed her postcards home – 'sun, sea, sand and cheese!'

'Watch out, there goes Dolly Parton!' hissed Felicity as the man with the big bosoms she'd seen at the Welcome Drink passed the pool.

Tessa described the Root family, from the first night's dinner (Radish and Parsnip, the boy Turnip and baby Swede); and they christened Dolly's friend, the puce-faced drunken woman, Red Rum. And all those who'd been here a week longer were christened the Nutty Browns, which made them the Bright Whites – but not for long.

*

A montage of cleverly edited short filmclips of the other holidaymakers follows, with voice-overs where necessary. 'Walking On Sunshine' by Katrina and the Waves is playing in the background.

BONNIE
There was one dad there, stank of booze, morning noon and night.

MICHELLE
Yeah, and he couldn't keep his hands to himself neither.

FELICITY
We called him Alcopop.

Over lunch, they talked about the men in their lives. Or rather, Felicity cross-examined Tessa about her personal life. 'So what about Sammy's father' – she forked in a large amount of waldorf and chomped – 'Where's he?'

Tessa did her best to tell her whole life story the way she'd told it to Fabio the night before, in a few painless sentences. But Felicity was too clever to be glossed over, and was having none of it.

'So let me get this straight. You met Jeremy when you were both eighteen, you got pregnant and he became an airline pilot, flying all over the world to glamorous destinations, while you stayed at home and poured all your energy into your daughter. Then, so predictably that it makes me want to weep, he fucks off with an air hostess because she's managed to get herself pregnant, whilst telling you he's only doing the decent thing – and you believe him? And as far as I can tell, you're still in love with him now, hmm?'

It did sound a bit stupid when it was put like that. 'No, no,' protested Tessa, 'it's not like that at all. I mean, he had no choice, did he? He couldn't leave those babies without a father, and Sammy was ten, old enough to understand.'

'Oh – I thought she was five, the same age as Spike is now. I don't think he'd understand if Cliff or I had an affair . . .'

'No, I reckon he met Mona about then. But he didn't actually leave us until she was about ten.'

'God, so he really dragged it out.' Felicity shook her head. 'Bloody men, they just can't keep it in their trousers, can they? Thank god Cliff's not like that, I wouldn't stand for it. But what about you? It doesn't sound like you even got angry. What about losing your husband to another woman? Doesn't that make you fucking furious? It would me.'

'Well, yes, of course, but it doesn't help anyone to just go around being angry all the time, does it? And anyway, by that time I was more relieved than anything else. He'd been leading this sort of double life for ages, it was exhausting.' Thankfully it looked like Felicity's indignation was subsiding. 'But the great thing is that we've managed to stay friends, which is more than can be said for some couples who separate under such circumstances.' With any luck she wouldn't have to say exactly how friendly they still were ...

'Yes, fair enough,' chewed Felicity, nodding, 'Cliff certainly isn't on good terms with his ex-wife, that's for sure!'

Spotting an escape route, Tessa enquired, 'Christabelle's mother?'

'Yes, Penny.' She sighed and shook her head. 'Real old witch. Does everything she can to fuck up Cliff's life. Consumed with jealousy, just won't let him go. Sad really.'

'Yes, poor woman.'

'Er, no – poor us. She absolutely hates me. She can't seem to get it into her thick skull that we deserve a good lifestyle, god knows I – we – work hard enough for it. And

96

I wouldn't mind, but she's only got a little part-time job, as a secretary; she still thinks Cliff should be financially supporting her and her sulky daughter. I think she's still after him, actually, but he says he's just not interested. Silly cow can't see that she's just got to move on, and leave us alone.'

Feeling uncomfortable, Tessa tried to move on too. 'So,' she said, as she tried to pick out the remaining walnut pieces from the rice salad, 'how did you and Cliff meet?'

'Oh, it was about what, eight years ago now; he was a very successful photographer at the time – well, you know, still is, of course – and I'd just started my own PR company. I'd heard of him, naturally, but never actually met him. We hit it off straight away; he asked me out to lunch, and then we went out for a drink after the next shoot and bang – that was it really. We had a secret steamy affair for ages' – Felicity smiled at the memory – 'and then I left my first husband, he'd already left Penny years ago, and was only living with someone' – Tessa thought she detected a touch of artificial breeziness in her new friend – 'and then I got pregnant with Spike, and we got married!' She put her knife and fork together on the plate. 'Right, I think we deserve a big bowl of fruit salad after a hard morning's sunbathing, don't you?'

They queued for their dessert in silence, both slowly digesting the new information. In truth, they were each fraternizing with The Other Woman. Only this was different, wasn't it?

*

It took me a while to realize that the
barmen were twins.

We just thought it was one bloke on a
very long shift.

So we called them Ice and Lemon.

*

Tessa wanted to spend the afternoon on the beach, as
that was what she 'always' did, even though it was only
Day 3. Felicity had her first waterskiing lesson booked
for that afternoon, and so they chatted some more after
the delicious Jamie had come to tell her they were running
a bit late.

As she watched his Bermuda'd bottom disappear back
down the beach towards the waterfront hut, Felicity said,
with more than an acceptable amount of lust in her voice
for a woman of her age, 'Cor!'

'I know.'

The two women stared after him, until he disappeared
into The Shack.

'I call it Michael Owen syndrome,' sighed Felicity. 'At
that age, you don't know whether you want to breastfeed
them, or fuck 'em.'

Tessa nearly choked on her funny foreign ice cream.

'If only they stayed like that,' Felicity continued. 'Have

you noticed, all the men here look exactly the same? Every single damn one of them – they wear the same clothes, they're all the same type, they're even all going bald in the same place. And you can see how fast they deteriorate too – it's definitely an age thing, you've got to really work hard to keep yourself fit after thirty. No wonder Fabio's treated like a god.'

Hooray! thought Tessa, she's mentioned him at last. 'So he's your brother-in-law, is he?'

'Yes, poor old Cliff,' said Felicity, with unexpected sympathy.

Tessa pretended not to understand. 'But . . .'

'It's not fair, is it? They don't even look like they're from the same family. Can you imagine how I felt when I met Fabio? Talk about going for the wrong one. Mind you, once I got to know him . . .' She checked her watch. 'They'd better get a bloody move on, or I'll have to miss my lesson – I've got a conference call at half past three . . .'

'Got to know him?' Tessa prompted.

'Who?'

'Fabio.' She still couldn't quite manage to say that name without wincing.

'Oh yeah, he's a bit crap once you get past the looks.'

Oh no. 'Really?' TOLD YOU SO. *Oh hello, you again.*

'Standard stuff really – commitaphobic, no respect for real women, shags slags for his country, blah blah blah. Really only any good for one thing only, though legend has it he's pretty good at that. Mind you, so he bloody should be, he's had enough practice . . . you can't see Cliff anywhere, can you?' She was rummaging in her overlarge raffia bag.

Tessa looked around. 'No.' She wanted to know more. 'So is he – um, married or y'know, with anyone?'

Felicity lit a cigarette and dragged on it heavily, shut her eyes in ecstasy and eventually exhaled, by which time Tessa was already wanting to kill herself for asking such an obvious question.

'Good God no, he's never had a relationship longer than five minutes.' She peered at Tessa over her Gucci sunglasses. 'Why, Miss Scarlett, I do believe –' she said with wide eyes, laughing. 'You're blushing – you don't want to – oh my god!' she screeched, loudly. 'Fabio? You're joking! Oh no, you can't . . .'

Tessa tried to mutter stuff about of course not, but it didn't work.

'Mind you,' Felicity dragged again, 'he'd be perfect for a holiday romance. Now he'd take your mind off that ex-husband of yours, that's for sure.'

Tessa tried not to agree, but that didn't work either.

'Only one snag though.' She frowned as she flicked her ash on to the sand. 'He does tend to prey on the very young. In fact, I think he's having a thing with that silly little beautician.' Tessa had suspected as much last night, Michelle had been velcro'd to his side all evening.

TOLD YOU! shouted the enemy within, YOU'RE TOO OLD AND HE'S ALREADY TAKEN. WHAT WERE YOU THINKING? HA HA HA, YOU SILLY OLD FOOL!

'But you needn't let that get in your way.' Felicity brightened. 'In fact, I will do anything I can to help you get rid of her. I think your need is greater, don't you?

But don't even imagine we're going to be sisters-in-law. I don't think I'll be bothering the hat shop, not on this occasion.' She grinned at Tessa excitedly. 'Ooh, I'm going to enjoy this little project! Yes, a good seeing-to, that's what you need.'

'Huh, speak for yourself!' retorted Tessa.

Her friend's expression changed, and Tessa thought she might have gone too far; but Felicity had evidently seen someone coming towards them over Tessa's shoulder, and was quickly burying her fag end in the sand.

'And there's also another woman on the horizon,' she said, as she gathered up and stood up, 'who's going to be far harder to get out of his life. I've gotta go,' she said as she packed up her bag, 'I'll see you later. Jamie, oh Jamie, are you ready for me and my breasts, my little babyman?' she comically wailed, as she hotfooted it up the beach.

Felicity was quite nice really, thought Tessa to herself as she watched her make her way back along the beach. Just a bit – well, different, that's all. Larger-than-life, 'full-on' as Sammy would say. Not what Tessa was used to. Probably a better person to have on your side, than against you. Jeremy would have hated her, called her a show-off, she was far too boisterous –

'Good afternoon.' Gina the grandmother must have been the person walking along the beach towards them. 'How are you today?'

'Oh I'm fine, fine, thank you,' said Tessa.

And they had a little chat, and then Tessa invited Gina to sit down a wee while, and they chatted a little bit more, and really got on very well, remarkably well considering the generation gap. It turned out they had a lot in common. They chatted about being a mother, and how childhood was getting shorter and shorter these days, and how Gina's husband wasn't around now, and neither was Tessa's. And it was hard to be in love with someone who wasn't there, wasn't it?

But to know he's never going to come back – well, that was so *final*. Tessa spoke real sympathy, she felt true compassion for the older woman. But there was too much kindness in her voice, and suddenly, much to her horror, Gina was in floods of tears. Old people's tears, the worst kind of all.

'It's so silly,' she sniffed, once she'd managed to gather herself together enough to talk, 'I keep forgetting he's not here any more. It was terrible at first, I used to just wander round the house, round and round, from room to room, I didn't know what to do with myself, you see. Sometimes I'd just sit on the bed, for hours, feeling nothing. Or I'd stand at the window, looking at the other people getting on with their lives, knowing that because Alfie's was over, mine was too.' She blew her nose, dabbed her eyes.

'I haven't got a routine any more, you see, I don't seem to want to do anything for myself. But I always know when it's five o'clock, because I start to get a feeling of excitement in my stomach, it's time to put the dinner on, he'll be home soon. But then I remember that I'm never going to hear him open the front door and tell me he's home now' – she smiled – 'as if I didn't know.' Another tear sloped down her faded olive skin. 'I don't like it, you know; it doesn't feel right, being on my own . . .'

I know how that feels, thought Tessa, but she didn't say anything as she could see that Gina needed to get it all out. The poor woman must be desperate, they hardly knew each other. She understood that too, the need to talk to someone, just anyone, anything to release some of the pressure waiting to burst out of your chest. This poor, poor lady. Tessa busied herself with scrabbling about in her bag for a tissue, which she knew she hadn't got.

'It's all right my love, I've got a fresh one here.' Gina fished inside her summer dress, and pulled out a hanky which had been kept in place by her bra strap. Dabbing her eyes, she smiled crumpily at Tessa.

'It's so stupid,' she sniffed, 'I'm sure the boys are right, it'll do me good, being here. But I feel more alone than ever, and yet I'm surrounded by people all day. I just want to go back home, is that very bad of me?' If she heard Tessa's reassurances, she didn't acknowledge them. 'But when I'm at home, I get scared, I think I'm going mad. I do things as if he's still here, you see.' She smiled at her own insanity. 'I'm always putting two cups out beside the kettle, I can't help it. And I buy too much food, I can't get the portions right, I forget it's just me now. I haven't even got enough for a proper wash any more. It can take me a week, sometimes, to make up a full load . . . and if I hear a funny story, I think, ooh, I must tell Alfie about that later, and then I remember he's not here any more to tell . . .' Her voice crumpled again, she covered it up by blowing her nose one more time.

'And the garden's in a really bad state, I don't know what I'm going to do about that. I don't even know how to turn that Fly-me thing on, I'll have to pay the boy next door to do it, I suppose. Alfie would be so angry with me, if he could see how I'd let his lovely garden go to ruin. No, not angry; he'd be disappointed with me.' The thought of this brought a fresh onslaught of tears. 'I'm just so used to being two, you see. But I feel like I'm only half here, there's only half of me left . . .'

'Yes, well, I certainly know how that feels,' said Tessa.

It was as if Gina had noticed her for the first time. 'I'm sorry, you must think I'm crazy. It's just that you've got such a kind face, you see, and I don't want to bother the boys with all this, they're so busy, each of them.' She blew her nose. 'Well, you know, Cliff's not, but –'

'It's quite all right,' said Tessa in her most soothing tone, 'I do understand.'

'Really?'

'Well, sort of. I know my husband didn't die, but – well, I still lost him in a way . . .'

They spent the rest of that afternoon gently comforting each other – what women do best, when there's trouble.

They decided that the worst thing of all was having to put out the rubbish yourself. That was most definitely a man's job.

*

CLIFF

```
There was this really trendy couple
there, who got on everybody's tits.
They were head-to-toe in designer
gear, and obviously rolling in it.
```

He was a big cheese in the music
business, and she made it her job
to let everybody know that. They were
known as John and Yoko.

                    FELICITY
They had three very badly-behaved
kids called Feather — I ask you —
and Mink, and poor little Bo — I made
the mistake of asking if it was after
Bo Diddly and she said, 'No, Peep.'

                      *

Felicity and Tessa soon established a daily routine. They'd
meet around the pool in the morning, first one there
would bag two sunloungers; and then they'd have lunch
together. Felicity was so bad at waterskiing it was funny,
and Tessa didn't want to miss the spectacle, so after-
noons would be spent on the beach. Tessa would man
the mobiles, as Felicity screamed up and down the
coastline.

Then they'd take a couple of early evening hours off
from each other, during which they'd go up to their
rooms to shower, and they'd change into a selection of
outfits that each had bought and brought for the specific
purpose of showing off their tans.

At 7.30 precisely (both detested lateness), they'd meet
for a drink in the Bucket and Spade, before having dinner
at what had now become universally recognized as the
Cliftons' table. Tessa always sat next to Gina, much to
the relief of everyone else. If Fabio was free, he'd sit on

the other side of his mother, and Felicity would make remarks about what a jolly threesome they made, just to make Tessa blush.

Then, after dinner, they'd either join in with the evening's arranged entertainment – which could be anything from an appalling show starring the whole staff in the Village Hall, to a martial arts display in the circus tent – or they'd stay behind at the table and provide their own entertainment, getting gloriously drunk and girlishly giggly. Occasionally they'd brave the School Disco in the Village Hall, but the DJ (Robert from Maintenance) would only play chart stuff, and actually laughed in Felicity's face when she requested Abba.

They covered most of the important subjects quite quickly: Periods, Childbirth, Men, Work, Men, the joys of Staying In (Tessa), the joys of Going Out (Felicity), Other People's Relationships, a little bit more on Men and other sundry subjects such as *Dallas* v. *Dynasty*, Cherie Blair's teeth, other women's figures and suntans, their obsession with their own figures and suntans, and My Mother is Worse Than Yours Because.

They shared secrets too. Felicity confessed to Tessa that she didn't fancy Cliff any more; and Tessa confessed to Felicity that Jeremy was the only man she'd ever slept with. By the end of the first week, at the beach party laid on for the Nutty Browns' last night, Felicity nudged Tessa and said, 'You do realize,' and she was a bit pissed, 'that not only do I feel like I've lived here for ever, but I also feel like I've known you for ever. And yet, in real life, we've only known each other for seven days. But it's like you're one of my best friends. You know things about me that I've never told anyone back home.'

'Well if you think about it,' reasoned Tessa, who was only marginally less pissed, 'back home, we'd only meet up once every couple of weeks or so, for what, two or three hours or something – we must have spent at least a year together by now, in real world time.'

'That's what I like about you,' smiled Felicity as she retrieved a sticky cherry from her befreckled cleavage, 'you're so logical, and good at working stuff out – you're just like me! You must be so pleased . . .'

'I'm so not at all like you, how dare you?!' Tessa protested as she slurped the rest of her cocktail loudly up the straw. 'You know exactly what you're doing, where you're going, whereas I'm still fumbling round in the dark. I may have good intentions – sorry, did I slur that? – but I don't seem to be able to actually do anything about them.'

'Which is where I come in – Followthrough is my middle name,' said Felicity Followthrough Clifton as she plopped the cherry back into her cocktail, a Screw You. 'Now look. I've had my own companies for what, about ten years now, but I only started Guru PR five years ago, just after Spike was born. After a year, I bought my partner out. Within two years our annual turnover was over two million pounds, and that didn't come about by having good ideas and not making them happen.' She slurped the last of her drink and held both their glasses out to Ice or Lemon to be refilled. 'I propose a brainstorming session, first thing tomorrow morning. I know – a breakfast meeting!' (They both knew this would never happen, but the point was that the intention was there.) 'We're going to get you back on line, girl, so that by the time you go home you'll know exactly what you want and just how to get it!' Tessa could see why Felicity was so successful – her whole face lit up when she talked about work, she was animated and lively and infused with dynamic energy. It was very attractive. And infectious. In just a week, Tessa had felt herself thawing out under the bright light of Felicity's personality, she was beginning to remember the person she used to be . . .

'So that's that. Now then, have I told you about the time I farted during oral sex?' asked Felicity.

'Oh my god!' squealed Tessa with mock horror, hoping to disguise how shocked she really was when Felicity came out with statements like this. 'You didn't – what did he say?'

'What makes you think it was a "he"?' smiled Felicity, smiling out of the corner of her eye, just like Samantha from *Sex and the City*.

At last this holiday was becoming enjoyable, they each thought, separately but together. In fact, it was really good. Fun, even. They had everything they wanted and needed – but it wasn't the sun, sea and sand that was making them happy. (It could have been something to do with the drink, but it was certainly nothing to do with the food.)

No, it was the joy of close friendship that was wrapped around them, and all that came with it – intimacy, affection and respect, comfort and safety, all of which had been missing from both their lives for far too long.

Yes, this was fun, and they still had a whole week in Paradise left. Life was pretty good – for now.

*

FABIO
Every year Seaside Villages has a competition. The best catchphrase is used
for next year's advertising, and the
winners get a fortnight's free holiday. This year it was won by Stewart and
Fran, who'd come up with 'The holiday
that's home from home.'

FELICITY
Well – as soon as I heard that, they were
immediately christened the Slogans, of
course.

FABIO
And apart from one particular inci-
dent . . .

(THE SLOGAN BOY is shown brandishing a toy gun
out in the playground – everyone freezes in
horror, the smaller children start crying, a
plucky father disarms the boy)

FABIO
. . . I think they fitted in very well.

*

There was someone who was even more pleased than Felicity that she'd found a new best-friend, and that was Cliff. Thank fuck for that, he thought, as he laced up his new Nikes, he wouldn't have to worry about keeping her happy any more. Well not for a bit, anyway. Not until she decided she didn't like the Scottish bird after all, which could happen at any minute.

Women, thought Cliff, as he shut the room door behind him and made his way down to the ground floor of the hotel. Can't live with 'em, can't live with 'em. Bloody nightmares, the lot of them.

So why couldn't he learn to just leave them alone? Ever since he could remember, he'd had a woman on the go. He'd even had a crush on his nursery teacher, Miss Booker, because she'd got great legs. That was in the days of linoleum and stiletto heels, he could still smell her perfume and feel the little dents she'd made in the floor as she moved around the room. He'd trace round them with his finger when all the children had to sit on the floor, while she read them a story. She'd had lovely red lips, too.

He'd been a bit of a lad at senior school as well, always was a snappy dresser, even then. His dad had called him a 'bleedin' poof' when he'd come home in a pair of lime green loon pants and a Mr Freedom T-shirt with stars all over it. (That'd be a collector's item now, worth a fortune. Wonder if Mum still had it?) But they both knew he wasn't a shirtlifter, in fact Alfie had even encouraged him to sow his oats while he was young, told him not to get hitched too early. 'Not that I don't love your mum, son, but I'd hate to see you done up like a kipper all for the sake of a quick fuck behind the bandstand.'

He'd ignored his dad, of course. And it wasn't only behind the bandstand, it was behind anything that didn't move, with anything that did. Bloody hell, thought Cliff, those were the days. Then art college had given him access to the wilder women, and assisting the most swinging photographer in London during the late sixties (now dead unfortunately, an early casualty of HIV) had given him a taste for the posher birds. Beautiful, classy women. Highly-strung thoroughbreds. Private education and all that bollocks. Mad as a fish, every one of them.

It would have been fine if he'd managed to just shag and go, like his bloody brother. But he'd insisted on making it official, hadn't he? And weddings led to children, and children needed money, and so the older he'd got the more money he'd had to earn, and the more trapped he'd become. Yeah, there was no doubt about it, his life would be much easier if he could just learn to leave the women alone.

'All right?' Cliff smiled at the pretty brunette receptionist as he passed through the lobby of the hotel on his way to the so-called football pitch, a three quarters' size patch of yellowing grass way out past the car park.

'Ooh, Mr Clifton!' she called as she stood up to catch his attention. Which she didn't need to do.

'Yes, darlin'.' Cliff smiled his most crackin' smile and turned back, 'What's your name, by the way?'

'Dawn.'

'Ah, that's a lovely name, Dawn. Lovely name for a lovely girl, Dawn.' He smiled, in the hope that she fancied him.

'I've got lots of telephone messages here' – she ignored him – 'for your *wife*.' And she waved a bundle of little papers to prove it.

'Sorry, love, but I don't know where she is.'

'But they're all very urgent!' she appealed. She was very appealing.

'Oh, don't worry about it, lovely Dawn, she'll get them in the end. See ya darlin'!' And he left the reception area, jogging down the hotel steps as he went, like an impatient boxer. A little bit like that scene from the first Rocky movie, in fact.

Cliff had discovered that exercise was the best way to get rid of the frustration that was steadily rising in him, a bit more every day. Somehow things didn't seem so bad in the open air, he didn't feel so cooped up. He breathed in the sunshine and breeze as he jogged past the Kids Kottage, holding his tummy in just in case that dippy nanny bird with the big tits was watching. Now she was gorgeous – he always had a cocky word or two with her, when he dropped Spike off in the mornings. Nah, she wasn't there. Probably just as well.

Cliff had spent most of his life avoiding feelings, as he knew, to his cost, that they just got you into trouble. In fact, it made him angry that he even knew he was angry; the result of some bloody weekend couples workshop Felicity had made him go on. 'Let's all celebrate Cliff's frustration!' the wrong-kind-of lesbian in the crochet waistcoat had said. 'It's nothing a good shag wouldn't sort out!' he'd wanted to shout back, but he'd let them all dance round him like wankers anyway. But he hadn't liked it; the trouble with getting in touch with your feelings, is that it gets harder to make the fuckers go away again. And his old mate Alcohol just didn't do it no more, in fact it just made everything worse, bigger, more obvious. Didn't mean he had to stop trying though – the beer was free here, after all. Someone had to drink it, didn't they?

As he Rocky-jogged his way over to the football pitch, Cliff realized that he had no idea just what he was so fucked off about these days. Felicity probably knew, but he was buggered if he was going to ask her. True, he hated the fact that he hadn't had so much work recently, but it only made sense that the younger guys had to break into the business somehow, he'd done the same. But he still had to pay for his kids, didn't he? Couldn't have them going without. Specially not little Spike, god love him. Once Cliff had crunched the numbers, and he'd worked out that he was going to have to work full-on until he was seventy-three ... well, didn't bear thinking about.

But until then he was going to have to be like a fucking hamster running round and round on the money wheel, he couldn't afford to stop working. Trouble was, there just wasn't any work to be had. And let's face it, he was bloody knackered. Tired of the job, tired of his life. A bloke his age should be thinking of retiring soon, not licking the arses of twenty-three year-olds (well ... no), on the off-chance that they might hire him to take a picture of a radical newly-designed box of bloody soap powder. It was lucky Felicity's company was doing all right, that was a bonus.

'All right mate?' That bloke who won the competition, Mr Slogan, was already there, sunbathing on the
bench – only he'd never have admitted that's what he
was doing.

'Yeah, you?' Cliff did some warm-up exercises, even
though it was blisteringly hot. Well, that's what you did
before playing football.

'Yeah.'

There was a silence, the kind of silence that men are
comfortable with, and women are not.

'You enjoying it?' Cliff was standing with his legs apart,
swivelling from the waist up.

'Yeah, y'know. S'OK.'

'Yeah.'

More silence. More exercises. More burnt pates.

'The wife hates it.'

'Oh yeah?' Cliff was getting a bit puffed out. 'Why's
that – then?' Best sit down, don't want to overdo it, peak
too early.

'She don't like the other people here, says they're too
up their own arses.'

'Right.' He smiled. 'She has got a point, I'll give
her that.'

'And she's taken really badly against one woman, some
redhead bird, who's always shouting and laughing. Says
she's stuck-up.'

She's got a point there too. 'That's my wife.'

'Oh.' The other bloke didn't move. 'Sorry mate.'

'That's all right, forget it.' Cliff lay back and rubbed
his sore eyes, the suncream Felicity had insisted he use
was melting into them, it was stinging like fuck, but it

wasn't manly to say 'ow', so he didn't. He blotted it with the corner of his T-shirt instead.

Silence again. It was too hot to get all bothered.

'In that case,' the bloke on the bench went on, 'it was your kid that belted mine the other morning, in the middle of Craftwork.'

'Oh was it?' Cliff shut his eyes. 'Sorry, mate.'

'That's all right, forget it.' He turned on to his stomach. 'I ain't sure boys should be sticking beads and feathers and that on to pictures anyway.'

'Too right, mate,' laughed Cliff.

And that was them bonded. Nobody turned up to play football, as they'd suspected – this lot were probably more into rugby. Or lacrosse. The two men laughed at this, they understood each other. 'Apparently volleyball's the thing, dahling!' mimicked Mr Slogan, in a very passable posh accent.

They should really have gone back if there was no football to be played, but having secured some precious man-time away from their families, they stayed there anyway, enjoying the peace. After a couple of days, they'd found enough 'decent blokes' to form their own volleyball team, and from then on an unspoken class war was fought out on the beach, at eleven o'clock sharp, every morning.

*

SAMMY

Neb was, like, one of the nicest guys
ever. He was really big for his age,

well over 6 foot and really, like, wide,
and at first everyone was terrified of
him. Then we discovered that he was
actually a big softie, and not nearly
as scary as he looked. And he couldn't
do much either, because he had really
bad asthma. So one of the boys called
him The Nebulizer. He liked that.

*

'Where's Mamma?' asked Fabio, as he approached the
Clifton table.

'Mum,' said Cliff, through a mouthful of food, so it
didn't sound as pointy as he intended, 'says she's too
tired to sit round the table, and so she's taken a plate of
antipasta up to her room. She said she'd see you in the
morning. Where've you been, anyway?'

'Waiting for the doctor to turn up.' He sat down next
to his brother, opposite Tessa. They really didn't even
look related.

'Doctor?' asked Felicity as she pierced a poached plum
with her fork. 'Have you caught something nasty, Fabio?
Got a drippy willy?'

Tessa nearly gagged on her cream-filled brandy snap.

'No,' replied Fabio, patiently, 'one of the nannies has
got a very high temperature, some sort of bug, probably
– he's come to see her.'

'Which one?' asked Cliff.

'Alison. Why?'

'I just wondered.'

'Why?'

'Well, if it was any of Spike's lot, you know – don't want him to catch anything just before we have to fly home, that's all,' replied Cliff. 'Jeez, I was only asking.'

'Maybe I should ask him to take a look at Mamma, while he's here . . .'

'Why?' Cliff went back to peeling his orange in one piece, it was his party trick. 'She's not ill, for fuck's sake, she's just sad.' He began to separate the segments. 'Like you bloody care, anyway.'

'And what's that supposed to mean?' asked Fabio.

'Well,' Cliff leaned back in his seat and popped a piggy in, 'where the fuck were you when he was dying? She really needed support then, from both of us – I went down there every single bloody weekend, while you were off gawdknowswhere doing gawdknowswhat with gawdknowswho –'

'But I asked her, and she said she didn't need me –'

'Oh right, no, well why should she, she had Muggins here running round after her like a blue arsed bloody fly –'

'Boys!' Felicity's tone was sharp. 'Please! Shall we leave this until a more appropriate time? I'm sure Tessa doesn't need to experience the dirty linen of the Clifton family right now –'

'Tessa?' Lovely Dawn the receptionist was standing at their table. 'I've got through to that number for you, he's hanging on right now.'

'Oh right!' Tessa got up so quickly she knocked over her glass of wine. Luckily there was very little left in it. 'Oh god, sorry, oh shit – did I get you?' she asked Fabio.

117

'Not yet . . .' he oozed.

'Right, OK, um right – shall I come with you?' And she quickly followed Lovely Dawn out of the restaurant.

'Look, Fabio,' Felicity said as he looked round for a member of the restaurant staff to come and remove the tablecloth, 'how's it going with Tessa?'

Cliff shot a look skywards, a here-we-go look, as he licked his fingers clean.

'How's what going?' Fabio was confused.

'Well, you know, are you going to have sex with Tessa?'

'What?!'

'Look, I know she's too old and too clever for your usual type, but I just wondered if you could make an exception in this case.' Felicity leaned in, conspiratorially. 'She just needs a bit of fun, that's all. And I thought you might be the perfect person to provide that for her . . .'

'But she's married!' protested Cliff.

They both looked at him. He shut up.

Felicity continued. 'But she can't seem to get that bloody ex-husband of hers out of her system. She just needs to break that spell, I don't think she's slept with anyone else since him. You know the score . . .'

Fabio still looked doubtful. 'Well yeah, but –'

'Look, Michelle will never find out – we're going home the day after tomorrow, you'll never see Tessa again. Oh go on, she's gagging for it! Seriously, you'd be doing her a great favour, it would be an act of kindness . . .'

'Now I've heard everything,' groaned Cliff. 'My wife, pimping for my brother!'

'We got cut off!' Tessa was back, beaming. 'But

he did manage to say that the weather back home is terrible, they've had thunderstorms and everything. Poor old Jeremy.'

'I'll drink to that!' said Felicity, raising her glass, and shooting Fabio a mischievous wink.

*

TESSA

There was a very annoying boy who must have been about twelve, I suppose. I probably wouldn't recognize him if I saw him now, because I don't think I ever got a good look at his face – it was always behind a video camera. He just filmed everything, all the time. I'm afraid we called him the VD Boy, because he was all over you like a sexually transmitted disease.

*

Sammy was holding teenage court around a can of 7Up in the Bucket and Spade. As their parents were preparing for an après-déjeuner snooze in the shade, the teenagers had been turfed out of their beds by Housekeeping who had to clean the rooms. So they'd shambled down to breakfast, only to discover that it was lunch, which had just finished; and now they were gathered round their usual table at the beach bar, to discuss last night's activities, and to plan tonight's.

Which was done with as little eye contact as possible. Even though none of their mobiles worked out there, due to parents' total non-understanding of the global importance of pay-as-you-go communication, mobiles were still required items. So it was heads down, while some played games and others honed their texting skills to impress friends with when they got home.

Having scored a new best ever score of 1,386 on The Worm, Sammy actually looked up. 'Where's Neb? He has got so much to answer for, that bro, did you see him last night? First of all he drank bare amounts of rum and coke, then Chris saw him trying to pull one of the minging nannies, dintcha, Chris?'

Christabelle nodded. She understood the language, of course, they all did. Nobody knew exactly where it came from, but even though it was a big city thing, the ones who lived in the countryside were catching on quick, because they had to, or they just wouldn't be bo selecta, right?

Reports of the Nebulizer's drunken progress were duly filed, and then the more easily-led looked to Sammy, to decide what they were going to do next. There was an official programme of daily events all planned out for them, of course, but Kevin the Cretin – the member of staff supposedly in charge of the Sunflowers (such a crap name, so childish) – was in bed with a really bad cold, the gimp. But as they had yet to follow anything on the programme, it didn't really matter anyway. Being one of the stronger personalities there, Sammy had become their unofficial leader, a role she was more than happy to take – if you waited around for this lot to make a decision, nothing would ever happen. There were, however, various subdivisions of the teenage crowd:

the Clueless girls, the Needy boys, the Horsey Lot and the lowest of the low, the Babyish. But Sammy had the majority.

'So listen guys, I've had an idea. Let's go snorkelling!'

Smiles were wiped off faces quicker than you could say 'tidy your room'.

The prettiest Clueless girl, Angelique, seized this wide-open opportunity to overthrow. 'Er, excuse me?'

'You heard – snorkelling.' The two girls eyeballed each other.

Angelique, whose hair was perfect and going to stay that way, tinkled a laugh attractively. 'Er, no, I don't *think* so!' Her idolizing followers sniggered.

But Angus, who was from Aberdeen and had made much of his kinship with Sammy, said he thought it was a great idea. (He'd also realized that no matter how much he hung around the girls, trying to pick up flirting tips, they really did spend all day talking about nothing, and quite honestly he was bored shitless.) Fortunately his vote counted for something, as he was only a borderline Needy.

The Babyish were divided on this; some hated the idea, they thought it might be scary; others were overly-enthusiastic, and started requesting harpoons and other underwater weaponry.

One of the Clueless girls wondered out loud if there were octopuses down there, which could reach up and drag you down by the ankle, and make you drown.

Then Yoko the trendy mum came by, wearing that gorgeous Quiksilver bikini from the Village Shop, which all the girls had been lusting after. As she waited for Ice or Lemon to re-surface from the icy bowels of the freezer, she tried to join in, quoting lyrics from bands even they'd never heard of. So that got them all up and out of there, and after even more debate and wrangling, Sammy somehow got a large enough group of them to agree to accompany her to The Shack, where the snorkels were kept – and members of the Waterfront Team were known to hang out ...

She had a difficult job hiding her irritation when she found out that it was Jamie's day off, and he'd gone scuba diving.

*

CLIFF
There was this couple, right, who just never smiled. Never. Miserable as sin, they were – and this was before they had anything to be miserable about. Their kids were always bloody whingeing and crying, they were real downers that family. So I started off referring to them as 'Keep Death Off The Roads', and then it sort of grew into other old road safety campaigns, like 'Dip Don't Dazzle', and 'Clunk Click Every Trip', etc. They were just known as The Tufty Club in the end.

*

'EXCUSE ME, CAN I HAVE A WORD?' Bonnie gave

Christabelle a terrible shock, leaping out of the kitchen into the corridor right in front of her like that.

'Well, I'm just taking him over to children's supper,' the younger girl said, trying to pass, keeping her head down and her hand clamped around her step-brother's wrist.

'Spi-ike,' said Bonnie in her special kids' voice, 'would you like to watch a video?'

He didn't need to think about it, he'd been wanting to watch TV ever since he got here, even though nobody else wanted him to. 'Yes!'

'Yes, what?' said Bonnie, looking down really fiercely at him, like the Red Queen from *Alice in Wonderland*.

'Yes what please!' Undaunted, his little legs jiggled with excitement.

Having plugged him into the secret TV in her office, Bonnie led Christabelle into the kitchen. 'Cup of tea?'

'I'd prefer a coke.'

'Sorry, we don't have that sort of drink here. I could do you an orange squash with no added sugar if you like?'

'OK.' Christabelle sighed.

'You OK?'

'Yes, why?'

'Well, I just wondered.' Bonnie stretched up to the top shelf inside a cupboard to get the glass out. 'You don't look very happy, whenever I see you.'

'Well I am. I'm fine.'

'Oh. Right. You're very good with Spike though, aren't you?'

'No. I'm not. I'm crap at kids.' Even though Christabelle was looking down at the floor (which Tania hadn't

123

swept today) from underneath her Simpsons baseball cap, Bonnie could tell she was blushing.

'Oh.'

'He prefers his nannygranny to me.'

'That's Fabio's mum, isn't it?'

'Yeah, and she's my grandmother as well.'

'Oh right, I see,' said Bonnie, hoping she sounded like she didn't know that already, when in fact of course she did. 'D'you get on with her?' she asked as she poured not too much squash into the glass.

'She's OK.' Christabelle folded her arms. 'I hardly ever see her. She's my dad's mum.'

'You're not a very close family then?'

Christabelle snorted disdainfully. 'You could say that.'

'But your dad seems quite nice?'

'Yeah, he is. He's really nice. When he's around.'

'You live with your mum then?'

'Yeah.'

'Right.' Bonnie handed Christabelle her drink. 'And d'you get on with your mum?'

'Not really.'

'Oh dear, why not?'

'Just don't.' She took a sip and shot Bonnie a look which said, 'And don't ask any more'.

'Right.' This really wasn't going very well, Christabelle seemed immune to Bonnie's charms. 'Sorry, d'you want ice with that?'

'Nah, s'all right.'

'It's not too much trouble, honest.'

'OK, then.'

As Bonnie wrestled with the ridiculous rubber contraption, which made ice come out in the shape of Mickey Mouse's head, she decided to try a different tack.

'So have you made any friends here?'

'Yes, thanks.' Christabelle was sighing again.

'Oh yes, I thought I saw you the other day with that girl – um, let me see, Samantha wasn't it?' Bonnie was impressed with her own acting skills, she really sounded like she didn't know.

'Sammy, yeah. And?'

'Well, she looks nice.'

'She is.'

'And is her mum nice?'

Christabelle shrugged. 'I dunno.'

Go for it. 'She seems to be getting on very well with your Uncle Fabio, doesn't she?'

'I s'pose so, I dunno.'

Bonnie watched, powerless, as Christabelle downed her drink in one. Bloody hell, what was she going to report back to Michelle? She'd found out nothing. 'Would you like some more?'

'No, thanks.' She wiped her mouth with the back of her hand. Bonnie felt her mouth move towards a ticking off, but managed to cough instead. 'Sure?'

'Yes.' Christabelle looked down at the floor again. She was wearing Doc Martens, if you please, in this heat. No wonder she was prettily pinkened, had the bloom of a rosy apple. 'Can I go now?' As she lifted up her head and peered out from under her cap, Bonnie noticed for the first time that this girl had the most beautiful mouth, all squashy and plumpy.

'Yes, of course.'

'Cheers.' She didn't look up again, but she did add, 'Thanks for the drink.'

What is it about teenagers? You can't shut kids up when they're small, but as soon as the buggers hit adolescence you don't get another word out of them. Although, Bonnie realized – as she shut the kitchen door against the protests of Spike at being taken away from the TV tranquillizer – whilst their conversation had produced little information, in another way she'd learned quite a lot.

*

TESSA
There was one couple we really liked,
Jill and Stuart.

FELICITY
So we called them Jill and Stuart.

6. The Last Night

SPIKE is talking to camera. He seems over-
confident for his age, and a touch precocious.

SPIKE

I liked it when we were on our holiday.
It was a bit like being at school,
and I had chips every day. And my
nannygranny used to buy me lots of
ice creams –

Quick cut to a long shot of the vine-covered
terrace of the restaurant.

*

'I can't wait to have a night in on the sofa with the telly,
how pathetic is that?' giggled Tessa.

'Completely understandable. I have to say, I'm really
ready to go home now. I'm so fed up with having to
look nice all the time,' moaned Felicity, 'I can't wait to
slob out in m'big baggy comfies. Gina?'

'I'm looking forward to being back in my own house,
sleeping in my own bed . . .'

'Too right, Mum. Personally, I can't wait to have a
bloody good curry when I get home.'

'Oh honestly, Cliff, that's so predictable. D'you know,

I've actually got used to the food here now,' said Felicity as she tucked into her Black Forest Gateau. 'If you blindfolded me, I don't think I'd be able to tell the difference between custard and crème anglaise. Either the food's got better, or my palate's shot to pieces.'

'Don't let's forget the fish pie . . .' ventured Tessa.

'Why, what was the matter with that?' asked Fabio.

'They'd left the eyes in, that's what,' said Felicity, through her mouthful.

'Ugh!' said Spike, who immediately dropped his knife and fork on to his plate with a loud clatter. 'That's horrible!' And he began to cry.

'Now now,' said Gina to him softly, 'remember you've got to be big and grown-up tonight, Mummy said you could only stay up if you were good . . .' But she put her knife and fork together on the plate. This was a good excuse for her to stop eating too.

'So could you see them?' Sammy (who had been forced to attend this last supper) looked at Chris, who'd been a vegetarian for some time.

'Oh yes,' said Felicity gaily, 'they were dotted all over the plate, like little fried silvery currants, staring up at you.'

Tessa diverted. 'What about you, Christabelle? What are you looking forward to doing when you get back?'

Christabelle adopted that hunted look favoured by people who don't like to be in the spotlight. 'Um . . .' She looked to Sammy for support, but her friend had been distracted by a foursome who'd just arrived in the restaurant.

'Isn't that Beauty and the Beast, being wined and dined

by Robert Redford and Brad Pitt?' observed Felicity, who'd turned nicknaming into an art form now.

They all looked, of course, they had to. And what they saw was Michelle and Bonnie, on a double-date with Jamie and Bruno. And Michelle's little gel-bra'd cleavage was just loving the attention. As was she – she had obviously spent a lot of time getting ready for tonight, and was at her sheeniest.

'Hmm,' tutted Fabio, 'I don't think they should be doing that. Staff are only allowed to eat in the dining room in the evenings if invited to do so by villagers. I'm sure that's the rule, what are they up to?'

'Oh for god's sake, Fabio,' scorned Felicity, 'lighten up. It's the last night!'

'Maybe for you, but not for us,' he replied distractedly, still looking over at the offending table.

'Fabio is only doing his job,' said his mother.

'Yeah well, good on 'em I say,' said Cliff, blissfully unaware of any of the difficulties this particular combination was causing the rest of the table. 'That Bruno's bloody good at tennis y'know, he wiped the floor with me the other day in the mixed doubles . . .'

'Can we go?' asked Sammy, who'd stood up anyway. 'Come on, Chris.'

'Don't be too late tonight, please,' Tessa called after them, 'you haven't done your packing yet . . .' She sighed. 'Oh what's the point, she knows as well as I do that I'll do it for her. D'you know, she didn't get in until well after five a.m. last night; I only know because she woke me up, bumping into the furniture.'

'Good god, what did you say to her?' asked Felicity.

'Well nothing, what's the point? To be honest, I'm just glad she's enjoying herself, she deserves it.'

'You spoil that girl,' pronounced Felicity.

'Well at least nobody could accuse you of spoiling Christabelle,' muttered Cliff.

Felicity put down her spoon. 'I beg your pardon?'

'Well,' said Cliff, fortified by the wine, 'you haven't exactly done your best to make sure she's had a nice time, have you?'

'But she's your daughter –'

'What difference does that make?' He drained his glass. 'You're not much better with your own child. Spike's spent more time with Mum on this holiday than he has with you.'

There was a split second's silence, during which Looks were quickly flashed between Fabio, Gina and Tessa, dreading what was to come. Felicity, however, had fixed her steely gaze on her husband. 'Anything else to add, Cliff, while you're at it?'

'Yes,' said Cliff, whose eyes were a little bloodshot, 'you're not much of a fucking wife either.'

'And what,' Felicity was scarily calm, aware that all eyes were on her, 'is that supposed to mean, precisely?'

'You know.' And not taking his eyes off her, he stood up, grabbed the rest of the wine bottle and left the table, to stunned silence.

'I wish he wouldn't swear like that in front of the boy,' said Gina, shaking her head.

'What's a fucking wife?' asked Spike.

'Time for bed,' said Felicity.

'Am I a fucking wife?' asked Spike.

'I'll take him up,' sighed Gina, 'I'm tired, and it's going to be a long day tomorrow.'

'Night night, darling.' Felicity kissed her son. 'Make sure you get a good night's sleep, we're going on the aeroplane again tomorrow!'

'Are you a fucking wife?' Spike asked his nannygranny, as she led him away.

'Thank God we're going home tomorrow,' sighed Felicity to Tessa as Fabio moved over on to Gina's seat, 'I don't think our marriage can stand any more of this – we're so much better together when we spend more time apart.' She smiled, only too aware of what she'd just said.

Tessa thought she could detect a tiny tear in the corner of her friend's eye, but knew not to let on.

'So you're not having much sex at the moment?' asked Fabio.

'Not much, no.' Again, Felicity smiled. 'In fact, none at all. I mean, we had a drunken quickie a while ago, but it wasn't what you might call a love thang.'

'But isn't that normal, in a long relationship?' asked Fabio. 'I thought that after you got married, the sex dried up completely.'

'Oh no,' said Tessa. 'It never did with us. In fact, if anything, we did it more and more . . .' She trailed off, aware that perhaps this wasn't the right thing to be saying right now. Felicity swilled her red wine around its glass, and stared into its gloomy depths.

'Is that right?' asked Fabio, turning to Tessa with a glint in his eye. 'You must miss it now, then?'

'Well, um, yes – um –' She really didn't know what to say. She'd drunk a bit herself, and was having trouble keeping up with events. Much as she was fond of the Cliftons, this family were sometimes a bit too modern for her.

'So how long has it been since you were last with a man?' asked Fabio.

'Gosh, um, yes, now let me see . . .' Tessa was shocked to be asked such a direct question. 'Er . . .'

His hand moved under the tablecloth, on to her thigh.

'Would you ever take a lover?' He tightened his grip. She wanted to burst into flames.

Desperate, Tessa looked to Felicity for help. Felicity seemed to be looking over at the foursome, who were looking back at them.

'Well yes, if um, yes – no, definitely, yes – maybe.' She smiled. I'D HAVE YOU FOR ONE NIGHT, IF THAT'S WHAT YOU'RE ASKING. Oh god. 'Sure, why not?' She hoped she sounded as carefree as she wanted to.

'Oh dear, is that the time?' Fabio studied his watch. 'I'm sorry to leave you girls, but I've got to get ready for the Awards Ceremony. I hope I'll see you later?'

And then he did something extraordinary. As he pushed his chair out, ready to stand up and leave, his hand moved up to Tessa's crotch and somehow, through the diaphanous films of her best dress that she'd been saving for the last night, he found just the right little button to press, gently but firmly. An electric charge zinged right up inside her.

'Do come, won't you.'

It was quite the most erotic thing that had ever happened to her, and if she had been one of those passionate, forceful women in a foreign film, she'd have grabbed his wrist and made it stay there; but as it was she could only manage to blush right down to the soles of her feet, and go more than a bit funny. He flashed that Ginola smile, and left.

'. . . wait till I get him home!' Felicity was saying. 'You all right, Tess?'

'Er, yes – sorry – just remembered something.' That was just so rude! She could hardly believe it had happened. Or that she'd enjoyed it.

'What?'

'Oh nothing – so look, come on, what're we going to do about Cliff? Are you going to go after him, or let him stew in his own juice, as my mother would say?' As Felicity ranted and raved, Tessa realized that she was yearning to get back to the safety of normal, where men didn't ask her sexy questions or touch her in sexy places. Much as she had grown to love them, these people were all mad.

She'd really missed her little life, and she couldn't wait to get back to it.

*

Cliff had rolled up his linen Versaces and was sitting on the beach, miserable as fuck. He swigged more wine from the bottle, and looked out to the dark sea. What the hell was he doing here? Why had he stormed off like that? What was the matter with him?

'Are you all right?' It was Tania, the dippy nanny with the big tits. She was bending down to talk to him, he could see right into her breasts, which were both beautifully lit by the moonlight. They looked like ripe, luscious globes, just gagging to be taken out and played with. 'I'm sorry,' they said to him, 'I won't disturb you if you don't want me to, I just saw you walking down here, and –'

'Nah, that's fine love, stay if you want. I'd like the company.'

'OK.'

She sat down beside him and played with her finger in the sand. 'How long have you been here now?'

'Two weeks.'

'Oh, right.'

'Going home in the morning.' Thank god, he could go back to hiding behind the garden and the dog. And Felicity would be back at work by tomorrow afternoon.

'Is this your last night then?'

He smiled. 'Yes.'

'Oh.' She carried on making a pattern in the sand. It was a heart shape. 'That's a shame.'

'Is it?'

'Yes.' Her turn to smile now. 'I'll miss the silly things you say to me in the mornings.'

'You will?'

'Yes.' She looked at him. 'You're funny.' She smiled. 'And you're a very good dad, you know.'

'Am I?' He wanted to stop asking questions – 'really?' – but didn't seem able to. This was ridiculous, he was sounding like someone in *EastEnders*. (*Seen Pat? Who's askin'? Wossit to you?*)

'Oh yes. I see all sorts in my job, I can tell you're a good father.'

'How?'

'Well, you know, you're kind.'

'How d'you know that then?'

'Easy. You've got kind eyes.'

'Have I?'

'Yes. Nice, kind eyes.'

'So've you.'

'And your little boy loves you.'

Ah, Spike. The emotion welled up inside him, he couldn't bear for anything to hurt that little kid. And that included Felicity, who had changed since she'd become a mother. He'd thought a baby would soften her up a bit, but no, she'd spent more time at work, and less time at home. He was everything to little Spike, the poor lad hardly knew his mother. 'Yeah, well, I love him to bits.'

'Yes, I know.' She flicked her long blonde hair back over her shoulder and leant towards him, leaning on one arm. She lowered her chin. 'I can see it in your eyes.'

'Really?' If Cliff didn't know any better, he'd say she was coming on to him. Can't be. She was a bit out of his league, this one. 'That's clever of you, Tania.'

'Yes, well, I am clever. Much cleverer than they think.'

'Who's they?'

'Oh, you know, Bonnie and all the other nannies. They all just think I'm a dumb blonde. Did you know they call me the Village Idiot?'

'No,' Cliff lied, remembering Felicity screeching with joy at this information one day, jealous that she hadn't made it up herself.

'Well they do.' She lowered her chin again, looked up at him with those sexy spearmint-rhino green eyes. 'It's very hurtful.'

'Yes,' said Cliff, 'I'm sure it is.'

'I mean, I'm not going to be a nanny for the rest of

my life – oh no.' She puffed herself up, ready to impress. 'I'm going to be a teacher.'

'Are you?' She was beautiful, this girl, she didn't need the moonlight to soften her curves. 'What are you going to teach?'

She laughed at him. 'Children, of course!'

They chatted for a little longer, until they heard the Awards Ceremony being announced from the Bucket and Spade, further up the beach.

Tania had to go then, because it was part of her job to be present at this particular event. Reluctantly, Cliff got up and went with her. But as they made their way over to the Village Hall, she mentioned his kind eyes one more time. What a shame it was their last night. But then again, thank God. The last thing he needed right now was another ex-wife.

*

'Eh, Cliffie, my man!' Mr Slogan slapped Cliff hard on the back and handed him a beer. 'Ready to get the medal then?'

'What medal?' asked Cliff, looking round to see if anyone had seen him come in with Tania.

'For being the top volleyball team, mate, that's what! Yay, up The Workers!' And suddenly Cliff found himself swept up into the mob mentality of blokey gangwork, and acting all tanked-up geezer, like the rest of them.

'God, it's pathetic!' hissed Felicity to Tessa, as she watched the men being boys.

But Tessa was busy looking at Fabio, who was presenting the Radish and the Parsnip with the award for Best All-Round Family – they'd won everything, from the backwards dinghy race to the Pop Quiz to the prize for the best kids fancy-dress outfit, which of course they'd brought with them.

As the Root couple walked hand in hand up the steps to collect their bottle of champagne, Tessa did her best to analyse exactly why she was feeling such lust for someone who was so – well, 'cheesy', as Sammy would say. But he was irresistible, he just was sex. Everything he did just reeked of it. As Fabio kissed the perfect wife and mother, even the audience went 'whoo-ooo!' in a very childish way, which made them all laugh at themselves.

Christabelle was trying to talk to Sammy, but she wasn't listening as she was too busy giving Jamie the evils, staring at him with narrowed eyes.

And Michelle wasn't listening to a word Bonnie was saying; she was far too taken up with raising one eyebrow at Fabio, whenever she could catch his eye. She was feeling very pleased with herself, his face when she'd walked into the restaurant was a picture. That'd teach him to ignore her.

At the back of the hall, Red Rum was dancing with Bruno, even though there was no music.

Alcopop was invading Tania's personal space, breathing all over her.

The Tufty Club were tutting at everything, muttering about football hooligans and the British abroad generally, listing, once more, the points to be raised in their letter of complaint.

Yes, it really was time to go home.

*

Bonnie left Michelle to it in the end. She'd done all she

could to help, but Michelle wasn't sticking to the plan of ignoring Fabio, and so it was just not worth her trying to help any more. As everyone poured out of the Village Hall and made their way down to the farewell beach party, she signalled over their heads to Michelle that she was going to bed. She'd had a long day, as they were short-staffed due to illness, and tomorrow was their only lie-in of the week, it being changeover day. Sundays were Bonnie's favourite day.

She made her way across the village green, her path lit by mushroom lamps, crawling with insects attracted to the warmth of the nightlight. She was just passing the playground, when she noticed a teenage boy sitting on his own, about to break one of the swings. 'Oy!' Bonnie said loudly, as she made her way over, 'get off that, now!'

'Sorry,' said a girl's voice. It was Christabelle.

'Oh – I didn't know it was you.' Bonnie sniffed as she neared. 'Are you smoking?'

'Might be.' Christabelle sucked in, noisily. The red dot on the end of her mouth glowed.

'It's a really stupid thing to do you know, you shouldn't smoke.'

'Yeah yeah, whatever.' Christabelle stood up and ground the fag end to death with her boot. 'I didn't put that out because you told me to, by the way; I'd finished it already.'

'My mother died of smoking.' Bonnie didn't know why she suddenly said that, she never talked about it.

'So did my grandad.'

'So why are you doing it?'

'I dunno really' – Christabelle sat down on the bench for parents – 'something to do I s'pose.'

'Can't you find something else to do instead?'

'Like what?'

'I don't know' – Bonnie sat down beside her – 'take up a sport, perhaps? Go cycling? Mountain climbing?'

'What, every time I want a fag? It'd be a bit of a bother – I don't live anywhere near a mountain, I'm from Twickenham. Middlesex is quite flat.'

They both smiled at that.

There was a pause, not an uncomfortable one.

'So how old were you?' Christabelle asked.

'When?'

'When your mum died.'

'Oh.' Bonnie thought about it. Why not, the girl was going home tomorrow, she'd never see her again. 'Ten.'

'Ten? So you remember it then?'

'Oh yes. I remember it all right. It was horrible, really scary. It was really awful for my little brothers . . .' Bonnie trailed off, she didn't want to go there, she didn't want that feeling, that hole that she'd have to try and fill up again. 'What about you, how old were you?'

'When?'

'When you lost your grandad.'

'Oh – seventeen, it was only about three months ago.'

'I'm sorry to hear that,' said Bonnie, and she really was, she had a pathological fear of death and all that came with it, 'were you very close?'

'No, not really. Used to be. Not any more.'

'Right.'

They fell into silence again, the tsing tsing of the crickets filled the space between them.

'You must be looking forward to going home tomorrow, see your mum again.' Bonnie tried to imagine how normal that must be to normal people.

'Huh!' She was surprised by the force of Chris' reaction. 'You must be joking! I'd rather stay here, thank you very much.'

'Oh? Why's that?'

'Well at least nobody's nagging me here, I can do what I want.'

'Yes, but it's not real life, is it? Your mum's probably only strict with you because she cares.' Christabelle's mum was probably quite nice, they usually were, other people's mums, better than they said. 'Listen, I'd rather have a strict mum, than no mum at all.'

They both thought about that.

Bonnie persisted in trying to find a bright side for this girl. 'And surely you're missing your friends, aren't you?'

'Well not really, no. They're all a bit shit back home, Sammy's about the best friend I've ever had. But she's more interested in boys than me. I'm just someone for her to hang out with, when there's no boys around.'

'Yes, well, I know how that feels,' said Bonnie. 'Listen, you should get to bed, you're up early tomorrow.' She laid her hand on Christabelle's arm, just because she really wanted to. 'Unless you want to talk a bit more?'

'Well – d'you mind? I'm not at all tired. But you don't have to, I don't care, y'know.'

The two girls smiled at each other. At last, someone

who might understand me, thought Christabelle. At last, someone who may appreciate me, thought Bonnie. What a pity it had taken them until the last night to find each other.

*

When Felicity heard him fumbling with the lock on the other side of the door, she automatically shut her eyes, so that she could fake deep sleep when he came in, her usual ploy. Despite exhausting the subject with Tessa all evening, she still had no idea what she wanted to do about this little tantrum of his, and so she'd decided to pretend it hadn't happened. Everything would be back to normal within twenty-four hours anyway, once they were home.

We nearly made it, she said to herself, we nearly got through the whole two weeks as an ordinary couple. But old loose-lips just had to cause a scene, didn't he? It hadn't taken a genius to work out what Cliff had been implying, Fabio had caught on quickly enough. An overwhelming wave of shame flooded Felicity's thoughts, and, one by one, tears of embarrassment crept out of the corner of her eye and seeped into the pillow.

He'd made her feel unattractive, old, ugly. He used to tell her how lucky he was to be with her, now he didn't bother. And yet, even though Felicity knew it was probably just a question of a few Botox jabs and an eyelift, she just didn't feel willing to do it. It was as if she didn't want to be attractive for him any more.

Cliff was still fiddling around outside, swearing at the key. Felicity tried to remember the last time they'd made love, intentionally, meaningfully. Ah yes, it had been her fortieth birthday, nearly two years ago. Two years! She had no idea how this had happened, how either of them had let it get to this sorry state, but these days she preferred her pyjamas to her husband in bed. In fact, the very thought of him humping up and down on top of her, all red in the face, made her feel quite sick.

It sounded like he'd got one of his volleyball mates to help him with the lock, they were both acting like bad Ealing comedy drunks out in the corridor now, for all to hear and discuss over breakfast tomorrow morning.

She had to do something about this. But what? She only had to get them to the sexy place, surely once they'd done it like they used to, they'd be able to do it again? Couldn't she just try really hard to recreate the old days? Surely once they'd broken through that barrier, it would get easier and easier each time? She'd drunk quite a bit tonight. Would it be that hard? (Although as Kathy might say, would he?) There was only one way to find out.

'Get inside, now!' she ordered as she flung open the door. Cliff fell in key first, with a sizeable crowd grinning behind him. 'Good night to you all!'

And with a flourish, Felicity Followthrough Clifton slammed their bedroom door behind her, and set to work on reclaiming her marriage.

*

'Fancy a nightcap?' Michelle asked her sexmachine, as he shook the ninety-ninth villager's hand at the bar in the Bucket and Spade, and wished them a safe journey home tomorrow morning.

'No, thanks, I've still got a bit more to do here – you go on ahead, I'll see you in a bit.'

Safe in the knowledge that Tessa had gone up to bed over an hour ago, Michelle pressed her lithe, bendy little body up against him as she said goodnight. 'I'll stay up for you, don't be too long!' she trilled, as she tottered off in those follow-me-home-and-fuck-me shoes she knew he loved.

Red Rum was face down on one of the tables, fast asleep and snoring like a cartoon character of an old drunk. Either Ice or Lemon was doing his best to rouse her, but she was dead to the world. So it was down to Fabio to scoop her up and carry her over the village green, past the pool area and into the hotel.

'What – room number?' he puffed at Nikki, who had volunteered for the late shift on Reception in case her boyfriend phoned.

'You can't be that desperate, surely?' she smiled as she eyed the comatose corpse in his arms. 'What's her name?'

'Just show me – the room list' – she did – 'and – give me a key.' (Unbeknownst to the villagers, all the bedroom doors had the same lock. This helped avoid any problems when guests took their room key home with them, which they often did. And of course, if they were unthinking enough to do that, they were unthinking enough not to post it back to the hotel.) 'Cheers.' Clenching the key between his teeth, Fabio somehow made it up the stairs and into her room, to deposit Red Rum on the bed. Her husband was fully clothed and snoring on the other side, also out for the count.

As she landed, the woman opened her eyes and stared up at the beautiful face above her. She quickly closed them again, afraid that she'd died and gone to heaven.

*

Tessa thought she heard a knock on her door, but she was always hearing things when she was trying to sleep. At home it was usually the bedroom radiator knocking as the heating went off, but that couldn't be the noise she'd heard just now. Maybe it was rats, running around behind the skirting boards? Cockroaches, signalling to each other that it was all right to come out, to crawl all over her face while she was asleep?

Tip tap. There it was again. Tessa consulted her watch. Just past two o'clock. Maybe it was someone looking for Sammy, who wasn't back yet, of course. She had been talking about staying up all night, which made perfect teenage sense, they did have to be ready to go at a ridiculously early hour in the morning. At least she'd sleep on the plane, instead of hurling the usual abuse in her mother's direction.

As predicted, Tessa had done all their packing, which had been much easier than on most holidays, as this time they hadn't actually been out of the grounds to do any local shopping. She and Felicity had been meaning to go and explore, but somehow they'd never found the time. So she hadn't had to sit on the suitcases, as usual.

Tip-tappy-tap. Right. Tessa swung her legs out of bed and grabbed a towel from the bathroom. She opened the door. 'Hello?'

In one flowing movement he came in, held her round

the waist, shut the door behind him, and kissed her long and hard, pressing his body against hers, up against the wall. WOW!

Tessa didn't say anything, she couldn't. She didn't want to. Not a word was spoken between them, they communicated with their loins and groins instead. He pulled her towel off impatiently, and she didn't mind that he could see her tanned breasts now, in fact she wanted him to see all of her. His hot and wet mouth slid down over her nipple, and bit it, exactly enough to arouse, but not enough to hurt. Just right.

He moved her backwards into the room, guiding her expertly, she knew she wouldn't fall. He lowered her smoothly on to the bed, his licky-slippy tongue never leaving hers. As he kneeled across her, straddling her, she could see the burgeoning bulge of his cock beneath his mediterranean blue jeans, straining to burst out of there and into her. With one hand he expertly played with her clitoris, with the other he searched his back pocket for a condom; she began to undo those bursting buttons of his, one by tantalizing one.

WHAT DO YOU THINK YOU ARE DOING? asked the voice. *Oh shut up.*

He found what he was looking for, and kept it in his hand as he ripped his shirt off.

It was a beautiful sight.

HELLO? CAN YOU HEAR ME? *Go away. It's the last night, I'll never see him again. I can do things like this, I can.*

Tessa admired the body before her, as he swiftly stepped out of his jeans, no underwear, and climbed back on top of her. Broad, tanned chest with just enough hair to play with, strong arms for holding close, just the right amount of soft hair on his navel, leading a silky dark path down to his urgent cock, which didn't look like Jeremy's at all.

Ah.

GOTCHA!

Tessa shut her eyes. And saw Jeremy's face. Frowning.

He parted her legs, and trailed his way down her body with his long hair, licking her all the way down to – oh god, Tessa shut her eyes, but Jeremy was there again, furious.

'Look, Fabio, I don't think I can do this.' She opened her eyes and looked up at him.

He was tying his hair back. Into a bloody ponytail. Like a girl. He'd got a hair tie out of his pocket, not a condom. In preparation. So that he could get to work on her. Ugh. What a turn-off.

WHAT A WANKER.

I can't do this.

'Sorry, babe?'

'I can't.'

'What d'you mean?'

'I just – well, y'know, I don't think –'

'But look, I want you really bad . . .' And he placed his cock at just the perfect place, to show her.

But it wasn't right. It wasn't the one she was used to.

YOU'VE GOT TO ADMIT THOUGH, IT IS VERY BEAUTIFUL. Oh give me a break, whose side are you on?

'Oh no, don't get me wrong, it's not you, or – that – it's because, well –'

I'm still in love with my husband, she was about to say, but didn't get the chance.

'I'm sorry to interrupt, but I think you'd better come quickly, Fabio.' Bonnie, standing at the end of the bed, white as a sheet. 'It's one of my nannies, Alison. I think she's dead.'

7. Day of Departure

MR SLOGAN is talking to camera.

MR SLOGAN
We couldn't wait to get home, back to
the real world. I wanted a proper pint,
the wife missed the shops and the kids
were knackered.

*

WHAT THE BLOODY HELL WERE YOU THINKING? ARE
YOU COMPLETELY MAD? SHE'LL HAVE TOLD EVERY-
BODY. *Shut up, don't you think I feel bad enough already?*
'Mum? You OK?' Sammy, still in last night's clothes,
stinking of stale smoke.

'Sorry, yes.' Tessa took a sip of her cold coffee. 'Have
you had breakfast?'

'No, Mum, you know I don't eat breakfast. Where's
Chris?' They both looked around the dining room. This
week's Nutty Browns were all dressed in their travelling
clothes, a bit hot and bothered in their unfamiliar long trousers, even socks in some cases. Last week's Bright Whites
were positively flaunting their shorts, smugly going about
their breakfasting business, another day in paradise stretching ahead of them. AND THEY'RE ALL LOOKING AT YOU,
THEY ALL KNOW WHAT YOU DID LAST NIGHT. 'Mum.'

148

'What?'

Sammy sighed, parents were so shit at everything. 'Have you seen Christabelle?'

'I don't know.'

'Well, where's Felicity and that lot?'

'I don't know.'

Sammy sat down at the table. 'Are you all right, Mum? You look like death warmed up.'

'Yes, I'm fine. Just a bit tired, that's all, I didn't get much sleep.' SLAG! LOOK AT THEM ALL, TALKING ABOUT YOU! *But we didn't do anything, we didn't have sex!* she wanted to shout.

'Neither did I,' Sammy grinned.

'I should hope not,' said Tessa.

'What?'

'What?'

'Don't you want to know why I didn't get any sleep?'

'No, not really. You can tell it to your father.' AND WHAT'S HE GOING TO SAY WHEN HE FINDS OUT? YOU KNOW YOU'LL TELL HIM, YOU CAN'T KEEP ANYTHING SECRET FROM JEREMY. *Oh god, you're right.*

'Tess!' Felicity made an entrance in the doorway, looking very elegant in what the magazines call palazzo pants and matching white jacket. She told Cliff to put the luggage out in the lobby, and sat herself down at Tessa's table. She looked great, tanned and sparkly, with her beautiful hair framing what looked like a newly stress-free face. 'We did it!' she hissed, under her breath. 'We actually had sex last night!'

Not wanting to hear any more thank you very much, Sammy got up from the table and diverted Christabelle on to another, so that she could divulge last night's details to her friend in peace.

YOU'RE NOT THE ONLY ONE! shouted Tessa's evil little voice, WAIT TILL SOMEONE TELLS YOU WHAT SHE DID LAST NIGHT . . .

'Really?' asked Tessa, trying very hard to look normal. 'Wow, that's great!'

'Isn't it?' Felicity was obviously thrilled. 'He tried to push for it this morning as well, of course, but I told him easy does it . . . God it feels good, I'd forgotten how great sex is.' She leaned forward. 'Don't suppose you did anything naughty last night . . . ?'

'NO!' Tessa virtually shouted, too quickly. 'I went to bed the same time as you, you know I did!'

'OK, OK – good grief, it was just a thought, calm down.' Tessa really hated her right then, she hated everybody, she wanted to go home.

'I'll tell you what, I bet they're pleased to be leaving.' Felicity as good as held her nose, as one of the Pongos passed their table. This was the family whose luggage had never turned up; they'd been nicknamed accordingly.

Suddenly, there was a loud clapping noise. 'Ladies and gentlemen, may I have your attention, please!' It was Fabio, standing in the doorway, with a grim-faced Bonnie right behind him. Tessa dived head-first into her handbag, and found her sunglasses. She didn't need to turn round, she could feel Bonnie's eyes burning into her already peeling shoulders. And she couldn't even *look* at Him. Thank god she was never going to see either of them again.

'Now I've got some good news and some bad news for you – which would you like first?' asked Fabio.

'The bad news!' shouted half of the Tufty Club, with undisguised glee.

'OK – now I know that some of you are looking forward to going home today' – murmurs and groans from his audience – 'but I'm afraid that due to an unexpected strike by the air traffic controllers, your flight won't be able to leave the island today.'

There was shocked silence, whilst people took this information in. What? So they weren't going home after all? What strike? What? What's going on?

'And the good news, is for those of you who didn't want to go home anyway.' (Cries of 'yay!' from the teenage table.) 'There are no planes landing either, at least not for the immediate future, which means that our new villagers won't be arriving today. So, on behalf of Seaside Villages, I'd like to offer you all another night here at the resort, as our guests, at no extra expense to yourselves. Hopefully the situation will be cleared up very soon, and then you can all go home as planned.'

He held up his hand to halt the increasing hubbub. 'Now, if anyone has any questions, please form a queue outside my office and I will deal with each of you one by one. Thank you.'

'Bollocks,' said Felicity, 'I was really looking forward to that tomato juice.'

END OF PART ONE

PART TWO

HOLIDAYS FROM HELL

8. The Staff

FABIO is talking to camera.

                FABIO
. . . yeah, that was a tough time. [He
flashes a white smile. He really is
very handsome.]

           INTERVIEWER
How did people react, when they heard
they couldn't go home?

                FABIO
Oh, I think most people were quite
happy to have an extended holiday,
they just went with the flow, relaxed
into it . . .

           *

'Now look here, you prat!' The red-faced man grabbed
Fabio's T-shirt and pulled him across the desk, 'I have
to get off this island right now, do you see?! I have a
company to run, and unless I get back, there won't be
a company *to* run when I get back, d'you understand?'

Fabio calmly released the man's grip. 'I'm very sorry,
but I really can't do anything about this, I'm sorry –'

'Sorry? SORRY?!' Another man who'd been waiting impatiently outside came in, harumphing. Others behind him filled the doorway. 'You will be bloody sorry, when I get hold of my lawyer! I'm going to sue the arse off you people, you won't know what's hit you! You can't do this, you can't just keep us here –'

'I've got three meetings tomorrow,' said a third angry man, 'and I can't get hold of my secretary to cancel them because it's a Sunday, so I'll have to wait until she gets in to the office tomorrow morning by which time I should have finished the first and be on my way to the second. This makes me look unprofessional, and that's your fault! So what are you going to do about that, eh?'

He didn't wait for an answer, which was probably just as well because Fabio didn't have one.

'And I'm supposed to be flying to San Francisco on Tuesday afternoon, am I going to make that flight? Well am I? How long are we going to be stuck out here? I'm losing money hand over fist right now. I can't be on holiday for the rest of my life, I have work to do! Just what do you propose to do about all this? Do you have some sort of compensation package to offer us?' The rumblings of discontent around him, coupled with Fabio's blank expression, fired him up to furious. 'Right! I want to speak to your superior right now, get him on the phone immediately! This is intolerable –'

'Oh I know,' sighed Fabio, 'it must be really annoying for you. I'd be furious, if it was me.'

That shut them up, they hadn't expected him to agree with them.

'But unfortunately, right now, there's nothing I can do about it, is there?'

Well, no.

'So let's just chill out, and keep cool about it, and not lose that relaxed holiday mentality you came here for in the first place. Hopefully you'll be out of here soon. Believe me' – he straightened his T-shirt and smoothed his hair – 'that's what we all want.'

Eventually they left his office, somewhat pacified by the offer of a free cold beer at the Bucket and Spade for everyone, plus full secretarial services from Nikki and Lovely Dawn, plus 24/7 use of the hotel email and telephone, and the company would surely reimburse their mobile phone bills – but the men still weren't very happy about all this. And neither were their wives.

'But I've already paid for the kids to do an Outward Bound course with an SAS instructor when we get back, and it's supposed to start tomorrow! I had to put their names down for it a year ago, it's very over-subscribed. We'll never get on it next year, they'll be furious about this . . .'

'The children are in tears, they miss the nanny!'

'And who, may I ask, is going to keep feeding our hamster/guinea pig/rabbit/cat/dog/horse/au pair?'

And so it went on, for over two hours. Fabio found himself smoothing over potential problems, fending off difficult questions, and occasionally making up the answers when, in reality, he had no more information than they did.

Once he'd shut his office door on the last woman ('but we haven't got any more clean clothes!') he rang the hospital. It took him a while to find anybody who understood English, but eventually he got through to the pretty little nurse who remembered him from last night. She said the doctor would call him back, but if there was anything she could do, here was her home phone number, he could call her anytime . . .

Fabio buzzed through to Nikki to ask her to call his boss at Head Office.

'What, again?'

'Yes.'

'But it'll be the fifth time this morning. That's more than you've spoken to her since the season began. You're not –'

'No, Nikki I'm not. Have you seen her? She's old enough to be my mother. And just because she's a woman, doesn't mean to say –'

'OK, OK, keep your hair on! Blimey . . .'

Michelle stuck her head round the door, without knocking first. (He'd tried to tell her, but she saw it as a Girlfriend's Perk.) 'Everythin' all right, babe?'

'Yes, thanks.'

'I missed you last night.'

'Yes, I was busy.'

'So I heard.'

OK. Here it comes.

'Bonnie told me.'

'Right.' Fabio steeled himself.

'I don't believe you sometimes.'

'No?' Fabio doodled on his pad. Trying to put the moment off. He hated it when women were angry with him, he usually managed to avoid this kind of thing.

'No. Honestly, what are you like?'

'Um, well, y'know, er –' Oh no, she had tears in her eyes.

'You're so kind.'

'Sorry?'

'Going in that ambulance with Alison last night, you didn't have to, you know. That was such a sweet thing to do, Fabio. She wasn't really dead, was she?'

'Steve Davis on the line for you,' shrilled Nikki through the speakerphone.

'What, Steve Davis the snooker player?'

'No, Steve Davis the managing director of Seaside Villages.' She sighed. 'Calling from London.'

'Oh, right.' Fabio cleared his throat. 'Put him through, would you, Nikki?'

'Is that the big boss?' mouthed Michelle.

Fabio nodded at her and picked up the phone. 'Mr Davis, hi!' He waved goodbye to Michelle, who had popped open her beautician's overall to show him her perfect tits, encased in a white lacy bra; she did this from time to time, as a special treat for him. Fabio winked at her and swivelled his chair away from the door, so that he could focus properly. 'Yes, bit of a tricky one this, isn't it?'

*

Bonnie hated the disruption. She liked things to be normal, to know what was happening next. Routine equals Safety, and Safety equals Happy Children and Satisfied Parents; they used to drum it into them at college, routine and safety, that's what everyone needs. Well, she was already out of her routine, and so were the other nannies who'd had to work today. It was a Sunday, which was normally their day off, so they were very grumpy about it. And as for safety – well two of her staff were off sick, very sick – Alison was even in hospital. What if it was something catching and they all went down with it?

And It was back again. She hadn't had It for a few days, she'd even allowed herself to think that It might have gone away. But no, It had been lurking in the shadows, waiting to pounce. It was back with a vengeance.

She'd already had two breakfasts. One with the early shift, and then she'd taken another one, on a tray, telling Mandy as she left the restaurant that she was taking it to Kevin, who was still malingering (as her dad would say) in his bed. He'd probably caught something off Alison, his room was next door to hers. Perhaps they'd been doing it? No, unlikely, she wouldn't fancy him, nobody would, he had very bad acne, it was disgusting. All yellow pustules, which needed squeezing. Nah, he was probably worn out, having to look after those teenagers – this lot were particularly horrible. They even called him Kevin the Cretin to his face. And he just laughed, he thought it was funny. He had such low self-esteem, it was pathetic.

But she hadn't taken the breakfast to Kevin, of course, she'd eaten it herself. Secretly, in her room. Cereal, toast, fry-up with two eggs, she'd even licked the jam out of the tin foil carton. She knew it was mean, but she couldn't help it. That was what It was like, you see. The more she did it, the worse she felt. And the worse she felt, the more she had to do it.

Kevin was a big strong lad though, he wouldn't miss just one meal. And the last time she'd popped her head round the corner of his bedroom door, he'd said he wasn't that hungry, just desperate for a fag. Which of course, she couldn't give him no matter how much he begged, because that wouldn't make him any better, would it? Besides, if she got him one, that might be the very one that actually kills him, the one that starts the cancer off. (He was looking rough, though, this morning – but smokers were always more ill than everyone else, weren't they? Served them right.)

Bonnie had no patience with people who were sick. She didn't like it, they were weak, pathetic. Lying there, feeling sorry for themselves. Of course she was never ill. Never. She was always the last one standing, she wasn't going to let some silly bug get her. Or cancer. Or anything. People needed her, and she wouldn't let them down, never. She knew what that felt like, she wouldn't do that to anyone.

Not like her. That old tape, the one full of stuff about Mum, began to play in her head again. How dare she decide to smoke? She must have known she'd die, leave her three children and her husband to fend for themselves. Only it had been down to Bonnie, the eldest, the only girl, to do all the work, looking after the boys. Doing her mum's work, what her mum should have been doing. Dad was too taken up with Marion, his 'lady friend' to notice. Of course, Marion pretended to him that she was happy to look after the house and kids, but she wasn't. She was horrible to them when he wasn't around, the boys used to come to Bonnie if they needed something. And she'd damn well get it for them too. But if she tried to talk to Dad about it, he wouldn't listen, he'd say she was a bad girl not to like Marion, when Marion did so much for her out of the kindness of her heart, blah blah blah. The kindness of his wallet, more like. Dad was so stupid, he couldn't see through her, she was a cow. And this was all Mum's fault, for deciding to be a smoker. Bonnie could still remember the actual day she found out that smoking kills you – she was twelve years old, it was at school, she saw that poster on the hall noticeboard, she didn't know until then. Overnight she'd gone from loving her mum, and really missing her, and feeling so sad, to being angry with her, hating her for doing that. She had chosen to kill herself. That was really selfish. And Dad could have stopped her, couldn't he? And that was when the hole inside Bonnie had suddenly become much bigger, it was like her insides were being eaten away, and so she'd had to eat more food, to try and fill it up.

That's why no one loves me, because I'm fat. And until I get thin, nobody's ever going to love me. Everyone knows that fat people have no control over themselves, that they're weak-willed. Why would anybody want to be with someone like that? Someone who just sat on her bed stuffing her face, crying as she ate, hating herself more and more, for not being able to stop.

Bonnie knew she was horrible, she thought bad thoughts, she was a bad person, everybody found that out sooner or later. Michelle would find out soon, maybe today even. She'd go off her, they'd all go off her. They'd find out that she was a fraud, that she wasn't in control at all. Some of them probably knew already. That's why they all laugh at her behind her back, she knew they did, she could sometimes hear them, that's why – stopit*stopit*STOP

IT! For once, Bonnie remembered what that lady doctor had shown her; how to pull away from her crazy mind when it got too much, and so she looked at her watch, to bring herself back to today. Quarter past nine, it's a quarter past nine on a Sunday morning. Back into your box, everybody. Deep breath in; and relax.

Right, the emergency staff meeting wasn't for another couple of hours, so she just had time to supervise Tania sterilizing the baby bottles. (She'd caught her bleaching them yesterday, it was amazing any of the little ratbags were still alive.) And she'd be sure to go the long way round to the Kids Kottage, to avoid the Village Shop and all its chocolatey temptations. Although, she could always write off the rest of today and start eating properly again tomorrow . . .

*

'No, we haven't got any newspapers today. There's no planes, is there, so they can't be flown in, can they?'

For once, Michelle wasn't bothered that it was her turn to serve in the Village Shop this morning. Everyone was buzzing with it, the punters were complaining like mad, moaning and groaning away, but she could tell they were loving it really. And anyway, they were getting a free extended holiday, weren't they? Ungrateful bastards. Besides, it'd probably all be over by tomorrow.

And if she was being honest, Michelle didn't mind the occasional drama every now and then neither. Ever since she was a tot, she'd been the centre of attention, as her nan used to say. Her mum and dad had framed photos of her and her brother dotted all round the front room:

Michelle in her white bunny costume when she went to her first fancy-dress party; Malcolm in his too-big uniform outside their front door on his first day at school; Michelle as a dancer in the local pantomime, age eleven; Malcolm grinning out of his school photograph, with the blue swirly background and no front teeth, but lots of freckles and great big sticky-out ears. The FA Cup, Dad used to call him.

Bloody Malcolm. He'd only gone and become a drug addict, hadn't he. Caused so much trouble, so much pain to Mum and Dad. Michelle had spotted it straight away, of course, because he'd stopped taking care of his appearance. Dead giveaway. And now he lived in his bedroom, all the time. Well, most of the time. Excepting when he'd gone and done one of his disappearing tricks, making Dad get in the car and drive round the streets for hours on end, looking for him. He never found him, of course. Malcolm would either just walk in through the back door as if nothing had happened, or the police would phone them, to get him picked up from the station, or whatever gutter they'd found him in this time.

She'd had enough of it, Michelle had. Which is why she'd decided to come out here. Do you good to get away love, her parents had said. Mum had come shopping with her, they'd chosen some lovely outfits together, and then Mum had adjusted the hemlines and waists and anything else that needed taking in, so that they all fitted Michelle really properly. Dad had stayed in the car at the airport, he couldn't take it. Mum had slipped some cash into her hand as they'd hugged byebye, told her she'd rather Michelle took it than Malcolm stole it.

She'd missed Mum and Dad a little bit at first, but

they wrote every week, leaving out the sordid details of Malcolm's activities, of course. They knew she had no time for all that. Wonder what they were doing now? Hmm, ten o'clock English time, Sunday morning; Dad would be out washing and polishing his beloved Rover, as per usual, and Mum would probably be popping the Sunday roast in the oven. Mmm, Michelle could smell it right now, she could kill one of Mum's roasties. Anyway, then her Dad would go off to pick up Nan, and Mum would start cleaning the house from top to toe, she always did that on a Sunday morning. Well, she used to until Malcolm started complaining recently that the noise of the vacuum was waking him up. Nobody ever had a go about him playing his music really loud at night though, did they? (Mum always put some Sunday dinner on the table for him, even though he never came down to eat it. Michelle didn't know why she bothered.)

So Mum would be doing Michelle's room with one of those carpet sweeper thingies, swishing it backwards and forwards over the shagpile. Michelle had made her promise not to move any of the cuddly toys on her bed while she was away – Mum knew Michelle was very fussy like that, she had lots of them, and they were all in order; from the little teddy in the 'T'-shirt saying 'Hug Me' which she got given from her first boyfriend, right up to that giant panda with the red ribbon Derek had brought round for her the day before she left. Honestly, like she could fit something that size into her new suitcase with wheels and flip-up handle. What was he thinking? And how'd he smuggled it out of the house without the wife seeing? Ooh, that's a thought – maybe it belonged to one of his kids ...

'Right, I'll have one copy of each of the broadsheets, please,' announced a thick-set man with dark curly hair.

'I'm sorry, we don't sell sheets,' retorted Michelle. Honestly, you had to wonder.

'Yes, ha ha, very funny. Could you just get them for me?' He was obviously bonkers. 'I'm a stockbroker you see, and I have to keep an eye on the markets.'

'Oh, you can arrange a day-trip to go sightseeing around the rest of the island at Reception.' She smiled at him, helpfully. 'Though there's nothing to see really, most people don't bother. It's such a tiny island, there's nothing going on out there, I can promise you that. It's dead.'

'He wants all the big papers,' explained his wife, who'd been looking through the children's flippers, to see if they'd had any new sizes in since yesterday.

'Well, he can't have them, can he?'

'Why not?'

'Because the papers didn't come today, that's why. The airport's on strike, remember?'

'Oh yes, of course.' She came over to her husband and put a hand on his shoulder, sympathetically.

'Well look, is there a TV I could watch? Sky News, perhaps?'

'Ooh no, there are no tellies here. It's company policy. You're supposed to be on holiday, getting lots of sun, sea, sand and sex!' The man raised his eyebrows at this, and grinned. 'It wouldn't be right to be indoors all day, staring at the goggle box, now would it? Not after spending all that money on a de luxe holiday like this. You're supposed to be getting away from it all!'

'But there's a TV in the Kids Kottage,' said his mousy

little wife, trying to stick up for her mad husband.

Michelle recognized her now. This was Olivia, the poor exhausted woman with the bad skin who'd been stiff as a board on her first day. 'Yes, I know,' she said, patiently, there was nothing worse than a know-all punter, 'but that one only plays videos, all right?'

'Oh, I see.' That told her. In actual fact, she looked much better now, she'd obviously been following Michelle's handy hints. Oh yes, it looked as if her sex life had really improved . . . 'When's it due?' she asked, winking.

Olivia looked blank.

'The baby?' Michelle indicated Olivia's stomach, which was definitely a lot bigger than when she'd arrived. To her surprise, the woman didn't answer her, just ran out of the shop instead.

Her husband tutted, and gave Michelle a look that said, 'Typical!' 'Have you got yesterday's *Financial Times* then?' And then he added, with a smile, 'It's pink.'

As if. Nutter. But just to humour him, Michelle pretended to look for a pink newspaper on the returns shelf, underneath the counter. 'There's an old *Daily Star* here, will that do?'

'Well . . .' he looked torn, 'it's not really the same thing.'

'I know' – she tried to be sympathetic – 'it's just black-and-white. But sometimes they have nice colour pictures inside.'

He thought that was funny. But he bought it, she knew he would. Dad always said she could sell a surfboard to a shark, if she put her mind to it.

'Incidentally, I must thank you,' Mr Pink said, as he handed over two shillings, 'I told my wife she'd put on weight. She always does on holiday.' He grinned. 'Now perhaps she'll do something about it. Bye!'

'What a fucking nerve,' said Yoko, who had come into the shop during this exchange, and was now busy emptying out the Chupa Chups hedgehog stand. 'That sort of comment makes me bloody furious, I just can't believe people can still think like that. Narrow-minded git. Fucking tory bastard.' She heaped all the lollipops on to the counter. 'I'll have all of these, please, and a *Daily Mail.*'

'Haven't got one, no papers today,' said Michelle for the millionth, trillionth time that morning. 'No plane, no delivery.'

'Oh yeah, 'course, sorry, I forgot.'

Michelle studied the disappointed face in front of her. 'You could make so much more of yourself, you know.'

'Really?' She ruffled her hands through her sticky hair.

'Yeah, the Meg Ryan look's a bit pastay now. Tell you what,' and she leaned forward conspiratorially, 'pop by the Village Gossip this afternoon and we'll see what we can do.'

Well, she had to drum up some work for herself, didn't she? As a commission-based employee of Seaside Villages, Michelle Bloxham was damn well going to reach her sales targets, no matter what.

*

'Don't tell anyone, but this strike could go on for quite a while, apparently. Head Office says we've got to keep the villagers distracted.' Fabio had been told to call an

168

emergency meeting. 'Anyone got any bright ideas?' The Heads of Department scratched their collective head, trying to think of some way to help.

Silence.

'Craig?' Fabio decided to go round the room. 'You're a pretty creative kind of guy. Surely Entertainments have got lots of tricks up their sleeve?' (They had almost as big a budget as Childcare, and a whole store-room full of costumes and props.)

'Well, yeah,' replied Little-Craig-with-the-Big-Personality, who was busy cleaning out his ears with his finger, they were still full of shaving cream from last night's Flan Flinging Fiesta. 'But as you know, Fabby, we only do a two-week rotation. I mean God knows what we're going to do tonight, it's normally the Welcome Drink on a Monday.'

'You're going to have to think up a few new ideas, I'm afraid. People are getting very angry about having to stay out here, we've just got to keep them happy, or we'll have a riot on our hands.'

'How long's this bloomin' strike going to go on for?' asked Craig.

'I don't know, how long do they normally last?' Fabio asked the rest of the room. Nobody knew. 'So, what can we do to keep everyone's mind off it? And don't even suggest karaoke, Craig, that was my first thought. Head Office went mad. Apparently, we've got to keep looking classy, whatever that means. Bruno?'

Bruno had almost nodded off, due to a late-night woman-chasing exercise. Last Nights were his favourite, the ladies were usually more up for it then. He was probably more pissed off than the rest of them about all this, he'd been looking forward to some fresh legs arriving today. 'What?'

'Any ideas as to how we can keep people entertained tennis-wise?'

Bruno's eyes narrowed. 'Are you saying I don't do a good chob?'

'No.' Fabio was confused. 'I'm just asking if there's any way we can make tennis more fun?'

'We could do a red-nose Charidy Tournament,' piped up little Craig. 'I could get my boys and girls to dress up as clowns, give the money to Comic Relief.'

'No,' said Bruno and Fabio at the same time. 'Head Office says we mustn't make the villagers part with any money. Then they'll have the right to complain, apparently.'

'And tennis is a serious sport,' sniffed Bruno.

'What about this, Fabio?' Kenton, Head of the Waterfront. South African, big, burly, capable. 'Day trips round the island in the speedboat! That should take up a few days, we can only take four people at a time.'

'Good idea, Kenton. Brilliant. But how long would it take to go right round the island?'

Kenton didn't know, no one had bothered to venture very far yet. He promised to get one of his guys on to it.

'Mandy?'

'What?'

'Any ideas?'

'Well, y'know, I suggest we keep feeding them.' She was in one of her awkward moods. 'Three meals a day still all right?'

'Oh, look, don't be like that,' Fabio sighed, 'this is difficult enough as it is.'

Mandy folded her arms in a huff.

Fabio addressed the rest of the room. 'I know this is boring, folks, but I've got to report back to Head Office by the end of the day, tell them what we've come up with, OK? Apparently, they normally have a Crisis Management Team that flies in when this sort of thing happens, but they can't get here, so we're doing it all by phone.'

'You think they would hev thought about that!' grinned Bruno.

'And it turns out I also have the power to send home anyone who isn't helpful!' said Fabio, with a sideways glance at Bruno, who immediately stopped grinning. The last thing anybody wanted was to go back to the real world, where bills had to be paid, and meals cooked, and public transport taken.

Luckily, nobody asked how they would actually get home, if that happened.

As they were all filing out of the room, Fabio asked Bonnie to stay behind. Unfortunately, this prompted Bruno to make inappropriately childish faces, and so Fabio had to push him out of the room before shutting the door.

'Of course, I don't include you in this, Bonnie,' he said, smiling his dazzler. 'You don't have to come up with any new ideas. You're doing a brilliant job already, so you just keep doing what you're doing and I know those kids will be fine. They're in very capable hands. The best.' He looked her straight in the eye. 'Thanks.'

Ignoring him, Bonnie said, 'When's Alison coming back to work? What with her and Kevin being off, we're very short-staffed, you know. It's not easy.'

'I know, I know. But you'll be fine, Bonnie, I know you can do this. You're a true professional.'

What a creep, thought Bonnie, as she pinched a lonely couple of ginger nuts from the hospitality plate of biscuits which had been just sitting there, asking for it, on the trolley. 'I only haven't told Michelle what you were up to last night because I don't want her to be hurt,' she sniffed, as she slipped them into her pocket. 'But I can't promise that I'm going to keep quiet for ever. So you'd better start being a good boy from now on, hadn't you? Bye.'

As Bonnie made her way over to the Kids Kottage to discover godknowswhat going on in her absence, she realized that she wasn't so scared any more. In fact, she was going to enjoy having Fabio sucking up to her. Long may it last.

*

'What's the matter, pussycat?' asked Michelle. He wasn't responding so well tonight, it'd taken a bit longer than usual to work him up.

'Nothing, why?'

'You feel all tense, a bit stressed-out.' She climbed on top of him. 'Is it work?' She straddled him with her thighs, and fished about for his cock with her nimble fingers.

'Well, yes, ooch!' She'd stuffed him inside her, a little too early. 'This is quite serious, Michelle.'

'What is?'

'This situation.'

'You – mean – us?' she asked, rhythmically. 'You want – to get – serious?' She flicked her hair out of the way, so that he could see her tits bouncing up and down.

'No!' replied Fabio, too quickly and too loudly. 'No.'

'Thank god – for that,' said Michelle, also too quickly and too loudly. 'I couldn't – think of any – thing worse!' And she threw her head back, attractively, to scoff at the very idea.

Fabio looked up at her snaking away on top of him, her youthful little body twisting itself inside and out, her nipples erect with excitement. It was a view he'd seen many times now. Too many times soon, but not yet.

As Michelle trailed a fingernail down from her nipple to her pubic strip, she asked, 'So – what's bothering – you, honey?'

To Fabio this was just as bad as the 'what are you thinking' question. He squirmed, internally and externally, and said, 'Nothing.'

Michelle gave him one of her Looks as she massaged herself, with her French manicured finger tips, for him to see.

'I'm fine, really I am.'

She raised her eyebrows, and her hips, balancing him right at her luscious entrance. Jesus, she was good, she knew just how to play him.

'I suppose work is getting me down a bit, that's all.'

She took him in and up and down and round again. 'Why?'

'All the aggro – it's like they think this strike is all my fault, they're all shouting at me about it. I mean, I can't

173

do anything, can I?' He held her hips and rode her from underneath. 'Oh, yes, babe, yes . . .'

'How long – d'you think – it'll be – now?'

'Er, well, let me see, when it's fully erect it can be up to –'

'No, silly – how long until – everything's back – to normal?' She tickled his balls with her pricky fingernails. 'Honestly, what are you like?!'

'Oh, right,' and he pushed himself hard, right up her, right up to the end to show her the point anyway, 'um, oof, yeah, well, I don't know, it all depends on the doctors . . .'

'What?'

Bollocks. 'Look, do we have to talk about this now? Let's just –'

'What doctors?'

'Does it matter? C'mon, babe, let's just move and groove togeth—'

But Michelle wasn't going to leave this alone. She stopped her jiggling and looked directly at him. 'Is this something to do with that Alison?'

'What?'

'You've been in to see Alison, haven't you?'

'Well of course I have, she's a member of my staff.'

'When?'

'This afternoon.' He tried to carry on, but for some reason she was refusing to play.

'You went to see Alison in hospital this afternoon?'

'Yes.'

'Without telling me, behind my back?'

'What?'

'I don't believe this' — Michelle was outraged — 'and I suppose you had a right cosy little chat, with her, just you two, didn't you?' She moved her face in to his, her hair was tickling his chin, making him smile. 'Didn't you?'

'Not really, she didn't say much —'

'What the hell d'you think you're playing at, Fabio?!' Ignoring his answer, she sprang back from him, leaving his cock stranded in mid-air. 'Was she good?'

'What d'you mean?'

'Did you fuck her?'

'What, in her hospital bed?'

'No, before she got ill.' She was scrutinizing him now, piercing his conscience, he shut his eyes and turned his head away.

'I'm not even going to answer that. This is ridiculous.'

'She told me when we arrived out here that she really fancied you, y'know.'

'Did she? I didn't know that,' he lied.

'Tell me the truth, Fabio. D'you fancy her?'

'Not now,' and he was telling the truth, 'definitely not. She'll never be as good as you. I fancy you though, I really fancy you, babe, you know how much I want you, c'mon, Michelle, make it with me, let's come together, you and me, babydoll . . .'

Now that she'd heard what she needed to hear, Michelle could get back to the job at hand. Wrapping her fingers around the root of his dying erection, she allowed him back inside her, simultaneously tightening her grip on him with her well-lubricated, well-exercised internals. 'Now listen,' she said as he grew back into her power, 'don't you go and see her again, not without me.' She smiled down at him. 'I mean you don't want her getting the wrong idea, do you? Poor Alison, she might think she's still in with a chance ...'

Fabio knew this not to be the case, but let it go. 'OK, babe, whatever you say. I won't go and see her again.'

Pleased with him and wanting more pleasure for herself now, Michelle began to feed him in and out of her, warmly sliding up and down on him, expertly grinding him round at the same time. They were soon back on track.

'That's better,' Michelle said, silkily, 'that's my man.' But just as he was about to come, she sprang off him in one catlike movement and lay beside him, her legs wide open, her arms stretching behind her, gripping the wooden posts of the headboard. 'Now fuck me,' she ordered, in an entirely different voice. A voice that was steely, cold, commanding. A voice that turned Fabio on so much, he forgot all about work and got to work on her instead.

*

The strike at the airport wasn't resolved by the next day. Or the day after that, by which time the villagers had split into two camps of those who didn't care, and those who did. But by the third 'extra day', even the most laid-back of the Nutty Browns were getting a bit twitchy, much to the amusement of the Bright Whites who were only in their second week, and still very much enjoying their holiday.

The queue for the office computer was getting longer

and longer earlier and earlier, as more and more people checked and sent emails; both phone lines were jammed with either incoming or outgoing calls to and from the British Isles; Dawn and Nikki were becoming more and more resentful about their extra workload, and had taken to calling the airport, every hour on the hour, for any news.

And the complaints and requests were getting even more petty and even more bizarre. ('We've used both our complimentary bars of soap, will we need any more?' 'Do you have three chess sets?' 'The tumble drier in the laundry room doesn't seem to be working, how do you suggest we dry our clothes?')

The Heads of Department had done their best, and the Crisis Management Team said that Fabio was doing really well. There was something for everyone on the programme now, no one could claim to be bored.

One of Bruno's Athena poster girls had come up with the Frying Pan Challenge, which was self-explanatory, although Howell the chef had gone berserk about this abuse of his precious equipment.

Fortunately catering queen Mandy had distracted him, and everybody else, by coming up with the bright idea of a Men versus Women Cooking Competition. (This was brilliant because it had given Howell a much-needed night off, during which he'd got so drunk he'd had to be forcibly extracted from the bushes outside the nannies' bedrooms, but he'd been a little happier since then.) Unfortunately, Mandy had let herself down by declaring the result a draw, and was still being given a hard time about it from the competitors many meals later.

Kenton had found out that the island tour was completely unfeasible, as it took much longer to circumnavigate than anyone had thought. (Jamie had been out in the speedboat for over four hours, much to the fury of many waterskiers. And he said it was mostly very boring, as they had the best bit of sandy beach, the rest of the coastline was just rocks, there was nothing much to see.) But the Waterfront Team had put on a dazzling midnight display of synchronized windsurfing in the swimming pool, floodlit underwater, to the tunes of an old Hooked On Classics CD. This had had a double benefit: the ladies had loved seeing those toned bodies gliding so smoothly and effortlessly across the water, and lots of the men had signed up for lessons the next morning. There was something very calming about rippling muscles and rippling water, it was a beautiful thing – Kenton had really pushed the boat out this time.

And Little-Craig-with-the-Big-Personality had really gone to town too. The Entertainments Team were on the go from first thing in the morning, until last thing at night. One day they'd burst into breakfast dressed as farmyard animals; the chicken had pretended to lay the eggs, both ends of the cow had moo'd obligingly beside the milk churn, but unfortunately the pig had only served to put the smaller children right off their bacon.

Then, after their early morning antics, they'd tour the camp, looking for fun and mischief. People would be pushed into the pool, towels and clothes would be hidden and divebombs performed to great effect; all those they'd managed to splash got a free slice of water melon and a photo taken with a hilarious watersquirty camera, just for a laugh.

There was no end to their fun, they worked really hard at it. One peaceful afternoon down on the beach, they put on a comedy waterskiing display, with multi-skilled circus performer Otto wearing a tutu and Craig dressed up as a Keystone Cop; two or three times they started a food fight with the leftovers at the end of lunch; they hosted a Beauty Pageant in which all the contestants were men in bad wigs and bikinis, and even held a summer seventies Halloween Fancy Dress Abba Beach Barbecue party.

Yes, in Fabio's mind they'd excelled themselves, even he couldn't have predicted this outcome. They'd done exactly what they'd been asked to do. After just a few days, everyone hated the Entertainments Department so much that it was all they could talk about. As a result, much of the villagers' anger and frustration at their involuntary internment was diverted towards the hapless Craig and his boys and girls. Everybody hated them.

They in turn took this negative reaction as a sign that they weren't doing their job properly, and so the Entertainments team tried even harder – with, in their minds at least, hilarious results.

9. The Kids

SAMMY

All the other teenagers were really
sad.

INTERVIEWER

Why? was it because they wanted to go
home?

SAMMY sighs and looks skywards.

SAMMY

That's sad as in no life, not sad as
in crying. [She shakes her head and
smiles.] They all thought I was really
cool, and so did I, at the time.

*

Most of the teenagers were really pleased about having
to stay on, this was bare good. More time to talk, more
time to hone their texting skills, more time to break the
rules. More time to not spend with their parents. Safe.

'My dad left me a note this morning,' reported the
Nebulizer, as he slugged a Bacardi Breezer with one
hand and played Space Invaders with the other. 'It

said that he wasn't going to pay for any more drinks. Apparently my bar bill for last week was over a hundred quid!' He snorted with pleasure at the achievement.

'God, that's so harsh,' sympathized a pretty girl called Dido, who had thought being called Dildo was the worst it could get.

'Dido.' It was Angus, who everyone knew fancied her. 'I just want to thank you, for giving me the best day of my life.'

'Oh sod off,' she said and went back to her game.

'Yessss!' celebrated one of the Babyish, '927!'

'What the fuck are you playing?' asked Sammy, looking up in horror.

'Snake!' cheered the boy, 'and I just got a brilliant score!'

The cool bruvs all looked at each other. 'That is *so* toy,' declared Sammy. 'Nobody plays Snake any more.'

There was silence as they all got back to their game. (And some people may or may not have changed what game they were playing.)

'Ah, here you all are!' said a cheery woman's voice, with an unmistakable Antipodean twang. 'Hi there!'

One or two of them looked up, just to see who it was. It was a tanned woman in uniform, with a little pink nose and button brown eyes. She had short blonde hair scraped back into a high ponytail.

'I'm Donna!'

They stared at her.

'I'm one of the nannies, I've been assigned to look

after you as Kevin still isn't better!' She said this as if it was good news. 'So what are you all doing?'

No reply.

'Does anyone want to play a nice game of catch?' She held up a tennis ball hopefully. Even the Babyish went back to what they were doing.

'I guess not.'

She thought for a moment.

'What about doing some painting, or drawing? No? Perhaps if I take you on to the beach and let you bury me? What about a water fight? Um, perhaps we could have a swimming race, out to the pontoon and back, last one home's a sissy?'

'Go away,' said Sammy, who was nearly past her top score so far.

'I'm sorry?'

'We're fine, thanks,' said Angus, quite nicely.

'But I've been told –'

'Look.' Sammy put down her mobile, she'd blown it thanks to this interruption. 'We, like, don't want you here, we're perfectly capable of looking after ourselves. Now piss off back to Australia and leave us alone, OK?'

'Um, it's New Zealand, actually,' said Donna, shocked. She'd never been spoken to like this by children before.

'Speak English there, do they?'

'Yeah, of course.'

'Well then you'll understand the expression "fuck off and die", won't you?'

That got rid of her.

*

Spike woke up and looked over at Christabelle's bed. He knew not to wake her up as she was really really grumpy in the mornings, and he wasn't allowed to wake Mummy and Daddy up until the big hand of his Monsters Inc clock was on the o'clock and the little hand was on the eight, but they hadn't brought his clock with them, it was still at home, and he was boiling hot and he wanted a drink and his bites were itching. And the sun was coming through the wood curtains in bits of stripes, so he knew it wasn't the middle of the night still.

He got out of bed, taking his cuggie with him, and padded softly out of the room, being good and remembering to close the door behind him. He banged so loudly on the next-door door with his little knuckles that it hurt a bit. He could hear babies crying in other rooms, and so he knew it was time to get up now.

The door opened and his nannygranny looked very sleepy. 'Spike!' she said. 'What are you doing up and about on your own? Where's Christabelle?'

'Still sleeping,' he said as he looked up at her, and put on his cute photo face.

'Lucky her,' muttered Gina under her breath. 'What about your father?'

'I don't know.'

Gina looked at her watch, the one she'd inherited from her mother. It was small but elegant, and it kept good time, just like her mamma. 'Oh, Spike, it's half past six!'

'Is it?' said Spike, not knowing if this was good or bad.

Gina looked down at her only grandson, her *poverino*. He was wearing his favourite Buzz Lightyear T-shirt, had no pyjama bottoms on and was clutching that filthy blanket. He looked like an orphan from a Charlie Chaplin film. 'You'd better come in.'

Her room smelt funny, but Spike didn't mind.

'Now why don't you try to get back to sleep, there's a good boy.' And she peeled back the untouched covers on the other bed for him.

'I don't want to sleep in that bed, I want to sleep in yours.'

'But I'm in that one.'

'Yes, but then we can snuggle up.' The little boy hugged his cuggie. 'I'll be really good, I won't wriggle, I really promise.'

'Oh come on then,' said Gina, who didn't need asking twice. She'd been stealing hugs and cuddles from her grandson ever since they'd got here.

'What's this?' asked Spike as he pulled some stripy clothes out of his nannygranny's bed.

'Oh, er, that's your grandad's pyjama top.' There was no point in lying to children, she knew that.

'Why have you got it in your bed?'

'Well, so that I can cuddle it at night.' It sounded so foolish, now that she'd said it out loud.

'So is it like your cuggie, like mine?' asked the little boy as he wriggled down in the bed.

'Yes, love, it is,' replied his grandmother as she got in beside him and held his little heart close to hers, 'that's just what it's like.'

Christabelle had heard Spike leave the room, and knew she should really go after him. But she also knew he'd only cry if she did. He didn't like his half-sister. He'd told Bonnie, who'd told him off for saying such a rude thing, even if it was true.

She'd tried with Spike, she really had, but she just didn't have whatever it was that made people good with kids. And she reckoned children were like animals, and wasps, they could smell your fear. Spike knew she was nervous around him, which was probably why he was so naughty with her, he just became out of control, and got her into trouble. Only yesterday morning, he'd slipped her hand when she was talking to Bonnie at the Kids Kottage, and run off somewhere. In fact, it wasn't until Felicity had dragged him back, kicking and screaming, that Christabelle had even realized he'd gone missing. Apparently he'd run back into the hotel and found his mum, who'd been forced to say she'd have him for the whole morning. And she hadn't spoken to Christabelle since. Neither had Spike, come to think of it.

She'd watched how Gran was with him, to see if she could pick up any tips; but she'd ended up feeling jealous, because she wanted Gran to speak to her like that too, with all that warmth and love in her voice. Make her feel cuddled. Like before, when she was a little girl. Gran used to really love her then, she knew that. Well, she thought she did.

Christabelle used to stay with her grandparents for a fortnight every summer. Sometimes it was for three whole weeks. Mum would go on one of her hippie holidays, to find out more about herself with candles and bearded men on remote Greek islands, and Christabelle would be pushed off to Leigh-on-Sea to stay with her grandparents. But it didn't feel like that, in fact, she used to look forward to it.

Grandad was great, he was kind and funny and used to buy her lots of silly presents and far too many sweets and call her Tinker, short for Tinkerbell. No wonder Gran was missing him so much, he was lovely. Everybody loved Alfie. He was like a big bear: cuddly most of the time, but he could also be a bit scary.

Anyway, he had to be at his butcher's shop six days a week, and so most of the time it was just her and Gran. Every morning they'd make the beds and do the housework and tidy up, and then they'd take the bus to the shops, for bits and bobs. They'd always pop in to see Grandad of course, who'd proudly announce to all his customers that she was his granddaughter, and everyone would be so pleased about that, for some reason, that Christabelle almost got a round of applause – they'd all turn to look at her, and make admiring noises, and go 'ahh' a lot. Her cheeks were burning even now, just thinking about it. It was one of those things that you love and hate at the same time. You sort of want everyone to look at you, and yet when they do, you can't bear it.

Then after that, they'd go back home and make a delicious picnic, with bad things in it like scotch eggs and salad cream, stuff Mum wouldn't let her eat at home. And they'd walk down to the beach, with Christabelle carrying the big tartan rug under one arm and Gran's little folding chair tucked under the other; and Gran would sing at the top of her voice as they walked, mad Italian songs that made no sense, but Christabelle sang along anyway. And Gran would actually watch her trying to do cartwheels on the sand, not like Mum, who was Too Cross for everything, Too Upset to look, Too Mad to say well done. Or even worse, she'd sometimes pretend to be interested, thinking Christabelle couldn't tell that she wasn't really. 'Oh yes, well done', she'd say, but she wouldn't mean it, she'd be all wound up in her own problems, too caught up in her own life to be able to take any interest in anybody else's.

Sundays were best. Sundays were when Alfie would take them on a Magical Mystery Tour in his car. Only he would know where they were going, all they had to do was to 'be ladies', as he said. Which meant wearing a dress, which Christabelle hated, but she did it for Grandad. And anyway, it was sort of worth it in the end. Over the years, he'd taken them all over the south-east of England; Christabelle had souvenirs from stately homes and zoos and museums, and Alfie always bought Gran a tea-towel from wherever they went, because that was all she wanted.

And even though they were far too old, Christabelle had sometimes kidded herself on these Sundays that they were her real parents, that she had a mum and dad who wanted to take her out, together, just the three of them. She'd lie down in the back of the car, watching the trees whizz past through Grandad's little sunroof, and listen to them chattering away to each other. And she'd pretend that she was their little girl, and that this was just another day, it was quite normal for them to be doing this. Like a real family.

As she lay in her bed and listened to the sounds of other people's families getting up, Chris despised herself for having been so stupid. Of course that wasn't true, of course they weren't her real parents.

Her mum was, well, different to other people's mums, which was sometimes good and sometimes bad. Christabelle loved her, of course she did, but it was getting harder and harder these days to keep on loving her.

Mum had an anger problem, they were both aware of that, she had 'issues', as her therapist said. When she was in one of her rages, Christabelle knew to keep very quiet, not say anything, keep herself to herself. Sometimes she'd hide in her room, but she didn't do that any more as Mum would come thundering down the corridor, screaming, and barge into the room. And if it was really bad, she'd throw things, or break stuff. Once, she'd picked up a mouldy glass of orange juice and thrown it in Chris' face; another time she'd shoved all the clothes on Chris' floor into a bin bag and taken them to the dump, making Chris watch as the metal jaws of the machine chewed them up. So Chris had learned to keep quiet, to stand still and look like she was listening, even though in her head she was listening to Nirvana, wishing she was there.

When it was over, Mum was very apologetic, very ashamed of her behaviour. She'd cry, and beg Christabelle's forgiveness, and they'd hug, and it'd all be better. It was as if Penny had flicked a switch inside her, and she'd be in a really good mood suddenly. She'd done mad, crazy things, fun things, like she spent all day Saturday tie-dyeing all their whites that had gone grey in the wash and then sold them at a car boot sale on Sunday; they'd had a snow picnic in Richmond Park; once she filled the house with two hundred sticks of burning jasmine incense she'd bought from the pound shop – that sort of thing. Christabelle wouldn't join in with all her madnesses, of course, but she'd smile at her mother's fun.

Occasionally, there'd be a bloke hanging about, as Penny was still quite pretty, when she wanted to be. Life became easier for Chris then, as Mum was less on her case, being busy with the new man; but then she'd do one nutty thing too many, and he'd leave quite soon after that, if she hadn't managed to push him out already. But Mum would get really upset, even though the guy was usually a loser, and she'd cry all day and all night, and nothing Chris could do was enough to make her better. Mum would make her sleep beside her, and all she could do was lie there and listen, deep into the night, as Penny told her everything, too much, far too much, more than she needed to know. But it did seem to help her. Eventually, Mum would start getting at her again, which was a sure sign that she was on the mend. Christabelle preferred the shouting, she could deal with that. She couldn't bear to see her mum crying, like a little girl.

And as for Dad – well. Don't even go there. He certainly didn't. He was a good father and everything, and she knew he loved her, but he just wasn't around enough. Never had been. Chris couldn't really remember her parents ever living in the same house together, but she could remember them fighting a lot in the kitchen, just below her bedroom. She'd heard them say things to each other that nobody said sorry for, things about her, horrible things that she didn't want to remember now. One thing she knew for certain, though – it was because of having her that they split up. It was her fault.

Today's Christabelle tried to burrow back down into her bed, like she always did when she didn't want to face the world, but it was different when there was only a sheet. She loved her duvet back home because it was warm and squashy and dark; this sheet didn't even cover her properly and usually ended up wound round her ankles or her neck, sometimes both. And Mum hadn't let her bring her bedsocks, so her toes were curly cold, as usual.

Yes, she was one of those people who was always hearing things she wasn't supposed to. It was probably because she was awake a lot at night; she couldn't even get the sleeping thing right.

That's what had gone wrong with Gran and Grandad. She'd heard them.

She hadn't been intentionally listening in. It was a Sunday night, she was about ten and a half, and she'd heard them say that they were going to watch David Copperfield on television at 9 o'clock. (Gran always made her go to bed too early.) So Christabelle had quietly crept out of her bedroom to sit on the stairs outside their front room, so that she could at least listen to it. (She'd only just discovered Dickens, they'd read a little bit in English and she'd gone to the library for more. They were good stories, but in quite hard language, so maybe the film would be easier to understand.)

But they weren't watching that after all, they were watching a magic show, and you couldn't exactly listen to that. So Christabelle got up, to go back to bed; but as it was the adverts, Gran began to talk. (Alfie wouldn't let anyone make a sound during the actual programme, he said it was a waste of his licence fee. You could speak during the ads though, in fact he wanted you to, he hated people flogging him things he didn't want.) So Gran had developed this brilliant technique of picking up exactly where she'd left off during the last adbreak.

'I don't know why he gives her a penny,' she'd continued. 'I mean, it's not as if he planned to have a child with her, she just got herself pregnant to try and pin him down. God knows why he bothered to marry her. I still say she was after his money.'

Grandad had laughed at that, saying what money, she'd probably had more than him stashed away in a trust fund somewhere, posh people were like that. And then they'd mentioned someone called Eileen, she hadn't been able to understand that bit, and then Gran had said '. . . but Christabelle's nothing like those two, she's not − you know − very feminine, is she? Not a very pretty little girl, that's for sure.'

'Yep, takes after her father in that way,' Grandad agreed. 'She does her best, but − well, of a Sunday, it's like looking at a bulldog in a frock.' He'd laughed at that, he thought he was very funny. She could still hear him laughing now.

'Alfie!' scolded Gran, but you could hear that she was smiling as she said it. 'Poor love; she's one of those children that's always in the wrong place, standing just where you need to be, you know, right in front of the fridge door . . .'

And then Grandad had sort of agreed with her again, but he said that whatever way you looked at it, she was Cliff's daughter, and even if she wasn't the sort of child you took to straight away, they had to do what they could. 'And it's not her fault that nobody wanted her, she didn't ask to be born, did she?' And he reminded Gran that Christabelle was only here for another week, and that she enjoyed having her granddaughter to stay, she liked the company. Then the programme had started again, and so they shut up.

Christabelle had run back up to her dad's old bedroom then, acid tears pricking at her not-very-pretty bulldog eyes. But she didn't cry, she refused to. She pulled out all her eyelashes instead.

*

'Ah, there you are, Mum! I've been looking for you all over the place.' Cliff began to run along the beach towards Gina, who was just coming back from a walk along the shoreline. She'd not been able to go far, it had become too stony underfoot. So she'd perched on one of the big rocks, and looked out to the calm, flat sea, searching for a bit of peace. But there were only waves of turmoil inside her, and she'd had to come back before the pain drowned her completely. She looked at her watch, and was disappointed to see she'd only got rid of an hour.

Despite enduring more than a fortnight of intensive volleyball, Cliff was still a bit unfit, and so he stopped short of his mother and waited for her to reach him. 'Everything all right, Mum?' he panted.

'Yes thanks, love,' she replied, automatically.

'C'mon then, I'll walk you back,' Cliff said as he linked arms with her.

'I'd prefer it if you'd walk back with me, Cliff,' said Gina curtly, 'I'm not a dog.'

'Sorry, Mum.' How did she do this? He was over fifty years old, and yet she could still make him feel like a five year old with one swift lash of the tongue. 'So how are you doing, then?'

'What d'you mean?'

'Well, y'know, are you enjoying yourself?'

'No.'

'Oh.' He looked down at his toes, and curled them into the wet sand as he walked, so that they made footprints behind him. He hadn't done that since he was a boy.

'I'm ready to go home now.'

'Yes, I think we all are, Mum. Pain in the er, whatsit, all this, isn't it?'

They walked on, in silence.

'Dad would have liked it here, wouldn't he?'

'No, I don't think he would.'

'Oh? Why not?'

'He always said he didn't need to go on holiday, he lived every day like he was on holiday.'

'Yeah, he loved the beach, didn't he? D'you remember, crafty sod used to make me go for a walk down there with him every Sunday morning when I was a kid, no matter what the bloody weather was like.' Cliff smiled at the memory, even though it made him sad to remember. He'd loved those cold days, just him and his dad. ''Course it was really so's he could stop by the pub, for a quick pint – and he'd make me sit and wait for him outside, in the car park. Me and Bobby Stokes, freezing our arses off, taking bets on the progress of ants down concrete gullies while our dads were inside the boozer. You didn't know about that, did you?' Cliff chuckled. 'Every bloody Sunday. He made me swear not to tell you. And I wasn't even allowed a bag of Smiths crisps, you remember, those ones that had the salt in a twist of blue paper inside,' he laughed, 'in case they spoilt my dinner. Which meant you'd be upset, and he wouldn't have that, never.'

Gina didn't reply.

Cliff went on. 'I really miss him too, y'know.' He swallowed. 'He was my dad. My dad.' He stopped walking, his voice was strangled with emotion. 'I still can't believe he's not coming back. Doesn't seem right without him, does it?'

Gina looked down at the sand, and drew her cardigan around her shoulders.

They walked on.

'I suppose we're going to have to let him go, Mum. We've got to say goodbye to him sometime.'

Nothing.

'I know this is hard for you.' Cliff felt his eyes flooding, he looked out to sea. 'I just wish I could help you, I can see how sad you are. He asked me to look after you, he kept asking me – I, er' – a chubby tear rolled down his cheek – 'well, the thing is, Mum, I don't know how to do that.' He stopped, held her by the arms and turned her to face him. 'Is there anything, and I mean anything, I can do, Mum, to help you?' He swallowed again. He sounded desperate. 'I hate to see you this unhappy. And I don't think Dad would want you to be like this neither. Let me in, Mum, eh? I can help you, let me help you, please?'

But Gina wouldn't look at Cliff. She couldn't raise her head to meet his sorrowful puppydog eyes. She just couldn't do it. How could she tell her son that she couldn't stand to be near him, couldn't even look at him, because he reminded her so much of his father, her husband, her love that had been destroyed so slowly, with such painstaking cruelty? She wanted to get away from Cliff now. He was too close, and Alfie was too far away. She wanted to go home to him.

She started walking again, looking ahead at the shining sand of the shore, being swept clean of its memories again and again by the sea. 'It's all right, son,' she said, eventually. 'I'm not ready to move on yet. I thought the hardest thing I'd ever have to do was to bury your father. Now I know that it's going to be even harder than that to carry on without him. And besides,' she added, 'for as long as we're stuck here, we can't move anywhere very fast, can we?'

*

'Sammy! Wake up! It's two o'clock in the afternoon, for

goodness' sake.' Tessa was shaking her shoulder, it was really annoying.

'Gerroff, Mm.'

'Oh honestly – it's such a waste of a beautiful day. I can't believe you're still in bed; I only came up to get a new book because I've finished that other one, it was quite good but it tailed off at the end; still, if you want to lie here all day, then that's up to you, I suppose.'

Nothing.

'OK, well, I'm off. As long as the sun's out there, so am I. I must say, that's one good thing about having to stay here a little longer, I'm getting a really good tan now – I'm on Factor 4 you know.'

Like I bloody care, thought Sammy, as her mother selfishly slammed the door loudly as she left. She had a raging hangover, courtesy of many Malibu and pineapples alternated with many more Red Bull and vodkas. And the best thing was that Dad was paying for it, so Mum couldn't stop her, even if she wanted to. She probably didn't care anyway, and she certainly had no idea how much her daughter was drinking – they hardly saw each other these days.

So much for this famous mother-and-daughter 'quality time', then, that wasn't going to happen. Surprise surprise. Mum was always saying she was going to do things, but never did. So no fat lecture about Respect, or The Importance of Thank You Letters, or The Facts of Life (which would have been a real crack-up actually), thank God for that. But they'd have to talk properly soon, as Sammy had something to tell Mum.

She hadn't told her yet, there hadn't been the right

moment. But Dad had made her promise to have sorted it by the time they got back. Typical Dad, leaving it all up to her. But he was right, she was the right person to explain. And it was for the best.

Only the plan had gone wrong, because Sammy was supposed to tell Mum just before they left here, and then go to the South of France with Dad and Mona and the kids the next day, and then Mum would be over it by the time they got back. But now she didn't know when they were leaving, did she? And Dad had probably gone on holiday without her now. Oh well, whatever.

And anyway, there was lots more important stuff to deal with at the minute, such as how she was going to pull Jamie. Through the fuzz of her befuddled brain, Sammy tried to remember what had happened last night. Oh yeah.

It had all got a bit out of hand. Angus had got really pissed and threatened to fight the Nebulizer for Dido, who wasn't even there because she'd gone to bed early anyway, at one o'clock, because she had really strict parents. One of the Clueless girls had been sick after her first ever cigarette, all over head Cluelette Angelique's new dress and so she'd been instantly relegated to the ranks of the Babyish. And they'd had to carry yet another lightweight, a girl called Isis this time, all the way up to her bedroom which wasn't easy as she weighed a ton, and they'd had to go round the long way to avoid Parents.

But she was making some sort of headway with Jamie. At least he'd probably noticed her at last. They'd gone to the School Disco, to watch Parents' Dancing, when he'd come in with some of the other sports bloods. She and Chris and a couple of the others had been having a laugh doing the wrong letters for YMCA with their hands, (XTLV in fact, hilarious) and these really bo guys went up to the bar.

So they did too.

The guys ordered four beers.

So they did too.

Then nothing happened.

So Sammy grabbed Chris's fags and offered them to the guys.

They all said no, so Sammy made a great show of giving them back to Chris, so that the guys knew they weren't hers.

As the Parents danced like windmills on acid, their daughters remained glued to the bar, watching the bopping gimps in silence. Waiting for the guys to start talking to them.

Then that bloody Becca walked in, didn't she.

Now Becca was a bit older than them, but too young to socialize with Parents. (Rumour had it she was eighteen.) She was here on holiday with her dad and his new girlfriend, who was only a year older than Becca! Eeyou, as the Clueless girls would say. What was that girl thinking of, shagging a bloke old enough to be her father? Yuk. And Becca's little brother Anton was in the Bluebells, like Spike; and even he wasn't very nice, he was a biter.

Anyway. Becca hung out with the teens from time to time, if she felt like it. Graced them with her presence. Truth be told, they were all either a bit scared of her, or a bit in awe of her, mostly both. Anything they'd done, she'd done more. And she was really confident (even though she was a bit of a minger to look at), and she was fully developed.

And she was here, rocking up to the bar looking like Jessica bloody Rabbit in a tight red dress which Sammy wouldn't have worn if she had a hench arse like that, but anyway. And it seemed she'd had a Michelle Makeover too, her hair had fat white streaks in it now, she looked like a badger.

'Hi, guys,' she smiled at them and winked at the barman, who seemed to know what she wanted, she didn't even have to ask.

Well, that was it, wasn't it. They all crowded round her, and laughed for too long at her stupid stories, and it was as if Sammy and the other girls weren't even there.

This was really bad. She had to get off with Jamie soon, they could be going home any day now, time was running out. She had to do something, and she had to do it now.

So Sammy had slammed her bottle down on the bar very loudly, and without even saying 'come on' to Chris or goodbye to anyone else, she'd just walked out. That'd teach him to ignore her.

*

There was a rumour, on the third day of the strike, that it might be resolved by the next morning, and they could be going home tomorrow afternoon. So the villagers relaxed a little, and the atmosphere around the campus turned to one of uneasy acceptance.

To the staff, however, the notion of dealing with a new

lot of villagers arriving the next day without having a day off in between was completely unacceptable. Fearing a mutiny, Bonnie refused to open the Kids Kottage. 'My staff need a break,' she had informed Fabio and any parents who'd had the cheek to complain, 'and besides – don't you want to look after your own kids?' (Of course they didn't, or they wouldn't have booked this sort of holiday, Bonnie knew that. But they'd never admit it.)

Taking his lead from Bonnie, Fabio also shut down his office for the day, telling Nikki that he was going to spend the day at the airport, gathering information on the strike, seeing if he could hurry things along a bit. Coincidentally, the Village Gossip was also closed, and Fabio and Michelle spent several pleasurable hours on a private rock further down the coast, nakedly sunning and sexing themselves, blissfully unaware that Crisis Management in London was desperately trying to contact Fabio as a matter of some urgency.

And Craig and his boys and girls were enjoying a well-earned break too, they were exhausted from the Egg Olympics of the previous day. They were busy dodging Robert from Maintenance, who was furious – there were eggs ranging from raw in the shade, to scrambled in the sunny spots, all over the compound. Who was going to clear this mess up? So to all intents and purposes, the villagers were left to entertain themselves, just for that one day.

The children were fine, it was the parents that caused all the trouble. Some mothers had tried to persuade the fathers to look after the kids in the morning, in a do-their-bit kind of way. Which would have meant missing volleyball, and the men had organized a tournament for themselves, in an attempt to take their minds off the frustration they were all feeling. 'It's a very positive way of getting rid of our aggression,' they justified.

They'd split themselves into various teams: by country – England, Scotland and Ireland (Wales was too poorly represented to form a team, and holiday homes didn't count); by profession – The Long Arms (a few local solicitors, a barrister and various other legal professionals); Money (several bankers, too many financial advisers and some people from the City); The Arts (publishing, music, advertising and an estate agent for some reason); and the Dot Coms (internet entrepreneurs, known as the Dot Cunts behind their backs). Others had taken comedy names – The Netball Team (who should really have been called the Friends of Kathy); The Rotters Club (after some book they'd all read and heavily identified with); The Piss-heads (who Felicity renamed the Fish-heads), and The Workers (which wasn't a comedy name at all, but the posh twats were too up their own arses to realize that). And those who didn't fall into any of these categories were in either the Nutty Browns or the Bright Whites, depending on how long they'd been here.

So there was a bit of a hoo-hah when the women demanded that the dads look after their own kids. Some men claimed that they really wanted to, but just couldn't let their fellow team-mates down; others just gave a flat no. One brave man from the Arts said yes at first, but retracted his offer after allegations of being pussy-whipped. In the end they adopted their 'in a meeting' stance, and would not and could not be moved.

There were a handful of decent blokes who weren't in any of the volleyball teams, and they did nice wholesome things with their wives and kids, like build a very complicated sand citadel with underground water tunnels, and an electrically engineered windmill involving shells and a plastic water bottle, that sort of thing; but they were very much in the minority.

These men's wives were perfectly happy, being used to doing activities together, as a family, but the majority of the women were furious. The whole point of coming on a holiday like this was to give the mums a break, couldn't the dads see that? Yes, well of course they could, and any other day they would, but it was the tournament and it was really important and – oh, just forget it.

Next, the mums tried to bribe the teenagers to look after the little ones. But the teenagers refused, what was in it for them? Money? Didn't need it. A longer lie-in the next day? Don't be pathetic. I'll let you send a text message from my mobile to one of your friends? No thanks. Why not? I've done that already, you've run out of battery by the way.

But some of the mums had begun to feel guilty about trying to palm off their kids, and the kinder ones caved in quite quickly, volunteering to look after the offspring of the militant hardnuts in an irritatingly selfless way. And so in the end, all the women looked after their own children, some through gritted teeth and some with a beatific smile the Madonna herself would have been proud of.

But it was hard work. Not only did Bonnie refuse to

open up the Kids Kottage, but she wouldn't let them use any of the facilities either, and they'd only brought enough of their own distractions for the flight here and back. Added to which, the sky was a bit cloudy and it wasn't as warm as it had been, which made the pool chilly and the beach too windy for comfort. Some of the kids watched their dads thrash the other side, but soon tired of it. And a toddler was knocked unconscious by a misplaced ball, so that put an end to that.

Even catering was running out of steam. Lunch seemed to consist entirely of leftovers, not-so-cunningly disguised in either a thick tomato sauce or a pie.

And then there was the whole afternoon stretching ahead of them. Some of the smaller ones obligingly took a nap, but the bigger kids wouldn't go to sleep as they were just plain bored by now, and so they began to whinge.

Word soon got round that John and Yoko had brought their kids' laptop with them, plus around fifty DVDs, and so the other mums cunningly appealed to their socialist nature, resulting in an impromptu showing of *The Little Mermaid* in the dining room. That was a lifesaver, it bought the run-ragged mothers ninety minutes of absolute silence. The mums went up to their rooms for a shower and a lie-down. Bliss. Peace at last, as Jill Murphy would say.

But the movie finished earlier than anyone supposed, and within five minutes the little darlings (led on by John and Yoko's Feather and Mink) had begun to trash the dining room, building caves and mountains with the tables and chairs, making trails with the salt and peppers. Then they opened all the cupboards behind the breakfast bar and discovered the whole season's supply of sauces and mustards in big squeezy bottles, which were just asking to be liberally squirted around the room like poster paints.

Howell the chef, fucking one of the older nannies who was perched on top of the deep freeze in the kitchen next door, managed to simultaneously ring Mandy's room from the phone on the wall to alert her to the chaos unfolding in her precious dining room. Mandy, in the middle of dyeing her hair Flame Titian with a home kit (didn't want that Michelle anywhere near it, thank you very much) had to come down and read the riot act very loudly to the little buggers, who didn't take her that seriously as she was wearing a funny plastic hat on her head and had dribbles of orange running down her face. In fact they laughed at her, which made her even more angry, which made them laugh even more.

Kids' supper was only tiny sandwiches that night. Three triangles each. There didn't seem to be anything for pudding, except many banana yoghurts, which nobody liked. And the orange squash wasn't out, so they had to have plain water. Which was probably why they found it so hard to settle at bedtime, the mums told themselves, their little tummies weren't full. Or was it that they hadn't done enough today to wear themselves out? Either way, the little darlings took even longer than usual to get to sleep that night.

So by the time the mums joined their husbands for dinner, they were too exhausted to listen to tales of triumph and testosterone on the volleyball pitch. They just wanted to go home, to get back to normal. Send the men back to work, climb into their 4-wheel drives and drop the kids off somewhere. One of them even said they'd rather do their own cleaning for a year, than stay out here any longer. The lives they had been so glad to leave behind only a couple of weeks ago, suddenly seemed more attractive. Appealing, even.

Which was a shame, because when they got back to their rooms that night, they found that a letter had been pushed under their door. It was on Seaside Villages headed paper, informing them that there was to be a public meeting in the Village Hall tomorrow at twelve, to discuss the present difficulties.

In the meantime, Seaside Villages hoped most sincerely that they were enjoying their extended holiday, and assured the villagers that they were doing everything they could to resolve this matter as soon as possible.

10. The Parents

TESSA

Before the meeting, the rumours were
circulating like wildfire. I remember
someone telling me that the airport
had been blown up by terrorists, and
somebody else said they'd heard the
airline had gone bust. I didn't know
what to think.

*

Bonnie knocked on Kevin's door. No reply. Little shit.

'Kevin?'

Silence.

She'd had enough of this. He'd taken too much time off already, it was only flu after all. She hadn't been to see him for a couple of days, she'd been too busy. But now it was time to get up and get back to work. Those teenagers were getting completely out of hand, she was going to have to take control of them herself at this rate. *'Kevin!'* She kicked the door as well this time.

Nothing, lazy bastard. Right, that's it! Bonnie fumbled around in her pocket for her key and let herself into his room.

He wasn't in his bed. He wasn't in the bathroom either.

And all his stuff had gone, there were no clothes hanging in the wardrobe. Kevin had gone. It was as if he'd never been there. He'd disappeared.

*

'It's just as well we're English,' said Felicity.

'British,' corrected Tessa. 'Why?'

'Because we specialize in this kind of wartime mentality, don't we? You know, pulling together, staying cheerful, jolly good teamwork, what! It's what we do best. Supposedly.' She sipped her usual breakfast coffee, and grimaced at the taste, as usual.

'What d'you mean, wartime? Honestly, Felicity, you're being a bit overdramatic, aren't you? We'll probably only be here for another couple of days at the most, we're hardly at war!' Tessa smiled at her friend's excess.

'Ah, but how d'you know? We've got no radios, or TVs, or even newspapers. No contact with the outside world at all.' She drained her cup. 'They could be making this whole thing up – anything could be going on out there!'

'Ach, don't be mad, I'm sure we'll find out everything at this meeting. And anyway, some of us brought mobile phones on holiday with us, didn't we? Some of us even brought two ... Besides, Jeremy would know if there's anything to worry about, he works for the airline. He'd have made sure we're all right.'

'Has he called you back yet?' Felicity's eyes narrowed in suspicion.

'No.'

'Ooh, the plot thickens ...' But before she could

launch into her usual Time To Move On speech, Tessa diverted her by indicating the longer-than-ever queue stretching all the way from Reception, past the dining room doors, and out on to the sun terrace, mainly consisting of grumpy-looking holidaymakers thinking only negative thoughts. 'I tell you what, they'd better have some good news to announce at this meeting, people are getting really angry now. In fact, Fliss, you seem to be taking all this very well – suspiciously well, if you don't mind me saying . . .' She looked at her friend with a question mark.

Felicity smiled. 'I know, I'm amazing even myself. But to be quite honest, what can we do about it? I mean, just look at all those people in that line, blood boiling, seething with anger and resentment, giving themselves cancer – what's the point? Far easier to sit back and enjoy the ride, that's what I say!' She was positively beaming.

'Good God.' Tessa was open-mouthed at her friend's laid-back attitude. 'You still having lots of sex?'

'Sadly not,' Felicity drained her coffee cup and winced, 'that seems to have been a one-off. In fact,' and she leaned forward, 'that's what worries me most. Forget the business side of things, that I can handle – but I'm not sure our marriage can stand being stuck out here any longer! I'm working at it, but Cliff's driving me mad, I'm just not used to spending this much time with him – oh damn, hang on –'

Her tiny silver cellphone was doing its diddly-dee.

'Hi, thanks for getting back to me, Seb.' She winked at Tessa. 'Yes I know, bloody nightmare, we're permanently packing and unpacking . . . god knows, hopefully not too much longer, I'm going to go over there and give the controllers a pay rise myself at this rate – d'you think they take American Express?! . . . well, apparently we're going to find out at lunchtime . . . still nothing on the news over there? No, I suppose there wouldn't be, it's not exactly world-threatening . . . not a clue, darling, but all sorts of conspiracy theories flying about – some girl's been taken to hospital apparently, probably gastroenteritis, salmonella and bloody botulism all in one big bug, if the food's anything to go by . . . but, listen, I'm going to phone Joe right now, and see if I can get hold of Alex, and then with any luck I'll have an answer for you by lunchtime, OK?'

As she snapped her little phone shut, Felicity said to Tessa, 'Ooh, d'you know, I could get used to this, running the business long-distance from paradise!' She laughed. 'After all, I can think of worse places to be marooned . . .'

Tessa tried to laugh too, but couldn't. Something didn't feel quite right.

*

Over on another table, Cliff was still waiting for Spike to finish his Coco Pops. Yet again, it had been decided by Her Majesty that it would be his job to take the lad over to the Kids Kottage that morning. He was outwardly pissed off about this, but inwardly excited. Pissed off because he was doing what Christabelle was here to do, but she was never awake to do it; and excited because it meant he was going to see Tania.

He'd been trying to avoid her, since the moonlit tit

night. Not because he didn't want to see her, but because he did. Very much so. A bit more of her, in fact. Much more. He'd imagined what she'd look like naked, of course; trouble was, he had this overwhelming desire to see if he'd imagined right.

Bollocks. He knew how this would go normally, he'd done it so many times before. You start it all up by asking her out to lunch. Not dinner, lunch. Dinner is at night-time in the posh totty world, he'd learnt that very quickly. If she's a tricky bird (and they were Cliff's favourite), you use a clever move; for example, you make a bet with her which you both know you'll win, the pay-off being lunch.

Then you do it again, only you meet a little earlier and part a little later. She begins to see what a nice bloke you really are, but keeps it to herself.

Next, you meet for a quick drink, early evening, straight after work. If she's wearing more make-up/has changed her hair/lowered her neckline, then she's up for it. But you don't make a move then. Oh no. That's what she's expecting you to do. No. You sit, you pay good attention, and then just when she's a bit pissed up and about to reveal too much about herself, you leave. Well, you did say a quick drink, didn't you?

(This makes them feel safe, you see. It shows them that you stick to what you say. They like that. And you leave them wanting a little bit more of you, hopefully a lot more.)

So within a week, she'll call you. Not because she wants to see you, oh no, she wouldn't ever say that. She'll give some dodgy reason which refers back to one of your earlier conversations (this is why you have to pay attention), or she'll flatter you with something like 'I want to ask your advice'. Whatever you do, don't ever question the reason she gives for seeing you again, just say yes.

At your next meeting – she chooses when and where, let her think she's in control – you ask her one or two questions about herself, and then you shut the fuck up. Just listen. This is important information she's giving you, it's going to come in handy later on. (If she stops talking, which is unlikely, then you're required to share something a little bit personal back. Don't matter what, make it up if you have to. Something sad, if you can. Then look a bit upset, but don't let her comfort you, ask her another question about herself instead. Shift the focus back on to her. This will start her off again, and she'll think you're both sharing.)

By the end of the evening, you will have been awarded qualities you don't necessarily have, but that's all right. Who would deny being 'kind', 'generous', 'funny', or even 'sweet' (which has to be the worst) if it meant there was a chance of a bloody good shag at the end of the night?

Cliff sipped his orange juice. Yep, that's how he'd do it if he was at home, but all that malarkey was impossible out here. Which could be a good thing in the end. Perhaps it was just as well, not being able to sneak around; he might manage to stay out of trouble. He knew it was wrong, to have sex with other birds, but he just couldn't help himself. And anyway, it was only sex, he didn't love them or anything. He just adored beautiful women, and they didn't seem to mind him too much neither ...

But it was after he'd fucked 'em that things started to go a bit pear-shaped. He'd never mastered the next stage, he'd always got in a bit of a mess at that point, so he'd let the women take over then. It had usually sorted itself out, one way or another. The 'friendship' had either fizzled out and they'd lost touch, or she'd met someone else; there were a couple of women he still saw now, once in a while, when they were in between boyfriends and husbands, there was no harm in that, was there? And of course, he'd ended up marrying the more pushy ones. But all that was way down the line; he could only think as far as the getting-them-into-bed bit. And what a lovely bit it was too ...

'Spike!' Felicity's voice shrilled over the heads of others trying to have a quiet breakfast.

Spike was drinking the leftover Coco Pops milk straight out of the bowl, which was Bad Manners, as he'd been told by his mother a hundred times before. She was always on his case, poor little sod. Cliff looked over at Felicity. He pretended to look surprised, as if he hadn't seen her sitting there with her little mate, trying to look like ladies who lunched at breakfast.

Felicity shook her head vigorously, wagged her finger, mouthed 'no!', looked up at the ceiling, looked back at them, eyes bulging with horror, lips pursed tight as a goat's chuff.

Cliff was tempted to mime 'shut-the-fuck-up-or-look-after-your-own-kid-why-don't-you' back at her, but shrugged his shoulders instead, in a 'what-can-I-do' way.

Spike put the bowl down and a dribble of chocolate

milk ran down his chin, splodging into his new Oilily T-shirt. He looked over to the breakfast buffet table. 'Um, next I'm going to have . . .'

'No, Spike, no mate – you've had enough!' Cliff scraped back his chair and got up.

'But I'm still hungry . . .' wailed the little boy.

'You can't be – you've had two bowls of cereal, one and a half bananas, two yoghurts and a boiled egg with a whole army of soldiers. You'll burst if you eat any more!' He picked up Spike's little Winnie-the-Pooh rucksack from where it was hanging off the chair. 'Blimey, mate, what've you got in here? It weighs a ton!'

Spike tried to snatch the bag from his father, but Cliff had already opened it.

'What's Mum's jumper doing in here? Spike?'

The boy looked down, squidging his finger into the remaining banana, smearing it on to the table. 'It's my new cuggie.'

'I don't think it is mate, it's Prada.' Cliff slung it, carefully, on to his shoulder. 'And anyway, you can't take a cuggie to Kids Klub, all the other boys will laugh at you.'

'Anton does.'

'Who's Anton?'

'My friend.'

'What, he laughs at you?'

'No,' said Spike, irritated, 'he's allowed to have his blankie.'

'Isn't he the one who bit you the other day?'

'Yes.'

'And he's still your friend?'

'Yes.'

'Oh.' Kids. Mad.

'But she won't let me have my cuggie.'

Cliff sat down again, exasperated. 'Who won't?'

'The fat lady.'

'Bonnie?'

Spike nodded.

'Why not?'

'She says we can't be babies.'

'But Anton's allowed his?'

'Yes.'

'How come?'

'What?'

'Why? Why's he allowed to, and not you?' Not that, in his father's opinion, Spike should even have a bloomin' cuggie whatsit; but his mother said it gave him comfort, and so –

'*Because*,' Spike was losing patience, 'he *bites us*!'

'So let me get this straight –'

Spike threw himself back in his chair and shut his eyes tight, he was fed up with this now.

'– Anton's allowed to have his blankie because he bites people, but you're not because you're a good boy. That's mental, that don't make sense.'

'And she lets the bad boys watch videos, when we have to go swimming.'

'What?'

'And she makes us all lie down for ages, on the floor, even when we're not tired. Mink tried to sneak out, but she got hold of him and smacked him on his bottom, really hard and he really cried, for ages and ages.'

Trying hard not to sound as furious as he felt, Cliff said in an even tone, 'OK, Spikey, let's go and sort this out.' He stood up.

'No!' There was a fear in his voice that Cliff had never heard before, 'I don't want to go!'

Cliff looked down at his son's little face, trying to read it. The boy looked genuinely terrified, this didn't seem to be just a moody.

'Please, Dad, please?' He blinked the baby tears out of his eyes.

A surge of protective fury coursed through Cliff's body, it looked like someone had been upsetting his boy.

'Right. Let's go and have a word, shall we?' And he scooped up little Spike in his big daddy arms and marched out of the door, barely acknowledging Felicity as he left. She was on the phone, of course she was, but she did manage a mini-wave and a busy-smile as they passed.

As they crossed through the Reception area and marched down the stairs, Spike buried himself in his dad's chest and sobbed. Then he curled a little arm around Cliff's neck. By the time he arrived at the Kids Kottage, Cliff was ready to kill.

One of the nannies managed to prise Spike off his dad, with the promise of Circus Skills later that morning, his favourite – and Cliff found Bonnie in the kitchen, surprise surprise. 'What the fuck do you think you are doing?' he shouted at her.

'Sorting out the snacks and sugar-free drinks for elevenses,' she replied calmly. She even had the nerve to smile at him. 'Please keep your voice down, we don't want to frighten the children now, do we?' she said, like an air hostess on an anti-terrorist training course.

'Spike tells me you're making them have a nap in the middle of the day. Is that right?'

Bonnie prised the lid off a large Tupperware box marked 'Kids Kooking'. 'Yes, that's right. A lot of the parents don't seem to be able to provide their children with enough sleep, and by lunchtime the poor little things are exhausted.' She peered into the box, and sniffed it. 'So unfortunately, it's down to us to make sure they catch up on the Recommended Daily Sleep Allowance for Small Children during the day.'

'But then they don't go to sleep at night, if they've had a nap in the afternoon!' Cliff protested.

'Not my problem, sorry. As you know, after 6 p.m. the children are Parents' responsibility.'

'And is it true that the bad boys get to watch the telly, when everyone else has to go swimming?'

'*Has* to go swimming?' she echoed. 'Wouldn't you rather your son was outside, enjoying the fresh air and beautiful sunshine, participating in interactive waterplay?' She jiggled the contents of the box, searching for a little something. 'Don't you want little Spike to learn how to swim?'

'Of course I do, but –'

'Or would you prefer,' she plumped for what was supposed to be a gingerbread man, 'that he was in the pool with badly-behaved children, dangerous, bad boys who want to drown him?'

'Of course not. But –'

'Anything else?' She picked a cherry off the ginger-bread thing's chest, and ate it.

Last try. 'Their cuggies.'

'I'm sorry?' Bonnie looked as if she had never heard the word before. The little raisin eyes were next to go, plucked and eaten.

'They should be allowed to have their cuggies.' Nope, nothing. 'Their blankies, blankets?' He cleared his throat. 'Comfort things, you know.'

'Oh, yes. Now, I might be wrong, but weren't you one of the men who complained about their boys doing too many "girlie activities"? That we were encouraging them to go – ahem – soft in the head? I believe the word "poof" was mentioned?'

'Well yeah, but . . .' he trailed off, pathetically.

'Exactly. And I don't think Spike turning up with a scrap of dirty security blanket is going to help persuade anybody here that he's a big butch boy, now is it?'

Cliff couldn't think of anything to say quick enough.

'So. I hope that's helped put your mind at rest.' That fucking smile again. 'Now, if you'll excuse me, we've got a difficult enough job to do here as it is. Time to get on!' She pointed her biscuit in the direction of the door. 'Perhaps it is your other child you should be worrying about, Mr Clifton. Goodbye!' And she bit the gingerbread man's head off.

Cliff found himself doing what he was told and walked away, down the corridor, thinking. What the fuck did she mean by that? Other child? Christabelle? Peering through the one-way mirror in the Kids Klub door he was relieved to see that Spike was absolutely fine, he was happily being wrestled to the floor by the Slogan girl.

Satisfied, Cliff turned to leave, but bumped straight into Tania's bosoms. Bloody hell, he'd forgotten about them. Her.

'Hi!' she whispered. 'How are you?'

'Fine!' he whispered back, and then he couldn't help himself, 'All the better for seeing you!'

She smiled, no, beamed at him, flashed those green eyes at him like a naughty kitten. She was so fresh, healthy-looking. It was nice to be looking at a different female face close-up for a change. No stressful frown lines, no crow's feet, no meanly thinning lips – big soft squashy ones instead, and her tits can't have been withered by childbirth either, they were probably still meaty, big and bouncy. She made him want to be all energetic again.

Tania didn't say anything more, and so he did. 'I just had a bit of a barney with old Fuckface in there –'

'Ssh!' she puckered that sexbud mouth, all shiny and wet inside. 'She's got really good ears!'

'Well, that's the only thing that is bloody good about her!' Cliff muttered under his breath.

'Oh I know,' whispered Tania, 'she's always roof-dropping on us, it's awful.' Smiling at Cliff's puzzled face, she said, 'My dad's a builder.' And she winked, knowingly.

Cliff still didn't quite get it, but never mind. He was beginning to get an alert in his shorts, it was time to go. 'Listen darlin', I've got to get on – catch ya later, yes?' But his legs didn't move, he seemed to be rooted to the spot.

'When?' she asked, and she was all breathing at him, making her bosoms go up and down, they were just bursting to get out of there.

And then he went and said it, didn't he. 'Lunch?'

You must be stark staring raving fucking mad, Cliff said to himself as he walked back to the hotel block. How are you going to get this one past Her Maj? It's not like we're in the middle of bustling central London, where you can tuck her away in a discreet, dimly-lit bistro. There is only one restaurant here, and the whole bloody village will be in it.

What was worse, was that Felicity had recently started collaring him at lunchtime, making sure the two of them ate together. One of Felicity's New Age mend-the-relationship tactics. Which was OK, but they were in danger of turning into one of those holiday couples who had nothing to say to each other, just stared out into space instead. And of course, the big sex revival hadn't lasted very long, she was back pretending to be tired again, and so was he now. Even though they hadn't actually done anything all day.

So how was he going to wriggle out of this one? Supposing he did manage to shake off the wife, as soon as Felicity spotted him with Tania she'd be over there like a bat out of hell, knowing her. Causing a terrible scene, threatening the poor girl with private detectives and so on, like she did when she caught him having lunch with Denise. Screaming at the top of her voice about trust and communication, going apeshit in front of the whole restaurant, even though it was perfectly innocent. He'd told Felicity she was a client, over and over again, and she'd believed him in the end, thank fuck.

Perhaps he could put Tania off? Change it to dinner? No! Another day? But what other day – all the days here were the same. And all mealtimes were the same. And all the same people were in all the same places, there was no skulking around to be done here. Not that he was planning any, of course. He just liked Tania, that's all. They got on well together. Nothing wrong with that.

The knot of anger in Cliff's stomach began to grow again. He was still trapped, boxed in, under surveillance, even out here. More than ever. He was condemned to working his arse off at home in order to keep everyone happy, and now he couldn't even have lunch on holiday with a friend without everyone thinking he was having an affair. They'd be down on him like a ton of bricks. He hadn't even done anything wrong, yet, but they'd all assume he had. And bloody Felicity would know he fancied Tania, she was like a witch, she had super-psychic powers when it came to that sort of thing. Cliff loosened the collar of his polo shirt, he was beginning to feel claustrophobic, panicky even.

The lift doors finally swooshed open and a hot-and-bothered Cliff went marching up the landing. Time to kick some arse. He banged on the door, hard. 'Christabelle! Wake up! Get out your lazy bed and open this fucking door, right now!'

Eventually, after more hollering and banging with both fists, the door was pulled back to reveal his lard-arse of a daughter, squinting in the daylight. 'What?' was all she managed to say.

'What the fuck is going on with you?' He marched past her and opened the shutters, letting in a stream of sunlight so brightly piercing that Chris had to dive back under the sheet and pull it right up over her head. 'Why aren't you getting up for Spike any more?'

'He goes in to Gran when he wakes up,' came the muffled reply.

'Yes, I know. And then she brings him back in here, gets him dressed, and hands him over to us. Early. Too bloody early. And you sleep through the whole bloody thing!'

'So?'

'So that's not the deal, is it?'

Silence from the white mountain.

'Is it?!' Cliff stripped the sheet off her, and noticed for the first time that she was wearing a long-sleeved T-shirt and baggy combats, in bed. 'Have you only just got in?'

'No,' she said, all on the defensive.

'Then why are you wearing all this clobber?'

'I get cold,' she replied.

'Well then turn the bloody air conditioning off!' Bloody hell, could it be that a child of his was really this thick? He went over to the dial on the wall, flicked it to 'off'.

'But Felicity,' and there was an undeniable sneer when Christabelle said her name, 'said I had to keep it on.'

'Why?'

'She doesn't want Spike getting too hot.'

Bloody hell. Her again. She who must be obeyed, or she'll unscrew your balls and have them fried on toast for breakfast. 'Listen – oh, what's the bloody point.' Cliff had been up for hours, he was exhausted. He felt old, he was too tired to deal with all this shit. If he made someone happy, someone else would complain. It was a never-ending, self-defeating, one-man battle that he just couldn't fight any more, not today.

He surrendered by sitting down on the end of his daughter's bed. 'Look, you have it how you want it, OK?' He patted her feet, which were wrapped in thick black socks. 'Leave Felicity to me. But for God's sake tidy this room, it looks like a bloody anarchist's HQ.' She was looking a bit funny, so he smiled at her. 'I love you, darlin', you know that, don't you?'

But instead of smiling back, her face collapsed. She immediately covered it with her hands, but Cliff moved up the bed and prised them away. For the second time that morning, Cliff's heart went out to the child in front of him.

'Hey, hey,' he soothed, 'what's the matter?'

'Nothing,' she said, biting her lip.

Women. They cry, they say nothing's wrong. 'Look, don't let Felicity upset you, you come and tell me, I'll sort her out for you –'

'No, no,' there was a flash of anger in Christabelle's eyes, but no tears, 'it's not Her. I couldn't give a toss about Her, she doesn't scare me.'

'No, I suppose your mum's ten times worse than that, isn't she?' Cliff smiled, they both knew what Penny was like; she made Felicity look like Mother Teresa.

'No she's not, Mum's OK!' Her face was flushed with instant defence. 'You just can't remember her nice bits, that's all, you've forgotten –'

'All right, all right, keep your hair on.' Blimey, talk

about getting your head bitten off. Maybe she wasn't old enough to see it yet. 'Well then, what is it, what's bothering you?'

'Nothing, it doesn't matter.'

'Right,' Cliff got up from the bed, 'I'm off then. I've got to get changed for volleyball.'

'You shouldn't be mean about Mum.'

(Always worked, that getting up and going thing.)

'She's much nicer than you think. Than anybody thinks. She doesn't have an easy life, you know. It's really hard for her – she's got no money, well, not enough, and I'm very expensive to keep. And if it wasn't for me, she'd be living somewhere really exotic, like somewhere abroad, running a retreat or something – it's only because of my education that she's got to be here. There. Whatever.' She was biting her lip very hard now, it was turning white. 'She can't afford to have a nice life, so she gets angry, that's all.'

Well, it was quite obvious to Cliff what had been going on here. So Penny had been poisoning his own daughter against him, had she? Filling her young head with details of his financial shortcomings, instead of pointing out his better qualities, was that it? Making out that everything was his fault. Bitch. She probably hadn't said a word about how he'd stuck by Christabelle, fought through the wall of aggression her mother threw up, worked really hard to keep some sort of contact going with his daughter. And the rows he'd had with Felicity about all this – it would have been so much easier to walk away, but he hadn't. He would never abandon his children, never.

'I just want to go home, Dad. I miss my room,

I actually miss Mum.' They both smiled at that, but inwardly, not to each other.

'But you've got me, haven't you, your old dad? I'm here, aren't I?'

Christabelle didn't say anything. More lip-biting.

'Look, Christabelle, I know –'

'I prefer to be called Chris. I've told you that.'

'Right, sorry, er – Chris. Now look, Chris, I know I've not been around a lot exactly this holiday, Chris, mate, but, well –'

'Not ever, you mean.'

He didn't need to ask, they both knew what she meant.

'I only wanted to come here so that I could be with you. I haven't seen you properly for months, Dad. You never have time to see me any more. Sorry.' She looked down again, shook her head, 'Sorry.'

'What for, what are you sorry for?'

'Well, you know, I don't want to be a pest to you. You've got enough people to look after, you don't need me bothering you as well. Look, never mind, it doesn't matter, we'll be home soon, back to normal.'

'No.' Cliff sighed. 'You're right. I'm sorry, love, it's just that – well, you look so bloody grown-up these days, it's hard for me to remember that you're still my little girl! But you are, aren't you?'

She almost nodded.

'And you're so quiet, you never ask for anything. Not like the others, who never stop asking. So I just assume you're OK. Which isn't right, is it?'

She nearly looked up at him.

'So, here's the plan.' Yes, this felt good, it was the right thing to do. 'I want us to use these next couple of days to get to know each other properly, hang out together, play a game of tennis now and then, whatever.'

Christabelle slumped her shoulders.

'OK, not the tennis thing. Not today. But let's give it a go, shall we?'

She looked a bit wary.

'Chris?'

She frowned.

'Look, I don't mean spending every bloody waking minute of the day together, you can still hang round with all your friends.'

Pause.

'I haven't got any friends.'

'But I thought you were big mates with Tessa's girl.'

'Well, I was, I am, but Sammy's a bit busy these days.'

'Busy? Doing what?'

'Chasing boys.'

'Well you should be doing that with her, shouldn't you, at your age?' He tried to nudge her in the ribs, but couldn't quite get round there. 'Eh?' he winked, 'eh?' He was going to say 'an attractive girl like you', but stopped himself in time. No need to go too far, she'd lose faith in him.

'Stop it, Dad.' She was half-smiling. 'Bonnie says they're all idiots, all the boys out here.'

'Bonnie? Big fat-bastard Bonnie?'

'I wish you'd stop doing that!' defended Christabelle once more. 'She's my friend.'

'Oh, is she now?' asked Cliff, trying not to look as surprised as he was. What the fuck? 'Really? That's an, er, odd choice, isn't it?'

'Not really, no. She's much nicer than you think. Honestly Dad, you're not a very good judge of character, are you?' There was a faint trace of a smile on her face, a flicker of humour, a little girl being brave, being a cheeky monkey with her dad. Crisis over, whatever the crisis was.

'Friends again?' he asked.

As Christabelle chattered on, Cliff discovered to his surprise that she was much more – well, sorted, than he'd thought. Quite bright in fact, maybe this bloody expensive education was paying off. And this was a much better thing to do than chasing a bit of skirt he'd never see again. He determined to make sure he spent some time with his daughter every day, starting right now. Which was probably why, before he knew what he was saying, he'd promised to have lunch with her too.

*

Like most of the other women assembled in the increasingly stuffy Village Hall, Tessa found herself gazing up at Fabio, marvelling at his everything. He was up on the stage, standing in the middle of a long line of Seaside Village staff, addressing his captive audience with the aid of the DJ's microphone. Unfortunately, this meant that every time he spoke, the disco lights on the front of the turntable console flashed on and off, which was a little distracting. The DJ himself (Robert from Maintenance) was doing his best to fix it, but in the meantime they'd swung it round to face the back of the stage. As a result, Fabio's words were heralded by very dramatic multi-coloured flashes of light sweeping up the backdrop, making the whole spectacle look like 'something out of "Lord of the Bleedin' Dance"', as Mr Slogan remarked loudly to Cliff. Other men sniggered, but the women hissed them to 'ssssh!' as Fabio was doing his best to field some quite tough questions from the audience, poor man.

'What if this strike goes on for another week?'

'Well, let's hope it doesn't . . .'

'Are Seaside Villages taking any measures to try and hurry them along?'

'Oh yes, I'm sure they are.'

'What measures, exactly?'

'Um, I don't know – exactly.'

'Surely there are other ways of getting to the mainland – by boat, for instance?'

'Yes, we're still looking into that –'

'But you can't just hold us here indefinitely, we have to get home!'

'Yes, I know, it must be very frustrating for you.'

'Are you aware that some of us have already formed a Legal Action Committee?'

'Er no, I didn't know that.'

'Why is there nothing on the news about this back home?'

'Isn't there? Well I suppose it's not very big news to the rest of the world, when you think about it . . .'

'Are you sure this supposed strike really exists?' asked the female half of the Tufty Club.

'It's real all right,' Mr Slogan stood up. 'I hitched a lift over to the airport early this morning, it's all closed up, nothing doing.' He spoke to Fabio, up on the stage. 'Listen, mate, as far as I can see you don't know any more than we do, you haven't got any answers for us – so what d'you think we should do, swim for it?' Much laughing, men only.

Fabio laughed too, he was clearly out of his depth.

Alcopop, who Sammy noticed was sitting next to the Nebulizer, so he must be his Parent, stood up. 'What about the cost of all this?'

'Ah! Yes! Your accommodation and food will be provided free of charge for the rest of your stay, that I can guarantee.' Fabio smiled, triumphant.

Amidst mutterings of 'so I should hope', Alcopop stayed standing. 'Yes, but do we still have to pay for extras, like, for example, I don't know, drinks from the bar?'

Absolute pindrop silence.

'Er, we'll have to let you know on that one. Any other questions?'

'Are there any planes landing, or does it only affect departures?' Mr Pongo was near tears at the thought of never seeing his luggage again. 'Can you provide us with at least another set of clothes? We've been wearing these for over two weeks now.' (A group of teenagers sitting near the Pongos rudely held their noses and poowee'd, sniggering.)

'Does this mean no newspapers for the foreseeable future?'

A low rumble of discontent began to spread through the audience.

'What about fresh food supplies to the island? Are they affected?'

'Is that why someone's in hospital?'

'No, that's just the cooking!' shouted out Felicity, much to Tessa's embarrassment. Fabio shot her a look; further down the line-up Howell, the chef, committed her face to memory.

'How long will it be, once the strike's over, until the first plane can take off?'

'When do you think we can tell them we'll be back at work?'

'Are you going to compensate us for loss of earnings? OK if I charge you my daily rate for being here?'

But Fabio had nothing more to tell them, all he could do was smile. The rumble turned into a dull roar, signalling the dissatisfaction of the badly led.

'May I make a suggestion?' Felicity stood up, hands on hips, and turned round to address the rest of the hall. 'I think it would be a good idea,' she said, as the roar descendo'd down to a murmur, 'to make sure that we are kept fully informed of all developments from now on. I propose we nominate a representative, chosen from the clientele, to work alongside Fabio and help him out in what must be a very difficult situation.' Fabio tried not to look as relieved as he felt. 'This way we can ensure that all our needs will be taken into account, and that we are fairly represented, for however long it lasts. And of course the person you nominate will absolutely make it her business to ensure that we are at the front of the Departures queue, when the time comes.'

Once Felicity had been voted in, the questions stopped. (Under her breath, she claimed to Tessa that it was because everyone knew they were in safe hands now, but Tessa was sure it was because everyone was hot and hungry.) They all began to file out of the Hall, still muttering, but glad to get out of there.

'Oh, I nearly forgot, I have got some good news!' announced Fabio, loudly enough to stop everyone in their tracks. They looked up at him, expectantly.

'Yes, Craig and his boys and girls will be putting on a special production of Robinson Crusoe the Musical tonight, here in the Village Hall, at half past nine –'

The villagers carried on filing out of the hall.

'Oh don't look so worried, Cliff,' said Felicity to her husband, 'it's all going to be fine.' And she kissed him on his shiny forehead. 'I'm really sorry, darling, but I'm going to have to have a working lunch with Fabio now, I've got to find out exactly what's been going on.'

'Oh,' said Cliff, being Crestfallen, 'that's a shame. Never mind, I'll have a look round, see who else is about.' But Felicity didn't hear him, she had already gone to grab Fabio, eyes bright at the prospect of a New Project.

'I'd keep you company, Cliff, but I've got a date with Gina,' commiserated Tessa.

'I'll be fine, thanks, love.'

'And I forgot, Dad, but it's Aberdeen Angus's birthday and they've arranged a special barbie on the beach for him . . .'

'That's great! Well off you go, Chris, you enjoy yourself with your friends,' said Cliff, with a big smile. She left with

Sammy, who walked off asking if she'd heard right, did her dad just call her Chris or what?

'Oh dear, are you sure you'll be all right, Cliff?' asked Tessa, kindly. 'It's a shame you'll be eating on your own. I'd say come and join us, but –'

'It's women's talk, you wouldn't like it,' interjected Gina.

'Ugh, no thanks,' said Cliff ungraciously, as he looked around the room. 'I'm sure I'll find someone, I'm a big boy now. Go on, off you go to your ladies' lunch. Just don't spend the whole time talking about me, that's all!'

'He's up to something,' said Gina, as they were walking over to the restaurant. 'I'm sure of it. I know that look.'

'Really?' asked Tessa. 'D'you think so? Cliff?'

'He's not as honest and decent as he seems, you know.'

Tessa was shocked. She knew Fabio was Gina's favourite, that was obvious. But to hear a mother speak with such disloyalty about her own son, well, it made her feel very uncomfortable.

'I'm beginning to think all men are a bit like that,' said Tessa, to try to take the sting out of this particular subject.

'Yes, but some are worse than others,' said Gina, knowingly.

As Tessa was desperately thinking of something else to say, something to change the subject, Gina blurted out, 'He's like his father, you see.'

'Alfie? But I thought –'

'That he was perfect? No. Nearly,' she smiled, 'nearly. But he just had this one weak spot, especially when he was a younger man. He had all sorts of secrets then, only they weren't so secret.'

Tessa could tell from the tinny tone that had crept into Gina's voice that whatever it was, still hurt. She seemed to be bitter about whatever he'd done wrong, and probably with justification. From information gathered during her conversations with Gina, Tessa knew that Alfie had demanded her full attention at all times. He was the sort of man you didn't argue with, he did what he wanted to do. A like-it-or-lump-it person. And Gina had given herself wholeheartedly to her husband and his sons. To hear that Alfie wasn't necessarily worthy of such dedication was, strangely, distressing. Even though Tessa hadn't ever met the big man himself, she felt as if she knew him pretty well. 'What do you mean, secrets?'

'Well, he was very popular with the ladies.' Passing a glowering Mandy waiting at the entrance to the dining room, Gina hooked her handbag on to one of the chairs at their usual table. 'They used to love a chat with him you see, he'd brighten up their day. He always claimed they were after him, and I think some of them probably were, but I know of at least one example when it was round the other way.'

The two women went their separate ways around the buffet area, and having helped themselves from the increasingly predictable selection of cold meats, pasta salads and accompanying foliage, they sat down opposite each other.

'There was one particular woman, you see, who was always in the shop every time I went in. Jam jar blonde she was, tiny waist. Cliff was about nine or ten then, and little Fabio was still in his pram, bless him. We'd pop by on the way back from school, just to say hello, you know. And she was always there; either coming in, or just leaving, or – well, just there.'

'But couldn't that have been just coincidence?'

'Yes, that's exactly what he said,' said Gina, as she parcelled up a thin piece of greying ham with her knife and fork. 'And he got angry when I asked him about it. Said she was a young widow, it was just her and her little girl now, her husband had been drowned dead, he was a fisherman, you see. Alfie said she was very lonely, that was all. So she'd started hanging around the shop, with Alfie and the lads, because she said she missed the sound of men's voices.'

Tessa raised her eyebrows.

'I know,' agreed Gina, 'that's what I thought.' She toyed with a chunk of beetroot. 'So one night, when he thought I was at Bingo, I paid her a visit. I knocked on her door, and told her right there on the doorstep to leave my husband alone. I told her she could steal someone else's man, this one was not available. She tried to deny it, of course, but I knew she was guilty. I shouted at her, I called her every name under the moon; then I pushed her back inside the house, and slammed her own door in her face. She moved away after that, I never saw her again.'

'Good for you!' said Tessa. 'That showed her!'

'No.' Gina's brown eyes lost their fire. 'It's only now that I know how she felt. And so do you. She was lonely, Tessa. She'd lost her husband.'

Tessa swallowed her misplaced enthusiasm away.

'I was horrible to that poor woman. She didn't deserve it.'

Tessa really hoped Gina wasn't going to cry, yet again. To be honest, it was getting harder to be sympathetic nowadays, she was running out of comforting things to say. 'No, Gina, you did the right thing.'

'I thought so. But when I met with the solicitor about Alfie's will, she was in it. It seems her name was Moira, and he'd left her a thousand pounds.'

'What?!'

'It turns out there was something going on between them after all. She'd only moved down the road, to Southend, and they met up, every Wednesday afternoon, right up until he got sick.' She shook her head. 'And I always thought he was going in each week for supplies.' Gina sighed. 'The strange thing is, I wasn't even angry when I found out. That's typical Alfie, you see, he chose just the right time to let me know – when I was too sad to be angry with him!'

Tessa was amazed at Gina's capacity for wifely love, she hadn't been quite so positive when she'd found out about Jeremy's wandering willy.

Gina leaned across the table and gripped Tessa's arm. 'You won't tell anyone, will you, Tessa? I haven't said a word about it, not even to Fabio. There's no need for the boys to know that sort of thing about their father. And anyway, they've got their own secrets to keep. Which reminds me, I keep forgetting to tell you' – she took a sip of water and lowered her voice – 'I think there is trouble between Fabio and Michelle!'

'Oh, really?' said Tessa, trying very hard not to sound

at all interested. WHO ARE YOU KIDDING? shouted the little voice inside her.

'Yes, I think she's beginning to get on his nerves. And I can see why.' She sat back, waiting for Tessa to ask why.

So she had to. 'Why?'

'Well, it's these modern women – I don't understand it, it's crazy. They want to go out with a powerful man with an important job, because these men earn the big money, you see? Then, once these girls have got all their diamonds and sports cars and what-have-we, they have the cheek to complain that their men work too hard – they feel neglected, you see. It doesn't make sense to me. These silly girls can't understand that it was working so hard that got the men the money in the first place!'

'Has Fabio bought Michelle a car, then?' What?

'No, nothing like that, of course not! But she thinks she's inside with him – he told me the other day she left out a magazine with the address of a plastic surgeon circled in red pen. She's expecting him to pay for a booby job!'

'No!' Tessa suspected it had probably been his suggestion. It made her blush to think of how he'd enjoyed hers, which were definitely bigger than Michelle's. WAY HEY, RUMPY PUMPY! *Oh, please.*

'He won't give her the money, of course.'

'No?'

'Ooh no, not Fabio, he wouldn't do that. Oh no. He's not a big spender' – she smiled with pride – 'he's a big saver.'

UGH, MEAN WITH HIS MONEY, WHAT A TURN-OFF.
Shut up.

'And anyway, he's not a rich man either, but she doesn't know that. But he'd never waste his money on a woman's chest.'

'No ... so what does he spend it on?'

'Well, he's got a very big motorbike, which thank God he hardly drives, he keeps that in our garage; and you must have noticed his beautiful clothes? Oh yes, he takes good pride in his appearance, always likes to look nice, our Fabio. And he's got hundreds of videos, and CBs, and those VDV things, you know, the usual things a young man needs.'

HIMSELF. HE SPENDS IT ON HIMSELF.

'He's always said that he would buy me and Papà a house one day, a big one, right on the sea front, but now – well, I don't suppose that's going to happen any more, is it?' Gina's dark eyes became crystal clear. 'If only he had found the right woman before his father passed away, Alfie would have been so proud of him and his little *bambini* ...'

Tessa knew the signs and changed the subject before the tears came. So they talked about men and their fascination with wheels, Billy Connolly going round Australia on a motorbike, Alfie's favourite comedian Benny Hill, milk deliveries in Edinburgh up all those stairs, keeping fit without paying all that money to join a gym, and then Gina left the table to go upstairs for her nap.

After coffee, during which Tessa noticed with amusement that Cliff had been lumbered with the Village Idiot for company, she went in search of Sammy. They'd hardly seen each other since they'd been here, perhaps they could spend a couple of hours together now. That was what they were here for, after all – a bit of quality time together. Maybe they could take a walk, or go for a swim in the sea. Perhaps they should both take up snorkelling, learn something new, together. She should use these extra few days wisely.

As she neared the beach, Tessa could see the birthday barbecue still smoking away, but there were only a few teenagers left lurking around it. Christabelle was there, but without Sammy. Odd.

'Any idea where she could be?' asked Tessa.

Christabelle crimsoned. 'Um, no, not really.' She looked down at her feet, or rather her boots.

'She's further along the beach, that way,' said a very pretty girl, with an 'A' on the front of her pink T-shirt, picked out in little diamonds.

'Thanks.' Tessa made her way towards the waterski hut, picking her route through the sunloungers neatly arranged in rows along the shore. It was blisteringly hot, the sun was stinging her skin. It was too much; Tessa never thought she'd catch herself thinking this, but she was getting a bit sick of the sun. She'd never complain about Edinburgh summers again.

'Ah, Jamie!' she said, he was hanging up some wet life jackets, 'have you seen Sammy?'

He didn't reply, he just grinned and pointed towards the sea. There, in the knee-high water right in front of them, was a young couple clamped together, oblivious of the other swimmers. As they came up for air, Tessa recognized them. Sammy and the Nebulizer. Sucking their faces off each other, as if they hadn't eaten for days. Tessa was no body language expert, but it looked as if her sweet sixteen-year-old daughter had both hands down the front of his shorts; and Neb had one hand up her wetly transparent T-shirt, and the other spread across her daughter's schoolgirl arse. In broad daylight. In front of the whole beach.

'Sammy!' she shouted, aghast.

Sammy opened her eyes, saw her mother, and went back to what she'd been doing, with renewed fervour.

Tessa ran to the edge of the water. 'Sammy! Stop it!'

But Sammy took no notice, and Neb's grip on her bottom seemed to increase. As did Sammy's interest in the contents of his trunks.

Shocked, Tessa waded into the sea, and pulled them apart. Sammy fell backwards into the water, and resurfaced, spluttering. Neb laughed at her. So Sammy pushed him backwards, and he too went under. But instead of coming back up, he grabbed Sammy's feet under the water and pulled them out from under her and she fell in again, with a loud shriek. People on the beach must have thought it was yet another slapstick display dreamed up by the Entertainments Department.

Up in the privacy of their room, Sammy turned on her mother. 'What is it with you? Are you jealous or something? We were only having a bit of fun, god, honestly.'

'What do you think you were doing?' Tessa asked. 'You were acting like a common tart – what on earth must everyone have thought? We could all see what you were up to, you know. Doesn't that worry you? Aren't you ashamed of yourself?'

Sammy didn't say anything. She just hardened her face to no expression, and stared at her mother.

Tessa continued. 'Oh, Sammy, this isn't how we brought you up. Why are you being so awful these days? This isn't like you, this isn't my little girl. I can't understand it, it's as if you don't care any more. You throw all your clothes on the floor, you come in at all hours of the day and night – you treat this place –' Tessa stopped herself just in time.

'– like a hotel? Oh please.'

Tessa tried to ignore her. 'The thing is, Sammy, I don't think you're turning into a very nice person. You have to admit, you are being a bit selfish at the moment – you don't care whether you wake me up or not, you crash around the room anyway. You haven't got a single nice word to say to me, in fact I think you're avoiding me – and now I find you behaving like a prostitute in front of the whole world!'

'Hah!' Her daughter's face, a picture of insolence, had a certain ugliness to it that Tessa hadn't seen before. 'That's a bit rich, coming from you!'

'What's that supposed to mean?'

'Well, you're not exactly behaving like a nun yourself, are you?'

'What are you talking about?'

'You and Fabio. We all know.'

'Know what? There's nothing to know.' BUT YOU'VE SEEN HIS WILLY! *Oh fuck off, not now.*

'Then why are you blushing?'

239

'I'm not.'

'You are.'

'Oh, Sammy, wait till Dad hears about all this, he's going to be so disappointed . . .'

'Yes,' said Sammy, going into the bathroom, 'isn't he? He's not going to be very impressed with you shagging the staff, now is he?'

'Oh don't be so stupid,' blustered Tessa, 'what utter nonsense.' Her face was burning now, pulsating, throbbing with shame.

'I know all about it, Mum. Bonnie told Chris, who told me, of course.' She started to towel dry the ends of her hair. 'They all think it's rather sweet. I think it's disgusting.'

'What d'you mean, *they*?'

'The guys. All my friends. Everyone. They all know.'

Tessa couldn't bear to even think about that. She tried to fight back. 'And now "everyone" has seen for themselves that you're a total slut.'

'Ah well, like mother, like daughter,' sniffed Sammy as she changed sides with the towel. 'And they don't think that at all. All the girls know why I was doing it.'

'Why?'

'To make Jamie jealous, of course.'

'Well, I don't think that little plan's worked, he didn't seem at all impressed, he was too busy laughing. Perhaps you should face up to it, Sammy, he doesn't want to be with you. I'm sorry, but I can understand why; no man wants to be with a tart.'

'Well it doesn't seem to bother Fabio, does it? He's got Michelle, and Becca on the side, and even Angelique wants him to take her virginity. Face it, Mum, he doesn't actually like you, you're just another willing body to him.'

There was a silence while mother and daughter each considered their hurt from the other's stinging words. Sammy threw the towel over her head and started to rub vigorously. Tessa moved quietly round the room, straightening things, tidying, trying to work out where to go from here. What would Felicity do?

Eventually, Tessa said, 'Look, Sammy, can we start again? I just want us to be friends, that's all. That's why I came to find you in the first place, I wanted to check that you were happy, see how you felt about having to stay here, that sort of thing.' Her voice was a bit shaky. 'I don't want us to fight.'

Sammy came out from under the towel and stared at her. Her eyes were rounded, she looked like a baby rabbit caught in her mother's headlights. Tessa decided that all Felicity's strategies were too complicated for her, it was best to just come out with it.

'I miss my little girl.'

That was it. As soon as she said it, she knew it to be the truth. That's what had been bothering her these past few months. Tessa wanted her baby back, and her husband for that matter. Her whole identity, the wife and mother she had so perfectly become, had been stolen from her and she couldn't bear it any more.

'Can I have a hug?' Tessa smiled a watery smile and held her arms open, but Sammy stayed put on the bed, dry-eyed, arms folded. 'Please?' Sammy scowled at the floor.

So Tessa went over and sat down beside her daughter, and embraced her. She stroked her baby's hair, just like she used to. But Sammy didn't soften, she didn't move a muscle, just sat rigid and stared straight ahead.

'What's the matter? You're not too old for a cuddle, are you?' Tessa tried to look into her daughter's eyes for a clue.

But Sammy looked away. 'Stop it, Mum. There's no point.'

'No point? There doesn't have to be a point, does there? It's just a cuddly hug. All I want is for us to be close again, that's all. That's not too much to –'

'– Dad's moving his family down to London.'

Stab.

'And I'm going with them.'

Twist.

Punch.

'No.'

Can't be.

'Yes.' Oof!

Kick.

Ow!

'You can't.'

'I can, it's all arranged.'

'No, I won't let you.'

'You can't stop me. I'm old enough to decide for myself now, Dad asked a solicitor. I'm going to sixth-form college down there, to do my A levels. I've already got a place, starting in September. Next month.'

'But school –'

'Dad's sorted it all out, they know I'm not coming back.'

'But, but, I thought you hated Mona the Moaner . . .'

'I won't see much of her, will I? I'll be at college all day, and out partying all night, hopefully. It's going to be so cool!'

Hurt and pain, hurt and pain. More hurt and pain. 'Why didn't either of you tell me?' *Why am I always last on both your lists, when you both know you're first on mine?*

'Look. We knew you'd be a bit upset, which was why Dad said it was best to tell you on holiday, in a nice place, you know.' Now she looked at her mother. 'Don't worry, Mum, it'll be fine. You should be happy for me and Dad, not sad. We're going to be out of your way at last, you won't have to put up with us any more!'

Choking, need air. Need space. Need to be on my own. Need to get out.

'Mum?'

Go.

'Listen, I'll come up and see you in the holidays, Dad said I could fly back . . .'

Door slam.

Run.

Run.

*

By the end of the working day, Felicity was fully ensconced in Fabio's office. Her dear brother-in-law clearly couldn't organize a sick bucket for a hen-night, so she'd had to be quite firm with him. She'd quickly established that he hadn't a clue what was going on, or how long this strike was likely to last. And there was no evidence of any attempt to organize alternative ways for them to get home; clearly he'd been relying on it ending any day now.

And the Crisis Management Team weren't much help either. They'd sounded most put out when Felicity rang them in London to introduce herself. They said they were only able to deal directly with Fabio, as he was the company employee. But they hadn't been much use to him up to now as far as she could see. If only he'd got a move on a few days ago, when all this started, they'd at least have been able to ferry everyone over to the mainland in small groups on local boats, or something similar. But now, from what she could gather from one of the kitchen porter's uncle's cousin's pidgin English on the phone, they were only ferrying local people on business or dire emergencies. Nobody seemed at all interested in a bunch of frustrated holidaymakers. Some people she spoke to said that the strike could end any day now. Others said it could go on for weeks.

The whole thing was a bloody mess. Felicity decided to work on the basis that they were going to be here for at least a few more days, and that while Fabio and the staff kept everybody distracted she would work on a solution. Even if it meant booking the QE2 on her credit card, she'd get them home.

So she'd taken up residence on the other side of Fabio's desk, facing him, as that meant she'd miss nothing. She'd witness every phone call, see everything he wrote down, hear any news as soon as it came in. He'd protested about this, of course, saying that he really had done everything possible, it was just a question of waiting; but Felicity knew that eventually he was going to be very grateful for her help. Her brother-in-law was very handsome, but he wasn't a natural-born leader.

Her head was spinning by the time she left the office, and she was still bursting with ideas as she made her way up to the room, to get ready for dinner. There were so many things to think about, to work out, to organize. What about the navy? Had anyone thought of commandeering a submarine? How many could one carry? She'd already told Nikki to email all the cruise lines, to see if they could hitch a lift with one of their passing ships that regularly crossed the horizon. Oh yes, Felicity was really fired up, this was what she was good at – this was what she was for.

The door was unlocked, which meant her husband was already in. 'Hi, honey, I'm ho-ome!' Felicity sing-songed as she closed the door behind her. It was just like being back home in London, she always said that when she came through the door after yet another over-stressed, overstretched day at the office.

Cliff was lying on the bed, fully-clothed, asleep, with his mouth open. Which was just like back home in London too. He'd even managed to perfect the re-creation by snoring. His T-shirt was ruckled up, exposing his ever-expanding beer belly. There was a trail of saliva slugging out of the corner of his mouth, and his arms and legs were twitching, like an old dog dreaming of chasing young rabbits.

'Cliff!' Felicity shouted, perhaps a little louder than was necessary. 'Wake up!'

He came to with a snuttle, the sort old people do when they're roused from a daytime nap. 'Whassatime?'

'Time to start getting ready for dinner.' Felicity swung into her getting-undressed-to-get-dressed routine. 'Be a darling and run one of your famous baths for me, will you? I honestly don't think I've got the energy.' She kicked her sandals off. 'God, that brother of yours is – well, extraordinary. Just when you're about to lose your temper with him for being possibly the most disorganized man on earth, he gives you this smile which quite takes your breath away. You can't get cross with him then, it's most disarming. I forget, actually, how exquisitely beautiful he is. He really is one of the most handsome men I've ever met; he could be a male model, you know. He's in bloody good nick for his age. I can see why everybody loves him, especially all the women – he's just gorgeous, real eye candy, and so smooth with it –'

'Have dinner with me tonight.' Cliff was sitting on the edge of the bed, looking up at her with the imploring eyes of an abandoned hound.

Felicity tried to ignore the words that were running round her head; 'pathetic', 'lapdog', 'wimp', etc. 'Well I am, I mean we are, we're all eating together as usual, aren't we?'

'No, I mean just us. Please?'

'But why? It seems a bit anti-social, don't you think?'

'I just want to spend some time alone with my wife, that's all.'

Yes, she was afraid he was going to say that. 'But what about your mother? And Tessa?'

'They'll manage.'

'Well, yes, but –'

'Please?'

She paused. Looking down at her husband, with that horrible Battersea Dogs Home expression on his face, Felicity realized with a shudder that she couldn't think of anything she'd less like to do. She knew already how it would be. He'd just sit there, listening to her talking about everything she'd achieved today, not contributing to the conversation at all, but nodding. And then, when she tried to include him by asking him a question, he'd tell her some boring story that she'd heard a million times before, about some glamorous fashion shoot he was on thirty years ago. And then they'd have nothing else to say, and would sit in silence for the rest of the meal. She would have to make all the effort, and she was tired, she couldn't face it. Not tonight. Not any night, actually.

'I need to be with you, Fliss.'

'But you will be with me —'

'Alone.' He got up. 'Look, don't make me spell it out.'

'Spell what out?' she said, making him spell it out.

'I want to try and get us back on track, keep us going, you know — rekindle things.'

'Yes, well, you know, so do I, of course I do, and normally that'd be really nice, but —'

'But what?'

But out here we can't cover ourselves with the blanket of domestic details, she wanted to say. We haven't got anything to talk about. We haven't got anything to say to each other any more. 'Well, is there any point?' she asked, in a quiet voice.

'What d'you mean?'

'Well, I think we both know, don't you?'

'Know what?'

Felicity sighed and sat down on her side of the bed. 'Oh Cliff, I don't know how to say this.'

'Well don't say it then.' He came and sat down beside her, pawed her knee.

'No?' She looked into his eyes, sad, faded eyes, tired eyes.

'No. Just give me a chance, Fliss, just a little bit more time. Please?' He stroked the side of her face. She made herself let him. 'I want to hold all this together, I really do.' Good god, he was nearly in tears. 'I want to make this family work. I don't want to fuck up again, make the same old – well, you know, you and Spike are so important to me, but I need your help, I don't know how to do this . . .'

Someone knocked on the door. Thank god, thought Felicity as she leapt to answer it, she really couldn't deal with all this relationship bollocks right now. It was Tessa.

'Hi.'

'You all right? You look a bit shaken and stirred.'

'I am. Shaken, not all right.' She looked very vulnerable. 'Where've you been? I couldn't find you this afternoon, I thought you were going to try the monoski. Kenton was most disappointed, as was the rest of the beach.'

'I know, I was stuck in the office with the fabulous Fabio all afternoon.' She adopted a stage whisper. 'He really is gorgeous you know, you really must try a bit harder to get off with him.'

'Yes, look, can we talk later? I really need some of

your down-to-earth wisdom.' Tessa's voice cracked and she sniffed. 'Please, if that's all right.'

'Of course. Bucket and Spade, usual time. See you there.' She shut the door. Cliff had started her bath. 'That was poor Tessa,' she called out, 'she looked really awful, as if she'd been crying all day. Oh dear, I wonder what's happened?' Perfect. 'I'm really sorry, Cliff, but I'm going to have to ask her to eat with us, she looked distraught – and she is here on her own after all.' And before he could protest, she continued, 'And your mother always has dinner with us. We can't leave her to fend for herself, can we? She'll only start crying about being lonely, again.'

'Charity begins at home, you know,' said Cliff with the heaviness of self-pity, as he came out of the bathroom. 'You should look after your own family, before you start interfering with other people's.'

But instead of rising to his bait, Felicity pretended not to hear him. She couldn't be bothered to argue with him any more. God, tomorrow she was going to do everything within her considerable power to get them out of here, she wasn't sure she could stand much more of this.

*

Gina looked around the dinner table and despaired. They brought it on themselves, this generation, they really did. In her time they stuck with what they'd got in front of them today, they didn't waste their energy on the future. So they had time to enjoy their lives, you see, they didn't rush round like headless hens, trying to grab a bigger this and a better that, wanting more than they needed. They just got on with it – something this lot were incapable of doing. Getting on with it, enjoying today.

Tessa was all right, of course. In fact, Gina had become very fond of her. It was a pity one of her boys hadn't married someone like her; she was certainly one of the few sensible people here, and the one who reminded Gina most of herself. She had a kind heart, and the patience necessary to survive in this chaotic world. But she had a misplaced loyalty to that ex-husband of hers. How could she love a man who loved another woman more? But instead of getting on with finding herself a new husband, she was still hanging around this idiot, who could reduce her to tears without even having the blood and guts to speak to her himself.

'I just can't believe he's done all this behind my back,' she was saying. 'How could he do this to me? It's just so, so – *awful.*'

He can do this because you let him, Gina wanted to say. He has no respect for you, and why should he? Here you are, an attractive woman still young enough to be adored, wasting your time on a man who doesn't want to waste his time on you. After all, to live in the past is to waste the future. Until Tessa realized that, she was going to remain the family doormat. And no wonder that daughter was so rude to her mother, she had no respect either. If Gina's boys had ever, ever spoken to her or their father in that tone of voice, they'd have been beaten for it. There was too much liberal in life these days, children were being allowed to get away with manslaughter.

'Spike was wearing a bloody Snow White outfit when

I went to pick him up this afternoon, can you credit it?'

And Cliff wasn't much better. In fact, he was wasting his life too. He spent a lot of his time looking after everyone else, but he didn't do it very well, you see. Too busy promising everybody the world to deliver it. He always had a lot on, Cliff, but never anything to show for it. His father used to say he was like a Jack Russell, trotting around with a string of sausages dangling from his mouth, but never stopping to eat them. It was a shame, really, he tried so hard. But nothing he did ever came to very much. He was a good photographer, of course, but these days the cameras are so good it's hard to take a bad picture, apparently. Still, he had a good heart, and as Alfie said, he meant well. But people who only start things off, without seeing them through, leave a trail of unfinished business behind them ...

'I've just had a great idea – what about helicopters? They don't need an airport, they can just land right here, on the Village Green!' Felicity knocked her wine back. 'God, I am brilliant!'

No wonder he'd taken up with her, thought Gina, she was like a human whirlwind. She had all the get-up-and-go he wanted. Gina felt sad, she'd hoped that going on holiday with Felicity would bring them closer. She wanted to be friends with her daughter-in-law, it didn't seem right that they were almost strangers. She and Eileen had been very close. Still were. She'd even got on with Penny, at first. But Felicity – no.

'What d'you mean, permission to land? I'll give them permission.'

They had nothing in common, she could see that now. Felicity couldn't cook, but she was the first to complain about the food here. She was very good at her job, but wouldn't give the same commitment to her family. She was an expert on childcare, but didn't want to care for her own child. In brief, Felicity was the exact opposite of Gina.

'Oh for god's sake, what's the matter with him now?' Felicity read the room number on the little blackboard being paraded around by the Village Idiot, like a bimbo in a boxing ring. 'Have you noticed, Tess, that the board used to say "baby needs a hug in Room blah-blah", and now it says "baby needs parenting in Room blah-blah" instead? They're really getting arsey, aren't they? I'm going to have to have a word with Bonnie about that tomorrow morning, it's not on.'

'Poor little Spike is very upset,' announced Tania as she stopped at their table. 'I've done my best with him, but he says he wants his mum.' She looked at Felicity with those Miss Great Britain green eyes.

Felicity looked like she wanted to punch her. 'But we've just spent the last hour-and-a-half getting him to sleep!'

'I'm afraid he wasn't fully down when you left,' said Tania. 'I've been doing my best to pacify him, I even took him into Mummy and Daddy's room and got into your bed with him' – Cliff was choking, he seemed to have got something stuck in his throat – 'but no luck, I'm afraid. Perhaps his dad will come with me, we could see what we could do together?'

'Look, I'll be up in a minute,' said Felicity, as she

slapped the choking Cliff on the back, with rather more force than was necessary.

'He's in his gran's room now,' informed Tania. 'It's like musical beds with you lot, isn't it?!'

'I'll go and see to him,' said Gina.

'Oh Gina, are you sure, thanks,' said Felicity, a bit too hastily.

'Yes, I was going to go to bed myself soon anyway.' Get away from you lot, she wanted to say. Get a bit of peace. 'Goodnight, everybody.'

'Ooh, my arms are killing me,' groaned Tania. 'This blackboard is heavier than you think.'

'It's OK to put it down now,' said Felicity, 'you've found us.'

As Gina picked her way through the tables, waving and smiling to the other diners, she realized she'd made a lot of friends over the past couple of weeks. But there was nobody she wanted to be with down here. She needed a good chat upstairs, with Alfie; his voice had been fading a bit lately, she hadn't been able to feel him so much. She needed to make contact again.

'Mamma!' Fabio was walking into the restaurant, just as she was coming out. He greeted her with his arms outstretched. 'Where are you hurrying off to? Don't you want to eat with me?'

Michelle's tidy little head popped up from behind his shoulder. 'Evening, Mrs Clifton!' she said in her silly, tinny little voice.

'Michelle.' Gina folded her arms and clasped her handbag to her bosom. 'I'm going up to sort out little Spike,' she said to Fabio, 'he hasn't settled yet.'

Fabio linked arms with his mother. 'You go on ahead, get us a table,' he said dismissively to Michelle, 'I'm going to walk Mum to the lift.'

I'm not a dog, Gina wanted to say, but didn't. Fabio would be crushed by such criticism, he was a very sensitive boy. 'How's it going with Michelle?' she asked instead, as they walked slowly down the corridor.

He sighed. 'D'you know, Mum, I don't think there's a woman in the world who's right for me. There's something wrong with all of them.'

'What's wrong with her, then?'

'Oh, I don't know. Nothing. She's fine. Apart from wanting to spend money I haven't got, on things she hasn't got!' He laughed. 'No, I think it's me who's got the problem. I just get bored with them so quickly. Once I find out what makes them, er, tick – then I lose interest, and want to move on to the next one.'

'But I think that's very sensible, *mio piccino*. You don't want to marry the wrong girl, look at the mess your brother's got himself into. So, who's the next lucky girl?' Gina wasn't going to try to persuade him to stick with that gold-digger.

'Well, that's the trouble, isn't it? We're stuck out here for another three months at least.'

'What?' exclaimed Gina, panic-stricken. 'Is it that bad? *Dio mio*, what kind of people are they, these airport traffickers, that we have to –'

'Not you, Mum,' reassured Fabio, with a smile, 'us. The staff. You're all right, you'll be off home as soon as this stupid strike is over.'

'And how long will that take?'

'I don't know. Three, four days? If I set Felicity on to them, it could all be over by tomorrow lunchtime!' He pushed the button to call the lift. 'Don't worry about anything, Mamma, you're going to be fine. You're with your family, we're all here to look after you.' He bent down and kissed her on her forehead.

'And when are you going to start your own family, Fabio?'

He pretended he'd been winded by a blow to the stomach. 'Whoah! Mamma, please! Where did that come from?'

'Well, you know. Time is running out. You will have to start looking for a wife.'

'A wife?!' He looked at her as if she'd said a rude word.

'You could do worse than Tessa, you know.'

'Yes, thank you very much, Mamma, but I think I'll pick my own wife, if you don't mind.' He grinned. 'It's a tough job, searching for the perfect woman, but someone's got to do it!'

The lift ding'd its arrival. Gina hugged her big grown-up boy. 'She's very nice, and I think she likes you.' She kissed him, both sides, and got into the lift. 'And I like her. Perhaps you should try her next.'

'Night night, Mamma, love you,' he waved, smiling at her and shaking his head as the doors closed, '*Dorma bene.*'

Gina felt herself warming inside, as the lift took her up to the first-floor landing. They were all right really, her boys. Neither of them had good women in their lives, but who could blame them when you considered what was on offer? And they were honourable men, both of them. Cliff was a good father, and Fabio was an excellent son. What more could a mother want for her children?

The lift doors opened on the second floor to reveal Bonnie, sitting on a chair, reading a book and eating a Mars bar. Being an observant person, Gina couldn't help but notice lots more ripped-up chocolate wrappers underneath her seat. Litterbug.

'He's in your room,' said Bonnie rudely through her mouthful, hardly bothering to look up. Gina thought she said 'little sod' after that, under her breath, but she couldn't be sure.

She let herself into the room quietly. Spike was sitting at the pillow end of her bed, all hunched up like a garden gnome, hiding his face behind his cuggie.

'Spike?'

'Go way!' came the muffled reply.

'It's me. Nannygranny. Come on, *poverino*' – she sat down on the bed beside him – 'let's have a cuddle.'

But he pushed her away. 'No. I want my mummy.'

'Well,' said Gina, carefully, 'she's not here.'

'She's never here!' He was puffy and red in the face, he'd obviously been crying his little heart out for some time. 'Why isn't she ever here?'

Gina tried to think of a nice way of handling this. She couldn't.

'I don't think she likes me any more, does she?' His voice was quiet, his chin was trembling. 'I've been bad too much, she's cross with me. I'm a bad, naughty boy. Is it because I'm bad?'

'No!' Gina held his shoulders square, so that he had

to look at her. 'You are a good, good little boy. You have done nothing wrong. Never has there been a better boy, do you understand that? You are the best boy in the world, the most loved boy in the world.' She stroked his soft cheek, to calm him. 'I love you, we all love you.'

'Then where is my mummy? Why hasn't she come up to see me? Has she been shot by hunters?'

'What?'

'Like Bambi? We saw that today, his mummy died, it was really really sad.' He began to cry again. 'Is my mummy dead now?'

'No. She is not. She's downstairs. She's – busy, that's all.' Too busy to give you what you need, baby boy. She can't, you see. She hasn't got the love for you. Why do these women have children, if they haven't got time for them? Gina could feel the fear for her grandson welling up inside her heart now. She had to stop, keep strong for the boy. 'Come on, in you get,' she said, as she pulled back the covers for him. 'You get those little piggy toes inside, and snuggle down like a good boy.'

'Can I stay the whole night here, in your room, with you?' asked Spike, as he found the comfy place in the bed.

'Yes, you can,' said Gina, who'd been badgered non-stop for the last week by her grandson to let him do exactly this.

'Yessss!' hissed Spike, as if he'd won the World Cup. 'And are you going to sleep in the same bed as me?'

'Well, I don't know –' Gina was hesitant at the prospect of an uncomfortable night. It meant she'd have a bad day tomorrow.

'Please?'

Who could say no? 'All right. But you'd better be safe asleep by the time I get in, or I'll take you back to your own bed. OK?'

'OK.' He wriggled in anticipation, and yawned. 'Are we going to have a lie-in in the morning?'

'Yes, let's,' replied his grandmother, 'that would be nice, wouldn't it?'

As Gina changed into her nightdress in the bathroom, she realized how tired she was. Too tired to get angry at Felicity for neglecting her own son, too tired to get angry at Bonnie for letting them watch *Bambi*, too tired to get angry at Michelle for not being the right woman for Fabio.

Before switching the bathroom light off, she opened the wardrobe door in the bedroom. There was just enough reflected light to pick out the clothes inside. Now, what would it be tonight? His golf jumper with the diamonds on it, or one of his Sunday shirts, or perhaps that jazzy short-sleeved one he always wore on the August bank holiday . . .

In the end, she picked an old vest, as it was the least bulky item she'd packed for him. Well, what with Spike being in there too, there wouldn't be room for much else. And it still had a strong smell of his skin, of his hair oil, of him.

Gina wept quietly, just one more tear, as she carefully spread the vest out on her side of the pillow, and laid her head upon it as she tucked herself in to her sleeping grandson. Help me, Alfie, help me, she cried inside. I need you. We need you. We miss you.

There was no reply. But as she was dropping off to sleep, Gina felt a big heavy arm curl around her waist, and she could feel his hot breath on the back of her neck, just before he kissed her gently on her way.

*

Cliff woke up because nobody had woken him up. He'd woken up before, of course, in anticipation of Spike crashing in as usual, but he hadn't done that yet, and so Cliff had stolen a few precious moments and gone back to sleep. Sort of thing.

He'd been having one of those dreams that haunts in half-sleep, the ones where it's difficult to know if they're true or not. He'd been dreaming about Tania's tits. Last night, in his dream or for real, while everybody was busy in the Bucket and Spade playing Guess the Cocktail Concoction, she'd taken him by the hand and led him down to the beach. Then, very slowly, very very slowly, she'd unbuttoned her little top, smiling, licking her lips, as the little pearl buttons glinted in the moonlight. He could see her bra now, then a little bit more, ooh, yes, he could just see them, heaving with passion, bursting to get out of there and into his mouth. He felt his cock harden as they lay down on the sand, he threw his knee across her and went to mount her –

'Cliff!'

He opened his eyes, and found himself staring down at Felicity's horrified, over-moisturized face.

'What are you doing? I can hardly breathe – get off!' As he rolled away, she scrabbled about on the bedside table for her watch. 'Ohmigod, it's eight forty-five! I've got to get up, I was supposed to meet Fabio for breakfast before our meeting with the HODs.'

'Who?' he asked, as grateful as she was for this diversion.

'The Heads of Department,' she said, with a do-you-know-nothing look.

'Right.' He put his arms underneath his pillow as he turned on to his stomach, and waited for things to die down a bit. 'Where's Spike? He's sleeping late, isn't he?'

'Well I'm not surprised if he is, he was awake half the night. Gina must have gone up to him at what, ten thirty? I should think he's having a lie-in, don't wake him up yet.' She dashed round the room, climbing into clothes and putting on make-up simultaneously. 'What're you up to today?' she remembered to ask, but not to sound interested.

'Oh you know, the usual. Breakfast, drop Spikey off, volleyball, lunch, football, bit of a swim maybe, pick Spike up, take him to kids' supper, watch yet another boring kids' video in the Kids Kottage, give him his bath, put him to bed, have a pre-dinner nap, drinks, dinner, more drinks, bed. Bloody hell,' he said, 'makes me knackered just thinking about it. I thought this was supposed to be a holiday – I've got a full day ahead of me already.'

'Well I,' said Felicity as she shooshed her hair around in front of the mirror, tweaking bits here and there and tying the rest up with a Mont Blanc ballpoint, her usual arrangement for work, 'will be very busy all day and most of the evening, too. So I won't be around much today, I'm afraid.'

260

'Oh well, never mind,' said Cliff, into his pillow, 'I'll manage.'

'Right then, I'm off. You'd better go and get Spike soon-ish, or you'll be late for school.'

'It's not school,' said Cliff, turning round in the bed too late to see his wife disappear down the corridor and shut the door loudly behind her, 'it's a crappy little organization, run by a Nazi. But some of her commandants are a bit of all right ...' And he had a quick wank on the vision of Tania in a peaked cap, bursting out of a tight uniform, stockings, suspenders, the whole lot. Fucking brilliant.

Cliff was in a really good mood by the time he knocked on his mother's door. If he could manage to keep the Tania thing down to just a fantasy, then this might be the easiest way to stay faithful to Felicity. He could even make love to his wife imagining he was doing it to Tania, if he was clever. He didn't have to have the real thing all the time, did he? Well, he could try this first. Every time he wanted to do something with Tania, he'd do it to Felicity instead. He'd bloody well force her to have dinner with him tonight, just the two of them.

No answer. Maybe she'd taken him down to breakfast already. Don't know why she didn't do that anyway, Cliff thought to himself, as he jogged down the stairs, save me the hassle.

But they weren't in the dining room either. Nor at the Kids Kottage. Fabio was standing at Reception when Cliff came in. 'Seen Mum?'

'Not since last night, no. Why?'

'Can't find Spike. No one's seen either of them.'

The brothers frowned at each other. Without taking his eyes away from Cliff's, Fabio said to Lovely Dawn, 'Give me a room key. *Now!*'

They didn't wait for the lift, they walked quickly up the stairs two by two, and then broke into a run down the corridor to Gina's room.

Fabio knocked loudly on the door. 'Mamma?!' But they didn't give her time to reply, they went in anyway.

'Hi, Dad,' whispered Spike from the bed, 'we're having a lie-in. Ssssh! Nannygranny's still asleep.'

Gina must have died only a short time before, as her body was still warm. There was, however, a gentle smile on her peaceful face. She was happy, at last.

11. The Truth

FELICITY

I remember that day very clearly. It
was when everything changed. I woke
up that morning thinking there was
no reason to panic; by the end of the
afternoon I couldn't think of one reason not to.

*

'What do you mean, you don't understand English? For
fuck's sake, you bloody moron – hello? Hello? Bugger!'
Felicity slammed the phone down hard, hard and loud
enough to make Nikki the secretary actually get up from
behind her desk outside and knock on the door, coming
in before Felicity could say don't.

'Everything all right?'

'No, it damn well isn't!' Felicity rubbed her face in
her hands. She was tired, she'd not slept very well last
night due to Cliff's snoring, which seemed to be getting
louder every night. It had now progressed from small
tractor level up to the full combine harvester, and even
screaming '*Shut up!*' into his ear had had no effect. So
she'd lain awake most of the night, plotting how to
murder him without being found out. And then she'd
overslept, and then an ashen-faced Cliff had told her

about Gina, and just the thought of Spike lying there beside his dead grandmother made her stomach churn so much that she was feeling sick. And to top it all, Fabio had taken to his room and hadn't been seen since.

Which had left Felicity to handle everything on her own. She'd called both undertakers listed in the local version of the yellow pages, and both had come up with a different reason for not being able to deal with Gina's body. The first claimed they weren't taking any more work on until the owner of the firm returned from holiday; and the second had seemed quite interested, until they found out where they had to collect the body from, and then the stupid man had suddenly pretended not to understand English. Even the doctor had seemed unwilling to tell her when he'd visit to issue a death certificate. He'd said he'd call her back, if you please.

'Poor Fabio, is he really poorly?' Nikki looked genuinely concerned. 'Maybe I should take him some grapes, or something –'

'No!' snapped Felicity. 'He's shocked and upset, that's all, he's not ill! He's lost his mother, for christ's sake. We'll have to leave him be for the time being, I'm sure he'll come out when he's feeling better.'

'Well, OK then,' Nikki retreated, 'but tell me if there's anything I can do to help. It's just not the same without him.' And she shut the door, in a bit of a huff, too loudly.

Alone, Felicity wasn't sure what to feel. She was numb, she didn't feel anything yet, she'd gone into organizational mode. Truth be told, she wasn't too surprised that Gina had died in her sleep. Wasn't this quite usual with couples who'd been together for such a long time? One died quite soon after the other, apparently. Within three months in fact, according to Tessa, who'd seen several documentaries on the subject.

No, she'd been more surprised at Fabio's immediate reaction than anything else. Straightaway, he'd made them promise to keep his mother's death a secret. He'd said it would only worry people, even cause a sense of panic, which wouldn't help anyone, the situation was bad enough already. But once he'd left, Cliff had said she was his mother too, and he wanted people to know; she'd made a lot of friends here, she couldn't suddenly 'go missing'. So before long the whole camp was talking about it. And later on that morning, Nikki and Lovely Dawn had come into the office to offer their condolences; and that's when Fabio had visibly blanched, and gone to his room.

Leaving Felicity to deal with it all. But what was she supposed to do with the body, for christ's sake? She'd turned the air conditioning in Gina's room up to arctic, but they couldn't just leave her there indefinitely. On the other hand, if the airport was closed they couldn't fly the body home either.

For once, Felicity Followthrough Clifton was stumped.

*

Tessa just couldn't take it in. Gina, dead. Gina was dead. Gina is dead.

She'd seemed fine last night. Tessa had even thought she was cheering up a bit these days.

Gina's dead. Not coming to lunch. Never coming to lunch again.

Tessa left the buffet area with her plate and found another place – she couldn't bear the thought of eating at their usual table – and sat down. She couldn't believe it. Gina had died, she'd died.

Of grief, probably. The grief had finally overwhelmed her, swallowed her up. She didn't want to live any more, she'd often said that, no point; but Tessa had pretended not to hear, changed the subject.

What if it was suicide? Perhaps Gina had killed herself! No, she wouldn't, would she? Not with Spike there, surely. No.

Not sure what to do with herself now, or even how to be, Tessa opened her book. It was the last of the pile she'd brought out with her, a literary prizewinner which, to be honest, she'd hoped she wouldn't have time to read; now she couldn't work out what it was about anyway, the little black words were swimming on the white sea in front of her. But it gave her something to look at. Gina – dead. Not here any more. Incredible. Awful. Unbelievable, she just couldn't take it in.

'OK if we join you?' Mr Pink and his run-ragged wife were standing in front of her. Tessa gave up on her book and nodded.

'Isn't it awful about Fabio's mother?' asked Olivia, as she sat down on the chair beside Tessa. 'I can't believe it!'

Mr Pink didn't say anything, he was too busy yomping through his mountain of niçoise.

'You were good friends with her, weren't you?' asked Olivia.

'Yes,' replied Tessa, who really didn't want to talk about it, in case she made a fool of herself and cried in front of them.

'She seemed so nice,' commiserated Olivia.

'Yes, she was,' swallowed Tessa, 'she was lovely.' Oh god, her voice had gone all wobbly.

She saw Olivia decide to change the subject. 'Are you on a diet too?'

'No,' said Tessa, relieved, 'I'm just a bit sick of the food, that's all.'

'Me too,' said Olivia, who had less than a mouthful of everything on her plate. 'I must say, I don't want to sound ungrateful, it's jolly nice here and everything, but I can't wait to get back to Marks and Spencers.'

'Well, thank God you can't,' said Mr Pink. 'D'you realize being stuck out here is saving me a fortune? Mind you, the share price will have plummeted, now that they don't have the benefit of Olivia's custom!' And he laughed heartily at his own joke. It seemed so inappropriate today. 'St Michael – patron saint of extravagant housewives!' He thought that was hilarious too, he must be a very good Friend of Kathy's indeed.

'He'd be the first to complain if I went anywhere else,' confided Olivia, as her husband marvelled at his own brilliance, at his plateful. 'I'm a hopeless cook!'

'Oh I'm sure you're not,' said Tessa, who had begun to bolt her food, despite not being hungry.

'You haven't tried her salmon en croûte,' scoffed Mr Pink.

'Yes, well, that was impossible,' said Olivia, appealing to Tessa, 'I was trying to bath the children at the same time –'

'Don't let's discuss this!' Mr Pink held up his hand, to halt what was obviously Old Business between them.

Tessa knew better than to interfere. 'Oh well, never mind, we'll be home soon!' she said, trying to be cheery and positive, which was not how she was feeling.

'D'you think we'll still be here in September?' asked his wife. 'I do hope the children don't miss any school.'

'Aha!' Mr Pink leapt on that one too. 'I hope they do, I might get a discount on the fees!' His laugh seemed to be getting louder.

'Aren't you supposed to be going to the States in September,' she asked, pointedly, 'on your boys-only golfing trip? Shame if you missed that.'

He shovelled in more privet. 'Don't be ridiculous, of course we'll be home by then. The whole thing's preposterous! Besides, all the legal boys are working on it, they'll get us out of here.'

Tessa and Olivia exchanged a glance, they hoped he was right but they had a funny feeling he wasn't.

'D'you know, I never thought I'd say this, but I do miss the TV,' sighed Olivia. 'And so do the children.'

'Do 'em good, lazy buggers. Might throw the thing away when I get back.'

His wife ignored him. 'Well, you know, I think television's good sometimes, it can calm them down just before bedtime, for instance.'

'Turns 'em into bloody morons, if you ask me.'

And so it went on. Tessa got away as soon as she

could. There was no mistaking who was in charge of the remote control in that family, she thought to herself as she made her way down to the beach.

At least she didn't have to worry about all that any more. Nobody to question how much she'd spent on a new dress for his business function; nobody to challenge her on her childrearing methods; nobody to tell her how much she could and couldn't eat, where she could or couldn't buy the food from.

Perhaps it wasn't so bad being single after all. She only had herself to please, and Sammy of course. But not for much longer. She was going to be on her own soon, all the time. Completely alone. With nobody to look after. Nobody to need her.

She found her usual sunlounger, the one on the end of the middle row under the coconut shade with a hole in it, and lay down. Opening her book once more, she began to cry.

At least Gina's dead, she thought. At least Gina's dead.

*

Spike just didn't understand. 'But why won't she ever wake up?' he asked, as Cliff carried him over to the Kids Klub.

'Because she's gone to sleep, for ever,' said Cliff quietly, as he nuzzled his son's head. He was looking for that baby smell, but it had gone, of course, years ago.

'But she's got to wake up!' protested the small boy. 'She promised me I could bury her today.'

'What?!'

'In the sand.' He placed his little hands on to his dad's cheeks and swivelled his head round, a favourite trick. Looking his father directly in the eye, he said, 'She promised me.'

'Well I'm sorry, Spikey, mate, but – well, you can't do that now. Listen.' They had arrived at the door of the Kids Kottage. Cliff put his son down and squatted down to his level. 'She's not coming back, ever. D'you understand? Does that make any sense to you?' He looked at Spike's little face.

Spike shook his head.

Cliff tried again. 'Your nannygranny's never going to wake up, we're never going to see her again.'

Spike frowned, but said nothing.

Cliff could feel a lump forming in his throat. Bloody hell, one more try. 'She can't move, she can't, y'know, get up. She's gone away.'

'No,' said Spike, earnestly, 'she hasn't. She's still in bed. She's a bit lazy, isn't she, Dad?'

Cliff smiled a sad smile, and gave up. 'Tell you what, mate – how's about bunking off today, eh? Fancy spending the day with me, give the old Kiddies Klub a miss?'

'Yesss!'

Spike was unusually quiet as he sat on his dad's shoulders on the way up to the football pitch, and so was Cliff. He was horrified, disgusted with himself. He couldn't cry, well, not yet. Not a sodding tear for his old mum. What kind of an unfeeling bastard had he turned into? He knew he should, he wanted to, of course he did, but he just couldn't. Perhaps he was in shock. Yes, that was it, he was in shock.

Strangely enough, he'd cried like a baby when Dad had finally gone. Which was mad really, they'd all known he was ill, months in advance. It had been a nasty death, a slow crawling deterioration. Cancer. Horrible. Terrible to see such a powerful man reduced to nothing, wasting away like that. Rotting. Hadn't stopped him getting bad-tempered towards the end, bossing Mum about from his bed, shouting at her even. Only thing he had left, she'd said, so she took it.

And now she'd gone too, and he didn't feel anything. In fact, people he didn't even know seemed to be more moved by Mum's passing than he was. Lots of them had come up to him already this morning, said how sorry they were and all that. He'd tried to look properly sad, but he didn't really feel it. Bit sorry for himself, though, he was an orphan now. And head of the family. That ponce of a brother of his had better watch out, there would be no more of this dodging-his-responsibilities business. Mum had been so distraught at Dad's passing away, and Fabio had been 'too busy' to be there with the family, nancying about out here, 'preparing for the season' apparently. But he still managed to get all the glory without putting in any of the work, as usual. He'd phoned, hadn't he, during Dad's wake. Set Mum off so much she couldn't speak. All the old biddies passing the phone round, clucking like he was the most important person in all this.

Unable to deal with Cliff's family, on any level, Felicity had been out the back, organizing the posh caterers she'd squeezed into Mum's tiny but pristine kitchen. They were offering guests what Cliff called dollies' food, stupid stuff like mini dollops of porridge on tiny oatcakes. And that upset Mum because she'd been up most of the night before, making 'normal' sandwiches, like cheese and pickle, stuff people round here were used to. Cliff had busied himself with the details nobody'd thought of, like sorting out the funeral parlour boys, giving them enough for a drink after. And all the time his heart was breaking, because that sort of thing was normally Dad's job. It didn't seem right that he had to do it now. That was what Dad did.

But Mum's funeral, how was that going to work then? He couldn't get his head round this one at all. Mind you, if they had it out here, at least Eileen wouldn't be able to turn up and –

'All right, mate?' Mr Slogan was standing over Cliff, who'd been too self-absorbed to notice him coming up the well-trodden path to the football pitch.

Cliff tried to sound casual, not like he'd discovered his son lying next to his mother's dead body this morning. 'Yeah, yeah, I'm all right. You?'

'Yeah, y'know, usual bollocks. Wife moaning on about f—' – he just stopped himself in time – 'nothing, kids bickering at each other nonbloodystop, y'know.' He took off his T-shirt and laid it on the ground to sit on. He too stared out on to the deserted football pitch. 'I heard.'

'Yeah,' said Cliff, his foot scuffing some yellowing grass from the parched earth in front of him.

'Sorry, mate.'

'Yeah.'

'My nannygranny's been shot by hunters!' announced Spike, as Cliff took him down from his lofty perch.

'Is that right?' said Mr Slogan, giving Cliff a funny look.

Cliff shrugged.

'Yes, but there was no blood,' said Spike, proudly.

'Right,' said Mr Slogan. 'Listen, Cliff mate, if there's anything –'

'Right.'

'Right.'

Silence.

'Bloody hell, watch out, here they come, look out!' Mr Slogan scorned, 'load of bloody nancy boys ...'

Cliff looked over to the path, and could just pick out a few men making their way up to the football pitch. Their leader, John as in Yoko, was sporting a tasty designer 'Italia' shirt, and they looked well up for a bloody good game, one of them was even carrying a ball.

''Ere, Cliff,' said Mr Slogan, 'd'you fancy going out for a beer?'

'What d'you mean, going out?'

'Finding a local bar, there's got to be one near here somewhere. I could do with a change of scene, and you probably could too.'

'Leave the compound, you mean?'

'Yeah – quick, they're getting closer. C'mon, let's go.'

'What, now?'

'Yes, now!'

'What about Spike?'

'I love beer!' announced Spike. 'What's it taste like?'

'All right, lads?' Mr Slogan sprang up and adopted a fake matey grin as the eager men arrived.

'Fancy a game?' asked a puce-faced Alcopop, whose whole body seemed to be sweating gin.

'Nah, thanks, just put one out,' said Mr Slogan. 'Don't let that stop you though.'

'You escaped from here before?' asked Cliff, as they walked up the drive towards the big gates that opened out on to the main road, little Spike skipping in the middle of the two men.

'Nah.'

'Nor've I, dunno why not.'

'We've always been just about to leave, that's why,' said Mr Slogan. 'We're living out of suitcases, don't know whether to pack or unpack. And you don't want to go anywhere too far away, do you? I've thought about getting out before, but didn't want to miss the coach to the airport.'

'What if we miss it today?' said Cliff, suddenly anxious.

'Then we have to get on the next one,' replied Mr Slogan, who'd obviously got it all sorted. 'Which means the wife and kids go home on a different plane, and what a pity that would be, eh?'

'Right!'

The two men laughed, and then suddenly stopped laughing.

'What's that?' asked Cliff, stopping in his tracks.

'Fucked if I know,' said Mr Slogan. But he kept on walking.

As they got nearer, the scene ahead of them became clearer. Squinting into the fierce sunlight, Cliff could just pick out some men in a uniform they hadn't seen before, not that of the usual security guard.

A few more steps, and it was obvious. There were roadblock signs across the big gates, the car was a police car, and the officers had guns.

'If I didn't know any better, Cliff, mate,' said Mr Slogan quietly, 'I'd say our exit was being blocked by an armed guard. Looks like we'll have to think again.'

*

'Don't all look at me, how would I know what's going on?' Felicity stared back at the assembled crowd in her tiny office.

Tessa had turned up wide-eyed, to report that both ends of the beach had been sealed off by what looked like soldiers, who'd also taken all the fuel from the waterskiing boat, and their spare can too, despite Kenton's protestations.

And Cliff and Mr Slogan were there, to tell Felicity about the gunmen at the front gates.

Plus, a Nutty Brown woman had come to announce that she'd run out of shampoo, having only brought travel-sized bottles with her.

Outside, the phone rang.

'It's a Mr Blah-di-blah for you,' said Nikki, over the speakerphone, 'from the local thingy.'

'You see what I'm dealing with?' appealed Felicity as she picked up the receiver. 'Felicity Clifton.'

Her face changed almost immediately. 'But you can't –' she stuttered. 'I don't understand –', 'that's ridiculous, we can't possibly –' and 'I'd like to speak to your superior, please. No, I will not hold – hello? Hello? Ah, yes, now what exactly is going on?'

By the time she replaced the receiver, they were all agog.

'The bad news, ladies and gentlemen', announced

Felicity in a measured tone, 'is that the air traffic controllers' strike is not yet over.' She sighed. 'In fact, they think it's going to last a few more days at least, maybe even another week.'

Silence.

'And the good news?' asked Tessa.

'Is that it doesn't affect us any more anyway.' She took a deep breath. 'We can't leave here, even if we were able to. It appears that the local authorities have decided to close us down. From now on we're not allowed off the premises, under any circumstances.'

'What?!' exclaimed Cliff.

'Why not?' asked Mr Slogan.

'Apparently,' said Felicity, visibly shocked now, 'two other people from here have also died, it seems Gina's our third death. They reckon we've got a highly contagious illness here, a potential epidemic on our hands. And so we are now, officially, under quarantine until further notice.'

*

TESSA
That was when it all changed. That was
when it stopped being a holiday camp
and turned into a prison camp. That was
when we crossed the Paradise line.

END OF PART TWO

PART THREE

HOLIDAYS FROM HELL

12. The Prison Camp

TESSA

And as if that wasn't enough to deal
with, it rained the whole of the next
day.

*

It was Felicity's turn to fend off the villagers this time. She'd called a meeting in the Village Hall, and fortunately Robert from Maintenance had fixed the microphone. They'd been cross enough about the strike; now the news of the quarantine had made them absolutely furious.

'This is ridiculous!' shouted one man. 'We have jobs and homes and lives to get back to, they can't do this!'

'I'm afraid they can,' replied Felicity. 'Unbelievable though it may be, the local authority is legally entitled to hold us here. I've had my solicitors in London check it out. And I believe some of the law professionals here have come up against the same brick wall, so to speak.' The Long Arms volleyball team actually looked a tiny bit defeated, although they hadn't given up yet, of course.

'Quarantine, in this day and age – I've never heard of anything so archaic!' said an angry woman.

'I know.' Felicity sighed. 'The only consolation is that even if we weren't quarantined, we still wouldn't be able to go home – the air traffic controllers' strike is still unresolved, I'm afraid.'

'Excuse me –' Mrs Root had her hand up.

'Yes?'

'What was wrong with those two members of staff who died, what did they have?'

'Are we the only people to be quarantined?' asked somebody else.

'Yes, what about the other tourist hotels?'

'Um' – this was getting trickier – 'it's just us. There aren't that many hotels on the island, actually, it's mostly B&Bs, or rented villas. In fact we're the largest –'

'So whatever it is, it's only here. It's something inside the camp, is it?' asked the Parsnip. 'A sort of "enemy within" type scenario?'

'Well, it's certainly looking that way, yes.'

A low rumbling of anxiety started to circulate around the room.

'But what is this illness, exactly?' The Radish found it hard to disguise the fear in her voice. 'What do they think we've got?'

'Well . . .' Felicity had been dreading this question. The Village Hall was pin-drop quiet. 'Well, we don't really know very much at this stage.'

'But what do you know?' the woman insisted.

'Very little, medically speaking,' replied Felicity. She took a deep breath. 'The facts are these – both members of staff who were taken ill had very severe flu-like symptoms – aching muscles, headache, a high temperature, that sort of thing. Both were taken to hospital, and as we now know, both, unfortunately, died. We're –'

'Why weren't we told this at the time?' interrupted Mr Pink.

Good question, thought Felicity. 'I have no idea, I'm sure Fabio had his reasons.'

'And where's he, may I ask?' asked Alcopop. 'Is he dead, too?'

'No, he's in mourning for his mother,' said Felicity, curtly. Everyone turned to stare at Alcopop, who went redder than usual.

'Did she die of this mystery illness as well?' asked the persistent Radish. 'How contagious is it?' She gripped her husband's arm.

'No, Gina didn't have any flu-like symptoms. I had dinner with her myself that evening, she seemed absolutely fine. She died in her sleep, possibly of old age, god bless her.' The potboiler of anxiety was bubbling up amongst her audience, which was exactly what Felicity didn't want, she could sense fear in the room. 'Listen!' she said, sharply enough to get everyone's attention. 'The only reason we are under quarantine is because according to local rules if three or more people die in such a short space of time from unknown causes then that constitutes an epidemic; so they've sealed us off from the rest of the island, but only until they have determined the exact reason for these deaths. It's just a precaution, that's all. For all we know, they could all three have died of entirely unrelated, separate causes. It's unlikely to be anything major.' Even though she sounded convincing, she wasn't convinced. But it was vital to keep everyone calm. 'I'm sure that as soon as the results of these tests come back we'll be allowed to leave.'

'If the strike's over by then,' said the male half of the Tufty Club.

'Yes, well, hopefully it will be,' said Felicity, wanting to punch him.

'So if we get flu-like symptoms, we should start to panic, should we?' countered the female half.

'No, that's the very last thing you should do.'

'What if the children get ill?' asked Mrs Root. 'What should we do then?' More uneasy pre-panic panic swept round the room.

Felicity raised her voice to be heard. 'If that is the case,' she said, 'and it's extremely unlikely,' she hoped, 'then tell someone in the office, and we will make sure you see the doctor as soon as possible.' She managed to smile. 'Of course.' And then, brightly, 'We just carry on as normal!'

That seemed to put the necessary Bandaid on the problem. Felicity stayed up on the stage as she watched the villagers file out, their mood a mixture of disbelief, anger and horror, which equalled shock. Some of the men were even laughing. They shouldn't be, thought Felicity to herself, who could already sense that this was no laughing matter. It was looking much more serious than that.

*

TESSA
And it rained all the next day, too.

*

'The swimming pool's gone green, there's bits floating

282

about in it, my daughter's blow-up crocodile is covered in slime.'

'Nikki, call the pool guy, will you?'

'I have, he can't come in.'

'Why not?'

'They won't let him. We're in quarantine, remember.'

'Oh, right.'

'Felicity, there's something brown and sludgy coming up through the basement floor. It really stinks down there.'

'Nikki?'

'What?'

'D'you know what it could be?'

'Yes.'

Patient pause. 'What is it?'

'Poo. Something to do with the septic tank, I think.'

'What d'you mean?'

'I think some bloke comes in to empty it every few days.'

'What bloke?'

'I dunno, do I?'

'Well, where's Robert from Maintenance?'

'Trying to work out that lawnmower thingy the gardeners left at the front gates for us.'

'Right.'

'How am I to run a kitchen with no outside staff?'

'I don't know, but you'll have to find a way.'

Howell sniffed. 'Well I can't guarantee the food will be very good.'

Felicity resisted that temptation.

'Most of it's covered in shit, anyway.'

'What d'you mean?'

'The basement. It's our store room. It's where we keep all our supplies, didn't you know? Everything's covered in shit now.'

Felicity shuddered. 'We're still getting fresh food delivered though, aren't we?'

'Yes, they deliver it to the gates and Mandy picks it up every morning. She's not happy about it though.'

'Felicity, someone's lost his mobile phone. No one will lend him theirs. Can he use yours?'

'Felicity, Craig says he needs thirty metres of parachute silk, preferably yellow, for Lord of the Pies – where can he get that from?'

'Felicity, the washing machine's broken down. The repairman can't get in, obviously. So who's going to fix it?'

*

TESSA
And it rained the day after that. Three
days in a row.

*

'Felicity, the teenagers have taken over the Circus Tent and are bouncing up and down on Otto's safety net – he says it's going to break any minute and they'll be seriously hurt!'

'Felicity, someone's stolen all the clothes from Lost Property!'

'Felicity, they won't deliver our order for the Village Shop – the guy won't come near the place, he's frightened he'll catch something!'

That was the last straw. Felicity may not have had any working experience in the holiday industry, but she did know enough about human nature to know that it was exactly this sort of thing that could start a riot. This ignorant man's refusal to deliver, even to the gates, meant that they would very soon run out of basics like toothpaste, suntan lotion, tampons, soap powder, paracetamol – Calpol, heaven forbid – deodorant, Biros, postcards etc. And it was the little things that mattered in a big situation like this. There was only one thing left for her to do.

'Fabio?' Felicity knocked gently on his door.

Silence.

She knocked a little louder.

'Hello, Fabio?' She thought she heard someone moving around inside. 'It's Felicity.' Silence. 'Please, Fabio, I know you're upset, I'm worried about you. I just want to see that you're OK, it's been days since anybody's seen you . . .' She pressed her ear to the door. Nothing. 'Look, if you don't open up I'll get a spare key from Reception, or something. I'll break the door down, if I have to.' Yes, that seemed to do the trick, he was coming to open the door.

'What d'you want?' It was Michelle who opened it a crack, just wide enough to look at Felicity down her perfect little ski-jump nose.

'To speak to my brother-in-law, if you don't mind.'

'I'm afraid he's in bed, goodbye.' And she closed the door in Felicity's face.

Not one to be pushed aside by the help, Felicity opened the door and marched straight into the room.

Fabio was stretched out on the bed, naked, his perfect form resplendently enhanced by an enormous, glistening hard-on. He appeared to be handcuffed to the bedstead, and had been gagged with what Felicity immediately recognized as one of Michelle's cheap scarves. Michelle herself was a picture of perkiness in a very short nurses' uniform, made entirely of shiny royal-blue nylon with white lace trimmings, complete with a little upside-down toy watch, pinned at a jaunty angle to the breast pocket.

'Right, thank you nurse, that will be all,' said Felicity. 'I'll take it from here.'

'What?'

'You can go away now, I need to talk to the patient alone.'

They both watched in silence as Michelle gathered her clothes up from around the room and scrambled into something a little less medical. Felicity threw a handtowel over Fabio's disappointment as Michelle unlocked the cuffs, kissing him on the forehead as she left. She came back to whisper something in his ear that made the towel move a bit, but Felicity soon put a stop to that by holding the door open and hissing 'out!'

Once Michelle had gone, Fabio sat up on the bed and removed his chiffon gag. 'Oh, thank god you're here, Felicity, she's been holding me hostage for days now . . .' he trailed off, seeing that she was unconvinced.

'I came to offer my condolences, Fabio. I had a mental picture of you crying and pining and wailing with grief for your poor departed mother. I had not imagined that you would be fucking your way through this difficult time with the help of your friend Little Nurse No-knickers.'

At least he had the good grace to be slightly ashamed. 'I know, I know.' He looked up at her. 'The trouble is, Felicity, I can't deal with all this, I can't handle it.' His honesty was disarming. 'Don't get me wrong, I've done my fair share of crying and all that – the first day was terrible, I kept seeing her lying there, with poor little Spike smiling up at us beside her; it was like a nightmare, Felicity, like a bad dream. But then Michelle came knocking on my door and, to be quite honest, I was pleased for the chance to be able to focus on something else, I grabbed it with both hands.'

Felicity raised an eyebrow.

He didn't notice. 'I just can't hack it right now. I'm really stressed out with all this. I was going to come back to work tomorrow, honest.' He looked up at her, he did have some sadness in his eyes. 'I just don't want to think about poor Mamma right now, that's all. I can't. I'm supposed to be in charge here, I can't fall apart, can I?'

Felicity felt the urge to give him a hug, and so she did. Give him his due, he did seem to be coping with what must have been a terrible shock, albeit in his own unique way. And quite frankly, she could do with a hug herself.

As they parted, he said, 'So. How's the air traffic controllers' strike going? Is it nearly over?'

'No. Not that it matters now.' She looked at him, frowning. 'You don't know, do you? Hasn't Michelle told you?'

Fabio looked wary. 'Told me what?'

'That we're in quarantine.'

'Oh no.'

'Oh yes! We're not allowed to leave the holiday village until some tests come back or something – oh, Fabio, I've got to tell you, I haven't a clue what's going on, I can't get any sense out of –'

'Shit!' He buried his face in his hands. 'So they know now, do they? Oh god.'

'You knew this might happen?'

He nodded.

'Fabio!' Felicity tried to remain calm. 'I think you'd better tell me everything.'

It was a bit jumbled, but Felicity managed to make some sense of the chain of events:

Poor Alison had died in the local clinic, a couple of days after Bonnie had found her comatose. Kevin had been 'spirited' away to the local clinic, and he too had died. Their bodies had been flown home, but not before the local doctor had taken some samples to send to the mainland for analysis. (Their deaths were immediately treated as suspicious, as it was so unusual for otherwise healthy young people to die of what appeared to be just a heavy cold.)

The island's medical authorities were on full alert. Both Steve Davis ('the snooker player? What's he got to do with this?') and Crisis Management had instructed Fabio to keep the deaths a secret, to avoid any panic.

But the samples were taking a long time to process. It was the holiday season, and the whole country had virtually ground to a halt. The authorities had wanted to put the Village in quarantine there and then; luckily Fabio had managed to talk them out of it. Then, fortunately, the air traffic controllers had gone on strike, thus solving the problem. Nobody could leave, even if they wanted to.

Once Felicity had informed the doctor about Gina's death, and Cliff had told everyone else, Fabio had panicked. He knew they'd have to close the place down then, and that he'd be in big trouble with Seaside Villages for not handling the situation properly. Mamma's death meant, as far as the authorities were concerned, that they were in the grip of an unknown, fatal illness.

'But Gina didn't have any flu-like symptoms,' protested Felicity. 'I think her problem was that she didn't want to live any longer, don't you? She missed your father so much, she wanted to be with him.'

'Yes, you're probably right.' Fabio swallowed. 'I still can't believe she's gone, Felicity. She was my mamma. How could she do that, how could she leave −'

'I know, I know, let's not think about it now,' said Felicity, who'd not really had time to process the Gina thing yet. 'Look, Fabio, I can't seem to get any sense out of anyone about this wretched illness. How much do you know? Is it contagious? What've they told you?'

'Nothing. That's the worst part − no one knows what it is, and they won't until those test results come back.'

'And when will that be?'

Fabio just shrugged.

'Oh god, this is scaring me now.' Felicity shuddered, and got up. 'I mean it could be anything from bubonic plague to leprosy, maybe it's just plain pneumonia. But what if it is a bug we've got here? What if it's breeding right this minute, and we're all getting infected without knowing it?' She turned off the air conditioning, she was shivering now. She started to pace the room. 'Look, I think this is far more serious than we think. What if someone else falls ill? Everyone's watching each other for the slightest sniffle now – who's going to be next? They can't do this, can they? I mean, my god, it's like they've left us to die!'

'Oh Felicity, don't be such a drama queen!' Fabio smiled at his sister-in-law, who didn't smile back. 'I'm sure it won't come to that.' He sighed. 'I don't know what's going to happen. But one thing I do know is that I've got the sack.'

'What? Why?'

'Steve Davis said that if this got out, I'd be out.'

'But it's hardly your fault!'

'I know, but I'll have to take the rap for it, won't I? I suppose it's all over the papers back home?'

'Not really, just a tiny paragraph in the *Daily Mail* about "Holidaymakers Stranded In Paradise", apparently. I don't think anyone's that concerned, to be honest. From the outside, it doesn't look that serious, does it? No one's got any idea how it feels to be cooped up with all these bloody villagers, moaning on and on, complaining about everything.'

Fabio grinned. 'You've changed your tune!'

'Well, they're such bloody wimps, aren't they? I've had a terrible three days, dealing with all their stupid trivial problems. Whilst trying to run this place single-handed. Which reminds me, that's why I'm here. I need your help. Come back to work, Fabio, please?'

'I'm not sure I'm entirely ready —'

'Listen, if you're well enough to have bondage sex with that trollop, then you're well enough to help me keep everyone else under control.'

He looked unconvinced.

'Look, I wouldn't normally say this,' and she lowered her voice, 'but I haven't got a fucking clue what I'm doing.'

'Well, nor have I, really. I wouldn't be much help to you, babe.'

'Oh don't be ridiculous, Fabio, you're a trained resort manager. You must have done some sort of course on what to do in case of an emergency like this?'

'Er, well, I was supposed to, yes.'

'But you didn't?'

'No.'

'Why not?'

'Well,' his confession was accompanied by a sheepish grin, 'I got diverted.'

'Go on.'

'The admin assistant, Martine, just gave me the certificates, wrote them out herself.'

'Oh, god.'

'Look, I had spent a whole weekend in bed with her. She was a real screamer too.'

Felicity couldn't quite believe her ears. 'But you've done the rest of the management training courses, haven't you?'

'Well, yes.' Felicity stared at him. 'Sort of. Well, no. Oh come on, I had to spend a whole week in Malta with her for those qualifications.'

'What?'

'Look, it's not as bad as you think.' He reached over to his bedside table and brushed away various sex toys which were lying on top of a book. 'This has been fantastic, really helpful.' Fabio held up a thick, large paperback with the title *A Bluffer's Guide to Leadership Skills and Strategies* by Ted Nichols splashed across it in big gold letters. And underneath that was a photograph of a small, moustachioed man who didn't look like he could stand up to so much as a traffic warden, let alone steer them out of this crisis.

'Oh great,' said Felicity. 'So you know no more about managing a holiday resort in crisis than I do.'

'Not really, no.' He grinned. 'But you'd never know, would you?'

'Oh shit,' said Felicity.

Silence.

Eventually Felicity sat down on the bed, and looked her brother-in-law in the handsome face. 'Look, Fabio, I can't do this without you – and I suspect you can't do it without me. What d'you say to joining forces, doing our best to get out of this mess together?'

But before he could reply, there was a knock at the door. 'Felicity?' It was Nikki. She peered at Fabio's naked body behind Felicity's head, and blushed. 'Um, I just came to tell you that you've had a fax through from Crisis Management.' She tried not to look again, but couldn't resist.

'And what did it say?' asked Felicity, as she moved to block Nikki's line of vision, not feeling the need to explain anything.

Nikki was staring at Felicity, shocked. 'Um, sorry, that we're just to sit and wait for it all to blow over, that's all we can do now.'

'Oh really,' said Felicity, 'is that right? Hmm, we'll see about that.'

13. Felicity Followthrough Clifton

                FELICITY
    The first thing I did was to insist they
    take Gina's body away.

Footage of GINA's door, which is covered in
many beautiful and primitive paintings and
line drawings of flowers, some made out of
tissue paper, with loving handwritten messages stuck around the doorframe. Four men in
white boilersuits, with gas masks and protective gloves, enter the room. The door shuts
in our face. Cut to them leaving the room
carrying a body bag. A young girl, about ten
years old, stops in the corridor to make way
for them. Realizing what is happening, she
starts to cry.

                FELICITY
    It wasn't done in the most sensitive
    way, but at least it was done.

                *

Once Felicity and Fabio were back at their desk, there
followed a short period of negotiation.

Felicity claimed that the villagers needed a proper structure to live by in order to avoid the camp breaking down

into chaos. Fabio said that he thought people should be left to deal with the situation in their own way. Felicity tried to take his opinion into account, but couldn't. As Fabio was ultimately an anything-for-an-easy-life man, and Felicity was a perfectionist, they quickly settled into a method of working that suited them both: Felicity came up with the bright ideas, and Fabio agreed with everything she said. They made an excellent team.

Their main task was to find out who, exactly, they had here. Fabio hadn't even got a database of the clientele, if you please, just a list of names and room numbers. So the first thing Felicity had done was to make Nikki type up and print out questionnaires for each family and staff member to fill in.

First came the usual stuff: Name, Date of Birth (the best way to find out people's star signs, Felicity had a hatred of Sagittarians), Address, Occupation/Profesional Qualifications, etc. This information helped her to place everybody, socio-economically speaking. ('And with any luck,' as Felicity said to Fabio, 'one of our number might be a raft builder.' 'Wouldn't a doctor be more useful?' asked Fabio, oblivious to the fact that a doctor would have come forward by now.)

Then came Hobbies/Interests, which was purely for nosy purposes, as Felicity was always fascinated to discover how other people spent their leisure time. But she told Fabio that it was in order to start up some clubs and societies – people with hobbies liked doing that, didn't they?

Family Medical Record came next, as Felicity's considerable experience with big companies told her that

Seaside Villages would try to wriggle out of any compensation claims if they could. This way they could establish what each person came with already, and what, if anything, they'd caught out here. But it didn't say that on the form, of course.

Then they were asked if they were willing, able and qualified to serve on any committees that may be formed if necessary, e.g. Financial, Legal, Medical, etc. (Felicity was horrified when Fabio disclosed the food budget he had to stick to. 'Four pounds a head for three meals a day?! Good god, Spike's school lunchbox probably costs more than that!')

And finally there was a Suggestions Box at the end of the form, where villagers could fill in any ideas they may have about how to make this unpleasant period pass as pleasantly as possible.

'Now I think we should have a steering committee, don't you?' Fabio looked blank. 'A group of people who make all the big decisions? Like a government, but smaller ...'

'Oh, like a Parish Council, you mean?'

'Perfect!' Felicity clapped her hands with delight. 'That's so corporate, it's brilliant!' Fabio looked blank again.

They also decided (well, Felicity did) to operate a lending library, to pool all their books and use them as currency. So a paperback could be exchanged for something useful, like suntan lotion, or a clean T-shirt.

And anything left for longer than three days in the Lost Property basket would be passed on to the Pongos. (Most of it was unidentifiable anyway, as Felicity commented with a sniff; everything in there came from Gap, M&S or Boden.)

And later on that afternoon, Nikki was given a list of Rules to pin up, on the notice board in Reception:

1. No hoarding of food. (Even though it was a mystery to Felicity as to why anyone would want to, Fabio said that he'd seen people pocketing fruit and bread at lunchtime to take up to their rooms. This would encourage the rats to come back. 'Back?' 'Don't ask.')

2. All phone calls to be temporarily suspended, except in case of emergency. (They didn't want their two phone lines jammed with people attempting to let out their homes for the next few weeks, as Felicity had overheard someone trying to do that morning. The telephone was their only way of contacting the outside world, and their only way of receiving news and information. And, anyway, most people had given up queueing and had arranged their own mobile-borrowing system by now.)

3. No computer access, except in case of emergency. (That wasn't going to be popular, but it was necessary to keep the phone lines free.)

4. No hanging washing in public places; bedroom balconies only. Yesterday, one of the Nutty Brown women had hung out her family's laundry to dry on the volleyball net; there had nearly been a full-scale riot.

5. No paying nannies for private work on Sundays.

Felicity pre-empted that one, it having crossed her mind already. Bonnie would have a seizure.

And the good news is that all drinks are half-price! Felicity had insisted on this, even though it went against all budgets, as she said you had to pass on some good news after giving the bad. Fabio was horrified, as his salary was performance-related, and this wouldn't look so good. Nor did he think it was a good idea to encourage villagers to be drunk all the time. But Felicity said this was exactly what she wanted, as they would hopefully be numbed and oblivious to the potential hideousness of this situation.

In a last attempt to make a stand, Fabio had scurried off to fetch his leadership book, which Felicity had then literally thrown out of the window. The one thing she knew about was how to paper over the cracks of chaos, and put on a happy face. She was, after all, a Public Relations guru, which was why her company was called Guru PR, d'you see?

*

But although Felicity was very good at corporate cleansing, her people skills were tested to the full when she called Mrs Slogan into the office, to ask her to be in charge of Housekeeping.

'Why you askin' me?' the woman demanded, thick fat red arms akimbo, bubble perm a-wobble. 'Just 'cos I'm not posh, you think I should do your dirty work, do you? Is that it? You going all Upstairs Downstairs on us, or what? People who talk like me, they're only good for cleaning up after you lot, that's what you think, is it? You patronizing bitch!'

Felicity was shocked. 'No, no, goodness me no, it's not that at all. Quite the reverse – we've thought long and hard about this, haven't we, Fabio?'

'Yes, Felicity, we have. Long and hard.'

They both smiled at her.

She didn't smile back.

Eventually Fabio sweet-talked her into it. Apparently, she was a Domestic Science teacher, and not quite the working-class-salt-of-the-earth-Mrs-Overall stereotype Felicity had assumed her to be. But more amazing than that was Fabio's skilled charm; no wonder he had every woman he came across (so to speak) eating out of his hand.

The three of them decided that every female here would have to help with the housework (one thing they did all agree on was that the men would not be useful in a cleaning situation), and that a rota to that effect would be drawn up immediately. And not only did Mrs Slogan accept the job, but she said she'd be glad to show the likes of Her (pointing rudely at Felicity) how to do it. 'You lot couldn't clean a toilet properly if your life depended on it.'

Taking a leaf out of Fabio's book, Felicity said Mrs Slogan was absolutely right, of course; which is why she was the perfect woman for the job.

14. The Women

CLIFF

I just kept out of Felicity's way. I
know how she likes to focus, she has
to be very, y'know, concentrated. So
I kept my grieving for my mother away
from her, let her be, deal with my own
shit, you know.

Cut to:

TANIA

When Cliff first told me he'd lost his
mother, I said that was careless of
him, wasn't it; I didn't know he meant
she'd died. I felt sorry for him then.
I think he just needed a bit of womanly comfort, and people have said I'm
good at that. [She giggles.]

*

Bonnie flung open the nursery door. A toddler who'd
been playing behind it screamed. 'Where the fuck's
Tania?'

'Dunno, haven't seen her,' said the nanny who was
sitting in the middle of the floor on a Tweenies bean
bag, reading a dog-eared copy of *Heat* magazine.

'What?! But it's nine thirty-seven a.m., she's more than half an hour late!'

'God, is that all?' moaned the nanny, without looking up. 'Doesn't time fly when you're enjoying yourself . . .'

'Mind you, I don't know why I'm bothered, she's got to be the worst nanny I've got; you know she failed my Kinder Egg test but they let her in anyway, I couldn't believe it!' Bonnie sighed. 'Well, if she sneaks in without me knowing, tell her to come and see me will you? Angela?' She had to say it again, louder, it was hard to make herself heard over the yelling.

'OK.'

'And wipe this child's nose, it's getting blood on the carpet.'

Bonnie hoped to god that Tania hadn't got the dreaded Flu Thing. 'The last thing I need right now is more staff getting ill,' she thought, as she made her way back to her office via the kitchen. 'I am not going to look after these spoilt brats myself, and that is final.' Just as she turned into her doorway, she spotted activity out of the corner of her eye.

'And what time d'you call this?' she roared, pounding down the corridor towards the 3–5s room, the Lupins.

But it wasn't Tania. Yoko jumped, hand on her chest. 'Ooh, you gave me such a fright!' she said, as she hustled Mink into the playroom. Feather tried to hide behind his mum, terrified. 'Bye, gorgeous, have a good day!' she called, and waved at her little girl as she shut the door.

'You're late.' Bonnie stared at the woman with black and white streaks in her hair. Call yourself a parent? What kind of example is this? You look like Cruella de Vil. Or a badger.

'Yeah, sorry, hangover.' She smiled. 'Cheap booze, what can you do? C'mon, Fev, let's try to find your lot, mate.'

'I'm afraid that won't be necessary.'

'Sorry?'

'Your children are excluded, as from now.'

'What d'you mean, excluded?'

'They will not be welcome at the Kids Kottage any more.'

'What?!'

'You are persistently late, and your children are very badly behaved. We don't need people like you here.'

'But you can't do that!'

'Yes, I can.'

'But that's not fair –'

Ignoring her protestations, Bonnie marched into the Lupins, plucked little Mink out of the Barbie Beach Buggy and handed the bawling bundle back to her mother. 'Now are you going to leave, or will I have to escort you off the premises?' As she watched them walking away, she thought she heard Feather hiss 'hooray!' under his breath. The child was obviously stupid, and hadn't understood what was going on at all.

She was just doing her job, and she was in full control. She felt unstoppable now, and it felt good.

*

'Ooh, Bonnie, what are you like?' said Michelle at dinnertime. 'That means she's going to have to look after her own kids from now on! She's not going to like that, they're really naughty, aren't they? Bloody hell, I don't know where you get your nerve from, I really don't. Are you sure you're allowed to do that?'

'Who cares? What are they going to do about it, send me home?' Bonnie pushed a hardboiled egg into her mouth. 'Maybe this will show those lazy arseholes that I mean business,' she said through it. 'You finished with that?'

'Yeah, I'm not all that hungr—, blimey, steady on, Bonnie!'

'I need my strength, Michelle, for dealing with these bastards that don't know how to bring up their snivelling kids,' said Bonnie, as she gulped down the rest of Michelle's sausage roll in one.

Michelle sat back and watched as Bonnie quickly hoovered up her leftovers, finishing by soaking up Michelle's grey saladwater with the second baguette. 'They can't all be bad, surely?'

'Oh they are, Michelle, I can assure you.'

'In what way?'

'Well,' she chewed, 'some of them are so besotted with their little darlings that even if they fart it smells of roses. Honestly, it makes me sick. In their parents' eyes, these little buggers can do no wrong.'

'But isn't that normal?' asked an unsuspecting Michelle. 'My dad would do anything for me. When I first started going out and that, he'd drive me to the pub and wait for me in the car outside, all evening, just in case anything happened and I needed him. And my mum's the same, she adores me. That's just love, isn't it?'

'No, Michelle, it is not!' Bonnie slammed her fist down on the table, causing the other diners to look round. 'It is not a loving thing to bring up a child thinking that they're perfect, that the world revolves around them only, because that child grows into a self-centred, manipulative adult who will still throw a tantrum to get their own way! Can you not see that?' She was bright red in the face, spitting food everywhere.

'No,' said Michelle, genuinely, 'I can't. I think it's really nice to know that your family love you, no matter what.'

'But that's wrong, Michelle, it's wrong! If you murdered someone, would your parents still love you?'

'Yes.'

'No!'

'Yes, they would. And they'd come and visit me in prison – in fact, Mum would probably bake a cake with a nail file in it or something!' Michelle didn't like the way this was going. 'You OK, Bee? You seem a bit stressed out . . .'

'I'm fine!' snapped Bonnie, a bit too loudly. 'So you're one of Them, are you?' She reached over and took an untouched dessert that had been abandoned on the next table. 'Figures,' she muttered.

'And what's that supposed to mean?' Michelle drew herself up.

Bonnie shook her head, between shovelfuls.

'I hardly think you're one to talk about figures,' Michelle said, sniffily.

'Pardon?' Bonnie stopped eating, momentarily.

'I know it's your glands, and your metable crate, and that, but – well, you don't help yourself by eating as much as you do!' There, she'd said it.

'And what business is it of yours, what I eat?' Bonnie's eyes narrowed.

'Well, you know.'

Silence.

'I'm only trying to help,' smiled Michelle uneasily, shifting in her seat.

'Are you saying I'm fat?'

'No, no, god no, I'm not saying that at all!' Michelle laughed and laughed. 'No, no, dear me, no!'

'Then what are you trying to say, Michelle?'

'Nothing. It doesn't matter.'

'Say it, go on, you know you want to.'

'I really don't, honest.'

'Come on, Michelle, spit it out.' Bonnie had the look of a bull at the entrance of a china shop.

'I just think . . .'

'Yes?'

'That you could make a lot more of yourself.'

'Oh, really? In what way? I don't think there could be much more of me, could there, Michelle?'

'Ooh, Bonnie, you are funny!' screamed Michelle, in a desperate attempt to turn the conversation into a nice light-hearted one. 'No, look, all I meant was that if you cut down on the food and did some exercise, perhaps you would be happier with your shape, that's all.' She put on her sympathetic face, and laid a kind hand on Bonnie's arm. 'You might even be able to get a boyfriend!'

There was silence, while Bonnie drained her beer to empty. She slammed the glass down on the table so hard, that Michelle jumped. 'I'm quite happy with my "shape", as you call it, Michelle. At least I don't look like an anorexic breadstick, like you. And, anyway, isn't it in your interests to have a fat friend, so that you look even better? Even if I did get thin, you'd drop me straight away – don't think I don't know what you're up to, you scheming minx!'

Michelle was shocked, too shocked to find the right words to say so.

'And even if I did have a boyfriend, which I only don't have because I actually don't want one' – Michelle managed a splutter at this, but it didn't stop her – 'I'd make bloody sure I wasn't the last person to find out he's shagging one of the punters!' Bonnie wiped her mouth with the napkin. 'Now, if you don't mind, I have a life to get on with.' And she stood up, knocking her chair over backwards as she did so.

By the time people turned to see what the commotion was about, all they could see was Michelle's mouth stuck on open. 'What are you lot bloody staring at?' she screeched, before leaving the restaurant herself, muttering about power not suiting some people, she'd obviously lost the plot.

*

Felicity found Bonnie doing a picture crossword in her office. 'Ah, Bonnie, a word, if I may?'

'What d'you want?' She didn't even bother to look up.

'I gather you've excluded John and Yoko's children from the Kids Klubs?'

'That is correct.'

'I'm afraid you can't do that.'

'I'm afraid I can.'

'Look, Bonnie,' said Felicity, as she shut the door behind her, 'I know those kids can be a pain in the neck, but their parents have paid for your services.'

'No they haven't.'

'Er, they have.'

Bonnie looked up. 'Not any more – they only paid for two weeks. They've had their lot, OK?' And she went back to her puzzle book.

'No, it's not OK.' Felicity snatched the book away. 'You are an employee of Seaside Villages, you are contracted to provide childcare for their clientele.'

'And you are not an employee of Seaside Villages, so you can bog off.'

'I beg your pardon?'

'You heard. Now give my book back and get out of my office.'

Nobody spoke to Felicity like that.

'Just who, exactly, do you think you are? This may come as a shock, Bonnie, but you are not in charge here; your job is to look after our children and, to be honest, you're not even doing that very well.'

Bonnie didn't look up but Felicity carried on.

'D'you know what, I'm sick of being held hostage by you childcare people – you're all the bloody same. We work really bloody hard, us parents, to pay for an expensive holiday like this, so that we can relax, safe in the knowledge that our kids are being well cared for. But that doesn't seem to be the case any more, does it? I've had several complaints from the other parents – you nannies are behaving as if you're doing us some sort of favour! Well, we're getting a bit sick of bending over backwards to make your lives easier and easier, while ours get harder and harder. I, for one, have had enough of all this pussyfooting around you and your team of slags. It's your fucking job, just do it!'

Bonnie's face was like stone as she let Felicity carry on.

'And while I'm at it, I don't like your holier-than-thou approach to your job either. How dare you decide what's best for our children, when you haven't even got one of your own? We know what they like, we know what they want, they're our kids, and WE ARE THE BOSS, d'you understand? I think it's time you remembered that. You're just a nanny, and that's all you are!'

Nobody spoke to Bonnie like that. She stood up.

'If you don't like the job me and my team of "slags" are doing, then you can consider your Spike excluded too. It makes me wonder why you so willingly hand him over to us each day, if you think we're so crap. From now on, you can look after him yourself, see what we have to put up with. And if I see him or any of those other freaky kids in this building again, I'll close down the whole bloody place, d'you understand?'

Felicity stormed out, Bonnie sat and waited. Fabio was in her office within about five minutes. He pleaded with her to reconsider her decision, she replied no fucking way with knobs on. Eventually she agreed to let Spike stay, but only until the end of the week.

Her chance came later on that morning.

'How long's he been doing that?' Bonnie asked the nanny, who was having a fag in the plastic Wendy House, blowing smoke rings out of the little window.

'What?'

'Sniffing.'

'I know, I told him to use his T-shirt, but –'

'How long?'

'I dunno, since lunch? Yeah, that's right, they were all putting their chips up each other's noses, yeah, I thought his was a bit runny.'

Oh God. 'Right, get that child out of this room immediately.'

'What?'

'*Get him out!*' Spike looked up from his Lego.

'Well, where shall I put him?'

'Lock him in the toilet until I get back. I'm going to fetch his father.'

'Hiya!' called Christabelle, as Bonnie thundered past the tennis courts.

'Where's your dad?' Bonnie walked over to the wire netting surrounding the courts, where Chris was standing on her own, racket in hand.

'He's coming to play tennis with me, apparently,' she smiled, 'it's his way of showing he cares. He doesn't know I'm crap at it. Why, what's the matter? You look awful.'

'Huh, don't you start,' muttered Bonnie. 'Look, I need to get Spike out of the Kids Kottage as soon as possible. Can you come and get him?'

'Why?'

'He's got a cold. I don't want him infecting the other children.'

'It's not – well, you-know-what, is it?'

'I don't know, but it's better to be safe than sorry.'

As they walked back together, Bonnie said, 'Listen, I'm short-staffed at the moment, thanks to Alison and Kevin. And there's another one gone missing today. I've just had what I think is a brilliant idea. How d'you fancy being a nanny for me?'

'Ooh no, I don't think I could. I'm not very good with children.'

'Doesn't matter.'

'But kids hate me.'

'Not a problem.'

'And to be honest, I'm not mad keen on them either.'

'Perfect. My dad's in the RSPCA, he says you can't be an animal-lover and do that job, especially when you see how the owners treat their pets. It's much better to be emotionally detached.'

'Oh.' Chris considered that as they walked on.

'I just thought it might give you something to do with yourself, while you're waiting to go home. And I'd enjoy your company. We could have a laugh together.' The two girls looked sideways at each other, and smiled.

'Oh all right then, I'll give it a go.'

'Yay!' Bonnie did a hefty skip.

'When do I start?'

'No time like the present; just dump Spike with his mother in the office, and come straight back to Kids Kottage.'

'Shouldn't I do some training first? Aren't the nannies supposed to be qualified?'

'Nah,' said Bonnie, 'I'll teach you all you need to know.'

That's better, thought Bonnie to herself as she tried to finish her X-word Puzzle before lunch. Nice people in, crazy bastards out.

(From then on, not one parent was late to pick up their little darlings, and some even brought gifts for Bonnie: an orange, a glossy magazine, even a pretty little diamond bracelet . . .)

*

'Have you seen Cliff anywhere?' Felicity looked panic-stricken.

Tessa decided to leave the rest of her *Chicken Quarantina*, it was too rubbery. 'What's the matter?' she asked, 'has something bad happened?' Oh god, what now?

'No, no!' Felicity looked away. 'Just Spike wanting to spend some time with him, that's all.'

'Felicity?' Tessa knew her friend too well, she was holding something back. 'What is it? Sit down, speak to me. Have you had lunch yet?'

Felicity flumped herself into a chair. 'Oh, you're joking, aren't you? Time to eat? No, I'm too busy dealing with all these angry villagers – d'you know, you'd think it was my fault that we're stuck out here, the way they're carrying on! Everyone hates the new rules, but it's for the best.'

'I know,' agreed Tessa, 'it's funny how differently it's affected different people, isn't it? I think everyone's shit scared, but they've just got different ways of showing it.

Mind you, that's no excuse for Mr Pongo to be wearing a woman's blouse this morning.'

'He's not!'

'He is, but I don't think he knows he is. I'm sure it's from Next.' She leaned forward. 'I think it was the Pongos who stole the Lost Property basket.'

'Really?' said Felicity, nicking a swig of Tessa's rosé. 'Makes sense. And Bruno locked himself in the clubhouse yesterday, though he swears he didn't, he says the door was jammed.'

'No!'

'Yes. Thinks he's in a film, playing the part of the one who goes mad.' Felicity held her head in her hands. 'God! I thought it would be fun, a bit of a laugh, being marooned out here. But it's not, is it? Anything but.'

'I know what you mean,' Tessa agreed. 'I thought it would be like *Tenko*, you know, all the women would menstruate at the same time, there'd be a huge community spirit, heartwarming moments, that sort of thing.'

'Ah, Felicity, there you are!' It was Fabio, who smiled at Tessa, who blushed like a beetroot, no, two — she couldn't help it. 'Spike's getting bored, he wants his dad. And there's another problem.'

'Oh go away, Fabio, I don't want to know.'

'Craig's ill.'

'Sssh!' Felicity hissed. 'Sit down! Don't tell the whole world, for God's sake! What?!'

'He seems to have quite a heavy dose of flu, and he's got a bad case of the runs as well.'

'Well that doesn't surprise me, I'm surprised we haven't all gone down with food poisoning. I mean, what is that supposed to be on your plate, Tessa? Sorry, Fabio, go on.'

'He can't get out of bed – which, according to his boys and girls, is most unlike him.'

'Oh god.' Tessa hadn't seen Felicity look this worried, ever. 'Well, what do we do now?'

'Phone the doctor?' suggested Fabio.

'Apart from that. We've got to keep this quiet, the last thing we need is people panicking.'

'Oh god.' Fabio and Felicity looked at Tessa. She held her hands up. 'I'm not panicking, I'm not.'

'Look, please don't tell anyone about this, OK? It's probably nothing, maybe it's hay fever.'

Hmm.

Silence.

'Have you been looking for me?' Cliff approached the table, tennis racket tucked under his arm.

'Yes. Spike wants to spend the rest of the day with you.'

'But I'm supposed to be playing tennis with Chris.'

'Who?' asked Felicity, a little impatiently.

'Christabelle. My daughter.' His eyes flared. 'Your step-daughter.'

'Well Spike needs you more,' she said through gritted teeth.

'But –'

Felicity grabbed Cliff by his tennis shirt and pulled his head down to hers. She tried to say it quietly. 'He's got a cold!'

'What?' said Cliff and Tessa, together. Oh god, thought Tessa, not Spike. Oh god.

Cliff left immediately, to take the boy up to their room. Felicity left to ring the doctor again. Fabio sat down and ate his lunch with Tessa.

OH HELL-O, DING DONG!

*

'Well, how was it?' asked Felicity, as she joined her friend in the Bucket and Spade for their pre-dinner drink.

'How was what?' asked Tessa.

'Lovely Dawn said you got a phone call from Jeremy at lunchtime, but you didn't take it, because you were having lunch with the fabulous Fabio . . .'

'Oh, that.'

'Yes, that.' She waited for Tessa to fill her in. 'Well?'

'Well nothing, really. We had lunch together, that's all.'

'And?'

'And nothing, Felicity! There's nothing to tell.' Felicity looked almost hurt, but how was Tessa to say that he'd promised to finish off what he'd started, later on tonight, and that she could think of nothing else. Except the phrase 'life's too short' . . . 'How's Spike, anyway?'

'Oh, fine.'

'Really?'

'Yes, Tessa, really. He freaked out a bit when the doctor came in wearing a mask and gloves, but he's had a couple of sachets of Calpol, which Olivia very kindly gave me, and he's right as rain. The doctor said it's nothing serious.'

'So it's not –'

'No, it's not!' replied Felicity, rather aggressively.

It was Tessa's turn to look hurt now, she was only showing concern. 'And what about Craig?'

Felicity lowered her voice. 'He prescribed antibiotics, because it's looking like pneumonia.'

'But that's not infectious, is it?'

'No, I don't think so.'

'Does he think antibiotics will help? Is this mystery illness treatable? Is Craig going to die?'

'Oh please, Tessa, don't keep asking me questions like that, I don't know. I just don't know, OK? You know as much as I do, let's leave it, shall we?'

Silence. They both took a drink, both grumpy, both offended. Fortunately Sammy came rushing up, 'Mum! Have you seen Chris? Oh my god, you've got to come, quick, this is hilarious!'

'What is it?'

'Just follow me, quickly, or you'll miss it! This is going to be so funny . . .'

'Good,' said Felicity, getting up and taking her drink with her, 'I could do with a laugh.'

'This had better be worth it, Sammy,' warned Tessa, as they picked their way across the dark sand in their evening sandals, weaving a route through the moonlit sunbeds.

'Ssssh!' hissed Sammy, as they got nearer to the beach. Quite a crowd had gathered, some people giggling behind their hands in anticipation. 'They're in there,' she whispered, pointing to the waterskiing boat, which had been sitting redundantly on the sand ever since the soldiers took away its fuel.

As their eyes grew accustomed to the dark of the night, Tessa and Felicity could just pick out the younger members of the waterfront team, who'd surrounded the boat. They were noiselessly creeping nearer and nearer, moving so quietly that the only sound above the gentle lap-lap-lapping of the sea was that of rhythmic grunting, the unmistakable kind.

'Oh my god, how embarrassing for them!' whispered Tessa to Felicity.

'I wonder who it is?!' Felicity nudged back, with glee.

Together, the stealthy stalkers stood still. Jamie raised his hand, and then dropped it. Four torches went on, and their bright beams crossed as they shone into the boat. A white bottom stopped its bobbing immediately, and its owner raised his head.

'What the fuck –?' spluttered Cliff, dazed and shocked, as he squinted in the glare of the bright lights. 'What's going on?'

*

There was a Pub Quiz that night, during which one team was disqualified for having a teenager under the table texting someone back home for the answers. After the Pub Quiz, the Village Hall was turned into the School Disco, the trestle tables and chairs having been pushed back against the walls. Tessa surveyed the scene in front of her.

Tania, the disgraced nanny, was on the dance floor with Otto, the married circus performer, seemingly oblivious to the fact that everyone was talking about her.

Mr and Mrs Root were dancing in each other's arms, even though it wasn't a slow dance. (But they weren't looking at each other, they were looking over each other's shoulder, looking at people looking at them, looking smug.)

Red Rum was trying to drape herself around Jamie's neck. He was too polite to throw her off, despite being teased by his workmates and some of the teenagers, Sammy being the loudest and rudest.

Alcopop was propping up the bar, or rather, the bar was propping up him.

Michelle was deep in conversation with Mr Pink, whose head was virtually buried in her Wonderbra'd cleavage, nose first. She in turn was keeping an eye on Fabio, who was dancing suggestively with that young girl Becca. Becca was only a little bit older than Sammy, but could easily have been mistaken for a thirty year old woman with a great pair of tits and a trick pelvis.

As she looked around, Tessa realized she was tired of all this. She was fed up with the soap opera that was now their lives; same cast, different script. Join us again next episode, she thought, when Felicity sleeps with Fabio and Michelle gets off with Cliff. She was sick of this, sick of them, sick of being here. She'd had enough.

So she told Fabio that she was going to bed, and not to bother coming up to her room. He tried to look broken-hearted, but they both knew Becca was a more exciting prospect. She waved goodnight to Sammy and left the School Disco, each step feeling like a release from the relentless beat, beat, beat of it all. It felt good to be on her own, she felt a sharp blast of freedom in her lungs. Tessa kicked off her shoes, safe in the knowledge that they would still be there in the morning, and walked across the night-cooled grass with a kind of chilled relish.

She didn't go straight up to bed, but took a late-night stroll instead. She saw Bonnie and Christabelle chatting so earnestly in the kids playground that they didn't see her; she saw the moonlight reflected in the ripples of the sea, just like a photograph on a free Seasons Greetings calendar from a travel agent; she saw the flicker of a fire on the beach, teenagers egging each other on to jump over it; she saw a young mum sitting out on a balcony, quietly humming as she breastfed her baby under the stars; she saw rats scurrying around the bins outside the kitchen, stealing scraps of food for their own young. She could smell the night scents of the hibiscus, the jacaranda, the drains. There was a dead bird lying on the stone steps leading up to the hotel lobby. A scrawny cat ran away when she approached it. She could hear a couple arguing, a toddler crying, the crickets trying to drown everything out with their own songs of tsing-tsing.

How would Jeremy cope, if he was stuck out here? Surprised, Tessa realized that this was the first time she'd thought about him all evening.

And that was the first time she felt it. That was when it began to dawn on her that she was going to be all right. She'd coped this far without him, hadn't she? He hadn't been here to protect her, and yet right now, she felt very protected. Much later, she described this feeling as a kind of coming home, she was returning to her old self, the person she used to be. The person she'd turned her back on all those years ago, when she'd turned to face him instead.

As Tessa kept on walking, she could feel herself getting lighter. Her whole body began to ease up, her neck felt longer, her limbs more free, in her step a little skip. She felt good, she began to feel even better. It was the kind of confidence that came with the certainty that whatever she saw or felt or happened upon next, it wouldn't faze her. It was all part of the same life, her life. Her life, not his. She was stronger than she'd thought. She understood now that she was not afraid of very much, even though she was sure of very little. But this didn't worry her any more, not at all, it thrilled her, it gave her a little kick.

What was going to happen next? What would become of her? Who knows? That night, Tessa realized for the first time that it wasn't her job to write the script for the soap opera; all she had to do was to be in it, play her part as best she could. It was her job to show up, and that was all. The rest was out of her control. Thank god.

Now she felt like dancing. But not tonight. She wanted this feeling to last a little longer, to take her upstairs and send her to sleep. Tomorrow would be not only a new day, but a brand new day. Tomorrow she would be truly refreshed.

*

There was a knock on the door. Felicity opened it. It was the young mum from next door. 'I'm awfully sorry, I know you're having a row, but could you keep it down? The walls are so thin here, and I've only just got my baby off to sleep. If you could just not shout, that would be great.' And she smiled, sympathetically.

'Yes, OK,' said a weary Felicity, 'sorry.'

Before she went, the young mum whispered 'good

luck', and smiled again. Felicity tried to smile back, but couldn't.

She closed the door quietly, and went back into the room to face the piece of crap that was her husband. She'd been holed up in here for hours now, she hadn't had anything to eat or drink, they'd been arguing all evening, in between taking it in turns to check on Spike, who was asleep in Gina's old room.

'What I can't understand, Cliff,' she said, trying to keep her volume down, 'is why you chose to make a fool out of me so publicly.'

'It wasn't supposed to be so public,' muttered Cliff, although he knew this was no defence.

'Well it bloody well was!' spat Felicity. 'Have you any idea how it feels? To know that everybody's waiting to see what I'm going to do about this, to know that they're all going to be staring at me during breakfast tomorrow morning, trying not to talk about it to me and yet talking of nothing else to each other? Every single person here, Cliff, every single person knows now that you've not only been unfaithful to me, but that you've been stupid enough to fuck the Village Idiot! I don't know which is worse. Why, Cliff, I still don't understand, why did you do it?'

'I don't know.' He fiddled with the corner of the sheet.

'No!' Felicity ripped it away from him. 'Don't say you don't know, you're not allowed to not know. Give me a reason, give me something to hate you for, at least.' Felicity paced up and down the room, she couldn't keep still.

'I wanted a bit of comfort, that's all.'

'What?!' She spun round on her heel and glared at him. 'How much more comfortable d'you want it, Cliff? You don't even have to earn your own keep! I work all the hours god sends to pay for your food, your home, your clothes, your fucking holidays, I even paid for your sodding family to come here – and this is how you thank me, is it?'

Cliff got momentarily brave. 'Well, if you'd been giving me more attention, then perhaps I wouldn't have been forced into looking elsewhere.'

Felicity froze mid-pace. 'I beg your pardon?' she said, in a scarily quiet, deep voice.

'Tania was there for me when you weren't.'

'Oh well, excuse me,' she continued walking round the room, which seemed to be getting smaller and more crammed with furniture, 'I just turned my back for a moment to help your incompetent brother run this place, that's all. You know, helping other people? Remember that, Cliff? Thinking of others? Working selflessly for the common good? Does the word "teamwork" ring any bells?'

'I knew you were busy, which is why I didn't want to bother you – and anyway, you wouldn't come to dinner with me when I asked you to.'

'Oh, I see, this is all *my* fault!' Felicity did that terrible angry laugh, 'how silly of me – I pushed you into having an affair, is that it? If I'd just stopped trying to get us out of here for one moment and listened to your whining for hours on end, we wouldn't be in this position, is that it?'

She was getting nasty, he'd not seen her like this before.

'Well, I have just lost both my mum and my dad in the last three months . . .'

'Don't you *dare*!' She was screaming again, right in his face now, it was horrible. She reminded him of Penny. Scary. 'Don't you dare play the dead parents card, Cliff, I'm not having it!' She began to rummage in her beach bag. 'This is nothing to do with them, you leave them out of this.' And then, to his astonishment, she pulled out a packet of Marlboro Lights and lit one.

'When did this start?'

'What, smoking? About the same time your dad died of lung cancer, that's when.'

'But you can't –'

'Oh shut up! Don't you tell me what I can and can't do.' She took a deep drag, and sat down on her side of the bed with her back to him.

'Look, I'm really sorry, this isn't what I meant to happen –'

'I'll bet it isn't! I just wonder how many more times you've done this, sneaking around behind my back.' She took another drag. 'Honestly, Cliff, I just didn't expect this.' And blew out. 'You're as bad as Fabio. I just – well, I never thought you would be, I didn't think you were like that, I really thought you loved me . . .'

Cliff could tell that she was close to tears. This was a rare event, especially these days. Nothing seemed to get to her any more, she was hard as nails nowadays. Her struggle melted his heart, he was surprised to find himself feeling sorry for her, poor old girl, still trying to be brave, even now. He got up, and went round to the other side of the bed. He knelt at her feet, took her hand in his, and gently kissed it.

She snatched her hand back and looked away, dragging on her fag defiantly, as a lone tear slowly found its path down her tanned cheek.

'Look, darlin', I'm sorry. I didn't want this to happen, honest. I don't even know how it did. I just want us to be happy, that's all I want in the world; for you, me and little Spike to be a family. I love you, sweetheart, and only you.'

She sniffed, still not looking at him. 'Funny way of showing it.'

'Look, Tania means nothing to me – it was probably just a cry for help, that's all.'

'Oh spare me the clichés, please.'

'I do love you, I do. I don't want to be shaggin' all these women any more, I just –'

'What women?' She was staring at him now.

Bollocks. 'Nothing, y'know, I don't mean "women", I mean her, that's all . . .'

Her eyes narrowed. 'What about that one I saw you with in that restaurant, were you sleeping with her? She wasn't really a client, was she?'

'Which one was that, then?'

'You know perfectly well which one, Cliff, the one I caught you with, a few years ago – the one with the big hair and too much gold jewellery.'

'Oh, Denise?' He laughed with relief. 'Oh no, I've never slept with her.'

'Really. And I'm supposed to believe that, am I?'

But Cliff didn't answer. He just looked at her, trying to read her face.

'Cliff?'

He looked as if he was about to say something, but then changed his mind.

But Felicity wasn't going to let him get away with anything any more. 'What?'

'Nothing.'

'Come on, tell me.'

He broke her gaze, and looked down to the floor. 'It doesn't matter, it's all in the past now. Let's talk about the future, our future –'

'Cliff.' Felicity snorted the smoke out of her nostrils, reminding Cliff of a dragon, in more ways than one. 'Now would be a good time to confess all, if there is more to tell me. Have you been sleeping with this woman Denise?'

'No.'

But he looked very guilty. 'Sure?'

'Yes.'

'On Spike's life?'

'Yes,' he sighed, 'now just leave it.'

'I'm afraid I can't do that, Cliff. I don't believe you. I don't trust you any more. You just can't tell me the truth, can you? God, I can't believe this is happening to me; "Career Woman Cuckolded By Bored Husband", god, it's so bloody predictable . . .'

She started crying properly then, and Cliff couldn't bear it, so he said, 'Look, I am not sleeping with Denise, and I have never slept with Denise, OK?' He took a deep breath. 'She's my daughter.'

'What?' Felicity shut her eyes, squeezing the last of

the tears out as she ran this information through her exhausted brain one more time. 'No, I'm sorry, this is making no sense. Say that again?'

It was Cliff's turn to pace up and down now. 'I knew Eileen at school, she was the one we all wanted. But I got her in the end. I got her pregnant, you see, so we had to get married, you had to in them days. I was only seventeen, she was sixteen. Her family were furious, and Dad went bloody mental, but Mum really liked her, she thought I'd done well for myself.

'Eileen was bloody gorgeous, really beautiful, a natural beauty with huge —' Felicity began to look murderous again, 'but she wanted more than I could give her. She had dreams of marrying Paul McCartney, or Sean Connery, someone like that. So I thought I'd turn myself into David Bailey, keep her and the kids in the manner to which they'd like to become accustomed.

'Only it wasn't quick enough for Eileen, she didn't understand that you had to be a photographer's assistant for a few years before you could start making serious money. So she fucked off, didn't she, with the guy from Barry Motors, moved up to a big house. And the only time I was allowed to see my girls was once every summer, when she was off on holiday with him, driving round Europe in one of his posh cars. Then she'd let them stay with Mum and Dad.'

'So where are they now?' was all Felicity could think of asking.

'Well Denise is — hang on —' Felicity watched him do the maths on his stubby fingers, 'blimey — thirty-eight now! Fuck me. Which makes Jackie,' same delay, 'thirty-six!' He grinned. 'She was conceived during the World Cup in '66, you see – so I called her after Jackie Charlton. Though I never told Eileen that.'

Felicity noticed that he seemed to think this was all rather amusing. Clearly he couldn't see the gravity of what he had just revealed.

Cliff carried on, oblivious. 'They're both married now, with kids of their own. And I think Mum still sees Eileen every now and then, around Leigh, they keep in touch, swap Christmas cards, that sort of thing.' He smiled. 'I've just realized, this makes you a step-grandmother!' And he actually laughed.

That was it. 'And you a single grandparent. I want a divorce.' Felicity dropped her cigarette stub to the floor and mashed it to a pulp with her strappy gold Choo.

'What? But I feel so much better, now that I've told you all this. It's been awful, keeping this secret from you all these years. I've often wanted to tell you, but . . .'

'Yes,' she stood up, 'why didn't you tell me, Cliff?' She sounded horribly together, very calm.

'Well, y'know, I didn't think you'd be too pleased if you found out I had two failed marriages and three kids behind me. I thought it might put you off.'

'For once, Cliff,' she glowered as she towered over him, 'you're absolutely right. Although it's not the fact that you have two more daughters of my age that bothers me; it's the fact that you've been lying to me all these years.' Felicity suddenly felt very tired. 'I can't deal with this now. You're going to have to fuck off.'

'What d'you mean, fuck off?'

'Leave, move out.'

Cliff was confused. 'You're joking, aren't you?'

She wasn't.

'Where to?'

'I don't know, you should have thought of that when you were shagging your fourth wife-to-be, shouldn't you?'

'But we can't leave this place, there's nowhere for me to go. I can't move out – we're trapped here.'

'That's your problem, not mine. You may feel trapped, Cliff,' and she shooed him out towards the door, 'but I feel strangely liberated. Now fuck – right – off!' And with one final shove, she ejected him out of her room and into the corridor.

As she was chucking all his clothes and belongings over the balcony, watching him scurry around underneath in the dark, picking them all up again, Felicity felt quite proud of herself. Tempted though she was, at least she hadn't been cruel enough to tell him that she just didn't fancy him any more.

In fact, Tania might have done her a huge favour.

15. The Men

Eventually people sort of settled
down, and there was an uneasy air of
acceptance about the place. Looking
back, I can see that was probably the
lull before the storm.

*

'I think most of the forms are in now,' announced Fabio
the next morning, as he came into the office clutching a
wad of papers. 'Here they are.'

'Let me see.' Felicity looked up from the list she
was making. Not having slept a wink, she'd been in
the office since six o'clock this morning, avoiding the
breakfast gossips, focusing on the windsurfing poster
on the opposite wall instead of her work. Olivia had
been the only other person up at that time; she'd kindly
offered to look after Spike (having been reassured that
his cold had truly disappeared) while her own kids were
in the Kottage.

'You look awful,' observed Fabio.

'Thanks.'

'Really old.'

'Well, I am a grandmother, what d'you expect?'

Fabio looked puzzled.

'I take it you knew about Cliff's first wife, and his grown-up daughters?'

'Well, yes, but –'

'So why didn't you tell me?'

Fabio took the hair tie from his wrist and pulled his hair back into a ponytail. 'Well to be quite honest, I'd forgotten about them.'

'You'd forgotten?'

'Well he's so much older than me, I was only a kid when all that happened.'

'Of course.' She held out her hand for the completed forms. 'It didn't occur to you that your brother has based our marriage on a lie?'

'Well, no,' he replied, as he handed them over. 'I hadn't really thought about it. Sorry.'

In an attempt to forget about the events of last night and get on with the job at hand, Felicity scanned through the forms. 'Hmm – Horticulturist, Speech Therapist, Racehorse Trainer, a Seismologist . . .'

'What's that?'

'Not what you think it is . . . Furniture Designer, Financial Planner, another Financial Planner . . .'

'I heard about last night.'

'. . . Aha! Doctor! Yes! Oh. No, Doctor of Philosophy . . .'

'I can't believe Tania would want to have sex with Cliff . . .'

'Dentist, that might come in handy. Merchant bankers, lots of them, no surprises there then . . .'

'I mean, he's old enough to be her father – no, her grandfather!'

'Marine Biologist – good, he'll know how to sort the

pool out with all those chemicals we found – Nuclear engineer, Music teacher, Silversmith for god's sake . . .'

'What on earth can she see in him?'

'Fabio!'

'What?'

'Stop it. I've got enough to think about without you winding me up – just leave it alone, can't you?'

'So what are you going to do?'

'Right now, I'm about to start panicking. But not about my crumbling marriage, about the fact that whilst these people are all very marvellous high-earning respected professionals back home, they're not going to be very helpful to us out here, if this situation gets any worse. I mean, what use is an Underwriter in a desert island scenario? Or a Marketing Manager, for that matter? All any of these people can do well is complain.' She sighed. 'And it seems the closest thing we have to a raft builder is Mr Slogan, who's a kitchen fitter.'

'Steve Davis on the line,' screeched Nikki over the intercom.

'At last!' Felicity beat Fabio to it, and said into the receiver, 'How nice of you to return my calls, you rude bastard.'

The conversation didn't go very well after that. It appeared that Seaside Villages really couldn't do any more for them at this stage, and were more concerned about the financial implications than the welfare of its clientele and staff. In the end, Felicity lost it completely, and called Mr Davis a fuckwit, just before hanging up on him. Fabio rang him back.

The next couple of hours were spent in a similar style;

Felicity snapped at everyone, Fabio apologized. By about half past ten, Fabio escaped by volunteering to check on Craig, who said he wasn't feeling any better but neither was he feeling any worse. He was, however, in a high state of panic – somehow Fabio managed to talk him down, at least for the moment. On his way back to the office, he decided to find Michelle.

She was in the Village Gossip, chatting with Yoko, who now had rainbow-coloured streaks in her hair, and mysteriously, a bit missing from one eyebrow. Fabio watched them from the doorway.

'So John's always been faithful to you, has he?'

'Well, no,' replied Yoko, as she examined a zit on her chin in Michelle's mirror with handy magnifier and vanity light.

'Oh?'

'But he's never done anything with anyone behind my back, I've always been there too!'

The two girls laughed. 'That's what I like about you,' said Michelle, as she waved at Fabio to come on in, 'you're so modern.'

Eventually, he got her away from her friend and into his bedroom. 'Fancy a bit of elevenses, do you?' she said, as she stepped out of her white overall and lay down on the bed. 'I've got a bit of a treat for you, as it happens,' she said, as she pulled off her knickers. She'd cut her pubic hair into a heart-shape, and dyed it purple.

'Actually, Michelle,' said Fabio, pretending not to have noticed it, 'I'd like to talk to you.'

'That's OK,' said Michelle, 'I can do that. I'll start, shall

I? Um, OK, right – come on big dick, I want you to fuck my brains out, yeah, fuck my –'

'No, not like that,' said Fabio, as he sat down on the bed. 'I want to talk talk, about us.'

She sat up. 'You're not going to try and dump me again, are you? I told you the last time, I'm not having it –'

'No, no, nothing like that.' Fabio smiled at her. 'Completely the opposite.'

'What d'you mean?' asked Michelle, suspiciously.

'Michelle.' He turned round to face her. 'Since my mother passed away, I've noticed that I have nothing in my life of any value.'

'What about your motorbike?'

'Apart from that. And that's not what I mean.'

'Right . . .' She still didn't get it.

'And so, I wonder if you would – well, if you, y'know, could, ever, well now, in fact – oh look, Michelle, would you marry me?'

There was a short pause, during which Michelle just stared at him. Then she threw her head back and laughed and laughed and laughed.

'Oh don't – no, stop it, I don't believe – that's mad, you're mad – no, don't, what are you like?!' She caught her breath back, and said, 'Oh dear, Fabio, have you gone mad? Of course I can't marry you! Honestly, what are you like?!'

While she was laughing some more, Fabio said, frowning, 'But why not?'

'Because,' she replied, wiping a tear from her eye, 'you're just a sex toy, that's why! I wouldn't marry you, never! Are you completely mad?'

Fabio still didn't understand. 'But I need you, Michelle, I need a woman's love, I want to start a family, I want to settle —'

'No stop it, don't make me laugh —' She held up her hand to make him stop, while she regained her composure. 'Where d'you want me to start? I'm far too young, you're far too old; you're poor, I need to be rich; you've been unfaithful to me, mind you so've I to you now so we're all square on that one but anyway; you don't even own your own property —'

'What? When were you unfaithful?'

'I don't think that's any of your business, is it?'

'I can't believe you would do that, Michelle —'

'Well then it goes to show how little you know me, then, doesn't it? Yet another reason not to get married. Oh god, that's the funniest thing I've ever heard!' She looked at her watch. 'Now then, are we going to fuck or not? I've got a Brazilian at 2.30.'

'What?! Who's he?'

'Oh, just get on with it,' said Michelle, lying back down on the bed and opening her legs, winking at him in her own special way.

*

'Come on, let's do it again!'

Cliff was knackered, he'd only just rolled off her, he was fucking exhausted. Bloody hell, these young ones didn't half go; he'd been up, (well, awake) most of the night. He needed a few more hours' kip.

'I've never had anybody leave their wife for me before!' enthused Tania. 'It's exciting!'

And I've never been chucked out by a wife before, thought Cliff to himself, it's always been me who's dumped them. Tania's hand wrapped itself around his poor limp dick in a vice-like grip. There was going to be nothing doing down there for some time, he knew that much. 'Don't you fancy me any more, Cliffie?' she asked, in a little-girl voice.

'D'you know what, I'm starvin',' he declared, by way of a diversion. 'Come on, I'll buy you breakfast!'

'Oh no, you haven't been paying for it, have you?' Tania clapped her hand over her mouth, trying not to laugh. 'All meals are free here, didn't you know?'

'Yes, I did,' replied Cliff, wearily, 'it was a joke. What's the time, anyway?'

Tania consulted her digital alarm clock. 'God, it's eleven minutes past midnight!'

'What?! Can't be.' Cliff looked over to the bedside table and picked it up. 'No, you've got it upside down, it's eleven o'clock exactly.' A distant alarm went off in his muggy head. 'Bollocks, breakfast's over. Well, never mind, I'm going to have a shower.'

'No, you have to wait until I've had mine first!' said Tania, springing out of bed and into the bathroom in what seemed like one smooth, selfishly young movement.

Cliff crossed his arms behind his head and lay staring at the ceiling. He'd been in this situation a few times before, and yet this felt different. He normally had at least a few good months with the new one, with lots of great sex and new things to find out about each other; and yet here he was, only a couple of days later, asking himself what the fuck he thought he was playing at. He already knew he'd made a terrible mistake.

It wasn't hurting Felicity that bothered him so much. Even though he knew it was a bad thing to do, she'd turned into a bit of a monster over the past year or so, and part of him reckoned she kind of deserved it. She needed a bit of a shock, although he wouldn't have planned for it to have happened like this, if he'd had the choice.

She hadn't been even a bit understanding about his lack of employment. She'd just decided that as she was making all the money, she had the right to make all the decisions too. And so slowly, bit by bit, she'd been eating away at his manhood. (No, that wasn't right, that's exactly what she hadn't been doing – his manliness, y'know, his being the man.)

But he was missing her already, why was that then? Maybe it was just odd waking up next to someone else. Anyway, he'd get used to it, he always did. If he could stick it out this time, that is.

'Cliffie!' called Tania, from the bathroom. 'Could you pass me the soap, please?'

Now you see, Felicity would never ask him to do that, she locked the bathroom door these days, to keep him out. Cliff pulled back the mangled soggy bedsheet, and dragged his old bones into the shower-room.

As soon as he got in there, he felt better. There, right in front of him, were two perfectly good reasons as to why he'd done it. The finest pair of bazookas ever seen on a woman, and they were all his for the taking. And take them he did, in both hands, their slimy soapiness some-how managing to send the right message to his dick.

It was quick, but it was from behind, with her leaning over the basin. Luckily the mirror above it was all steamed up, so she couldn't see the reflection of his sweaty red face, panting more with effort than lust.

'Shit!' said Cliff, catching sight of the clock when he'd gone for a lie-down afterwards, 'volleyball! I knew 11 o'clock meant something. I've missed it! Jesus Christ, the lads are going to go mental. Bollocks!'

*

He was too late for volleyball, they wouldn't let him play. They hadn't got anybody else in his place, mind you, but they said it wasn't fair on the other side if he joined in half way through. So he cheered them on instead, but it was like he was invisible, nobody talked to him. (Except one of the younger Dot Cunts, who'd made a 'way-hey' type gesture with his fist and his elbow.)

Then Bonnie had sacked Tania, because staff affairs with the villagers were a sackable offence. Then she'd been immediately reinstated, because they were short-staffed. Tania had been very upset, she'd liked the thought of not having to work any more. So he'd tried to cheer her up over lunch, which hadn't been easy. She'd never heard of the Monkees, and he'd never heard of the Fugees.

He'd tried to get Chris to join them, but she was eating with Bonnie, who said she couldn't be seen associating with Cliff and Tania, in case people thought she approved of what they'd done.

So Cliff had checked Tania in to the Village Gossip,

for a makeover or whatever, his treat, while he hotfooted it up to the football pitch for a bit of peace.

'All right?' he said to Mr Slogan, who was stretched out in his usual spot, catching a few rays.

Mr Slogan didn't reply. Cliff thought he must be asleep. Mr Slogan coughed, so Cliff knew he was awake. He sat down on the hard earth, the sun having bleached all the grass away.

He left a small pause, and then Cliff said, 'How's the wife, OK?'

'Why, you gonna start on her next?' said Mr Slogan, without opening his eyes.

'What?!'

'Right bloody ladies' man you turned out to be, dintcha?'

Cliff couldn't tell if this was a good thing in Mr Slogan's view, or a bad one. 'Sorry about volleyball, I er, well, I er –'

'Had something better to do?' Mr Slogan turned over, to do his back. He didn't say any more.

Cliff decided to lie down too. With any luck, he'd nod off and catch up on some much-needed sleep.

They lay there, side by side, for an hour or so, in silence. But Cliff just knew that his friend disapproved.

In Cliff's experience, blokes usually split into two camps when this happens. On the one hand, you've got men who say things like 'phwoar' and 'good on ya, mate', claiming that they'd do the same if they got the chance, but somehow they never did. They made you feel brave, even though you knew you weren't.

And then there was the other kind of bloke who'd

stayed with his marriage, who reckoned he didn't mind if he'd never have sex with another woman, he 'couldn't do it to the kids'. They made you feel like a complete bastard, even though you knew you weren't.

And then there were people like me, thought Cliff to himself, who didn't fit into either category. The ones that actually did it. The ones who took themselves out of one situation and put themselves into another. And right now, for the first time ever, it felt like a pretty lonely place to be.

*

When he woke up, Mr Slogan had gone, and it was nearly dusk. Cliff made his way back to the hotel, just in time to see Olivia leading Spike to the office. 'Spikey, my little mate!'

'Daddy!' Spike came running over to his father and flung himself at his knees. 'Where've you been?'

'He's been busy,' said Felicity, standing in the doorway of the office. 'Come on, Spike, it's supper time.' She held out her hand.

'I want Daddy to take me!' he cried.

'Listen, Fliss –'

'What?'

'Why don't I have him tomorrow, I could look after him if you like.'

'No thanks, Oliva's doing him, aren't you?'

'Well, yes, if you like,' said Olivia, in that irritating 'but I don't really want to' way that the passive-aggressive do so well.

'Look, I'll have him,' volunteered Cliff, smiling down

at his son. 'I haven't spent any proper time with him for ages –'

'Yesss!' Spike punched the air, like he'd won the World Cup.

'– and Tania can help out too, he likes her, don't you –'

'No!' Felicity's voice cut a sharp note.

'Why not?' asked Cliff, and Olivia's face, and Spike.

'I will not have that woman anywhere near my son, d'you understand?' Felicity was almost shouting. 'Besides, I'm taking a day off tomorrow.'

('Are you?' came Fabio's question from inside the office.)

'I need a break. I'm going to spend the day with you, Spike. It's going to be just you and me, isn't that exciting?' Felicity smiled down at her son.

'Yes.' But Spike didn't punch the air like he'd won the World Cup.

'I don't mind having him, honestly,' said Olivia, who was feeling bad now.

'Please let me spend tomorrow with him,' said Cliff, who was feeling worse.

'No, he's going to be with me. Now if you'll excuse us, he needs to eat. Come on, Spike!' And she marched him off towards the restaurant, with Olivia running behind trying to keep up, saying that she really didn't mind, honestly she didn't, truly. Spike just managed to turn back and wave at his dad before they disappeared out of sight.

'Poor little boy,' said Fabio, from the doorway. 'I bet he feels awful.'

'Oh fuck off,' said Cliff, 'what would you know about it?'

The two brothers looked at each other.

They could have talked about it, they could have had it out there and then.

But they didn't, and they probably never will.

16. The Kids

THE TUFTY CLUB are talking to the INTERVIEWER,
both sitting on a chintz sofa with their arms
folded.

MR TUFTY
About the only good thing to come out
of the situatio was the fact that the
kids got really good at swimming.

MRS TUFTY
Yes, but that was about it, really.

They both sigh, gloomily.

*

Tessa, who had been waiting, put her book down when
she heard the key in the lock.

'Oh. Er, hi.'

'Hi.'

Not meeting her mother's eye, Sammy picked up her
baggy T-shirt from a pile on the floor and went into the
bathroom. Tessa sat patiently on her bed and waited for
her to come out.

'What?'

'Are you completely nocturnal now?'

Sighing, Sammy got into bed.

'It's nine o'clock.'

No reaction.

'In the morning.'

Sammy put the pillow over her head.

'Time to be getting up, not going to bed,' continued Tessa.

'Whatever,' came the muffled reply.

'I'd like us to have lunch together today.'

Nothing.

'Please.'

Not a sausage.

'Sammy?'

'Leave me alone.'

'No.' Tessa moved across to Sammy's bed and sat on it.

'Mu-um,' whined the muted teenager, 'go away.'

'No,' said Tessa, 'you're the one who's going away. Come on, Sam, have lunch with me, please? It's the least you can do.'

'Listen,' said Sammy as she tossed the pillow aside to glare at her mother, 'I don't owe you anything, don't you go laying all your shit on me. Anyway,' she turned on to her side and shut her eyes, 'I thought you'd be pleased to see the back of me.'

'Oh, Sammy, you didn't think that at all,' sighed Tessa. 'That's just it. I don't think you've thought about this for a moment. I just hope that Mona's nice to you. I'll knock her bloody block off if she isn't.'

'Look, Mum,' Sammy rolled on to her back and finally met her mother's gaze, 'she's really not that bad. In fact, I quite like her.' Tessa's teeth clenched. 'She's the one encouraging Dad to give me a bit more freedom, when we go to London. At least she's young enough to still remember what it's like to be a teenager,' Tessa's buttocks clenched, 'not like Dad who thinks I should still be wearing smocked dresses and having a nap after lunch.'

'But I thought –'

'I know. You've always thought she was a witch, haven't you?' She sighed. 'I suppose that's my fault, I could see how unhappy you were when Dad left, and so I thought that if I told you horrible stories about her it would give you someone to hate other than Dad. I mean, of course I'd still like you two to be together, and I used to wish and wish that it would happen at first, but now – well, I can see that it's just not going to be that way. Dad really loves Mona. He's not coming back, Mum, you have to accept that.'

Tessa's chin wobbled, she couldn't help it.

'Oh come on, Mum. Please don't. You're better off without him. I know he's my father and everything, but – well, you think Mona says nasty things about you to me, don't you?'

'How d'you know that?'

'Computers, Mum, they have memories.'

'Have you read –'

'Yes. You shouldn't be surprised; how am I to resist a file called "Highly Confidential"? Anyway –'

'I can't believe –'

'Anyway. Mona's never said anything bad about you, honest. In fact,' and Sammy took a deep breath, 'it's Dad who's always slagging you off to me.'

'What?!'

'He's awful, he does it all the time. Luckily I'm old enough now to be able to tell him to stop, I'm not scared of him any more. I think he thinks he's being funny, or something. Maybe he's trying to get me on his side. Or perhaps he's trying to persuade himself that he did the right thing by leaving you, making out that you're some sort of twat. I don't know why he does it really, but he's not very nice about you, Mum. It's not Mona who's the bitch, it's him.'

Tessa was horrified, hurt, she couldn't take this in.

'He sees you as some sort of defenceless woman, I suppose, an easy target. It's quite common, in fact, with second families, for the father to make out that the first wife was just a silly mistake. Makes them feel better about having fucked up everyone's lives.'

'How do you know all this?' Tessa asked, staggered at her daughter's apparent specialist knowledge on this subject.

'Oh we talk about it all the time, at school. There's loads of us now with parents who've split up – we find it all quite funny, really. You're the childish ones, not us.'

'Yes, you're probably right.' Tessa began to feel the betrayal, she knew Jeremy's ruthless side well. Oh yes, he was more than capable of being unkind about her to their daughter, in order to make himself look better. But god this hurt, it really hurt. She'd had no idea. She thought he still loved her.

'So it might be a good idea for you to stop sleeping with him as well, don't you think?'

Tessa stopped dead.

'I'm sorry Mum, but I know all about your little lunchtime sessions.'

'Oh my god –'

'Don't worry, I'm not going to tell anyone.'

'But you shouldn't know about things like this, you're too young to underst—'

'Look, Mum.' Sammy sat up in bed and faced her mother. 'I am not your little girl any more. I know you want me to be, but I'm not. We grow up really quickly these days, we're older than you think. I'm one of the few virgins left in my class, but that's not for lack of trying!'

'No, Sammy, stop it, I don't want to hear this –'

'So the sooner you start treating me like a person, and not a child, the sooner we can be friends, geddit?'

Tessa looked at her daughter, who looked back at her. 'Is that what you want?'

'Yes.' Sammy heaved a sigh of relief. 'I'd love us to be friends, I want us to have a good time together, I want to be able to tell you stuff, I need a friend right now, not a lecture! Come on Mum, we can do this, we can be kind to each other, can't we?'

Tessa found herself in the peculiar position of being in awe of her own daughter. Who was the grown-up now?

Suddenly, she felt excited. Yes, this could work, yes! 'So can we have lunch together today?'

Sammy smiled. 'Yes Mum, we can. But can I go to sleep now, please?'

'Yes, yes, of course. D'you want me to give you a tickleback?'

'Mu-um!' Sammy laughed. Then she said, 'Oh, go on, then!' and flipped on to her stomach, pulling up her T-shirt as she did so. 'One thing,' she said, as she closed her eyes.

'Yes?'

'I don't want you borrowing my clothes, Mum.'

Tessa smiled. 'Oh damn, OK then.'

'And remind me to show you how to secure your personal computer files when we get home,' she said, as Tessa lightly scratched her bare back. She opened her eyes. 'We will get home, won't we Mum?'

'Of course we will, baby, of course we will,' soothed Tessa, as Sammy closed her eyes again. 'Now go to sleep.'

Sammy soon fell asleep, but Tessa didn't stop stroking her. As her hand moved across her daughter's skin, she said goodbye to her little girl, whispering words of how she used to look after her, look out for her and look over her as she slept, just like now. She promised she'd try to embrace the young woman her daughter had now become, but a part of her would always cherish the baby she had once been.

As she silently left the room, she looked at her beautiful daughter sleeping so peacefully, and a tear slipped out of her eye and into her heart. What she didn't notice was that a little tear had slipped out of Sammy's eye too.

*

Felicity had woken up that morning with a five-year-old boy to amuse all day, no husband to do it for her, and an almighty hangover. She'd been so pissed last night, she and Tessa had actually danced to 'I Will Survive'.

As he knew he wasn't allowed to wake Mummy up, Spike had amused himself while he waited, by tipping out all her shiny make-up on to the floor; then he'd used it to draw a lovely picture, several lovely pictures in fact, all over the wall. Felicity wouldn't have minded so much if she'd been a cheap 'n' cheerful kind of gal when it came to cosmetics; or if the monster picture had been of Bonnie, and not her.

Once they'd got over the 'where's Daddy?' question, (to which Felicity replied 'he's gone for a swim in the sea' which was the beach version of a jump in the lake) they had the question of getting dressed to address. He wouldn't wear the as yet unworn Osh Kosh bib shorts she'd chosen, saying they were too crunchy; but she wasn't going to be spending the day with a child wearing his pyjama bottoms and one of her bikini tops either.

Eventually, they managed to catch the last five minutes of breakfast. Mummy had a coffee, so that she could start the day all over again, and become a better person. But there was more negotiation to be had over Spike's diet – he insisted on Coco Pops, saying Dad always let him have them, with extra sugar. Felicity felt plain old-fashioned corn flakes and fruit would make a healthier start to the day. In the end he did have Coco Pops, but with a sliced banana and no sugar.

'But I don't want to go to the beach,' whined Spike, as she dragged him there, 'I want to play with my friends in the swimming pool! Pleeeeease?'

Having dragged a couple of sunbeds to the farthest point on the beach, well away from the other villagers and their staring eyes, she spread out their towels, creamed up both herself and Spike, gave him his bucket and spade and told him to make her something lovely. At last, Felicity finally got to open her pristine copy of *Vogue*. She'd been saving it for a special treat, although she hadn't had time to read it yet, even if she'd wanted to. The essence of London life lifted off its glossy pages, the smell and touch of it smacked her senses, making her feel instantly homesick.

'Mum!'

The pages were full of chic must-have holiday items; pale palomino leather beach bags and mock rhinestone shades set with real diamonds, designer suntans and glossy long hair, frilly diaphanous prints and micro mini-shorts, a tiny fun beach tent for your tiny fun pooch, and an article on crisp white linen. Or you could khaki yourself, for the topical terrorist look.

'Mum, Mum, look at me!'

On page forty-three, a gay designer's Costa Rican beach house doors had been flung open for the good people of Condé Nast – it was a sea of white floorboards and spacious, neat and tidy pale blue walk-in wardrobes, with giant conch shells for handles; cool Indian summer saris hung from the ancient iron bedframe, wafting in the breeze that gently filtered through wooden weatherbeaten shutters; the bathroom had been inspired by the designer's favourite Moroccan hammam, each tiny mosaic tile having been lovingly salvaged from a condemned mosque; the heaving driftwood dining table was laden with blushed pears, delicious sweetmeats and crystal teardrop candelabra, the designer's dinner guests all beautiful in an utterly natural way and very, very young.

'*Mum!*'

'What?' replied Felicity, as she turned to the fashion pages – no! The legwarmer was making a comeback? That couldn't be true, surely. But oh yes, there it was, being modelled on a leg long enough to make even a kitten heel look flattering. They were legwarmers with a twist, though, mostly in soft pastel shades, a beautiful blend of cashmere, angora and pashmina with a bit of ermine gently woven through here and there; they bore no relation to those hideous stripy affairs of the past. But what would you wear them with, that was the question –

'It's all right, I'll get him!' shouted an urgent male voice, puncturing her aesthete's world of woolly warmers. There was lots of frenzied splashing, so loud that Felicity had to peer over the top of her magazine to see what was going on.

Oh my god. It was all too quick to take in, Waterfront chief Kenton had dived into the sea and was swimming as fast as he could towards little Spike, whose tiny head and arms were floundering about, somewhere in the middle distance. Felicity stood frozen with horror at the water's edge, clutching her magazine to her like some sort of shield, shrieking 'Spike! Spike!' helplessly, pointlessly, like

Sissy Spacek in a tragedy. Other people on the beach were standing up now, shielding their eyes from the hot sun as they peered out to sea and watched as Kenton carried the little boy back to the shore.

'Oh god, is he OK?' Felicity asked the burly South African as he waded out of the sea, Spike's limp body in his arms.

'He'll survive,' said Kenton, as soon as he'd cleared away the onlookers and the little boy began to cough up the seawater he'd swallowed. 'Keep going, mate, you'll probably spit out a starfish soon!'

'I just can't believe it, I don't know how that happened –' Felicity was horrified, appalled, shocked. Ashamed. 'I feel so bad, I was watching him, you know, one minute he was making sandcastles, and the next –'

'Yah, you've really got to keep your eye on them at this age,' said Kenton, as the colour began to come back into Spike's cheeks.

'Oh, Spike, you could have drowned!' The horror of the situation was only just sinking in, he could have died – and it would have been her fault for not paying him any attention. How could she have faced Cliff, what would he have said?

'I was only trying to show you how good I am at swimming now, Mum,' said Spike with a feeble smile, which made Felicity feel even worse.

'But you've got to be very careful in the sea, hey?' warned big, beefy Kenton. 'It's not the same as swimming in a pool, is it now?' He looked at Felicity to agree.

'No, no.' She impulsively pulled Spike towards her and hugged him tight. 'Oh god, you gave me such a fright.'

'Yah, me too,' smiled Kenton. 'Don't make me have to do that again, OK, Spikey?' His eyes twinkled, Felicity noticed they were the same colour as the sea. His tanned skin had a salty, distressed-leathery look to it, but it wasn't unattractive. 'Right, I'd better get back to the kayak class.'

'Oh Kenton, thank you so much' – Felicity had never been this grateful to anyone in her life – 'really. Thank you, thank you. If there's anything I can do in return, then please –'

'You could always have a drink with me, tonight,' grinned Kenton.

It was one of the rare moments in her life when Felicity was lost for words. 'Well, er, I –'

'I'll come!' shouted Spike, 'I want a drink tonight, let me have one! Please, Mum, I'll be really thirsty, I promise!'

She accepted his invitation, flattered to be asked by such a fit, young hunk of man, and yet at the same time, embarrassed – after all, this was proof of her new-found singledom being public knowledge.

'See you tonight, then,' cheerio'd Kenton, who was more handsome than she'd previously noticed. As he walked back up the beach, he picked something up from the water's edge. 'D'you want this back now?' he called. It was a soggy mass of *Vogue*, which she'd obviously dropped into the sea during the panic.

'No, thanks,' Felicity called back, 'you can throw it away!'

Turning to her son, who was scratching his name backwards in the sand with a twig, she said, 'Right then,

Spike. I think I've had enough wake-up calls now. Let's get down to business. You and me, we're going to play together today, all day.'

'And tomorrow, and the next day?' asked Spike, so excited that it nearly broke her heart. How had she let it come to this?

'Yes, all those days too.' She looked at his little face, for what felt like the first time in ages. She hadn't even noticed how beautiful he was, he was just perfect. Little nose covered in freckles, hair bleached by the sun, dazzling smile. It was all there, waiting for her. 'We're going to be best friends now, and you're going to show me how to look after you.'

'Really?' shouted Spike. 'Yesss!' And he jumped up and down, like he'd just won the World Cup. 'I know, I've got a good idea. I think I need an ice cream. Can I have an ice cream?'

'Maybe. But first' – Felicity took off her expensive Gucci sunglasses and carefully put them back in their case – 'I'm going to have to bite that bum!'

And she chased the squealing Spike up and down the beach, and they both got covered in sand, and so did the disapproving onlookers, who eventually decided that she'd probably gone completely mad, what with the shock of it all and everything.

*

'Night, Mum.' Sammy kissed Tessa, who was leaving the Bucket and Spade to go up to bed, ready to start Lisa Jewell's new book, which she'd exchanged for her half bottle of Factor 4, now that she was on 2. Sammy decided to go over to Christabelle, who was sitting with some nannies, to say how sorry she was about her grandmother dying and everything. Bit late, but better late than never.

'Hi,' she said, she hoped sympathetically.

'Hi.' Chris was fidgeting with a cigarette lighter, sparking it up over and over again.

'Haven't seen you around, where've you been?'

'Around.'

'Oh.' Sammy tried a bit of humour. 'I thought maybe you'd found a way out of this place.'

'No.' She sniffed.

'I'm going to see Neb, you coming?'

'Er no, I've got to meet a friend.'

'OK, cool. Lates then.'

'Yeah. Lates.'

We're so not friends any more, thought Sammy as she went into the hotel, but Chris wasn't that much fun anyway, so, whatever. She'd expected the Nebulizer's room to be full of people, like last night, but Sammy couldn't hear any loud music or laughter when she got up to his floor. Sure enough, when she opened the door quietly, the room was empty. Neb looked like he was asleep, and so she began to tiptoe out again.

'Don't go.' His eyes were open, but he didn't move. His tan had gone grey, he looked really ill.

'Hi,' said Sammy, wishing really horribly that she'd got out in time. 'I just came to see if you wanted anything.'

'Yes, I do.' He tried to smile. 'You.'

'Ha ha, very funny,' said Sammy, deliberately misunderstanding. Well, how d'you tell a sick boy that you don't really fancy him, despite that romp in the sea? 'Has everyone been to see you already then?'

'No.' The Nebulizer tried to shift his huge frame into a more comfortable position on his tiny bed, but didn't quite manage it. 'My parents came in before dinner, gave me a beer; but apart from that, I've just been lying here on my own.'

'Oh,' said Sammy, because she couldn't think of anything else to say. 'God, we had such a laugh last night, after we left you!'

'Really?' Neb tried to sound interested, and not left out. 'What happened?'

'Well first, right, we jacked all the Clueless girls' make-up and graff'd the Kids Kottage, it was, like, so safe, Jamie did, like, a really enormous dub, right on the front door, it was wicked – and then, right, the Waterfront boys (who are now called the Waterboys, by the way) broke into the Fuckit and Raid again, and they like had a race and drank a bottle of port down in one, a bottle each, oh my god, it was –'

The door banged open and Red Rum came in, pissed as usual. 'Just checking on you, Jonathan, you OK? Hello, dear,' she said to Sammy. 'Right, I'm off for a nightcap!' And she slammed the door behind her.

'Is that your mum?'

'Yeah.'

Red Rum and Alcopop for parents, how crap is that exactly, thought Sammy. Poor Neb.

'Right. Well, if there's nothing I can get you . . .'

'I'm scared.'

'What?'

'I'm scared. I don't want to die.'

'Don't be mad, Neb, you're not going to die.'

'I am, I've got this thing, haven't I?'

'No, of course you haven't, it's just your asthma probably – you look fine to me.'

'Well I'm not, I'm boiling hot and I feel like shit.' Even though he was the biggest teenager, he looked like a little boy right now.

'It's really hot in here, that's probably why,' said Sammy, checking the aircon.

'It doesn't really work properly, but I don't want to open the balcony doors or I'll get eaten alive by the mozzies, end up with malaria,' explained poor Neb. 'I'm fucked, Sammy, I know I am, I'm fucked!' He was beginning to panic. 'I don't know what to do, I'm going to die, I know I am.' He was beginning to wheeze.

'Stop it, Neb, you're winding me up. Don't say things like that.' Sammy thought for a moment. 'OK, stay there. Do not move' – they both managed a smile at that – 'and do not die until I get back. I'm going to be five minutes, OK, five minutes only. You can time me if you like.'

As she'd hadn't closed the door properly, Neb heard her running off down the corridor. He also heard various other people coming up to bed, discussing Craig's condition, and though he couldn't quite hear every word, he just knew they were talking about him too, saying that he had the Disease and was about to die. By the time Sammy returned, he was rigid with fear, and had broken out into a sweat on top of his sweat.

'Right, Neb, we're going to get you out of here – spring him, guys!' She'd come back with the Waterboys, and Aberdeen Angus. Between them, they somehow managed to carry him down to the beach, where they propped him up on a sunbed, so that he would have a ringside seat for tonight's antics. Dido kept him supplied with drinks, whilst fending off Becca, who was scaring Neb with threats of pity fucks and sympathy shags.

'This is the best night of my life!' he declared to Sammy, as she took his bet on a midnight crab race.

'Good, I'm glad,' she thought, hoping to god that it wasn't also his last.

*

The next morning, Felicity woke up with a raging thirst because she was hungover yet again, and a raging sweat because she was hot. Really hot, sweaty hot, sticky blocked nose hot. But it wasn't because of the sun, she could see through the balcony door slats that it was barely light outside. Yes, quarter past five, told her watch. But there was something wrong, something different.

And it wasn't the fact that Kenton was asleep beside her. They hadn't done anything, she'd made sure of that, but it had been one in the eye for Cliff, seeing them leave the School Disco together. And Kenton hadn't objected to 'just a cuddle', he was very easy-going about it all. He'd understood that Felicity just wanted some male company, and that was all.

Which was just as well, because for all her feisty talk, Felicity was quite shy when it came to intimacy. Although she was a thoroughly modern woman in every other sense of the word, she found it very hard to be truly open with other people, especially men. She'd been entirely faithful to Cliff during their marriage, largely because she found it relatively easy. She just wasn't the affair type; not because she was particularly moral, but because she was terrified of leaving herself open to the wrong person. To Felicity, vulnerability was a weakness. So she was fussy about who she trusted. Or thought she was – now it turned out that she'd misjudged Cliff completely.

(Admittedly, he was with someone else when they'd met, that was a big clue right there, which she'd chosen to ignore at the time; but they fell in love straight away, their love was different. Wasn't it?)

God, why was it so hot? Felicity kicked off her sheet, and turned on to her stomach. The only good thing to have come out of all this so far, was that she was now fully bonded with Spike again. She'd lost track of him recently, she knew that now. If she was being honest, every time she'd left the house for work she'd breathed a sigh of relief, trying to ignore the nagging voice of guilt about children needing mothers, and not nannies. She'd promise herself that she'd spend more time with him once she'd got such-and-such done, they'd go to the zoo at the weekend or something, she'd take time off specially to see him at half term, or in the school holidays – which always seemed to be over before they'd even started.

They'd been close when he was a newborn, of course, but once she'd gone back to work things had drifted a bit, and she'd been too tired to deal with a demanding toddler, and anyway Cliff was there for him, wasn't he? Felicity winced as she remembered saying to Cliff recently that it was more important she catch up on her sleep, than play bloody Happy Families, Spike's favourite, yet again. ('Have you got Mrs Knackered the Working Mum?')

So she'd gone upstairs for a lie-down, with the Sunday papers, while Cliff patiently shuffled those cards and dealt yet again. He was good like that, she had to admit; he may not be a brilliant husband, but he was an excellent father. Mind you, he'd had more practice than she'd ever realized, hadn't he?

Now Felicity could feel her sweat soaking into the sheets. Ah! Of course, that was it – the air conditioning wasn't on, there wasn't the usual hum of stale air circulating around the room. Maybe Kenton had turned it off, in the middle of the night. She eased her heavy bones out of the bed and looked at the dial. No, it was still on. Must be broken, she'd get Robert from Maintenance to have a look at it. While she was up, she went into the bathroom – bloody hell, the light bulb had gone too, this place was falling apart. The tiles were nice and cool on her feet though. She wasn't sure whether to flush the loo or not, as Kenton might wake up. Then again, he might be a heavy sleeper. It had been ages since she'd had a new guy in her bed, she'd got so used to Cliff's ways over the years. He'd sleep through anything. At least Kenton didn't snore. But no one did, when it mattered that they didn't.

There was someone at the door, knocking. Spike! He

mustn't see Kenton! Oh god! Felicity wrapped a towel around herself and opened the door.

It was Cliff. 'I want to talk to you,' he said, his sweaty forehead shining in the gloom like a beacon. She knew that face so well, she could tell he'd had a sleepless night. 'Can I come in?'

'No!' said Felicity, sharply, putting her hand across the door to bar him from entering.

'He still in there, then?' asked Cliff, furious.

A row ensued, during which Spike came out of Gina's old room, bleary eyed; Kenton did the 'what's all the noise about?' thing, looking like one of the Dreamboys in a towel, much to Felicity's pride and Cliff's chagrin; the neighbours opposite opened their door to shout 'shut up!' and then slammed it so hard that Bonnie appeared from somewhere and roared, 'Go back to bed, all of you, it's not even six o'clock yet!'

There was peace after that, for about an hour. Then all hell let loose when Howell began to prepare breakfast downstairs in the kitchen, only to discover that they were experiencing a power cut. 'I can't do a bloody thing in 'ere without the 'lectric!' he roared.

All morning Fabio tried to call the electricity people, forgetting each time that the phone lines couldn't operate without the switchboard, which needed power – the one thing they didn't have.

*

```
                  FELICITY
     Having the electricity cut off was
     the last straw. The angry people became
```

scared, and the scared people began to panic. That's when it really began to fall apart. I knew then that I just had to get us out of there.

17. The End is Nigh

A spotty youth of about fourteen is talking to the camera, reluctantly. Like the others, he is very tanned, except for the area around his right eye, which is still white.

> VD BOY
>
> Luckily, I had a couple of charged batteries left, after the power went down. And I'd brought loads of tape with me. So I kept filming people. But even if I had run out, I would have kept filming. I wouldn't know what else to do.

*

Felicity and Fabio did their best.

'The freezers are defrosting, what shall we do with all the food?'

'My children can't sleep at night, it's too hot without the air conditioning.'

'I've shut down the Kids Kottage, I can't guarantee the children's safety any more.'

'There's no ice for the drinks and the beer's warm — people are complaining, getting really abusive.'

'How are we meant to wash our clothes without hot water?'

'I can't run a salon properly with dirty towels, I'm sorry.'

'We're running out of candles, I think people are hoarding them.'

'I've re-opened the Kids Kottage, the nannies are bored.'

'I need to make an urgent phone call, my mother's in hospital, I need to see how she is.'

'Haven't you got a mobile?'

'Yes.'

'Well?'

'The battery's flat.'

'OK, you can use mine, but don't tell anybody.'

'I hear there's a mobile we can use in here?'

'No, there's not.'

'But she just said —'

'That was an emergency.'

'But my call's very important too.'

'What's it about?'

'It's none of your business.'

'It is, it's my phone.'

'But it's private.'

'Look, we're trying to preserve energy here, if it's not urgent —'

'But it is.'

'How urgent?'

'Very.'

'What's it about then?'

'I've told you, it's private.'

'And I've told you, no.'

'But I'm telling you, I have to make this call –'

'And I'm telling you to *fuck off* and stop wasting my time!'

*

TESSA

It was awful. Everyone was really bad-tempered. Some people really couldn't cope –

Footage of people 'losing it':

RADISH and PARSNIP arguing loudly over the breakfast table, ignoring their frightened kids;

BRUNO doing the classic 'we're all going to die' panic attack in the Bucket and Spade, FELICITY slapping him hard and clearly enjoying it;

THE TEENAGERS trying to harpoon fish in the sea, one of them stabbing his own foot, blood everywhere, his friends laughing about it;

THE NEBULIZER, still critically ill, crying like a frightened child, alone in his bed;

BONNIE, ransacking people's rooms, looking for food.

TESSA

– and others acted as if nothing had happened.

```
Shot of volleyball match in progress, even
more competitive than usual.
```

```
But most people were just very de-
pressed.
```

*

Up at the football pitch, several of the men were taking a break. 'How long have we been stuck out here now?' Mr Slogan asked. Nobody seemed to know, exactly.

'All right then, when did the power go off? Couple of days ago?'

They reckoned that was about right, yes.

'Fuckin' 'ell, they've got to sort this out soon. I'm getting well fucked off with this.'

The men all agreed, and fell silent again.

'Hold up, 'ere he comes, look!' Alcopop was doing a funny half-walk half-run towards them, puce in the face, puffing and panting. 'Slow down, mate, you'll have a bloody heart attack!' jeered Mr Slogan, the other men cheering poor Alcopop on to run faster. But as he got nearer, they could see that he was clearly the bearer of some very serious news. 'What is it, mate, what's happened?' asked Mr Slogan.

'We've – oh god – we've – sorry, trying to catch – my – breath, um – we've – dear god, hang – on a minute . . .'

'Is someone else sick, is that it?' asked Cliff, who'd been sort of let back into the group, in an unspoken British male way.

Alcopop shook his head, wheezing.

'Are we still in quarantine?' asked Yoko's John.

Alcopop nodded his head, wheezing.

'I know, the air-traffic controllers' strike is over!' declared the Parsnip.

'No.' He held up his hand. They waited. 'We've run out of booze!' gasped Alcopop, eventually.

'What?!'

'Are you sure?'

'How come?'

It turned out that someone had been breaking into the Bucket and Spade and stealing the stock. And that they hadn't had a delivery of beer and wine for a week, nobody knew why. In fact, neither Felicity nor Fabio had even noticed. They'd be completely dry after tonight's session.

'Right.' Mr Slogan stood up. 'That's it.'

All the men stared up at him.

'Let's go.'

'Um, where?' asked Cliff.

'Shopping.'

'What?'

'You heard.'

The men all looked at each other, confused.

'Are you suggesting,' said Cliff, getting up, 'that we break out of here to get more drink?'

'Yes.'

The men all looked at each other, horrified.

'Where from?' asked the Parsnip.

'There's a village near here, didn't you notice it when we arrived?' Nobody had. 'There's bound to be a shop of some sort there, I can definitely remember a caff anyway, they'd sell us some booze.'

'But how will we pay for it?'

'Who said anything about paying?'

'What,' Alcopop was shocked, 'you're going to steal it?'

'No, you prat,' replied Mr Slogan, shaking his head, 'I'm going to charge it to Seaside Villages.'

'And if they won't do that,' said John, gleefully, 'I've got my company credit card!'

'See,' said Mr Slogan, 'now you're thinking.'

'Look, sorry, mate, I'm not doing it,' said Cliff, hands on hips.

'Why not?'

'Because, in case you haven't noticed, they've got guns.'

'So? You don't really think they're going to shoot us, do you?'

'Well, yes. That's what guns are for, isn't it?'

'Oh what's the matter with you, we're probably going to die anyway, aren't we?' He grinned. 'Come on; it'll be like *Supermarket Sweep*, only more dangerous!'

Mr Slogan had clearly not thought this through. 'But I don't want to leave my family, in case anything happens to me,' Cliff protested, nobly.

Mr Slogan, who Cliff thought was beginning to look like Sylvester Stallone, spat on to the dusty ground. 'Oh yeah, how would they manage without you? I mean, you've been great so far, haven't you? You've shagged a young girl in front of everybody, shamed your wife, embarrassed your daughter and you've fucked up your son to the point where he thinks his grandmother was shot by hunters! You're right, what would they do without you?'

Cliff looked down at the ground. Put like that –

'For god's sake, Cliff, for once in your stupid fucking life, why don't you just show a bit of courage?'

'Can I think about it, get back to you –'

'No!' Mr Slogan was red in the face. 'It's either now, or not at all.' He looked around the rest of the group. 'Now come on, who else is up for it?'

As all the others tried to discuss it further with Mr Slogan, Cliff walked away from the group, for a quick think. At least if I die, I'll die a hero, he reasoned. Dad would probably do something like this if he was here, he'd be proud of Cliff. So would Mum, she always thought he was a bit of a 'waste of gap', as she put it – this'd show her. And Felicity would have to admire him for it, and little Spike, he'd be proud of his dad. Even Chris would think it was stupid but brave. 'Right, you're on!' he said as he turned, and saw that everyone else was up for it too, having charged off back down the path in a purposeful posse.

Bloody hell, he thought, as he ran to catch up with them, we must be bloody mad.

*

At exactly that moment, another bombshell was being dropped.

'Bonnie's ill!' announced Chris in a shaky voice from the office doorway.

Felicity and Fabio looked across their desk at each other.

'Are you sure?' asked Felicity.

'Well she's going hot and cold all the time, and she's finding it hard to breathe, and she's coughing a lot, and she says she's got a really bad headache.'

'I'll go and see her,' said Fabio, standing up.

'Um, she's in my room,' said Chris, to the floor.

Felicity and Fabio looked across their desk at each other again. They knew each other well enough by now to know exactly what the other was thinking, and so they both looked away again, secretly smiling to themselves.

'Right, I'll phone the doctor,' said Felicity, picking up her mobile, 'those antibiotics did the trick for Craig, didn't they?'

'Yes,' replied Fabio, 'he seems much better. Come on, Christabelle, let's go and see what we can do to make Bonnie more comfortable.' He shot Felicity a wink as he left, and she smirked back.

But before Felicity could make the call, her other mobile rang.

'Oh thank god,' she said to the person on the other end, 'thank god.'

And then, Felicity Followthrough Clifton burst into tears.

*

This time Felicity and Fabio were up there together on the stage of the Village Hall, without a microphone but, as Felicity said, you didn't need amplification when you had good news.

'It's over,' she announced to her fellow villagers, 'it's over!'

A buzz of excitement went round the hall.

'Yes, they've had the test results back, and it's nothing to panic about, we're out of quarantine,' declared Fabio.

'What was it?' someone shouted out.

Felicity said they still weren't absolutely sure, but it definitely wasn't infectious.

'Which means, of course, that you're all free to go home!' added Fabio.

'But we can't, can we?' said one of the Tufty Club. 'What about the strike?'

'Oh, sorry,' Felicity laughed, 'didn't we say? That's over too!'

Nobody bothered to ask how this had come about, they didn't need to know.

'Yes,' she beamed, 'we're all going home tomorrow morning!'

There was actually a cheer. A big cheer, a roar. People stood up, hugged each other, laughed, jumped up and down with excitement. Some people cried with relief, others began to clap. They didn't know why, they were probably applauding themselves and each other, for having survived.

Up on the stage, Felicity turned to Fabio and said, 'Couldn't have done it without you, Fab.'

'I love you,' he replied. 'And I've never said that and meant it before!'

'If only I fancied you . . .' said Felicity, joking.

'And I wish I fancied you,' said Fabio, not joking. They laughed, and held hands as they watched the scenes of joy and relief being played out in front of them.

It was a most un-British display of emotion.

*

TESSA is talking. There is a tremor in her
voice and a tear in her eye.

TESSA
. . . it was strange. You'd think that
once we were free, everyone would want
to leave the compound, wouldn't you?
But no. We all stayed put. It was like
we didn't want to leave, even though
we could. Mad.

18. The Last Night, again

We got out all right, because for some
reason the guards had left their posts
unmanned. We ran to the local village,
bought up the contents of the little
shops, and raced back. So there's us
men, right, pushing these shopping
trolleys, all loaded up with booze
and food and torches and that, back
from the village, along the road. Mr
Slogan then says we're going to storm
the gates, OK, overpower the guards.
So I agree, because it seemed the right
thing to do.

He draws himself up in his seat, he looks
almost noble.

Cut to:

MR SLOGAN
What those b******s didn't know was
that I'd been watching the guards
over the last few days, and I knew
when they went to dinner - it was

the same time every day, and they were gone for at least an hour. [He cackles.] Cliff was absolutely shitting himself.

Cut back to:

CLIFF
Anyway, we get back, right, and – thank god – there's still no one there. We were really lucky. So we all run in quickly through the gates, and make a big entrance down the drive, all walking together in a line –

MR SLOGAN
. . . looking like something out of *Top Gun*, but with wobbly trolleys.

CLIFF
Then we found out that the whole thing was over anyway – that we'd risked our lives for nothing.

MR SLOGAN smiles, and winks.

*

The party was in full swing. The centrepiece of it all was a huge blazing bonfire on the beach, fuelled entirely by books. The good-as-new literary hardbacks had made good foundations; then there was a middle layer of all the big paperbacks, those ones that aren't serious enough to be hardbacks, but too grown-up to be relegated to the ranks of popular fiction; and all the smaller paperbacks, fattened from being read so many times, were being used as kindling. Tall, wobbly piles of non-fiction were stacked up nearby, for people to chuck on as they passed, if it looked like the bonfire needed a bit of a boost.

The whole of the village green was lit up by huge garden flares, staked into the ground at regular intervals from corner to corner; the men had got these from the village ironmonger, along with his entire stock of instant-barbecue-in-a-tin kits, on which Howell was roasting sausages and shrimps and chicken and bacon and pork chops, having been bribed to do so with a whole bottle of Scotch, all to himself.

Ice and Lemon, the twin barmen, had lit up the Bucket and Spade with a couple of hurricane lamps. They were doing their best to be fair about who got what to drink, but soon realized that people didn't care what was in their glass, as long as they thought it contained alcohol; once the beer and wine and champagne had run out, they moved on to the vodka, which went pretty quickly too. So they just filled up the vodka bottles with water for the rest of the night, and had a good laugh at people behaving as if they were completely pissed, when in fact they couldn't possibly be. (Unbeknownst to her, Red Rum was on plain orange juice from start to pass-out.)

Up at the pool area, Robert from Maintenance had

commandeered all the batteries the men had brought back, plus all the others donated by the teenagers and younger members of staff, and he reckoned he had enough to keep Bruno's bedside ghetto blaster (for seduction purposes) playing CDs for at least eight hours straight. He'd also used all the torches, and had placed them around the poolside, pointing into the water. This was not only for safety reasons, but also for atmosphere; he'd stripped the disco console of its coloured squares of gel, and had cut them down, fastening them over the beam of each torch with tiny pieces of gaffer tape. It looked fantastic. As Felicity said, 'You'd pay good money for a party planner to come up with that.' Even the Tufty Club had a quick bop at around midnight, despite previously condemning the place as a deathtrap, to anyone who'd listen.

Christabelle and Bonnie were watching the shenanigans from Chris' balcony. The erythromycin had begun to work, and Bonnie was feeling much better, but neither of them wanted to join in.

'Mad,' said Bonnie, through the hot dog that her friend had fetched for her, 'they're all mad.'

Chris was leaning on the balcony, looking out at the frenzy. 'I hate parties,' she said.

'Me too, everyone's so false, aren't they?' Bonnie smacked her lips, as she licked her fingers.

'Yeah, and there's so much pressure on to Have A Good Time. And yet,' Christabelle turned away from the party scene to look at Bonnie in her white plastic chair, a blanket around her knees, 'I don't really know what that means.'

'What, having a good time?' Bonnie asked. 'Well, it means enjoying yourself, you know, Having A Good Time.'

'So you don't know either.'

'No, I suppose not.'

Neither girl spoke, Chris watched and Bonnie listened to the screeching of drunken disco dancers instead. The air was heavy with things that had to be said, but neither seemed able to say them. There was a loud splash.

'Someone's gone in, then,' sighed Bonnie, shaking her head.

'Yeah.'

More silence over here, more splashing over there.

'They just don't know how to behave, it's indecent,' tutted Bonnie.

'Yeah.'

Pause.

'I might go to bed soon,' said Chris.

Bonnie cleared her throat. It was now or never. 'Listen, Chris, um – well, you know tomorrow you're going home, and everything?'

'Yes . . .' said Chris, still looking out across the Village Green.

'Yes, well, I was just wondering – I mean would it be all right to keep in touch? You know, swap phone numbers or something?'

'Yeah, OK.' Chris kept looking out, but scratched one boot with the other, nervously.

'Because when I come home at the end of the season, I think I'll probably have to come to London for a bit.'

'Oh yeah?'

'Yeah.' Bonnie swallowed. 'See the doctor.'

'That's a long way to come to see the doctor, isn't it? All the way from Birmingham? Don't you have doctors up there?' Chris smiled and turned her head to look at Bonnie, who wasn't smiling at all.

'She's a special doctor. In a special hospital.'

'Oh, right.' Eyes back out to the safety of the night.

'Yes,' Bonnie continued, 'I think I'll have to go and see her again. When I get back.'

'Right.'

'About my food thing.'

Chris nodded.

'My dad'll make me, I've got much bigger again, you see. He'll know, soon as he sees me. He hates it. He wants me to be thin and pretty, like my mum was.'

Chris wanted to say that she thought Bonnie was already pretty, but she couldn't.

'Over-eating isn't something you can hide from other people, you see.'

Oh god.

'Under long sleeves, and trousers.'

Chris stopped.

Bonnie didn't say any more.

Eventually, Christabelle turned round. 'How d'you know?' she asked.

'Oh I can spot a cutter at twenty paces!' Bonnie said. 'We had loads of them in the hospital last time, "self-harmers" they called them. They weren't even allowed biros, in case they tried to hurt themselves with the inky bit inside, you know, slash their arms, legs, whatever. It's all about self-loathing, isn't it?'

Chris nodded.

'Yeah well, I know how that feels. I'm the same, we've got the same thing!'

'What, you hate yourself?'

'Oh yes, really really a lot. And nobody knows how to hate me better than me, I do it really well.'

Chris looked down at the floor and sniffed.

Bonnie slowly got up from the chair, and came to stand beside her friend. She tenderly lifted Chris' chin up with her cupped hand. 'It's good, it's good, it means we know what it's like for each other.' She smiled, and looked over to the marauding villagers, running about like stupid children. 'People like that, they'll never understand us, they haven't got a clue.' She looked back at Chris' round tear-filled eyes, her perfect rosebud mouth. 'Come on, give us a hug.'

The two girls put their arms around each other, and held on tight, and tighter still. They clung to the sanity of each other, the safety each had to offer.

'You're the best friend I've ever had, you know,' said Chris, her voice muffled by the bigger girl's soft, squashy bosom. 'In fact,' and she looked up shyly at her bonny friend, 'I'm not being funny or anything, but I really like you.'

'Ah, thank you.' Bonnie gave her an extra squeeze. They separated, but kept touching with their eyes. 'I wish I didn't think you were just saying that,' she said, and the two girls laughed and laughed and laughed, knowing that only they understood exactly what that meant.

*

'Cliff? What are you doing here?' Felicity could tell it was him, standing in the dark hotel corridor, because he'd put just that bit too much aftershave on, as usual.

'Is that bloody beachboy in there?' Even without being able to see him clearly, she could tell he was a bit pissed. 'I've come to beat him up.'

'No, he's not' – Felicity tried not to laugh – 'it's just me and Spike.'

'Oh.' Cliff sounded relieved. 'Aren't you coming down to the party?'

'Oh yes, of course, once I've got Spike settled.'

'Hi, Dad,' said Spike, appearing in the doorway beside his mother, all wrapped up in a big white bathtowel, looking cute with his damp stick-'em-up hair. 'Have you come to put me to bed?'

'Yes,' said Cliff, who hadn't.

(Spike began to do his World Cup thing, which was beginning to get on everybody's nerves.)

'Er, I don't think –'

'Please? I've really missed him . . .' Cliff didn't like to sound as if he was begging, but he was.

Felicity sighed. 'Oh, OK then.' She led the way into the room, which was looking as pretty as it could, with a few little nightlights dotted around the place, it was twinkly, cosy and serene.

'Nice place you've got here,' said Cliff, marvelling at Felicity's ability to make anywhere feel like home. Tania's tiny room in the staff block was strewn with clothes and CDs and young people's junk. It was claustrophobic and smelled of parties. He realized now how much he hated it.

'Come on, Spikey, hop into bed.' Felicity held open the sheet for him, and for once he got in straightaway. She lay down beside him, as she had done for the past few nights, to help him get to sleep and take his mind off the sweltering heat. She blew gently on his face, he loved that.

'Shall I read you a story?' asked Cliff, as he sat on the bed beside Spike, on the other side.

'No, make one up, make one up!' Spike snuggled up to his cuggie and wriggled his little toes.

Felicity got up and closed the balcony doors, the partying outside was getting louder. To her amazement, Cliff began to tell Spike all about the latest adventures of 'The Dog With Woolly Trousers'. This was obviously a long-established tradition between them; she'd had no idea. She tidied the room up as she listened, and began to fold up their clothes, ready to pack.

'But the king was a silly man,' Cliff was saying, 'and didn't know how lucky he was to have such a good little dog.' Spike's little face had begun to ease, and his fingers relaxed their grip on his cuggie. 'And even though the queen was a bit of a bloody nightmare at times, the king really loved her, and so did the little dog. But the queen was cross, because the king had been naughty, and so she got cancer from being so angry all the time, and she died, and the little dog became an orphan, and he was sad for ever and ever, and —'

'Yes all right, Cliff, thank you.' Felicity looked over at Spike. 'Now that he's asleep, you can go.'

'But I don't want to.' He didn't move. 'I want to stay here, with my family.'

'There is no family any more, Cliff.' Felicity spoke calmly. 'You've made sure of that.'

'Don't I get a second chance?'

'No.'

Silence.

'OK then, forget that, what about a third?' Cliff knew that Felicity's sense of humour could usually melt her frosty façade.

But no, not this time. 'Just go.'

'I don't mind if you shout at me,' he said, 'I deserve it, I know I do.'

Silence.

'D'you want to hit me? Punch my fucking lights out?'

'No, I want a divorce.' But she didn't look entirely convinced.

Cliff went for the tiny chink in her steely armour. 'Look, at least wait until we get home, Fliss, please? You can't make a big decision like that out here, it's mad; everything's been blown up out of all proportion, because we've all been living on top of each other.'

'Huh! Speak for yourself!' Felicity carried on folding. But even though she wasn't saying anything, he knew she was listening.

'You know what it's like when you go on holiday, it feels like you've been away for ages. Since we've been out here we've been through hell and back – it would normally take years for all this to happen in the real world. One thing

I've got from it though, is that I really love you and the boy, and I'm not going to give up this easily.'

'But are you prepared to give up your womanizing ways? As you know, I don't share.' Felicity threw a suitcase on the end of the bed, and unzipped it. 'What about your stupid girlfriend?'

'I've already dumped her.'

'Really?' Felicity looked up. 'And how did she take it?'

'Well, you know, she was heartbroken. But she doesn't matter to me, she never did. It's you I want.'

No response to that, she carried on ferrying shoes from the bottom of the wardrobe to the bottom of her suitcase.

'Look.' He walked over to the bed, and got in her way. 'Give me another chance, please? Let's just wait until we get home, see what happens.'

'I know what will happen,' she said, as she pushed him out of the way. 'We'll go back to normal, and nothing will have changed. We'll carry on as usual, not really talking, not really communicating, we'll be too busy busying ourselves with other things.' She filled the gaps between the shoes with dirty underwear. 'The only trouble is, things aren't going to be the same. They can't be.'

'I know, I'm going to try really hard, I'm going to be the perfect husband, I'm going to –'

'Oh, shut up, Cliff!' Felicity slumped down on the bed, she suddenly looked really tired. 'You're right, I'll wait until we get back home to decide what to do.'

'Yesss!' excited Cliff, as he had when England won the World Cup in 1966.

'Sssh!' hissed Felicity, watching over Spike, 'you'll wake

him up.' She rubbed her face, pulled back her hair, and yawned. 'Now look, we're not back together or anything, we're just staying together, that's all – there is a difference.'

Cliff couldn't work out what that difference was, but it didn't matter.

'But if I do decide to give you another chance, Cliff, it won't be because I want to be with you. It'll be because I want you to be with someone else.'

He was confused. 'What's that supposed to mean?'

'I'm pregnant.'

'What?!'

'Pregnant, you know, having a baby.'

'Oh my god!' He didn't know what to think, or feel. 'How come? When?'

'Must have been that drunken quickie we had before we came out here. I'm not sure, mind you, I'll have to wait till we get home to do a pregnancy test, but my period's about ten days late, and my bosoms are sore, so –'

'Oh, Fliss, that's great! Isn't it?' He tried to read her face, normally so expressive, now completely blank. 'No? No. It's a bad thing, last thing you need, oh god. Well, er, you don't have to have it, you could always have an ab—, no, actually, you know what Felicity, I'd fight you about that one, I don't think I could let you do that, in fact, it's completely out of the question. God, help, shit – a baby! I'll need a bit of time to take all this in, bloody hell, er, fuck me, who'd have thought . . .'

'And you may as well know that I've decided that if I'm going to have this baby, I'm going to stop working.'

'Right.'

'Well, at least until it starts school. I'm not making the same mistake I made with Spike.'

'Right.'

'Which means that we will have to undergo some radical lifestyle changes. I think we should sell up, leave our stupidly expensive London lifestyle, move away, simplify our lives, get back to basics.'

'Great, brilliant, really good idea.' A light bulb went on in Cliff's brain. 'Hey! What about Mum's house, we could move there! Spike would love the seaside –'

'Don't be ridiculous, Cliff.' She frowned. 'Although Brighton might be good . . .'

'Yes, anywhere, as long as we're all together, that's all that matters.'

'I thought we could live off our cleverly invested capital, which will certainly see us through the first few years.' Which meant that Cliff would be off the money wheel. Or would it?

'Are you going to give up work completely, then?'

'No. I'll sell my business, and perhaps run a small consultancy. If I feel like it.'

Cliff was relieved, he knew her too well. There was no way Felicity would be giving up her career completely. If at all.

'One more thing.'

Oh fuck. 'Yes?'

'If I find out that you have so much as held hands with another woman, then you're out, OK? And don't think I won't find out, because I will.'

'I don't want anyone else, Fliss, I want you.' He went to hug her, but she stopped him.

'And I want to meet Eileen, and her daughters, and Christabelle is to come and stay more often, and we're going to do this family thing really properly, OK?'

'Yes, OK.' What a great woman.

'And, you'll know when I've started to trust you again, because our sex life will probably improve.' She shuddered. 'I hope. If it doesn't, then we'll have to go for sex therapy or something. I gather Viagra's quite good. For women, that is – it would appear – you certainly don't need it.'

'Right.' That sounded interesting . . .

And then she burst into tears. 'Oh, Cliff, I don't really know what to do. I don't want to be on my own, but I don't want to be with you if you're going to shag everything with big tits and a tiny arse. And I don't even know if I can fancy you any more. And I'm not sure if I want another baby, but it would be so lovely if we could start again . . .'

Cliff put his arms around her sobbing shoulders. 'Come on, darlin', we can do this. It'll be like the old days, when we were on the same bloody side. I know you might not like me very much right now, but I'm still your best friend, aren't I? I know you best, don't I, doll?' Felicity nodded into his chest. 'Look, tell you what, why don't you just lie down for a minute, put your feet up for a bit. Let's do what we always used to do, when we needed to work out the next bit; champagne and chips, right? I've got a bottle of bubbly stashed away in a secret place downstairs, and I'll see what I can do about the chips. You stay there, princess, I'll be back in a minute.'

Just as he had found the door handle and was opening the door, Felicity called out softly, 'Cliff?'

'Yes, sweetheart?'

'Are we going to be all right? Can we live happily ever after?'

He came back down into the room and looked at his wife, lying on the bed beside their son, her beautiful hair spread out on the pillow around her womanly face with its busy lips and flashing eyes, full of spirit, even now. 'I don't know, love, but I'm bloody well going to give it my best shot. I nearly lost you and Spikey back there, and I'm not going to let that happen again.' And I mean that, I really do.

Feeling each dark step with the back of his heel, Cliff made his way down the stairs and back outside to the party. Tania was dancing by the pool, laughing at Otto the married circus man, who was impressing her with his nifty moves. Cliff attracted Tania's attention, she whispered something in Otto's ear, giving him the opportunity to put his oily hand round her waist, the dirty bastard. 'Can I have a word, darlin'?' he said, as she tottered over.

'Yeah, quick though, I'm having a laugh. Where've you been, by the way?'

'Getting back together with my wife.'

'Oh. Why?'

'Because I love her.'

'Oh. Don't you want to be with me any more?' she asked, as she stuck her chest out, and looked at him in that certain way.

This is just a game to you, Cliff thought, it's like a game of musical bottoms. You have no idea what I nearly lost, what

I've got upstairs waiting for me. But why would you, you're only young, you don't need to grow up yet. But I do. Cliff took a deep breath and said, 'No, darlin', I don't want to be with you. I want to stay with my family, I'm really sorry.' He'd done it. It was as easy as that. Wow. Wow!

'Oh. OK then.' And she kissed him on the forehead, said, 'thanks for a nice time anyway,' kissed him again, and went back to the gurning Otto, who was waiting for her on the dance floor.

Bloody hell, she might have at least put up a bit of a fight, thought Cliff as he made his way back upstairs, clutching the bottle of champagne he'd hidden in a flowerbed, and a half-open tube of Pringles. But he'd turned temptation down. He'd been strong. He'd done the right thing. For the first time in ages, Cliff Clifton began to feel powerful again.

Felicity had gone to sleep, and Spike was curled up beside her. As Cliff put the champagne on the bedside table, and carefully placed the sheet over Felicity and their little baby small inside her, he thanked his lucky stars for being given one last chance.

And I won't fuck it up this time, Dad, honest. I get it now.

*

Every nerve in Sammy's body was tingling. She and Jamie were alone together, for the first time. Dido had decided to throw a last-night party for the Nebulizer in his room, to try and keep him hanging on in there, just for one more night. Sammy had popped out for a couple of minutes, to go and see Mum – but she hadn't said that of course. But

Jamie had come after her, and suggested a stroll on the beach, to get some fresh air.

So here they were, walking up and down the beach, past the bonfire and then back again, just talking. She didn't want this to stop, in fact she wanted it to go on and on and on. He was so nice, she hadn't realized how shy he was. And somehow his shyness had rubbed off on her, and instead of being what she'd thought was her usual loud self, she was being quiet too, letting his soft calming voice lap over her like the warm sea, listening to him talk about his family, how he missed his little sister, how he'd got an old Mini back home, how he'd thought all his dreams had come true at once, when he'd got this job before starting at Uni.

'Hey, what are we doing?' asked Jamie, as they turned at the end of the beach to come back again. 'We must have walked up and down here a hundred times.'

'I know, it's mad, isn't it?'

By the light of the bonfire, Sammy could see Aberdeen Angus looking for her. Bollocks. 'Fancy a swim, out to the pontoon?' she asked, before his arrival could spoil it all. But luckily, Becca had appeared from nowhere, took Angus' hand and was now leading him off towards the Bottyboat, which was their name for Cliff's little hideyhole. Tonight was Angus' turn to be shown Women's Ways, then. (Becca had also given Sammy a few tips on seduction, in the same way that old-timers pass on tips to younger criminals whilst in prison.)

'Yeah, a swim's a great idea,' grinned Jamie, even though it was against the rules to be on the pontoon in the dark. But it had become an unofficial pulling place for the teens, and it looked like nobody was out there right now.

So they stepped into the water, and waded out together until they were waist-deep. 'Ooh,' shivered Sammy, 'it's colder than I thought!'

'Here, I'll keep you warm,' said Jamie, and he held out his hand, and pulled her towards him until she was near enough to hold. Sammy could feel his heart thumping in his chest, or was it hers? Oh god, she thought, I think I'm going to be sick.

She'd snogged guys before, of course, but not like this. They both kissed the same way, it was so cool, it was so hot. He was gentle but firm, seeking and caring, calm and passionate.

Silently, he let go of her, and they swam together, hand in hand, towards the pontoon, which was bobbing up and down in the moonlight. He got up on it first, and pulled her on board. The dry, salt-weathered wooden floor was still hot from that day's sun, and once they'd taken their wet clothes off, it made a warm bed.

They kissed some more, and then some more, and then he said, 'What do you want to do? I apologize, I'm not very experienced, I haven't done a lot of this kind of thing before.' And then they laughed and laughed, because he sounded so formal, and they kissed a bit more, and together they found out how much they both knew already, and how much they could discover together.

'Why didn't we do this before now?' asked Sammy, during a break.

'I didn't even know you liked me,' was his reply.

*

Back at the party, Tessa had stolen a few moments for herself, and was lying on a sunlounger, cradling a now empty bottle of wine in her arms, gazing up at the sky.

'Hi Tessa,' said a familiar voice, 'have you seen Michelle?' Fabio was looking down at her. 'And by the way, what are you doing?'

'I'm starbathing.'

'May I join you?'

''Course.' She turned on her side, and Fabio expertly manoeuvred himself into position beside her, lying on his back. She fitted just perfectly into the crook of his arm, and rested her head on his chest. JUST LIKE IN BED. *Shut up, it's the only way to do two people on a sunlounger.*

Nobody else seemed to be that bothered about it either, and several villagers came up to thank Fabio for a wonderful party, as if he was the host, before they went to their rooms to pack and go to sleep. Half an hour later, they were virtually alone under the stars – apart from Howell, who was stumbling round, draining the dregs from any empty bottles he could find in the dawning half-light.

'Ah, Tessa,' sighed Fabio, as he stroked her soft silky sunstriped hair, 'why didn't we ever get it together?'

'I don't know, Fabio,' she replied, muffled into his chest, 'perhaps the timing was all wrong.'

He undid a couple of buttons on his shirt, and slid her hand inside. SMOOTH SKIN, TAUT TUMMY, WHAT MORE DO YOU WANT? 'Is it too late for us now?'

'Probably.' NOT, PROBABLY NOT.

He kissed her hair. She looked up at him, he kissed her nose, he kissed her face, he pulled her up to him and kissed her lips, perfectly, expertly. Inside his shirt, she let her hand wander up his chest, on to his shoulder and down his back. It was all prickly there. His back was prickly. Oh my god, HE'S GOT A HAIRY BACK. BAIL OUT, BAIL OUT!

'Michelle hasn't been able to wax it for me, because of the power cut,' he whispered into her ear.

Tessa began to get the giggles. 'I'm sorry –' she gasped, 'I shouldn't, but, oh dear . . .'

Once she'd got over herself, she kissed Fabio a smacker on the lips and said, 'I want you to know, Fabio, that you are one of the nicest men I've ever met.'

'Really?' he said, 'me?' He seemed genuinely surprised. 'Oh. I don't think a woman's ever said that to me before.'

'But I don't suppose you do much talking with women, do you?'

'Well – probably not, no. Most of the time we're having sex.'

'There you go then.'

He thought about that. 'Maybe that's what I'm doing wrong. But you see,' he shifted into a more conversational position, 'the kind of girls I fancy, I don't want to talk to. They're sluts, usually, not the sort of woman you'd want to settle down with.'

'Right,' said Tessa. 'Yes, I can't really see you and Michelle on the sofa with a pizza and a video every Saturday night.'

'No.' He paused. 'But I do want to settle down, Tessa, I really do.'

'Do you?'

'Yes, don't sound so surprised!' He nudged her in the ribs.

'Why?'

'I don't know, I've only just started thinking about it. I suppose I'm beginning to realize what I've been missing out on, that's all. I mean, you all get to go home now, with your families, together – and I have to stay out here until the end of the season, and then I come home, but to what? Nobody's going to be meeting me at the airport, nobody cares where I am or what I'm doing. Now that Mamma's gone, I haven't got anyone –'

'What about Cliff?' asked Tessa, in an attempt to stop him drowning in his own sea of self-pity.

'Huh, what about him? He doesn't care about me, he's got his own family. Well he did, until he threw it all away for the sake of a quick fuck.'

Tessa laughed.

'What?' He looked beautiful, but baffled.

'Well, it's so ironic, isn't it, that each brother wants what the other's got, and yet neither of you are happy.' She smoothed Fabio's hair back off his face for him. 'Don't worry, you'll meet a lovely woman soon, who'll be desperate to have your babies.'

'But that's just it,' he protested, 'that's the problem. I look at the women out here who are mothers, nice, kind women, who are good to their kids and their husbands, and I don't fancy them enough. I mean, I could do it for a while, you know, but I couldn't guarantee that I'd stay faithful, that they'd hold my interest. And that wouldn't be fair, would it?'

'No,' replied Tessa, on behalf of all womankind, 'it wouldn't.'

'So what should I do?'

'Talk to them,' yawned Tessa, who was getting tired.

'Talk to who?'

'Women,' answered Tessa. 'The ones you fancy, and the ones you don't.'

He thought about that. 'What about?'

'Anything.'

'I can't.'

'Yes you can.' She snuggled into his chest. 'You've been talking to me, haven't you?'

'Well, yes, but —'

'Well then.' She looked up at him, gave him her last bit of energy. 'The trouble is, Fabio, that you haven't got any female friends. You see women as either sex on legs, or baby machines. You don't see us as people.'

He was quiet.

'You'll know when you've met the right person, I promise you. You'll want to talk to them as much as you want to have sex with them. You've got the sex part down to a fine art, it's the communication bit you've got to work on.' She went back to his chest, and said into it, 'You're a lovely man, Fabio, and you deserve a lovely woman. They do exist you know, but it's up to you to find one.' She smiled again. 'And I do mean just one.'

He thought about all of that. Eventually he said, 'Tessa?'

'Mmm?' She was half-asleep.

'Will you marry me?'

She smiled. 'No.'

'Why not? We get along, don't we?'

She looked up at his beautiful face one last time. 'Because, Fabio,' she said, 'now that you know what you're looking for, you've got quite a few women to go and check out, haven't you? There's millions of them out there . . .'

'Well, yes, I suppose so.'

'And I think you'll enjoy the search, won't you?'

He grinned. 'Yes, of course, I haven't even started yet, I'd better get cracking . . .'

'Exactly,' said Tessa, as she nuzzled back to sleepy. WHAT THE HELL? YOU JUST TURNED DOWN THE MOST BEAUTIFUL MAN IN THE WORLD! ARE YOU CRAZY? *No, not any more. Now shut up and let me go to sleep.*

19. Going Home

A man who looks like a slightly smudged
Pierce Brosnan is talking to the camera.
He is wearing the uniform of a commercial
airline pilot. It suits him.

JEREMY

One of the journalists drove myself
and Mr Davis, the Managing Director
of Seaside Villages, from the airport
to the resort. We arrived at about
0800 hours, and, quite honestly, the
place was in a bit of a mess. Clearly,
they'd just been having one long party
during their extended holiday. It was
like a Bacchanalian orgy, we hadn't
arrived a moment too soon. There were
bottles, and food and clothing strewn
everywhere; the remains of what had
obviously been a huge bonfire still
smouldering on the beach; and some
very young children were swimming
by themselves in the pool, totally
unsupervised. They were ducking for
CDs, I remember thinking how deca-
dent that was. I had been given the

impression that these people might be
suffering a great deal of discomfort
from being detained – that obviously
wasn't the case at all.

  I eventually found my wife and daughter [he looks uncomfortable, for some
reason] who were very pleased to see
me, and then I duly flew the whole lot
of them home.

*

'Tessa!'

Tessa opened her eyes, and quickly shut them again. It was bright squinty sunlight out there, and she must have been in the middle of a dream about Jeremy.

'Wake up!'

Yes, no, yes, it was him, standing over her, face contorted with horror at what must look a bit shocking to him – she and Fabio closely intertwined on a sunlounger, an empty bottle of wine kicking about somewhere on the grass underneath them, along with lots of other empty bottles.

'Hi!' she said, for lack of anything else to say. Her head was all a-thump.

'Who's this?' asked both Jeremy and Fabio at the same time.

'I'm Tessa's husband,' said Jeremy, sternly.

'*Ex* husband,' corrected Tessa. 'And this,' she nuzzled up to Fabio, as she nudged him in the ribs, 'is my new boyfriend.'

'Yes, hi, I'm Fabio,' smiled Tessa's new boyfriend

in a way he knew pissed other men off, 'good to meet you. I've heard so much about you.' And much to Tessa's delight and Jeremy's horror, he stood up, took off his shirt and stretched his manly and tanned chest.

'Where's Sammy?' asked Jeremy, rather tetchily, looking round for his daughter.

'Oh, I don't know,' yawned Tessa, winking her thanks at Fabio while Jeremy wasn't looking.

'You don't know?' Jeremy echoed. 'But she could be anywhere – for God's sake, Tessa, she's only sixteen!' He looked round at the varying degrees of devastation around them – Red Rum was out for the count under a tree, legs apart, knickers on display; Howell was paddling up and down their stretch of sea in a kayak, singing something completely unintelligible; and some of the drunken teenagers and Waterboys were doing a spot of firewalking, over the still-glowing embers of the bonfire, and then hotfooting it straight into the sizzling sea.

Tessa stood up, and this being the only view she'd had for the past few weeks, immediately spotted Sammy's exact location, and stage of undress; they were both still asleep. Smiling, she hooked her arm into Jeremy's and turned him away from the horizon, walking towards the hotel. 'So why are you here, what's going on?'

'I might well ask the same of you!' retorted Jeremy, still outraged. 'I've come to take you home. One of you alerted the tabloids about all this apparently, and some bright spark thought it would make a nice story if I personally flew you back. Completely boring, I've had to leave Mona to cope with the kids on her own in the South of France, the airline insisted I do this. Ridiculous really, you've only been out here four weeks.'

'Four weeks!' exclaimed Tessa, aghast. 'Is that all? God, it feels much longer than that, I feel like I've been here for a lifetime . . .'

'Yes, well, lot of fuss about nothing.' He glared at her. 'And I had thought you might be pleased to see me.'

'Oh no, I am, really I am,' said Tessa, with as much enthusiasm as she could muster, which was only a bit.

'Where are we going?' he asked, as he followed her up the stairs.

'Up to our room, you can help me down with the suitcases, now that you're here.'

'Hi, Tessa, seen Fabio?' Michelle came out of a bedroom, which Tessa was pretty sure was John and Yoko's. She had just a sheet wrapped round her, toga-style, and her neck was covered in lovebites. Her hair was matted at the back and her mascara was smudged; she looked like she'd been up all night but had enjoyed whatever she'd been doing enormously.

'Down on the Village Green,' replied Tessa, hurrying Jeremy along the corridor. 'His sister,' she said, by way of explanation, trying not to laugh.

*

INTERVIEWER
Was it you who tipped off the papers?

FELICITY

Yes. Once we lost the electricity, the situation became untenable. I phoned a contact on the *Sun*, who immediately swung into action. They managed to speed up the medical tests, and as soon as the result came through they got us out as soon as possible.

INTERVIEWER

When did you find out what the illness was?

TESSA

Well, they didn't tell us until we were out of there and on our way to the airport, but apparently it was Legion-naire's Disease, wasn't it?

BONNIE

As they were in rooms next door to each other, Alison and Kevin shared an air-conditioning unit in the basement of the staff block. It hadn't been serviced properly before the season began, and so the water in it got stagnant or something. [She slaps her hand on to her chest, hitting her radio mike with a loud 'boomf!'] Craig and I shared an aircon unit as well, and that's what he had. Honestly, it makes

me shudder to think that I was nearly
next!

INTERVIEWER
What about The Nebulizer?

BONNIE [dismissively]
Oh, that was just asthma.

MR DAVIS
Once the test results came back from
the hospital, we evacuated and closed
that particular resort down, as it was
safer to get everybody out than to
leave them there, until the situation
could be rectified.

INTERVIEWER
What about Alison and Kevin's families, are they being compensated?'

MR DAVIS
Yes, that's all in hand. [He smiles,
a company guy smile.] I would like to
point out, however, that it's business as usual at all the other Seaside
Villages.

INTERVIEWER
And Mrs Clifton, senior?

MR DAVIS
The autopsy didn't reveal anything,

there was nothing physically wrong
with her. [He smiles, gravely.] Not
our responsibility, I'm afraid.

FABIO
I think Mamma died of a broken heart.
[He swallows.] She just wanted to be
with Dad, it was where she belonged.
So she left. [He smiles, with under-
standing.]

A shot of the tabloid photographer trying to
line everybody up on the steps of the hotel,
with difficulty. There is a close-up of MR
DAVIS shaking hands with FABIO, both are
grinning inanely.

FABIO
I left the company after that. Well,
actually, I was sacked.

INTERVIEWER
Was this anything to do with the fact
that the electricity bill wasn't paid
for that month, hence the power supply
being cut off?

FELICITY
No, I didn't know that! [She is visibly shocked, then gathers herself
together.] Well, all I can say is that
Fabio and I did our best, under very

difficult circumstances. [She raises
her eyes to the ceiling. Then she just
has to laugh.] He really was incompetent, wasn't he?!

INTERVIEWER
Was it just coincidence that the air-
traffic controllers called off their
strike at the same time?

FELICITY
I think once the Tourist Board realized that the British press were on to
them, they saw the error of their ways
quite quickly . . .

Shots of everybody giving luggage to the coach
driver, getting on to the coach, SPIKE sitting
happily on FELICITY's knee, TUFTY CLUB KIDS
crying, Pongo luggage still going round and
round on the carousel at airport, instead of
being put on their plane home again.

The Arrivals lounge at Heathrow: there are
journalists and news crews everywhere,
MICHELLE has a very tight grip on FABIO's
arm and is posing for photographs. Cut to
a double page spread, tabloid style. The
headline reads: 'My Nightmare In Hell By
Beautician Michelle'.

FELICITY

I didn't think saying goodbye to everybody would be so hard. We'd laughed a
lot on the way home –

CLIFF

Unfortunately Mr Slogan found out
from my passport that my real name
was Alfonso, which he thought was
hilarious.

FELICITY

We had the last laugh though, when we
found out his real name was actually
Stewart Logan; he had no idea why we
thought that was so funny.

TESSA

Felicity was mortified when she realized that she'd missed the most obvious nickname of all, for Robert from
Maintenance.

The INTERVIEWER obviously doesn't get it
either.

TESSA

Bob the Builder!

MR SLOGAN

Bloody Cliff, the nonce, actually told

his wife that there was never such a
thing as Football, we didn't even have
a ball. It was just somewhere we went,
to get away from the women. They didn't
find that funny at all.

*

'Honestly, you'd think Seaside Villages would have the
sense to send complimentary cars for us all, to take us
home, with all this press around. You wait till I have
my first meeting with them, I'm going to turn this
business around if it's the last thing I do!' Tessa and Cliff
exchanged a smile, as Felicity made a mental note to put
courtesy transport on the list for Steve Davis' attention.
'Can we give you a lift anywhere?' Felicity asked Tessa.

'No, thanks, we've got to rush off to Terminal 1,
catch our connecting flight to Edinburgh.' Tessa looked
at Sammy, who was standing there, uselessly staring into
the middle distance, in a daze.

'Ah, love's young dream,' smiled Felicity. 'Cliff, where's
Christabelle? Can you and Spike find her please, we'll drop
her off at your *second* wife's house on our way home.' Her
eyes glinted with mischief.

'I don't know what to say now,' said Tessa to her
friend, once they were alone.

'I do,' said Felicity, 'and it's thank you. I don't
think I'd have managed to get through that without you. You're a really brilliant friend, you're a top
bird, Tessa!'

'Me?' Tessa was astonished. 'But I don't know anything, you're the clever one.'

'We never did sort out your future, did we?'

Tessa smiled. 'Doesn't matter now, I think I know what I'm going to do.'

'But we're good together, aren't we? We made a good team.'

And the two friends hugged each other tight, until Cliff came back and it was time to go, time to get on with the lives they'd left behind.

*

TESSA

I haven't seen Felicity since then, we haven't spoken to each other. I don't know why not. But I suppose you never do keep in touch, do you, with the people you meet on holiday?

The author would like to thank

Jonny Geller and Louise Moore; Douglas Kean and everyone at Penguin; Tania Abdulezer, Lisa Aiden, Liz Anstee, Jonny Aris, Joe Barry, Simon Booker, Harriet Giles, Ted Giles, Vicki Giles, Benn Haitsma, Nichola Hill, Howell James, the Monday night girls, the Says family, Molly Ure, the V O'R and Kim Wilson-Gough;

and everyone I've met on holiday but haven't kept in touch with . . .